A LIGHT IN THE DEPTHS

AN EARTHPILLAR NOVEL

Christopher C. Fuchs

LOREMARK

PUBLISHING

VIRGINIA

A Light in the Depths / Christopher C. Fuchs – 1st edition
Paperback ISBN 978-1-946883-04-9
Hardback ISBN 978-1-946883-13-1
eBook ISBN 978-1-946883-05-6

www.loremarkpublishing.com

ALSO BY CHRISTOPHER C. FUCHS

EARTHPILLAR NOVELS

Lords of Deception
The Depths of Redemption

EARTHPILLAR HALF-TALES

The Fourth Messenger
The Revolution Machine

Coming in 2020:
Arcodum
The Feuding Tower

CONTENTS

2019 © Christopher C. Fuchs
Edinon
Ocean
IMPERIAL PROVINCES
Brewel
Velps
Leauvenna
Mt. Tremvig
Sea of Pemonia
Bronhildia
Calbrian Sea
Welkars
Rilhammor
Donovan
Bomlofoss Mts.
Mt. Elmbrel
Glombruk R.
Torfnabruk R.
Nore
Sea of Nore
Yoredgoyn
New Hovedollen
Castracane
Eglamour
Takumbyr
Barres
Gradhild
Nake
NAREN-DRA
Hrals
Ondirhar
Ardfalm
Sipadshur
Wallevet
Nalembalen
Rachard
GALLERLANDIA
Colbrint
Durgensdil
Bram
Ft. Rommested
RAHLAMPIA
Vayns
Bodamweym
Naren-Drg. Mts.
Pernadun R.
Woudenhod
Wadrulir Mts.
RAFFENIA
Birom
Gilgalem Mts.
Gilgalem
Cadentod

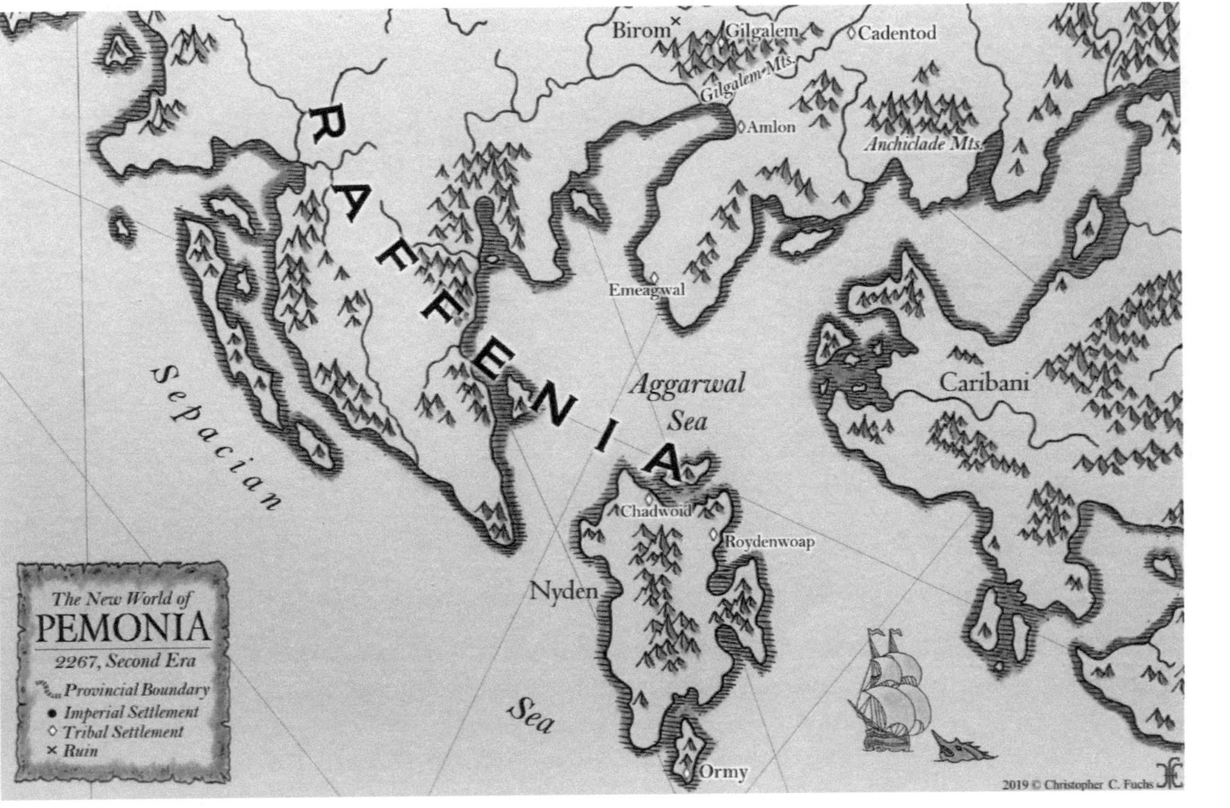
Birom
Gilgalem
Cadentod
Gilgalem Mts.
Amlon
Anchiclade Mts.
RAFFENIA
Emeagawal
Sepacian
Aggarwal
Sea
Caribani
Chadwoid
Roydenwoap
Nyden
Ormy
Sea
2019 © Christopher C. Fuchs
The New World of
PEMONIA
2267, Second Era
Provincial Boundary
Imperial Settlement
Tribal Settlement
Ruin

PROLOGUE

Thorendor Castle, Wallevet Ministry
Midautumn, 3032

"Very well," Arasemis said. "But remember, the second book—and my interpretation of it—will be quite different from the first."

Marlan nodded. Arasemis pushed up from his chair, leaning on his good arm, and returned to his cluttered table. He fished out Enildir's writings and handed the book to Marlan, who squinted at the title.

"*A Light in the Depths* . . . Is that a reference to the electrum of Gallerlandia?" Marlan asked.

"Enildir is using electrum as a metaphor for something far more valuable," Arasemis said. "Now, we previously explored Rildning's remarkable journey through Pemonia and watched him join the natives in resisting Brintilian colonial expansion. Enildir, the author of this second book, was later the keeper of Rildning's journal. These are his writings about Rildning's life after Marshal Hilsingor and his Frontier Corps burned Nalembalen."

"How did Enildir know so much about Rildning?"

"Enildir was Rildning's son, born to him by his wife, Eniri. He was only a baby when the events in the following pages occurred; he wrote his account later in life using tales from his father's companions. His writings will expose you to Rildning and the events of his day in much greater detail. Rildning was so much more than a tribal convert."

"Looks like it's written in Gali," Marlan said.

"Correct. Enildir was raised as a Gallerlander. This means there are many gaps in his stories. But I will rely on colonial records, dispatches, and some of my own studies to paint a fuller picture of Candlestone's origins for you. Now, let us journey back again to Rildning's time, about two years after the fall of Nalembalen . . ."

PART I

EXODUS

1

RILDNING

Plains of Bram, Bram Province
Luminebb, 2269

Rildning's shoulders slumped as he stared in disbelief at the torrent of blue-painted natives pouring out of the forest and down the slope. On horses and on foot they crashed into the flank of Gallerlanders in front of Rildning, thousands swarming out from their hiding places in the woods, screaming war cries and waving iron swords. *It cannot be*, he told himself.

"Rildning!" Owerdir shouted, jarring him out of his stare. "The Raffen! Where did they come from?"

Rildning saw the green-painted Gallerlanders panicking up ahead. The Raffen had clearly timed their attack to match that of the gray-armored Frontier Corps, which tore into the mass of Gallerlanders like a gleaming scythe through grass. Rildning could see Vaynking Tirgranir wrestling to command the scattering Gallerlanders. His ax whirled over his ivy-crowned head as he shouted to his tribesmen, but their courage was faltering.

"What hope do we have?" Owerdir asked.

"I will charge into the Raffen with most of our men and press toward Tirgranir," Rildning answered. "You and Urgamdir take the archers back down to the south and set up on that ridge to cover our retreat. We will meet you afterward in the valley. Do not fail us!"

Rildning and his tribesmen started running down the hill into the fray. He cursed himself for not having been able to persuade the tribe to adopt horses. The Gallerlanders had done well after Nalembalen, but the last few battles had shown the enemy had adapted to the Gallerlanders' tactics.

The Raffen saw them coming. Some diverted themselves from attacking Tirgranir's flank in order to absorb Rildning's charge. He threw his spear at a mounted Raffen, then drew the steel sword he had taken from a Frontier Corps knight after Nalembalen. It shone like a gem amid the dull gravel around him as the Gallerlanders' stone weapons crashed into the Raffen line.

Rildning ordered the tribesmen forward to Tirgranir, arriving just as his guard buckled. For a moment the Gallerlanders accompanying the Vaynking took heart, fighting bravely though greatly outnumbered.

As the Frontier Corps cavalry overran Tirgranir's position, Rildning and the Vaynking sounded the retreat, and Gallerlanders scurried south toward the valley, taking grievous casualties. But the surprise volleys from Owerdir's archers caught the corpsmen without their shields at the ready. Tirgranir was saved, but at great cost.

2

HILSINGOR

Frontier Corps Encampment, Bram Province
Luminebb, 2269

A soldier bowed through the door flap of Marshal Hilsingor's tent.

"Marshal, sir. A few more of the captives have confirmed Tirgranir will likely flee south into Vaynland."

"Just as we anticipated, Arnolf. Send a rider to inform Walpert that his Raffen should continue pursuing the heathens until nightfall and then promptly return to camp. That should ensure they go to Vaynland. And Arnolf, keep the provincial soldiers here and have them double-time on building the defenses. We must not underestimate the heathens, especially in light of their recent victories and their far higher numbers."

"Surely you don't expect them to counterattack after such a complete rout?" Firkas asked after the adjutant departed. The knight sitting at Hilsingor's table was weary and his armor battle stained. But his dirty face was proud, and his eyes steady. "Let my provincial troops chase the heathen king into the valley. The Raffen cavalry is small and not very good, anyhow."

"Not good?" Hilsingor scoffed. "They are not crusaders, but they showed great skill against Tirgranir. Walpert and your trainers have done well, more than making up for our losses from the disastrous battle in Ardfalm Forest."

"This time the Gallerlanders were surprised, outflanked, and without a prayer," Firkas said. "Like the crusaders, I'm afraid my provincial knights won't get the glory they deserve, now that all these Raffen folk are with us."

"Firkas, Firkas . . ."

Hilsingor sighed as he joined the stoutly built knight at the table, pulling off his mail coif and unfurling sandy locks heavy with gray. Hilsingor often thought the black-bearded Firkas resembled his own sons back in the Old World of Almeria, so he tended to think of bold Firkas as one of his own.

"Firkas, don't let your pride blind you," Hilsingor continued. "The spawn of Memelos have proven they are capable of great victory even on the heels of great defeat. You will remember Nalembalen, of course, and the antlered king's last battle. It was nearly two years ago that your predecessor's untimely death was a final parting victory for that old barbarian king Gratgofa.

"And Tirgranir's more recent string of success, probably a consequence of that damned heretic, should still be fresh in your mind. But don't worry," he said, gesturing to Gratgofa's antlered helm among his other trophies. "With patience and wisdom we will prevail and have enough glory to go around."

Firkas nodded. "What are we to do next then?"

"Your provincials and the Raffen footmen will return to the work of clearing the land and building roads, especially the route to the Raffen to increase the speed at which our new allies can be called to the frontier. I want you to do the same with the Bronhildi tribe as well. And here, on this very spot, we will build a new province greater than the prize of sacking Nalembalen. We shall build a city named Rachard, a monument to the elegant surprise of the Raffen on this day.

"As the commander under whom Walpert and his Raffen fall, your careful planning is to be commended. I will see to it that the exarch hears of your honorable deeds here on the Plains of Bram."

"So my provincials are to be rewarded with more earth digging, tree cutting, and stone paving? While the enemy regroups."

"Yes. Remember the Frontier Corps was founded not only to chase the heathens out of the interior of the continent but to enable its settlement and protection. I don't have to remind you we are in the service of the emperor and his servant the exarch and bound by oath to increase the greatness of the empire. The city of Rachard will be worthy of our victory today.

"The Gallerlanders will regroup," Hilsingor continued, "just as they always have. However, our strategy of march, settle, and protect cannot be otherwise, since we don't control their vast wilderwood yet. The provinces behind us are now free from the wild rule of Memelos, but the frontier ahead beckons us to free it from the fetters of the Depths."

"And what of the crusader legions?" Firkas asked. "When they join us from the north, will they press south into Vaynland and have the glory of dispatching Rildning and the heathen king?"

"Don't be so jealous, Firkas. Your noble birth and high honors on the field of battle are equal to Ravorglad's. There is still enough heathen blood for both of you, but we must first consolidate our gains. No provinces can be seeded and grown if we don't tend to the defenses and other necessities before we march onward. No one knows how deep the interior of Pemonia is. My Frontier Corps could burn a hundred villages and march across ten thousand fathongs before reaching the far side of the continent."

"So long as Rildning is left to me."

"As marshal, the honor of deciding the heretic's fate is entirely mine," Hilsingor said. "Do not forget that. And don't make Rildning your purpose. I know you seek vengeance for your brothers, but despite his many crimes, I don't believe he is responsible for the deaths of Onas and Rekef. He has no motivation to tell lies in this book." Hilsingor tapped Rildning's tattered journal, kept on the table with the marshal's maps and correspondence.

"You have seen the words yourself, but I can understand your doubt," the marshal continued. "Nevertheless, if he is captured as I've ordered, then I will have some important questions for him about something written in here. Afterward he will be sent back to the exarch and archbishop in Eglamour to be tried and burned at the stake. They will make him an example of how the paths of treason and heresy corrupt the soul. Is that clear?"

"Yes, sir."

"Very well. See to it that the provincials move the baggage trains from Wallevet to here, and see to the building of Rachard, the capital of the Province of Bram! We must focus on the coming harvest season and prepare winter quarters for what will be the largest massing of the Frontier Corps since Nalembalen. With the arrival of spring, our new campaign will hammer the heathens. You shall get your opportunity to capture Rildning, if I don't get to him first."

3

RILDNING

Brambruk Valley, Bram Province
Luminebb, 2269

An ominous sliver of moon had risen high in the night sky by the time Tirgranir and Rildning halted the exhausted Gallerlanders. They had fled well into the night, having crossed the hills and plains of Bram, which had once been the southern boundary of Umbyrland before the Frontier Corps arrived.

Their Raffen pursuers could not follow them farther into the darkness because the Gallerlanders too easily melted into the verdant shadows. They easily forded the Brambruk and entered the woodlands of Vaynland, where Tirgranir was king.

Owerdir, ever at Rildning's side, whispered in a low hush to his friend, "Our tradition prefers the early golden moon to the late silver. The full golden glow reminds us of the sacred electrum that calls from the earth for Thurondsogon. But when it becomes the fang of the great snake Demfrebra, we are reminded to hide, watch, and wait. The mist beneath the silver is also a bad omen."

"We suffered a great defeat today," Rildning said. "The omen came too late to be of any use." Rildning knew the sky omens were important to the Gallerlanders, but his patience for what he viewed as a distraction was beginning to wear thin.

Owerdir looked into the night sky. "It's certainly possible that worse awaits."

The march ended in the middle of a wood large enough to cover the remnants of the army. It was dark, but Rildning could see the eerie glow of the chieftains' electrum rings wandering about as the camp was made. Rildning remembered the moon-catching glow of Gofalnig's ring on his own finger in the Hral cave and in the depths of Ondirhar years ago. He had not worn electrum since surrendering the ring to High King Gratgofa. But he did not desire it, always remembering with disgust the hoarding greed of Hiltsfrad's men before Chief Wolf Yelgoram killed them.

Tirgranir permitted small fires to be built. The chiefs gathered round to discuss the day's events, and others came close or bent an ear to their steadily rising shouts amid the curling blue smoke of tabakat pipes.

"But it was ill-starred from the start!" Tirgranir said as the arguments flared.

"The flank should have been watching the forest," complained one chief.

"We were," another replied. "But what good does it do if your clansmen run like heath hens at the first sight of a howling Raffen?"

"Far outnumbered. No chance at all," another said.

"I accept responsibility," Rildning said. "I thought we had a chance to defeat them and open the way to rejoin Umbyrking Erambrin. But no man here or lying on that field expected the Raffen to be there."

"What you say is true," Tirgranir said. "We could not have known. But, if we had followed the sky omens correctly, we might have delayed an attack enough to learn the Raffen had chosen to side with the foreigners."

"We couldn't wait," Rildning insisted. "We are now completely cut off from Erambrin, as Goynking Odon was separated after Nalembalen. Today was our best opportunity to reunite the Gallerlander clans and halt the Frontier Corps. But now, with the Vayns, Umbyrs, and Goyns permanently divided, we—"

"Woe to Erambrin!" Tirgranir cried, his face twisting with anguish. "The Raffen, whom I do not fear, have turned against us. But the Umbyrking is surrounded by treacherous

Bronhildi, and his back is to the sea and mountains. They are likely to destroy him."

"Can they not escape by sea?" Owerdir asked.

"No," Rildning answered. "The sea lies in the hands of Admiral Arnasbirg. Erambrin would be better off hiding in the mountains."

"Hiding!" A tower of a man lurched up from his log seat, his firelit grimace aimed at Rildning. "Just as you wished to hide in the tree-root tunnels while Nalembalen burned?" Rildning could see Arbardir was fuming, his boar tusk earrings quivering with his fury. "I say you planned this to fail, as you planned the fall of Nalembalen. We should trust this foreigner no longer!"

"Hold your tongue," Urgamdir said as he stood. Arbardir was slightly taller, but Urgamdir was built like an aurochs. "I was there when Rildning warned Gratgofa's council. He said—"

"He spoke with words of poison," Arbardir snapped. "Tongue darts like the coiling Ondirhar asps, meant to make us flee into the arms of the tree burners. I have seen the asp venom that flows in his veins. He is the ilk of Ominchar in serpent form, Demfrebra's spawn sent to lead us astray!" He tightened his fists and stepped toward Rildning.

"Arbardir! I know better than any, having tested the blood in his arm with my own knife," Owerdir said. "He is no more a spawn of Ominchar than we are born of the foreigners' Memelos devil. But you have ever tried to trick or kill him, even under the gaze of our father, Yelgoram."

"Enough," Tirgranir said, pointing for them to retake their seats. "You may not be kin to Ominchar," he said to Rildning, "but I still think it's curious you abandoned your own kind, your fine clothes and steel, as you call it, for the people of the trees. For a hide tunic and stones."

"None of these suspicions have ever been a mystery to me," Rildning replied. "Neither the unbridled hate of Arbardir, for he has sought my death more than once, though I have given him no cause.

"I don't fault you for your suspicions, Tirgranir, King of the Vayns, given how my former countrymen have invaded your realm. But my actions since first encountering Yelgoram's village, and having been pardoned by your high king, and learning your language and customs, and fighting on behalf of your people these past two years—surely these actions count for something.

"And despite Arbardir's paranoid imaginings, my friends will attest that I've never left their side to conspire with the foreigners. As for the steel of the Frontier Corps, much as I have begged you to take up such weaponry and also horses, those things are second only to the strong will of your brave Gallerlanders."

"Again you are right," Tirgranir said with pride. He glanced at Arbardir and frowned. "But their bravery is wasted when the clans are scattered and surrounded. The path out of this darkness is hard for me to see. The Raffen alliance with the foreigners has worsened our situation. What has happened to Yelgoram? We've clearly received the Raffen answer from their swords before hearing from our own emissary."

"We've received no word that my father has returned from the Raffen capital." Owerdir's face was glum. "In his last message, he said the Raffen did not want to be involved in the conflict."

"Well, we know where they stand now." Tirgranir sighed. "And the Bronhildi, too. With the Welkars all but destroyed in the spring by the admiral's fleet, who else is left to help us fight the foe tide?"

"The Rahlampians," Urgamdir suggested. He looked sour and hesitant.

"Surely not," Tirgranir said.

"No other tribe can help us match the power of the foreigners," Owerdir said. "Even under the most favorable sky omens."

"Easy enough for Umbyr clansmen to offer," Tirgranir said. "But we Vayns have fought more wars with the Rahlampian Confederation than there are electrum nuggets glowing in the cold earth."

"Even so," Urgamdir said, "they will soon be forced to fight, flee, or ally themselves with the foreigners."

"If they haven't done so already," Rildning added.

"The rest of the tribes on our borders are simply too small," Urgamdir said. "I say we should again consider Rildning's urging to use horses. As he has said, we could easily steal them and sabotage the foreigners' supply lines, cutting off individual legions as we did in the Ardfalm Forest. We can also use the horses to—"

"I'll not have it!" Tirgranir shook his head and stared at the campfire. "Gratgofa was right to forbid those foul beasts."

"It's not just the horses and the metal," Rildning said. "Since Gratgofa's council I've advised we should cease meeting the Frontier Corps in battle upon the open fields, where their cavalry will always have the advantage. We must draw the enemy to where our advantage lies: hidden in the forests and wooded foothills, so we can strike them when they are near and hide ourselves again."

"Nalembalen wasn't an open field, yet you still lost it," Tirgranir countered.

"And the sky omens are rarely favorable to invite the foreigners into the forests," Owerdir added.

"I may never fully understand how the Gallerlanders deduce decisions of battle and other weighty matters from watching the heavens," Rildning said, "but this is my urgent advice. You must adopt the superior techniques of the enemy—horses, steel, and tactics of sabotage—or make the same mistakes that allowed Nalembalen to fall."

"Superior?" Tirgranir snorted. "Have you not spent considerable time learning our techniques? To run up into and across the trees. To throw stone knives. To signal among ourselves by calling like the birds of the forest. I would hardly call our techniques inferior."

"None of that is going to defeat cavalry on the field," Rildning insisted. "We must adapt or keep to the woods."

"Rildning's ideas worked well in Ardfalm Forest," Urgamdir said. "We destroyed a whole legion."

Rildning looked down, knowing Tirgranir hated to be reminded of a great victory that was not his. Rildning was also not proud of the deaths of so many soldiers at Ardfalm, though it had been necessary to permit the remaining Gallerlanders to flee to Vaynland.

"The Umbyrs and Goyns may have fought that way," Tirgranir grumbled, "but we Vayns have always met our enemy face to face and fist to fist. Even the metal-wielding Rahlampians have trembled at our stone blades. As king of the Vayns, I won't tell my men to throw stones while hiding in the bushes. And as for adopting horses and metal, we will hold to Gratgofa's command and keep our beliefs strong by shunning evil metals."

"One final plea," Rildning said. "As you have seen today, this is a powerful and merciless enemy. The Umbyrs and Goyns have lost their lands and survive in isolated pockets, surrounded. The same will happen to the Vayns unless you heed my advice about an enemy I know best."

"Enough," the Vaynking said. "We will seek out the Sage in Gilgalem, where the Gallerlander realm has its ancient origins. I'm sure his wise counsel will support my decision."

"Who is the Sage?" Rildning asked.

"You still have much to learn about our people. Perhaps your beloved Eniri and old Hegdir did not tell you every secret," Tirgranir said with a chuckle.

ço

As they dispersed to find rest under the ill-omen moon, Rildning thanked Urgamdir and Owerdir for their support.

"Arbardir is my half brother, but not my friend, as you are," Owerdir answered with a smile. "You are my brother, and in time the Vaynking will better appreciate your wits and cease listening to Arbardir."

"Thank you, my brother. Should we expect the Sage to appreciate a foreigner's wits?"

"The Sage is very old, very wise."

"Does he have a name?"

"What he was called before, I don't know," Owerdir said. "But he is now known by many names, such as the Questioner of New Graparins and the Wind Seer. He is also called Thuranmaret, Sky King, because none can read the sky omens as clearly as he can. His old eyes divine Wurumnak's answers to our most important questions.

"The Sage lives on Gilgalem," Owerdir continued, "a mountain at the center of the world. There the Maluram clan dwells in the belly of the mountain, where they forge and shape the electrum mined there and brought from every corner of the realm."

"Gilgalem . . . where our families fled after Nalembalen was burned," Rildning said, looking into the distance. "Do you think they are still safe there?"

"There is no safer place for the Gallerlanders."

For nearly a year Rildning had been away from Eniri, and he had never met his infant son. Letting her journey without him from Umbyrland to Gilgalem while she was with child was the most difficult thing he had ever done. He longed to see her and meet him. Then he recalled that Owerdir's own father was likely in grave danger.

"Owerdir," he said, placing his hand on his shoulder. "I'm sorry we've heard nothing from Yelgoram. Your father has a keen eye and quick wits. I'm sure he departed from the Raffen king's court as soon as he realized they were not going to help us."

"I'm not as hopeful," Owerdir said. "As our emissary, I think he would have stayed and bargained for as long as he could. He is in the hands of the king of the Raffen now. We must wait and watch."

4

YELGORAM

Woudenhod, Raffenia
Luminebb, 2269

Far south and to the west of the great forests where the wooden ark houses of Nalembalen long perched, there was a great plain of rich meadows, hills, and endless stretches of wide streams. These emptied into the valley of a deep-cut river, the name of which the Gallerlanders did not know. For this was the land of the Raffen tribe.

The blue-tattooed Raffen had not often found themselves at war with the green-painted Gallerlanders, as the latter did not stray too far south beyond their forests, and the Raffen did not venture too far north of the great river. So Yelgoram was surprised to find himself a hostage of the Raffen king, unaware of the Raffen raiders now in the employ of the Frontier Corps.

Yelgoram had pegged King Pendigied as an unwise youth with barely a whisker on his chin. The king was small of stature and with dark hair, as were most Raffen. But his green eyes were piercing, as if the young king could immediately deduce the character of those he met, even if he wasn't experienced enough to know what to do with that knowledge.

Yelgoram learned from talking with Pendigied's courtiers that the young king's father had left him the Raffen Empire at a pinnacle and that the chieftains supported the son's rule as long as they were allowed to continue pillaging the Nyden and Noric islands as they wished and keep the booty for

18

themselves. Even so, Yelgoram witnessed the chiefs' nervous deference to Pendigied.

The Raffen did not stuff Yelgoram into a cell or even chain him. He recalled throwing Rildning into the snake pit when he first met him and was glad the Raffen had no such habit. They simply did not permit him to leave the king's fortress. The Raffen took pains to make the aging Gallerlander comfortable. Overall it was tolerable, especially since half the Raffen spoke Gali. But it had been several weeks since they had seized him, and he was becoming anxious.

Yelgoram had volunteered to go to the Raffen, knowing that he was seeking an unlikely ally for the Gallerlanders. But someone had to try, and he would not send his sons, nor would he have encouraged Rildning to go. He believed in Rildning but knew the Raffen would never accept him. Satisfied with himself for trying, Yelgoram turned to depart from King Pendigied when they seized him without explanation. He wasn't surprised at their treachery but was sure they would release him once the threat from the colonists was clear to them.

On a bright and clear day, as the weather always seemed to be in the early Raffen autumn, Pendigied welcomed a colonial envoy into his court. Yelgoram was in his usual place, in a row of Raffen chiefs seated on a platform just below the king's ancient throne. He was sure this would be the moment that fear of the colonists would grip the Raffen king.

Pendigied's arms rested on two stalking wolves carved into the gray-blue limestone. The towering chair, with five vicious wolf heads snarling down from atop the backrest, made him look small. On the king's head was the grotesque iron crown of his fathers, said to have been fashioned from skystones, flaming rocks fallen from the heavens. To Yelgoram, it was strange for a lively youth who prized new faces and fresh news to sit in his fathers' old chair and wear their oppressive crown.

The oppressive throne did not deter the richly robed envoy from walking down the great hall, lit by tall windows set in the limestone walls. Yelgoram had stared at the light glistening through the glass, a curiosity his own people had never attempted to fashion, for hours. But now he kept his eyes on this foreigner, who had clearly been here before.

To Yelgoram's surprise, the envoy presented himself to Pendigied using Raffen speech, a faster-paced tongue that to Yelgoram lacked the emotion of Gali. The old Gallerlander turned to the chief nearest to him, who had become the closest thing to a friend Yelgoram had found in Pendigied's court.

"Wollem," he whispered, "what is going on?"

The chief listened a bit longer before answering. "He brings tidings of a battle. Our tribesmen were victorious."

Yelgoram's stomach turned. The splendor of his prison and the kindness of his captors made it too easy for him to forget that the Raffen were at war with his people.

The king appeared pleased with the news. The envoy bowed and showed elaborate thanks, then turned to wave forward the people who had gathered in the doorway at the end of the hall. At this point the king's wiseman, Alda, approached Pendigied with caution in his face, but the king turned him away with the flick of a hand.

The envoy was not alone after all. Yelgoram watched as a mixed train of blue-tattooed Raffen tribesmen and steel-armored foreign knights filed toward the throne. They were escorting small wagons stacked high with chests and boxes of every shape and size. The wagons' wheels creaked under their heavy loads. The last wagon had not yet passed through the doors at the end of the hall when the first reached Pendigied's feet.

The king rose and stepped forward as the envoy opened a long chest from which he drew a sword. Its gleam was bright and the hilt richly decorated. Pendigied drew two more swords from the chest, both sheathed in leather dyed with the same indigo of the royal standards that hung from the rafters high above.

Pendigied smiled at the steel as the envoy motioned for more. Two knights opened various containers to reveal jewelry and trinkets that shone a familiar light to Yelgoram.

"What is that?" he mumbled, but did not wait for Wollem to answer.

Yelgoram left his chair and approached the king and the envoy. As he drew closer, his fear was confirmed. He saw the envoy clasp a large electrum necklace around his own neck to demonstrate for the king. Many of the chests were filled with electrum.

Yelgoram lunged at the envoy, nearly striking him before being restrained by Raffen tribesmen. Pendigied was surprised, then angered at Yelgoram's rashness. The envoy, noticing Yelgoram's green-tattooed skin, rebuked him in speech Yelgoram could not understand. The king remained silent, his hands laden with the jewelry as he contemplated what to do with his once-docile prisoner.

"Curse them!" Yelgoram struggled against the Raffen gripping his arms. "Do not take this from them. It is sacred!"

"What is sacred, this gold?" Pendigied asked in Gali. "It is metal from the earth, as any other. Yet it is precious for its value. That is its power, you see? Not sacred, but rather a just payment."

The envoy opened a square chest. Inside Yelgoram spied foreign coins minted of electrum, an abomination that caused him to weep through his rising fury. The guards swiftly took him away to a small chamber under the great hall. There he was left behind a barred door.

He could not understand the Raffen. He did not expect them to share his faith in Wurumnak's electrum promise; only the Rahlampians and Welkars worshiped the god of the Gallerlanders, and his tribe was alone in keeping the electrum sacred and all other metals forbidden. But he had expected their respect, as they had shown when he arrived as an emissary. To openly desecrate what was most precious to the Gallerlanders confused and angered him.

He thought of his sons, Owerdir and Arbardir, as well as Rildning. He wished there had been some way to warn them about Pendigied's decision to align the Raffen with the foreigners. Yelgoram had been so sure—and the sky omens favored his belief—that he would be able to change the young king's mind.

He held his face in his hands in despair. His electrum ring glowed against his closed eyes as he asked Wurumnak to guide him.

5

PENDIGIED

Woudenhod, Raffenia
Harvesteve, 2269

"The Gallerlanders are true barbarians," said Genthus the envoy, "whereas the Raffen have shown themselves to be a civilized people. Look how you have mined and cut and built this fine hall of stone, a marvelous fortress unmatched anywhere in the forest dwellings of the northern folk. You have mastered the flame of the forge, tamed the mountain with your hands and even the sea with your ships. The empire is proud to have you as an ally."

"Yes," King Pendigied agreed. "The Gallerlanders are true wild men. They were once great, but the world has changed. Genthus, I want you to tell the exarch and the emperor that they have friends forever in the Raffen. Let our realm be a welcoming place in the eyes of your people, and let the swords of our warriors shine together on the fields of battle and upon the hills of victory."

"Your Highness is most gracious and wise," Genthus said.

"Now, how many more tribesmen will Marshal Hilsingor need for the spring campaign? You did not yet have a number when you last visited Woudenhod."

"The marshal bids me to ask you for another ten thousand."

"That is another legion, Genthus."

"Please excuse me, Your Highness." Genthus smiled. "I'm always frank and honest, as you know. The ten thousand won't be required until after the winter. The marshal has halted most of the current campaign unusually early this year. His latest victory, attained with your tribesmen, has secured the land of Bram, where he has encamped and will build a provincial capital. If I may, Your Highness, I'm certain your late father would have been proud of your accomplishments, not least of them the signing of our treaty."

"Give my thanks to the marshal," Pendigied said. "He will have his new legion by the spring. Half will be sent to him to overwinter in Rachard and consecrate its naming, and I will bring the other half with the thaw of spring. But I will require more horses."

"As you wish." The envoy bowed. "A new fleet from Almeria had just arrived in Pemonia as I was leaving the exarch's side, and at least thirty of the ships were dedicated to carrying horses. The exarch also ordered that colts be bred here, which will benefit you."

"The world is changing," Pendigied observed, stepping down from his throne. "Walk with me so I may fully satisfy my part of the treaty."

The two men walked up into the central tower of the blue-gray fortress where they found a Raffen man robed in indigo seated at a stone table by a sunlit window. In the middle of the table was a large wooden bowl, carved with animals twisted in intricate interlacing forms. The bowl was covered with a leather cloth.

"Don't worry." Pendigied smiled. "This is not another fermented meat dish."

"Thank you, Your Highness," Genthus said. He glanced at the serious face of the robed man.

"You have always remarked how beautifully our stoneworkers shape the limestone of the mountains," Pendigied said as they seated themselves at the table. "Now we have something new from the earth to show you."

The robed man snatched the covering off the bowl. Inside was a wooden model of a Raffen ship sitting on a pile of white powder.

"Very clever," Genthus said.

Pendigied knew the envoy was underestimating what he was about to show him. The king scooted his chair away from the table a bit. Genthus took notice but was not quick enough.

The robed man poured a small vase of water into the bowl. A popping and hissing was followed by a foul-smelling burst of pale steam. The men jerked back as the little ship burst into flame, and then the whole bowl was engulfed. The robed man tossed the vase into the fire, but the water left within in it made the flames leap higher.

Pendigied saw Genthus, his eyes wide with fear and wonder, had had enough. Only after the robed man dumped several buckets of sand on the flames did they subside. No trace of the bowl or the little ship could be seen among the smoldering ashen sand.

"We call it *firkerg*, something like 'quicklime' in your tongue," Pendigied said. "It quickly consumed one of our most productive limestone mines," he continued. "It is born from the burning of the stone itself, and our diggers found out the hard way that water feeds it. Only copious amounts of dirt or sand can stifle it."

It was clear to Pendigied that Genthus did not know what to say or did not fully grasp the significance of the Raffen discovery.

"The toy ship wasn't just an amusing demonstration," Pendigied continued. "This is how we defeated the Nyden and conquered the whole of their islands." Now Pendigied could see understanding begin to take root in the envoy's mind. Genthus was clearly not a man of war, but the king took great pride in revealing the ingenuity of his people to him.

"So you see, from a great tragedy we took a powerful gift from the earth. I'm pleased to share this secret with you, as agreed by the terms of the treaty."

"Thank you," Genthus murmured. "I suppose the imperial navy could make use of this mysterious—"

"Exactly!" Pendigied slapped Genthus on the shoulder. "Of course, there is no fleet that can seriously threaten your great ships, now that we are friends. But I'm sure the marshal has a use for such a weapon."

"After the Gallerlanders are defeated, we will return to fighting the Rahlampians," Genthus said, finally recovering from his awe. "Our battles with them on the sea did not go as well as planned, so this could be used against them."

"Will that be soon?" the king asked.

"No, the marshal remains focused on Gallerlandia."

"I will send urns of quicklime to Exarch Bredahade," Pendigied said. "And more will follow. I would like you to petition the exarch to grant me power over Vaynland after the marshal conquers it. Then my mines will supply any amount of quicklime he will need, and my people will move it from here across Vaynland and into Rahlampia with great speed."

Genthus bowed. "As you wish."

6

RILDNING

Brambruk Valley, Bram Province
Harvesteve, 2269

The Gallerlanders made quick time despite fatigue and low morale. Tirgranir and his Vayns led the march, as they were most familiar with the paths where the Brambruk Valley twisted its way out of the forested Wadrulir Mountains. It was not an organized march, as Rildning had been taught when he was a colonial knight, but rather fanned-out waves skirting through the undergrowth and around the hillocks. This was how a native army traveled, he told himself, much like they fought in battle.

As they jogged, Rildning wondered how he could convince Tirgranir that their traditional way of fighting would continue to prove ineffective against the Frontier Corps. But what more could he say that hadn't already been said?

Soon after crossing into Vaynland they encountered two men of Tirgranir's clan. These southern Gallerlanders had a distinct dialect, but Rildning could still understand them. They greeted their king warmly, but fear and fatigue circled their eyes.

"Where are the clans?" Tirgranir asked. Rildning caught the concern in his voice.

"Everyone has fled south," the first clansman answered. He leaned on his scouting staff. "We and the others were posted by the chiefs to watch over this land, but we are few and far between. The land is now empty of Vayns. You will find the villages and cities abandoned. The Raffen have scraped the life from our homes."

"The Raffen are here in Vaynland?" Rildning asked.

Tirgranir was also surprised. "Why did the clans not stop them?"

"We tried," the second clansman said. His quiver was almost empty of arrows. "But the blue-faced men were many, and with white faces among them. They were clothed in shining garb and rode atop snorting beasts of the breeze."

"Horses and armor," Rildning said. "And probably imperials with them. We will likely see many more."

"Not now, Rildning." Tirgranir turned back to his clansmen. "So you are defeated and scattered across empty lands?" The Vaynking stomped about, looking out over the lowlands. Rildning could see he was embarrassed and angered.

Rildning gazed out into the gray, still valley. A steady wind blew from the west, bending smoke rising from a village in the distance. He looked past the nearby foothills of the Wadrulir Mountains. Thick, low-hanging clouds hid the Gilgalem Mountains that the Gallerlanders said were just on the somber horizon.

"This is not the home I knew," Tirgranir said.

"Great Vaynking, let us guide you south," the first clansman said. "We have watched the movements of the enemy. They scour the land in search of battle and spoils, but we know a path they have not yet crossed, where the waters of the Wadrulir empty into the Fenthugren River. The log bridge there is the shortest route to Gilgalem."

"Then clearly they mean for us to take it," Tirgranir said. He grimaced as he looked out on the land again.

"I agree," Rildning said. "If the most direct route is unmolested by the Raffen, it's surely a trap."

"The alternative is to go back around the far side of the Wadrulir peaks, or else go over them," the sentry said. "But if we take that western path, we will meet the Raffen host in battle."

"I would sooner seek battle than run from them," Tirgranir said. Rildning knew the Vaynking became stubborn and reckless when frozen with indecision.

"We have a chance to retake Vaynland," Rildning said. "But not on their terms. We must first regroup with the others in Gilgalem. If that means we must either risk a trap at the log bridge or face the certainty of an army in the west, then we should risk the bridge. We have no chance of defeating the whole of their army right now."

"No chance?" Tirgranir glared at Rildning. "We are still a large group ourselves and have managed the Raffen raiders fair enough when passing through Umbyrland." He turned to one of his chieftains. "How many are we?"

"About ten thousand in the body and two thousand more in the rear."

"We outnumber a Raffen raiding party, to be sure," Rildning said. "But even if that is all we encounter at the start, they will harass and slow us until the Raffen host arrives. And we cannot hope to pick apart their campaign before winter. Let us keep our eyes on the horizon until we reach Gilgalem."

After a moment, Tirgranir nodded. "Then let's go swiftly. To the bridge!"

The sentries led them around the foothills of the western stretch of the Wadrulir Mountains. They camped early to take advantage of the rich bounties of a crabapple grove and well-stocked fish pools that served as an overflow of the Wadrulir River. The growing chill of Harvesteve did not deter the Vayns especially from bathing and spearing fish. Every pool was rimmed with sedges browned by the onset of cold.

"Look, Rildning," Owerdir said, pointing to a crowd of Gallerlanders around one of the clear pools. "There is the mighty Urgamdir." The chieftain had caught a fish in his mouth or at least pretended to.

Rildning laughed. "With that puffy beard and large belly, he resembles a painted walrus."

Clearly embarrassed, Urgamdir spat out the fish and dove again.

"It is good to see you smile again," Owerdir said. "If Urgamdir still has such spirit left in him, there is still hope."

"Perhaps," Rildning said. "But I cannot shake Nalembalen from my mind, even after all this time. I carry it with me.

The fires, the falling. The thunder of the great trees crashing down. All the people . . ."

"My friend, how often must I remind you that you did all you could to warn Gratgofa and the others? The enemy came so swiftly, and you've helped lead us to many victories."

"And more loss."

"You cannot continue this path," Owerdir said. "In time, we will find a way to honor the fallen of Nalembalen and those who have perished since. But for now, we must focus on what we can do today. The Sage will set a new light in you. You will see."

"Maybe," Tirgranir interrupted as he sat with the two friends. "Maybe the Sage will say Owerdir here is our savior." He smiled. "Or maybe this metal sword–loving foreigner." Rildning ignored the jab.

"It was my hope that my father could have convinced the Raffen to fight alongside us," Owerdir said. "That would have helped Gallerlandia."

"Don't fret," Tirgranir said, "they will want to barter Yelgoram back to us. We will take a worthy hostage or two and swap them. They will expect that, and Yelgoram will be returned."

As Tirgranir bit into a crabapple, yells were heard from across the river. Some of the Gallerlanders had crossed the shallows and camped within view so that the army would not be surprised during the night. Rildning and the others stood to see what was happening, then Raffen warriors ran out from the bushes, shiny swords and spears waving.

Rildning and the others organized their men quickly as more Raffen appeared, now on their side of the river. Rildning caught a glimpse of others fording the river farther up. The Gallerlanders on the far side of the river were already defeated and fleeing.

Rildning took Tirgranir by the arm and directed his eyes with his gleaming sword toward the Raffen cavalry across the river. The newcomers were descending a hill in formation, and a white face without blue paint was among them, the man's body in bronze-gilded armor. They and their horses were cloaked in mail, and all the Raffen carried bright swords. The lead knight's flag had a white field with the black starcross, the banner of the Frontier Corps.

The Raffen swelled across the river. The Gallerlanders held their ground, even when the Raffen from farther upriver crashed into their flank. When Tirgranir's guards became hard-pressed, Rildning and Urgamdir dashed toward the Vaynking. Urgamdir's shoulder took a glancing blow intended for Tirgranir.

"Bring him down!" Rildning pointed his sword as the lead knight crossed the river with the Raffen raiders.

Before Tirgranir could rally his tribesmen, the bronze-armored knight was upon them. Owerdir's archers unhorsed several of his companions, and Urgamdir was again in the thick of it, blood soaking his shoulder. The chieftain hefted a broken Raffen spear and pierced the chest of the knight's horse. He pushed up from the ground and pulled off his dented helmet as Rildning approached.

"Your name?" Rildning demanded.

"A pagan would not recognize it," the knight replied, smiling through broken and bloodied teeth. His gilded armor was caked with dirt. "But the high sum on your head is well-known to me."

The knight lunged up at Rildning. But his vigor was short-lived after being thrown from his horse. Their steel clashed a few times before the knight succumbed to Rildning's sword.

It was not long before the remaining Raffen realized their leader had been slain. They scattered despite their advantage. The more numerous Gallerlanders took heart, rallying their defense. After two small groups of Raffen cavalry were isolated and killed, the rest turned back across the river.

Tirgranir ordered his tribesmen not to pursue. Rildning thought this was wise, knowing they were tired, hungry, and weary of these raids.

⚬

"Lucky?" Tirgranir asked with surprise. He squirmed on the log beside the campfire. "I agree they were smaller in number this time, but—"

"You saw them," Rildning said. "The Raffen look more like the imperials by the day. They sign a pact, and steel arms and horses are their reward. We cannot defeat them with stone, especially out in the open. We must either fight hidden or use the same weapons they have." Rildning knew Tirgranir knew he was right.

"Our traditions and beliefs are sacred," Tirgranir replied.

"There is still honor in it," Rildning insisted. "Let us fight them together as I have said." He extended his hand to Tirgranir, and the Vaynking grasped it after a moment.

"If the Sage accepts your counsel, I will accept it. But not until then."

7

BREDAHADE

Eglamour, Donovan Province
Harvesteve, 2269

The old man could not stop smiling as he peered out the silk-sashed window of his carriage. The bustling town was newly paved with roads of stone that cut straight through new blocks of houses, markets, churches, and other public buildings. The place was a hive of merchants, soldiers, slaves, and craftsmen. The dialects of Brintilian, whether from colonies like Donovan or the imperial kingdoms of the Old World, filled the air as his carriage trundled along.

"Are you pleased?" asked the portly man seated across from him.

"You seek an answer for what you already know," the old man replied. "It is, of course, my great pleasure to finally see what you have built here, good Sarnaker. I knew your modest letters would understate your accomplishments, and Archbishop Ralmo told me as much."

"And Ralmo likely painted too fair a picture in his letters."

"Seeing it now, his praise was justified. We shall work on the details together, but from what you have shown me with this tour, it's clear you have turned this once tiny outpost into a fine city, one deserving to be called capital of the Brintilian Empire in Pemonia."

"Thank you, Your Eminence," Sarnaker said. "I hope you will be equally pleased with your palace. When everything is complete, it will be the grandest palace of any exarch in the known world, as will your court, where the Imperial Council of Pemonia will meet."

"And where will the chancellor live?" the exarch asked.

"There are several villas adjacent to the palace, ready for the appointment of the high officers of government."

Exarch Bredahade reached into the deep pocket of his richly embroidered cloak and produced a small scroll sealed with purple wax and matching ribbon. "His Imperial Majesty appoints you," he said with a wily grin.

"Your Eminence, I am humbled." Sarnaker's round cheeks blushed as he opened the commission. Bredahade had looked forward to seeing Sarnaker's surprise since first leaving Almeria a year ago.

"I knew you would be. It was on my recommendation. I have known you since you were a child, one of my most eager pupils. And your father before you, God rest him. The empire could have no abler chancellor during this Brintilian dawn in the New World.

"As exarch, I have the emperor's authority to build and govern the provinces in his name and under God, but I need an astute manager to help me tame these wild heathens and our headstrong Crusaders who sail here to confront them. As chancellor of the imperial council, you will be my high political officer, while the archbishop will remain the head of administration."

"Thank you, Your Eminence, for the faith you place in me. This service will be the honor of my life. And I would say, here at the beginning, that the passionate swords of the crusaders are likely the only thing to tame the feisty barbarians of this continent. We cannot expect all the painted men to submit quickly."

"No, you are quite right," Bredahade said. "But there will come a time, perhaps sooner than you think, that the heathen kings will grow weary of the war Marshal Hilsingor inflicts upon them. And we must make it easier for them to come to our table, as some already have.

"If the wars in Almeria have taught us anything, it is that some will submit for genuine peace, some for gold or lands, and some for positions of power. The chairs of the Imperial Council will surely fill with heathen chiefs seeking these things. But until then, yes, they must be pacified through the Crusade."

"Archbishop Ralmo would have it no other way," Sarnaker said.

"Neither would Hilsingor, nor the emperor. Nor myself, in fact," the exarch answered. "We must demonstrate our power on the most stubborn of the tribes, to teach them all not to test our resolve. A new era has arrived, thanks be to God, and they must be shown the path."

"Speaking of the true path," Sarnaker said, "you should know Ralmo has taken his responsibilities seriously, and rightly so. But, if I may, he has become as obsessed with the heretic Rildning as that commander, Firkas, who serves under Marshal Hilsingor.

"Ralmo insists I send a magistrate to Hilsingor to confiscate Rildning's journal. Hilsingor does not wish to give up the book for the church's investigation, preferring to keep it as a tool to study his enemy until the enemy is defeated. Nonetheless, the archbishop will likely ask you to press Hilsingor for it."

"Not to worry. The high churchmen back in Almeria also believe they still run the crusade. I'm well versed in dealing with these persistent souls and will ensure they don't get in the way of our soldiers' needs."

The carriage came to an abrupt stop. The exarch peered out the window again to see the shining marble columns of the palace. The afternoon sun gleamed off the bronze dome, and the new carvings threw sharp shadows. It was a formidable building.

The pair stepped out of the carriage and into the broad courtyard, where ornamental shrubs and fruit trees lined each newly paved path. Terraces flowed with crystalline water. The towering oaken doors of the palace opened slowly as they approached.

"Will it suit you?" the chancellor asked as they entered the great hall.

"Indeed it will."

8

HILSINGOR

Rachard, Bram Province
Harvesteve, 2269

Firkas found Hilsingor poring over a stack of weathered dispatches, quill in hand. The marshal's new quarters smelled of sweet incense, ripe cheese, and lamb shank, evidence of which lay half-eaten on a plate nearby. His new wooden stronghold was small but would provide warmth and protection through the winter until a permanent stone castle could be built.

"Sir, I have good news for you," Firkas said.

"Come, sit. I have good news as well." Hilsingor leaned back into his chair and rubbed his gray-stubbled chin.

"The wagon road to Wallevet is on schedule to be completed before winter," Firkas said. "The wall on its southern side—built of the felled trees as you instructed—should be done by week's end. Lastly, the road to the Bronhildi capital is now at ninety marqs in length, though it won't be finished by Frostfall."

"Continue the work through the frosts until the first snow. Any news of the crusader legions in the east?"

"The Umbyrking Erambrin remains trapped but won't surrender," Firkas said. "It has been impossible to fight them in the forests. Erambrin may have already escaped to the eastern mountains."

"I had hoped to hear of his defeat before winter," Hilsingor said. "But if not, we will set the torch to his forest in the spring."

"Shall we do so now? We'd be able to focus on Vaynland thereafter."

"No. There is little chance Erambrin's numbers will be reinforced during the winter. He could surrender during the snows. These people of Memelos thrive in the wilderness, but even they must eat. I think they have little provisions. In any case, we will have enough reinforcements and new supply roads to take our campaign east and south once Thawtide arrives.

"Now, as for my news, read this letter. It's from Genthus, the exarch's drigoman to the Raffen. He paid a visit to the Raffen king."

"Drigoman?"

"Linguists sent to allied tribes to facilitate treaties, trade, and the like," Hilsingor explained. "They are interpreters and advisers to barbarian kings, but remain loyal to the empire." Firkas shook his head and looked at the letter.

> Sir Marshal,
>
> Glory to God in the highest, Amen. I'm pleased to inform you that King Pendigied of the Raffen has agreed to your request for ten thousand tribesmen, half of whom will arrive to you before Winterfall. His only request is more horses, which I will arrange with the exarch in Eglamour. King Pendigied will lead the other half to you in the spring.
>
> You will also be pleased to know the king has, in his heart, converted to Messengianism. He will soon journey to Eglamour where the archbishop will crown him with God's mercy. His tribe is embracing the true faith. The first five thousand warriors you will receive have already converted by a confirming letter from the archbishop. The rest will overwinter in Eglamour.
>
> There is another matter, one God has surely ordained to be revealed to us through these new allies. The Raffen have a special weapon, a powder, which has mysterious properties. This quicklime, as they call it, causes an unquenchable

flame that is begun and sustained by water. Only heaps of sand or earth may smother it.

The Raffen have used this weapon to destroy the ships of their enemy, the Nyden, and now offer it for our use, however you may employ it. I highly recommend it to you, having seen it burn with my own eyes. We must be thankful God redirected these barbarians from their pagan ways to assist the crusade.

I will lead Pendigied to Eglamour at once. May your blessed legions regain strength over the winter and fulfill God's tasks in the spring.

In His holy name, Genthus

"Excellent news on all accounts," Firkas said. "My only doubt is the true conversion of all of the Raffen. The ones who already fight in my provincial legions can be seen conducting odd rituals at sundown."

"Do not doubt it, as it is God's will," Hilsingor replied. "The crusade isn't merely the conquest of the New World, but also the conquest of savage souls."

"But is it possible to convert souls so long tethered to the Dark Depths? Can the archbishop so easily pluck and cleanse souls still in the grip of Memelos?"

"Ralmo has issued the conversion papers himself, if what Genthus says is true. I know the Martinus himself desires this path for the heathens, or otherwise death. As the head of the Messengian Church, the Martinus is the top authority on such matters. War is the soldier's trade, Firkas, and we best keep to it."

They heard a call at the gates outside and went to the window. The sky was streaked with brilliant hues of crimson, amber, and lavender as dusk began to glow upon the land. Hilsingor's oak and alder fort, with its four squat towers, keep and palisade, was like a giant garnet set in the browning grasses of the table-plains and foothills around Rachard.

Hilsingor favored this time of year, when his campaigns—more often than not—culminated in victory and glory amid bountiful harvests. This season had been no different, with the fleeing of the Gallerlanders farther and farther south.

Down in the square, a dozen men on horseback had come through the gates. Thousands more were outside the palisade in the fields beginning to pitch their tents. Every man wore the starcross tunic of the Frontier Corps, but their insignia also had the red sash of the crusaders. This was the only symbol that distinguished the crusaders from the provincial knights led by Firkas. Hilsingor knew Firkas did not look forward to the arrival of Ravorglad and his Old World knights. But the marshal very much did.

"He is finally come, and not a day too soon," Hilsingor said. "We have much to plan."

Firkas did not respond.

That evening, the marshal, his commanders, and the dependable adjutant Arnolf dined in the main hall. The table was laden with stewed venison, juniper boar, and peppered pheasant. Silver cups were filled with good wine from Donovard vines.

As their plates were filled, Hilsingor ordered a server to bring a little box from a nearby cabinet. For a man known for his hard nerves and mind of war, Hilsingor sought out the finest food, particularly cheeses, whether he was camped on the aftermath of a battle or sleeping in a luxurious palace.

"This, brave men of the corps, is something truly special," he said. "Don't fill your bellies before you partake of it." He lifted the lid and pulled out a small cloth-covered wheel. "This came with me on the ship from Almeria." He unwrapped the cloth, revealing another layer of crinkled tobacco leaves and a heady aroma. "It is my last one."

"Pity that tobacco won't grow in the New World," Arnolf said.

"Not surprising," Ravorglad said. "These lands are continuously cursed by the dirty feet of the Memelos-men who walk upon it."

"Quite right you are," Hilsingor said. "I'll sooner smoke horse-hair before I touch the tabakat of the Gallerlanders."

"Tabakat has become popular in Almeria," Ravorglad said, shaking his head. "Ships leaving the ports of Donovan are stuffed with barrels full of it. The price per bundle competes with a sergeant's monthly wage after export."

"Are you a knight or a merchant, then?" Firkas sneered.

"Perhaps I'll be both if you finish your roads properly," Ravorglad countered. "How goes your stone-laying occupation?"

Firkas's face burned red, but Hilsingor could not stifle a smirk.

"Now, Ravorglad," the marshal began. "Do not look down upon the roads as merely a path to trample, nor dismiss the hands that lay it. For the roads will be the wings of the legions. The soldiers that are building them are battle-hardened veterans who have won the campaign here in the south as handily as you have in the north. Now, have you left the Bronhildi in good readiness?"

"Yes, Marshal." Ravorglad nodded. "As noted in the dispatches, Highchief Harkarom will arrive with his tribesmen by the spring equinox. He assured me that he has dedicated himself to the destruction of Gallerlandia, and he did fulfill his promise to send warriors ahead of him to fight Umbyrking Erambrin in the east."

"Bronhildi from the north, Raffen from the southwest, Ollohds and Hral wild-fighters from the western provinces, plus crusaders and knights of the realm," Arnolf said. "The spring campaign will surely be the largest yet seen in Pemonia."

"Perhaps we don't even need the crusaders," Firkas said, glaring at Ravorglad. "We have done well in lower Gallerlandia without volunteers from Almeria. Their swords are better used in the Far East. I'm certain the Arukan settlers will soon be overrun by the heathens there, and their properties will be free for the pilfering."

"There is no peril in overwhelming an enemy," Hilsingor said, "except our own arrogance. The crusaders and provincials can share the glories that await. Regarding the Arukans, the emperor has promised them free reign in the Far East, and we won't meddle with them. I have fought many wars with them, and they have lost all of them. I would crush them again if the emperor desired it, but he does not. He wants them to be out of our way, you see? So we will not needlessly kick that hive.

"The crusaders and provincials are the two arms of the Frontier Crops," he continued, "and each of you are my hands. Your respective legions are the organs of the same body, and I'm the head. So let your petty rivalry drive you to flawlessly execute my orders. Otherwise, with Arnolf here as my witness, I will sooner cut off a hand than see it harm the body. Is that clear to the both of you?"

"Yes, sir," they responded in unison. Hilsingor cut the little cheese into quadrants for the servants to distribute.

"Like us, the barbarians are strongest when unified. We are all like this cheese—potent as one whole, but when you peel away the protective unity, we're exposed and easily divided. As Arnolf noted, we have persuaded the Ollohd, bought the Raffen, enslaved the Hral, destroyed the Welkar, and harnessed the Bronhildi. Yet the Gallerlanders remain relatively united in battle despite the scattering of their petty kings. I don't expect to co-opt the kings, but we must keep them isolated and prevent their joining hands with other tribes farther east, specifically the Rahlampians."

"What do we know of them?" Ravorglad asked.

"Not enough," Hilsingor said. "The Raffen and our scouts say they are tireless fighters like the Hrals, with faces painted darker than the Depths of Memelos. But they are superior in mind and body to the Hrals, and are makers of siege machines and fine blades. They are longtime enemies of both of their neighbors, the Gallerlanders and the Welkars. And beyond them, we know nothing of lands or peoples."

"A modicum of skill then," Firkas scoffed. "And the Gallerlanders never even built machines beyond watermills."

"The Gallerlanders have built far more than you know," Hilsingor said, "if the tales in Rildning's journal are to be believed. But, yes, we should be wary of the Rahlampians. For this and other reasons, the castle we will build here in Rachard will have no equal on this continent.

"Aside from these defenses, I intend to push the legions farther south come spring. Spies tell me the Gallerlanders are seeking their mountain stronghold, like rats to their hole. Perhaps Genthus's quicklime will have some use for us."

9

BREDAHADE

Eglamour, Donovan Province
Harvesteve, 2269

Archbishop Ralmo and Chancellor Sarnaker joined Exarch Bredahade for dining and discussion, the first meeting of the trio since Bredahade's arrival. Many other officers of the new capital dined with them, welcoming Emperor Olskeroth's highest representative in the New World and apprising Bredahade of their many deeds and projects in turn. He was told the feast was the finest yet served in Eglamour, with fresh harvests gracing the many tables.

Bredahade thought about the rumors he had heard back in Almeria that the bounty of the New World's fields and orchards and woods were substandard. But now he wondered if the emperor's subjects were merely keeping the best secrets for themselves. He was glad to be in the New World and planned to die there.

Bredahade was also impressed with the many comforts of his new home. He found silk embroidered with silver and other expertly crafted garments in his wardrobe. Ornate tapestries of gold thread and laced jewels hung in every room of his palace. The sweet and nutty scents of the varied woods used to furnish his home were most pleasing, and he was fond of the many electrum decorations.

Bredahade learned smiths had hammered the electrum into every known bird, beast, and fish of the New World, fashioning the animals into handles and whole doors, lamps, and braziers, perched in the rafters and on bannisters, in fountains and innumerable other places. All of it reminded him of his purpose and his great dominion waiting wild and thick outside the new walls of Eglamour.

He knew many in the Old World saw the electrum as symbolic of the riches of Pemonia. It was melted down into bricks and ingots for shipping across the seas, along with iron, silver, silks, spices, timber, and many other goods. To see the unique metal now adorn every nook of his residence brought Bredahade great pleasure.

⁊

The next day, Bredahade was pleased to welcome Chancellor Sarnaker and Archbishop Ralmo into his palace again to discuss political and tribal affairs. These two men, plus the ever-absent Hilsingor, formed Bredahade's privy council, the men charged with the political, administrative, and military management of the colonies and imperial court. He was confident in their abilities, but Bredahade could see Ralmo was becoming increasingly agitated when discussing the commitment of some Old World nobles to the crusade.

"Pardon my saying so," Ralmo began, "but I don't think the grand master of Emmedollen fully appreciates my point. If he were to leave his safe castle in Almeria to join Marshal Hilsingor beyond the frontier, he would know we need his order of knights to make a greater contribution of men if we are to destroy all of these hideous tribes of Memelos."

"As I said," Bredahade replied, "before I crossed the seas, I urged the grand master to emulate the assistance of the other high knightly orders in sending a new flotilla to support the crusade. I think he will. No grand master can ignore the exhortations of the Martinus when a crusade is declared if he wants to remain an honored Messengian. Moreover, the nobles of the Old World are fully aware of the unique riches of Pemonia, if they needed further motivation."

"That may be so," Ralmo said. "But I cannot help but doubt whether he has the proper desire to destroy every last heathen here."

"He is a high officer of the temple, blessed by the Martinus and God," Bredahade said. "So I'm sure the grand master's heart burns bright for the crusade. Now, tell me of Hilsingor's progress in the east. I have not seen him since he departed for the New World three years ago, and only a few letters have found their way to me when I was across the seas. Will he come to Eglamour now that I have arrived?"

"Doubtful, Your Eminence," Sarnaker said. "The crusade consumes his time in full—"

"And so it should," Ralmo blurted.

Sarnaker glared at him before continuing.

"Hilsingor has much to show for his absence. For example, almost two years ago he sacked Nalembalen, the greatest Gallerlander city, in which perhaps hundreds of thousands of barbarians lived. Rather than see his army destroyed among the innumerable traps of the city's huge trees in the dead of winter, Hilsingor made the honorable decision to raze it. That momentous event was called the Furnace of the Wild, for when they marched in they found the earth had spewed up molten electrum and iron, and rocks cracked from the great heat.

"Importantly, the marshal's clever tactic scattered the enemy far afield, as the ashlands that remained of Nalembalen were broad and desolate, unsupportive of their numbers. Their highest king was slain by Hilsingor himself. This is to say nothing of his other victories over other heathen races and cities."

"Yet I hear one of our own blood, a convert to these pagans, led the survivors to safety?" Bredahade asked, eyebrows raised.

"Vile heretic!" Ralmo cried.

"Yes, Your Eminence," Sarnaker said. "That is Rildning of New Lorin. He was a knight and tutor at the academy in New Lorin, to the great shame of that former colony, which is now part of your Donovan Province. But Rildning isn't their only commander. There are three underkings, leaders of the Gallerlander subtribes. Each of them still leads a large following despite being scattered from each other thanks to the marshal's strategy."

"Vile heretic!" the archbishop wailed. "He should have burned in that cursed forest hole."

The exarch was amused by the way Ralmo could not contain himself. His brow coiled and his sapphire-studded miter quivered with indignation at the mere mention of heresy.

"I've instructed Marshal Hilsingor that, should Rildning be captured alive, he is to remit him to me at once," Bredahade said.

"I've also repeatedly demanded the marshal provide me with the heretic's journal, as it will be the best evidence of his crimes," Ralmo said. "Perhaps you—"

"I'm aware of the situation," Bredahade interrupted. "Tell me, what made Rildning turn against his emperor and his own blood? How could a man's mind be so completely corrupted by the painted men? In Almeria, some tales of Rildning claim he was bewitched by the Ollohds when he was a young knight. Others say the Hrals wounded him with a magical arrow that turned him into a wolf man. Still others say he was a simple murderer who made a pact with the Memelos kin."

"Simple murderer may be closest to the truth," Sarnaker said. "It was well-known that Rildning joined an expedition sent by the old governor of New Lorin to negotiate peace and trade with the heathens. But Rildning killed his companions when they found a hoard of electrum, preferring to keep the find for himself. He sold his soul to the Depths, mingling with the barbarians to gain more treasures."

"Vile heretic!" Ralmo screeched.

"They say there was one other who survived Rildning's treachery," Sarnaker continued. "A woodsman of some merchant skill. This man returned to New Lorin with tales of the heathens and the burning of Nalembalen. He soon came under suspicion as a collaborator of the convert, then he disappeared."

"Well," the exarch said, "fine bedtime stories for children. Killers and wolf men and treasures and such. I trust Hilsingor sees through this smoke to understand his foe. Rildning is clearly a survivor and is likely to be a step above the common heretic."

"The marshal certainly does," Sarnaker said. "The heretic's journal has helped him understand his foe."

"Which is all the more reason to pass on the evidence," Ralmo said. "I have requested it repeatedly, but he won't send—"

"Then I'm sure you will have what you need when the time comes for Rildning's trial," Bredahade said. "What else of Hilsingor's campaign?" He turned to Sarnaker, but Ralmo could not resist answering first.

"He makes peace with barbarians when he should be killing them. I don't have enough inquisitors in Pemonia to vet all the barbarians he has made into commanders, messengers, and the like."

"Well," Sarnaker began, "Marshal Hilsingor has defeated all of those you speak of. Notably the Bronhildi, dwelling in the northeastern peninsula, and the Raffen, who live in the far south and adjacent to Durgensdil Colony. With these victories Hilsingor gained treaties, exercising power over and through them. Thus he has requisitioned supplies, trained and fielded tribal armies, and learned the land of the frontier.

"The Bronhildi in particular have made excellent scouts, as they have extensive knowledge of northern and middle Gallerlandia. And they harbor bitter hatred of the Gallerlanders, having long been under the Gallerlanders' thumb. So they are well motivated by revenge and the spoils of war. As a result, Hilsingor has fashioned for them a province with significant autonomy, pending your approval, of course."

"And I've heard these Raffen folk are a great maritime empire?" Bredahade asked.

"Yes, they've proven to be a great asset with their shipbuilding, sailing, and knowledge of languages."

"And they are quickly converting to Messengianism," Ralmo added. "Glory to God!"

"Raffen King Pendigied is young but guided by one of our best drigoman, Genthus," the chancellor continued. "As you know, the drigomen are learned in the barbarian languages and culture, and are sent to broker and maintain talks with the barbarians.

"Hilsingor waged a short war with the Raffen before we won a treaty. Pendigied's father was on his deathbed, and his chieftains were torn between surrender and fighting. Facing the prospect of watching his empire inheritance collapse, Pendigied slew the chieftains who disagreed with his preference to seek favorable terms and may have even hurried his own father's passing. Our previous trade with the Raffen in Durgensdil Colony served as a foundation for a treaty, and the Raffen have proven to be loyal ever since."

"I was told the Raffen and Bronhildi have been enthusiastic about trading their warriors for our horses," Bredahade said.

"And we don't have enough," Sarnaker said. "We have requested increased shipments of horses from Almeria, and we are working to double the number of New World breeders."

"This is all well and good," Bredahade said. "We are building a realm worthy to be part of the empire. But I presume it has not been as easy as many in Almeria may believe?"

"There have been setbacks," Sarnaker acknowledged. "Hilsingor lost several battles after the burning of the treetop city. The Gallerlanders were weakened and scattered, but desperate and therefore dangerous. A few of the marshal's commanders underestimated them, and Rildning's followers completely destroyed one legion in Ardfalm Forest. So Hilsingor slowed the march of the Frontier Corps and took time to build supply roads. This year, he has already halted the campaign to focus on building and preparing winter quarters.

"Beyond Gallerlandia, we suffered a worthless victory against the Welkars farther east. Worthless because our defeat of those damn marsh-dwelling brutes cost us dearly, to the tune of half of Admiral Arnasbirg's men and ships. We were unprepared for the diseased-laden waters of that foul land. The admiral abandoned the effort and later helped quell the Bronhildi.

"Finally, the colonies and provinces continue to suffer relentless raids by the Hrals in the west. They are the most vicious beast men of the New World. They even occasionally attack Eglamour, but that will change as our ring of forts is nearing completion."

"The Hrals are the ugly right hand of Memelos," Ralmo added. "Chief minions from the Depths. Those whom our soldiers don't kill in battle are burned, though some have labored as slaves despite my proclamation that they be purged out of the realm."

"The Hrals are the only tribe that has been enslaved?" Bredahade asked.

"The Gallerlanders have served as laborers as well. Aside from slaves, the magistrate of Eglamour holds many chiefs of most tribes as hostages to guarantee peace treaties or sell back at great cost. This policy has worked well thus far."

"Very well," Bredahade said. The exarch considered all that they had told him before speaking again. "Have all the conquered peoples sent their representatives here to Eglamour to take part in the Imperial Council of Pemonia? The emperor wanted me to ensure all of the colonies, provinces, and tribes would participate in the historic event."

"Yes, Your Eminence," Sarnaker said. "I have worked tirelessly to not only erect this city but build the politics that will inhabit it. Many representatives have arrived and others will soon, but some faraway tribes such as the Raffen have not come yet. Our envoy, Genthus, another of your former pupils, is now in the Raffen lands with the young king, bestowing our rewards for their most recent assistance to Hilsingor in Gallerlandia. I expect Genthus to arrive with the Raffen king before the imperial council meets."

"Most excellent," Bredahade said with a smile.

"It seems your erstwhile students now fill the important roles of the empire in Pemonia," Ralmo said. "And that they have well prepared the path for their former teacher."

"It seems you are correct, good Ralmo," Bredahade said. "But don't worry, these fruits of my long labors rely more on the guidance of God than the lectures of old. None of the progress surrounding us would be possible without the mother church. You will find this exarch will lean on you in the months and years ahead."

At Bredahade's order, Eglamour held public festivities for a week to celebrate his arrival. This was followed by a second week of feasting to mark Hilsingor's recent victories and his founding of the Province of Bram. The grandfatherly exarch quickly became popular with the provincial lords, merchants, and commoners.

10

YELGORAM

On the Road to Eglamour
Harvesteve, 2269

Yelgoram was alone in a cramped cart. Trickles of rain blew though the stick-barred window. It was nearly nightfall on the first day of their journey from Woudenhod, but he could not guess where they were going.

Alone with his thoughts, the old chieftain wondered whether his sons, Owerdir and Arbardir, were still alive. And Rildning. Yelgoram's mind was heavy with guilt, having failed to convince the Raffen to join with the Gallerlanders. He prayed his sons and Rildning were safe and that Wurumnak would free him from his cage.

But he felt little comfort. He had been told he was in Pendigied's care and that he would be protected by the Raffen. He had believed them at first, when he came to negotiate with them, but not now.

11

PENDIGIED

On the Road to Eglamour
Harvesteve, 2269

Not far ahead of Yelgoram's cart, the massive iron-studded wheels of King Pendigied's wooden cabin-carriage pushed through the mud. More than a thousand Raffen tribesmen were ahead of him on the rutted road, and another four thousand followed close behind. On this evening, he dined with his drigoman, Genthus, in the carriage, which had two rooms, a bed, and a team of eight horses to pull it.

"How did my people ever do without these marvelous carriages?" the young king asked. "Bronze lamps of fine beeswax, walls of quilted goose feather, and every beam and post gilded with electrum. The exarch could not have given me a more luxurious gift."

"These cabin-carriages are crafted to specially suit their owners," Genthus replied. "Only the exarch and kings like you have the honor."

"And the noble horse beasts. They fly on the breeze as the ships on the sea. Have you ever seen a furred cow ridden warlike by men?"

"No, Your Highness."

"Neither have I." Pendigied smiled. "But tales of a faraway people say they ride furred cows of some sort. I cannot imagine riding one in battle, but they were the only people we had known to ride any beast. Your horses are made for travel and war."

"Thank you, Your Highness. Superior horses to match the superior warriors of your tribe. The exarch is most pleased with the alliance and eagerly awaits your arrival to Eglamour. If the rain blows away, we should arrive in time for the new assembly."

"Tell me more about this assembly," Pendigied said. "The Raffen Empire has many shores, islands, and inland realms. I look forward to learning more about how our peoples can cooperate against the many petty tribes on our frontiers."

"The Imperial Council of Pemonia will be the exarch's court," Genthus answered. "It will be the most powerful assembly on the continent, attended by the rulers of every colony, province, and tribe—or their representatives. You can bring any of your concerns to the council for the exarch to hear."

"I can hardly wait to meet the exarch and plot conquest together," Pendigied said. "I may be a young king, but my zeal makes up for it. And I am open-minded, Genthus, but not clay in anyone's hands."

"Of course, Your Highness."

"I know most of my chiefs support my decision to make peace with your people. I won them over by distributing the exarch's gifts of electrum, horses, and arms, which my chiefs used to settle scores with Hrals, Gallerlanders, Nyden, and others. But a few chiefs are still holding back even after seeing what happened to those who opposed me after my father's death."

"You are politically savvy, Your Highness, despite your youth."

"But it's not enough, Genthus. I want the Raffen Empire to not only be a partner of your emperor, but to truly be part of the Brintilian Empire. Everything about your world fascinates me."

"Thank you, Your Highness." Genthus smiled. "The exarch and the emperor are equally impressed with your accomplishments and those of your mighty people. They welcome the opportunity to embrace you in this partnership. As your exarch-appointed drigoman, I am your servant and adviser and will help you gain what you seek."

"As my adviser, I want you to navigate your world for me," the king said. "Its leaders, its people and customs."

"As you wish," Genthus replied. "I will serve for as long as Your Highness desires. We will come to know each other well if Your Highness finds my advice suitable."

"Thank you, Genthus. In truth, I tire of the old ways of my people, which are rife with division, pandering, pettiness, and dusty rituals. I feel my father's vast empire as a heavy chain wrapped around my neck. The decayed politics of the chieftains cloud my mind, and their bickering taxes me to no end. And even a few chiefs who do not agree with my actions are too many. They are fools, Genthus."

"Every great king has his jealous detractors," Genthus said. "What will you do to unify them?"

"Leave my people to me," Pendigied replied. "They will benefit from my wisdom, while the Gallerlanders and others will cling to the old ways until death. But I'll lead my people into a new era."

"Well said, Your Highness. I know you and the exarch will agree on many things. He too looks forward to a bright new era, with our people side by side in harmony."

"You are a good ambassador, Genthus, and the exarch's gifts have been many. I have another gift for you besides the urns of quicklime that follow in the wagons behind us. The Gallerlander prisoner is a great chieftain, well-known among all of the northern clans.

"He shall be given to the exarch, and I expect him to be dealt with harshly. I want Yelgoram to be made an example for any of the Raffen who may think of turning from their new religion. Yelgoram isn't one of us, so my people won't shed a tear. But they will see a symbolic end to the old ways in the punishment of the Gallerlanders."

"As you wish."

૭૦

The following day Pendigied and Genthus were seated on benches built into the top of the great carriage, enjoying the sunshine. They snacked on blackberries and brown bread. The journey now slowed as the road was partially washed away. But the young king and his drigoman traveled comfortably on their feathered pillows.

In their many conversations, Genthus tried to satisfy Pendigied's boundless curiosity about the Brintilian Empire. The king wanted to learn everything he could before he arrived in Eglamour. He also absorbed Genthus's old tales of Almeria, anything the drigoman could think to tell. But on religious matters of any depth Genthus politely deferred to the archbishop, who would instruct Pendigied as part of his official conversion.

A broad valley could be seen on the horizon above the treetops as the carriage trundled along. But soon the path narrowed and descended into a shady dell. Tree limbs now brushed the sides of the wagons, and more than once Pendigied and Genthus had to shift from one side of the carriage to the other to avoid the sweep of larger branches.

The path then opened into a tunnel-like glade where the sunlit canopy swayed in the chill breeze. Then the tribesmen up ahead cried out.

Pendigied and Genthus peered through the branches. They could see a few Raffen warriors break out of the marching line and rush toward the trees, steel swords and spears ready. But all of them were quickly felled by arrows from the woods. Mounted Raffen soon joined the scene, and the disruption steadily moved down the line closer to Pendigied's carriage.

"We are under attack," Genthus said, his voice breaking. "Are they trying to kill you? Or me? Perhaps they are trying to free Yelgoram?"

"Surely this isn't your first foray?" Pendigied said. "Don't worry. My tribesmen will prevail, like the sun shines after passing clouds." As he spoke, arrows plunged into the side of the carriage and the marching line behind.

"Shall we go down into the room?" Genthus asked, fear widening his eyes. "You must be kept safe."

"If you insist," Pendigied said, still calm.

"How can you be so unconcerned?" Genthus was panting with panic as they descended the small ladder. "We are halted in a narrow wood and under assault by unseen men. I saw two of your chieftains fall from their horses just now."

"I shall not mourn them," the king replied. "Sit down, Genthus."

A moment later one of Pendigied's personal guards opened the back hatch of the carriage and climbed in.

"They appear to be Gallerlanders," he reported. "Norbaer, Broen, and three other chiefs are already slain."

"How many?" Pendigied asked.

"Hard to tell. A handful have been killed. The others appear to be fleeing now."

The king nodded and dismissed the guard. Then he looked at Genthus.

"We no longer have a problem regarding chiefs who distrusted my wisdom," he said. "Norbaer was the primary one who encouraged others against me, and it appears his circle of supporters has fallen."

"You . . . arranged this," Genthus said. His astonishment was plain to see.

"Those attackers were mine, loyal men who answered my call to don the colors of the tree-dwelling people. Do your kings and emperors not make decisions that sacrifice a few for the many?"

"The exarch will have a worthy partner indeed," Genthus said. "May I congratulate you on your victory over your enemies, Your Highness."

12

RILDNING

Fenthugren River, Umbyrland
Harvesteve, 2269

When the Gallerlanders reached the log bridge, they found it occupied. Tirgranir's forward scouts had reported it empty a half hour ago. The steep hills on either side of the river hid both armies from one another until their paths through the long grass crossed.

"We've been out-scouted," Urgamdir said as the Gallerlanders watched the enemy form into battle lines.

"We knew they would be here," Rildning said. "And once again, these are Frontier Corpsmen leading the Raffen."

"Two, maybe three thousand," Owerdir guessed.

"And there is no place to ford across?" Rildning asked.

"Not for another two days' walk," Tirgranir answered. "No matter, we'll destroy them."

The Vaynking hefted his stone ax above his head, and the Gallerlanders around him cried out for battle. The Raffen and their imperial commanders responded with their own cries, but they did not budge from the bridge.

"Tirgranir, we should send a group downriver to ford across and attack their flank," Rildning shouted above the din.

"Nonsense," the Vaynking said. "They are concentrated on the bridge, so we will concentrate our charge and push them off!"

"Look there on the hills," Rildning said. "More cavalry. Even if we take the bridge, we won't hold it because most of our men will still be standing on this bank."

"I tire of your constant interference!" Tirgranir bellowed. "I won't have an outsider tell my men how to fight. My decision is made. Call forth your men!"

Tirgranir led the charge. As he did, the Raffen on the bridge raised a wall of spears, but it would not deter him. The Vaynking ran at full speed, shattering a cluster of spears with each swing of his ax. Several Gallerlanders were impaled, but their charge soon broke the spear line and they crushed together in a narrow melee.

Rildning gave the signal for Owerdir's archers to rain arrows down upon the Raffen who came forward to reinforce the bridge. He could see the fighting would be slow as no more than eight men could fight shoulder to shoulder. He could not get close to the fight.

Rildning saw an imperial knight lead a troop of mounted Raffen away from the main force at the bridge. The Raffen defenders backed off the bridge a moment later. As predicted, some of the cavalry rushed down from the hills and charged across the bridge.

They swept through the Gallerlanders with ease, wielding steel swords and war hammers from atop their heavy-mailed steeds. Then they circled and returned to the far bank as Raffen warriors surged back onto and across the bridge in their wake. Every Gallerlander on the bridge was killed, and many not near Arbardir and the other hard-fighting tribesmen protecting Tirgranir also perished.

Several foolish Gallerlanders attempted to swim the river and were promptly shot by archers, struck with stones, or drowned in the current. Despite their superior numbers, Tirgranir's men fell back. A few had even picked up the iron shields of the fallen enemy, disregarding their ancient prohibition.

The Raffen took the initiative and charged across the bridge, dividing the Gallerlanders. Unable to see or hear their chiefs amid all the horses and clanging metal, they panicked. Rildning corralled his commanders.

"The battle is lost!" Urgamdir cried. His bandaged shoulder, wounded from saving Tirgranir in the previous Raffen raid, was oozing blood again. His face was pale.

"Not while we stand," Rildning said. He led a charge into the fray. They did not get far, as more and more Raffen poured across the bridge, and fallen bodies choked paths to the bridge. The fighting was being pushed to the periphery.

All around Rildning the stone swords and axes of the Gallerlanders were splitting and shattering. His own steel blade was notched. Rildning prepared to shout the retreat when he heard a shrill scream behind him.

Men with black-painted faces and long dark hair streamed down from nearby hills on the Raffen side of the river. The enemy was utterly surprised, as were the Gallerlanders. These warriors wielded swords that easily cleaved the armor and helms of the enemy, but Rildning could not see the blades, just a glint of light swirl around each warrior.

Replacing them on the hilltop was a wheeled contraption pulled into place by six of these black-painted men. A moment later Rildning saw that a wooden arm laid across the wagon snapped forward. The whole thing jumped as it heaved a boulder into the air.

It struck the Raffen near the bridge, and a second stone swept into a cluster of mounted knights who commanded the Raffen. The corpsmen around them fled, and so did the Raffen. With renewed courage, the Gallerlanders swelled over the remaining Raffen and over the bridge. Now leaderless, the Raffen soon scattered.

As the battle waned, Rildning noticed a Gallerlander thirty paces from him brutally dispatch a wounded, struggling Raffen. When this tribesman had killed his enemy, his sharp eyes caught Rildning's glance, and he quickly looked away.

The lanky Gallerlander was familiar to Rildning, but his face was obscured by his shaggy hair. He was also a bit dirtier than the others. Before Rildning could approach him, a grunt from the Vaynking ended his distraction.

Tirgranir was being pulled up from the ground. His ax was shattered around him, but he still held fast to its broken, bloodied haft. Most of his protective chiefs had died, but

Arbardir was still alive. The Gallerlanders did not lower their weapons as the Rahlampians approached. Both sides glowered at each other.

Rildning saw that the Rahlampian tattoos were very different from the designs of the Gallerlanders and the blue splotches of the Raffen. This tribe's tattoos were thin lines on the face and wide black bands on the arms and legs, and many had images of simple boats with round objects tattooed on their shoulders.

They wore leather boots and woolen smocks, and their trousers were cut above the knee. Most, including their chief, had armor made of bundles of thick reeds and hammered bog iron plates. Their blades were glassy metal and without rust.

Rildning was surprised at the length and thinness of these swords. He reasoned that the oversized pommels were to balance the length of the blade. The sheaths were short and open-ended, with a clever latched assembly that opened lengthwise to swing the blade out for use. Rildning realized the Rahlampians might compete with the Frontier Corps.

"Who are they?" Rildning asked. He watched warily as the apparent leader of the black-painted men wiped blood from an extremely long, thin sword.

"Damned Rahlampians," Tirgranir muttered. Then silence as each side stared at the other. Finally Rildning spoke again.

"Well, they saved us. What do they want?"

"Blood. A fight. It's what they always want," Tirgranir answered. He turned to Arbardir. "Find that young chieftain from Elrid. He is from the east and knows how to speak with these foul people."

"He is there." Arbardir pointed to the mound of bodies on the bridge.

Tirgranir returned his eyes to the Rahlampians, who were murmuring among themselves.

"I knew the border town of Elrid, before the Raffen burned it," spoke the chief black-faced man in Gali. "Do not be surprised with my speech. The bloodlines, yours and ours, parted ages ago. But many of us still learn the old tongue."

"Did you build that catapult?" Rildning pointed up the hill. The man nodded. "Well done, and well aimed. But perhaps you can ask your men to unload it or point it away from us. We don't wish to fight you."

The Rahlampian chuckled. "Who is this white-face?" he asked Tirgranir. "A foreigner among you, as the Raffen have foreigners among them?"

Tirgranir looked at Rildning, who knew that if ever the Vaynking wanted to rid himself of Rildning, this was the moment.

"He was," Tirgranir answered. "But he is one of us now."

The Rahlampian smiled grimly. "Then you are no better than the Raffen."

"I'm foreign," Rildning said. "But I joined the tribe because of what has happened to Gallerlandia."

"We have a saying in Rahlampia: the answer to a riddle is not another riddle. Thus, any foreigner who says he will help us—the original peoples of these hills and valleys—is sent by the enemy to deceive and harm us. Do you want me to solve this riddle for you, Vaynking?"

"Put your cursed-earth blades away," Tirgranir replied. He had now stepped forward to Rildning's side and tossed down his broken haft. Urgamdir, Owerdir, and others followed. "You have helped us, but don't play games," he continued. "I recognize who you are, now, Mrigamad of Castracane. My tribesmen are weary, but we vastly outnumber you on this field. Choose now to leave or make battle, the ending of which will be no riddle or mystery to you."

"This is how you welcome your rescuers?" Mrigamad asked. "Perhaps you should test the omens in the sky before you spill rubbish from your mouth. Next will be blood from your gut."

Rildning could see Tirgranir's temper rise. Despite the restraint he had mustered, he was still hot with the battle and would have fought the Rahlampians with his next breath.

"Peace!" Rildning again inserted himself between them. "Let us have kinder words for allies who have defeated the foe."

"Allies?" Tirgranir was steaming.

"Let it be peace then, as your white-face says."

Mrigamad's abrupt acquiescence let Rildning breathe a sigh of relief. But now Tirgranir was the one who itched for a fight.

"Peace?" Tirgranir scoffed. "Why have you trespassed into Vaynland and at a time when my people are on their knees? If I had come upon you first, I would have killed you for pillaging my lands."

"The Raffen have raided our borderlands, too," Mrigamad said. "After your people fled and left your lands undefended, ours were left vulnerable. Cadentod, Rittonrewk, and many other villages have been sacked. We were sent by the domnitar to scout the enemy's encampments. The Raffen and their white-faced masters are our common enemy now, unless you prefer to lose on your own."

Rildning could see Mrigamad's return to jeering was angering Tirgranir further. So on a whim he surprised them both.

"Join us," Rildning said. "As you said, we face the same enemy. And as you have said, there is no time for games. I don't know the reasons for the deep mistrust between the Gallerlanders and Rahlampians, but only by uniting will you defeat this enemy."

"Rildning!" Tirgranir snapped. "We don't need these dark folk."

"Perhaps let the Sage of Gilgalem decide," Rildning countered. "I know our enemy. They won't stop until every Nalembalen is burned and every tribe quelled or enslaved. The empire views this continent and everything in it as its possession, with only us standing in the way. Let the Sage hear and decide on this alliance, as he will about our strategy overall." When Tirgranir relented, Rildning turned to Mrigamad. "And you?"

"I'll join you to Gilgalem, if only to judge your people's ability to guard the borderlands. Domnitar Anfinnan will want to know."

"So be it," Tirgranir said. "But I warn you, Rildning. We will be bringing these dark folk, who don't hold the electrum sacred, into our holiest place. And Gilgalem is our last refuge. If anything happens . . ."

"All will be well." Rildning nodded, though he wasn't sure why he was so certain.

❧

The Gallerlanders buried their dead with great care, as they did after every battle when able. The enemy's dead were stripped of any provisions and stolen electrum, then piled high and set alight. On a whim, Rildning kept a Frontier Corps banner, its simple starcross torn nearly in two. It was a symbol of his religion, which was still alive in his heart, though he knew in his head that it had been used as a trumpet to call men to fight for the New World.

He noticed Mrigamad's suspicious stare as he stuffed the banner into his tunic.

13

BREDAHADE

Eglamour, Donovan Province
Midautumn, 2269

"How go the preparations for the imperial council?" Exarch Bredahade asked. The chancellor and archbishop had joined him in the palace sitting room. The walls were decked with tapestries woven with electrum thread.

"The council is ready to commence as soon as the remaining barbarian kings arrive, Your Eminence," Sarnaker replied. "Highchief Harkarom of the Bronhildi and King Pendigied of the Raffen are still traveling. The governors of the provinces of Donovan, Leauvenna, and New Hovedollen have already arrived, as have the governors of Durgensdil and Brewel colonies. Marshal Hilsingor, of course, will not attend because he is forming the new provinces of Wallevet and Bram and preparing winter quarters."

Bredahade was always impressed by Sarnaker's promptness and thoroughness. His appointment had been a difficult sell to the emperor because Sarnaker's family was of middling nobility. But Bredahade had insisted his former pupil was the best fit for the office. Ever humble, Sarnaker had served with distinction as the mayor of Ramunhavin in Almeria.

Then there was Archbishop Ralmo, the middle-aged churchman who Bredahade felt was too easily excited and angered. He took a bit too much pleasure in burning heretics and heathens. Bredahade lamented that he had little influence over the archbishop, as Ralmo answered directly to the Martinus and the Temple Curia. Born in Donovan when it was merely a colony, Ralmo oversaw the entire Messengian Church in Pemonia, appointed bishops, and collected his own taxes.

Ralmo's insistence on serving as both religious and administrative chief of the Brintilian Empire in Pemonia was too much for Bredahade. The exarch had tried to dissuade the emperor of Ralmo's appointment, but the Martinus insisted, citing the necessity for an archbishop born in the New World to serve the flocks there. Ralmo's honorable service under the governor of Donovan had been spotless. So Bredahade was forced to accept him.

"What about the barbarians who signed peace treaties with the early colonies?" Bredahade asked.

"The Ollohds and the Teshi were long ago integrated into the provincial legions and courts," Sarnaker replied. "The Hrals have never yielded."

"Nor will they ever!" Ralmo snorted. "No unrepentant Memelos spawn has any place in the empire's legions, as I have counseled many times."

"The Hrals will remain subjugated," Sarnaker said. "But the others who have signed treaties converted to the true religion and have proven valuable. I've met with many Ollohd chiefs and a few Teshi that survived the war in Leauvenna. All of them are fully committed to the empire. Deprived of their old tribal power structures, they already have much invested with the provinces. The imperial council will be a powerful lever for the exarch."

"And you will lead the council well, Sarnaker," Bredahade said. "Ralmo, you must give this policy a chance. It is, after all, supported by the emperor."

"But not the Martinus," Ralmo countered. "The Temple Father in his letters makes clear he is wary of the imperial realm of Pemonia moving too quickly in befriending the unclean barbarians. More should be done to cull them."

"The Martinus has also written to me of his great joy upon hearing the news that whole clans and tribes continue to convert to Messengianism," Bredahade said. "A victory for God that is worked through our diligent hands. Now, let it not be said I have been too hasty in embracing the tribes. The Hrals and the dismemberment of Gallerlandia are only two examples. Our progress is swift, by God's will, and we shall continue this path."

"Well . . ." Ralmo muttered. "Well, the Martinus has also written to ask whether the heretic Rildning has been captured. Pending the progress of his actual arrest, if I could receive the journal that the marshal—"

"Speaking of progress," Sarnaker interrupted, "the land route between here and Durgensdil will likely be complete by next summer. The men of Alpening's legion will overwinter in Colbrint, a frontier town far south of here. They are well provisioned, and Alpening's courage and leadership, as you know, is second only to that of the marshal himself. The opening of this road will prove very profitable for the crusaders and the empire. Especially when the stormy seasons prohibit sailing the Sea of Nore."

"With the paths of Hilsingor and Alpening so well planned, I look forward to the spring," Bredahade said before dismissing them. After Sarnaker and Ralmo departed, Bredahade could still hear them arguing in the hallway.

"Why do you fill his old mind with so much rubbish?" Ralmo said. "You know this union with the barbarians will never work, regardless of their conversion. They are simply too tainted with evil. Or do you wish for the exarch to fail so you may take his seat?"

"What a preposterous—"

"Oh yes, I see though your veneer. You covet the old man's position."

"Hold your tongue!" snapped Sarnaker. "True, one day the student may replace the teacher, if you are unlucky enough. But I do believe his policy of standing up to the imperial council can work. How else do you think we Brintilians have ruled over the Arukans and the other Old World kingdoms? I suppose you, a Donovard, would have no knowledge of sophisticated politics, stuck as you have been tending church halls on the fringes of civilization."

"How dare you. Trifle with me and I'll see to it that accusations of heresy find their way to your doorstep."

Bredahade could hear Sarnaker take a step, then lower his voice.

"Trifle with you? Perhaps the exarch, or the Martinus, will hear of your forays with the Teshi women you have grown accustomed to. Or perhaps the clan-wife of that Ollohd chieftain? Oh yes, I know all about them. What scandal. In fact, you can thank me, or rather my contacts, for arranging your pleasures. Now, good Ralmo, I'll leave you to God's work, confident you will no longer meddle in the affairs of the exarch's chief politician. Good day!"

Bredahade heard Sarnaker walk away, but it was a while before the archbishop moved. The exarch wondered if he should stay in his chamber until Ralmo left, but decided on a whim to exit. There in the hallway he found him standing alone, great beads of sweat glistening on his brow.

"Are you all right, Ralmo?"

"Ah, yes, Your Eminence. I was . . . meditating. Solitary walks clear the mind."

Bredahade continued to walk past him as he spoke. "Good. I will require your mind to be clear to support our efforts, as God wills."

14

RILDNING

Gilgalem, Vaynland
Midautumn, 2269

When Rildning and the others exited the wood, the mountains of Gilgalem rose up from the earth ahead of them, their gently sloped shoulders carpeted with spruces, firs, and sugar pines.

"There it is," Tirgranir said, his eyes welling. "My seat of Vaynland, the great refuge and holiest place for all Gallerlandia. Beneath its great peaks lie the sacred mines and forge of the Maluram clan."

"It is good to see its gray stone rising above this sad realm," Owerdir said.

"Is it enough to hide all the Gallerlanders who have fled here, as well as our army?" Rildning asked.

"The Nalembalen of the south, and stronger yet," Tirgranir said with pride. "The tunnels, crevasses, and topmost woods of Gilgalem can provide shelter to many times more. And no one will go without food, even over many winters, for the understories of the mountain are cavernous and dug out long ago by ancient waters."

Mrigamad and his Rahlampians were awed at the sight but said nothing. Though the Rahlampians numbered several companies in size, Rildning had noticed they had largely kept silent and separate from the Gallerlanders. He guessed they were keen not to provoke Tirgranir's men. Rildning was curious about the rivalry between these two peoples, but he did not want to say anything to jeopardize his efforts to recruit them as allies.

With renewed vigor, the Gallerlanders trekked to the mountains where the foothills grew out of the brown plains of wild wheat. They greeted Vayn sentries as they made their way along the twisting footpaths. The joy of these guards at seeing their king again warmed Tirgranir's mood. Rildning's heart also stirred with eager hope.

"Is this the route Eniri and the others used?" he asked.

"Yes," Tirgranir answered. "When the Umbyr clans fled south, she led them here. I sent many Vaynland clans here as well before coming to your aid. There is no safer place in the world, and I hope knowing Eniri and your son have been with my wife, Sabani, has given you a measure of peace."

"It has . . ." Rildning recalled Eniri's reluctant departure from him. But her escape and survival had been paramount. Now, as he drew nearer to her, his thoughts and cares of fighting the Frontier Corps seemed so far behind him. He longed to be with her and see his child.

The Gallerlanders continued up the mountain paths. Miniature cliffs of snow-covered moss formed a dark overhang in many places. At last they came to a broad, rocky clearing. Here boat-sized boulders had fallen and were carved with many shapes, pits, and Gali inscriptions. They were too weathered for Rildning to read.

"It is the story of Wurumnak's revealing of Gilgalem to the ancient Gallerlanders," Tirgranir explained.

"Please, tell it to me," Rildning said.

"A fierce storm had driven a wanderer to shelter here. Then lightning struck the peak above, showering these boulders down around him. They glimmered with veins of electrum, which poured out at the wanderer's feet like molten blood. The liquid flowed into the cracked ground between the boulders, collecting in this depression here, where a shield of pure electrum was cast.

"Wurumnak said to the wanderer, 'Do not return to your village but stay on this mountain and harvest its blood. For at the End of Days it shall be forged into the sword that shall deliver the death to the great snake.' And so the wanderer became a miner and a smith, and the electrum shield served as a reminder of his duty to defend all of the peoples of Wurumnak."

As Tirgranir spoke, Rildning ran his fingers along the empty veins in the rock. He looked down to the depression, which lay in the middle between five boulders, where the shield had been forged by lightning. The place was now fissured and layered with lichen.

Tirgranir turned to Mrigamad. The Rahlampian and his men had kept their distance from the boulders. "You are fortunate to be the first Rahlampians to see this place," the Vaynking told them. Mrigamad did not respond.

At Tirgranir's word, most of the Gallerlanders rested on the boulder shelf. Here they would wait until their places were prepared for them in Gilgalem. Vayn women poured down the path into the clearing, carrying baskets of food. Old men also came with bundles of medicine for the wounded tribesmen. More tired warriors arrived throughout the day and into the night as the rear guards and trailing scouts reached the mountain.

Rildning walked out from behind one of the boulders to help tend to the wounded. As he worked, he felt as if he was being watched. His eyes drifted around the camp. Once again, like after the battle at the Fenthugren River bridge, he noticed the same tribesman staring at him. The lanky, sharp-eyed Gallerlander quickly turned away once Rildning took notice, as he had at the river. Rildning started across the clearing to question him, but Tirgranir intercepted Rildning.

"Follow me, Rildning."

He followed the Vaynking toward a large cleft in the mountain wall that curtained the clearing. They entered the cleft and walked not thirty paces through a narrow ravine before the rock gave way to a thick line of spruces. The air was clean and sweet smelling, and a breeze urged them onward from behind.

They stepped out of the boughs and onto a ledge that overlooked the massive refuge of Gilgalem, a sight like nothing Rildning had seen before. It was as if the peak of the mountain had been scooped out. Along the edge of the yawning pit were ten broad terraces carved from the rock leading from the tree ledge down into a flat courtyard at the bottom.

Children were playing at one end of the courtyard while tribesmen practiced fighting on the other. People mingled, ate, washed, and worked across the terraces as the sounds echoed upward. Every terrace terminated at the sides of a colossal natural tower leaning out over everything in the bowl.

Residents were already lighting torches set between the wooden doors and small windows that studded the terrace walls. The central tower had similar features, along with huge doors of whole tree trunks at its base in the courtyard and a large balcony near the middle.

On every surface of the terraces and walls and tower could be seen empty veins where electrum had once flowed. It was now that Rildning realized the painted designs and tattoos of the Gallerlanders mimicked these channels, rather than the vines of the forest as he had presumed. He looked at his own outstretched arms and the tattoos he had been given. He felt a sudden calling from the ancient past, a fateful feeling of welcome, like he was home.

Rildning turned his gaze to the sky as the sun set. The peaks of the surrounding ridge peered down into the bowl as if they were curious protectors of the natives within. The whole place was like a hidden basket of primeval origin, yet still so alive.

"Welcome," the Vaynking said with a satisfied grin. "Gilgalem has long been the home of the Vaynkings and the sages."

"An astonishing place," Rildning replied.

"Gilgalem's mouth is wide and its lungs deep, and the people are its voice. Come!"

The pair descended a small staircase to the topmost terrace. From there they wound their way down small ramps and staircases until they passed four more terraces. They walked toward the tower, at the same level as its balcony, which was part of the Vaynking's chambers.

The tower was full of small windows but lacked terraces. Soon they reached the end of the path and entered the tower. Above the door was a circular tile with weathered etching.

"From the plains and hills to the pit and caves," a man said as they entered the throne room. He was robed in red fox furs similar to the Graparins of Nalembalen, but without electrum or other fancy ornaments. He greeted Tirgranir warmly.

The vaulted ceiling rested on stone columns reaching up as high as two terraces. Rildning saw the simply made high-backed throne of polished spruce. Inlaid into the back of the chair was darker wood in the shape of a tree. On the wall above the throne hung a gleaming electrum shield.

"We have heard much about you, Parinsogon," the man said to Rildning. "Tales of your surviving the snakes and Hrals are well-known in the stone halls of Gilgalem. Welcome to you! I'm Rumban, Steward of Gilgalem when the Vaynking is absent, and Keeper of Pindoarig, the Tower of Steaming Stone, where you now stand. These halls have never witnessed a foreigner like yourself, but you are most welcome. Your wife the queen awaits you."

Rildning smiled and was about to speak but Tirgranir soured.

"Eniri is no queen," the Vaynking snapped. "She isn't the wife of a Gallerlander king, and the high king's chair is vacant—rather turned to ashes. She is a princess at best, but there is no Queen of the Gallerlanders in our times."

"I humbly beg your forgiveness," Rumban said, bowing low. "I meant no offense."

Rildning thought Tirgranir's reaction harsh, but he resolved to stay out of the debate. He knew Eniri did not consider herself a queen, not even of the Umbyrs alone.

"I have longed for two years to see her," Rildning said.

"Just this way," Rumban beckoned.

Before the steward could lead them on, several women burst into the chamber. Their hair flowed freely as they hurried to the men.

"Welcome home, my king." It was Tirgranir's queen. "You did not send early word of your arrival, but I know your voice from many mountains away."

As they embraced, Rildning's gaze fell upon the woman behind her. He whispered her name and she smiled, brushing her chestnut hair from her face. She reached out her hands and he took them softly. Rildning was lost in the emerald depths of her eyes as they drew near to his. Her lips were sweeter even than they had been on their first embrace in Nalembalen.

"I have waited too long for you."

"One day was too long."

The giggle of a girl broke their trance. Rildning and Eniri blushed as the others looked on.

"Now, Tirani," scolded the Vaynqueen, "do not act as though you've never seen love's blossom." The girl scampered off, and the queen approached Rildning. "I'm Sabani. I feel I know you so well. It's good to finally welcome you. Be assured that your family will always be welcomed here."

"Thank you," Rildning said. "The day Tirgranir came to us in the north was a great day, for he brought aid to our warriors. He also brought me comfort with the knowledge that my family had arrived here safely."

"Yes, and I'm sure you will want to see a certain little person," Sabani said.

"Go," Tirgranir said. "Spend the time with them while we have it."

Eniri took Rildning's hand. She led him out of the throne room into a series of halls and side rooms. The innards of Pindoarig tower were mostly unadorned but comfortable enough.

Rildning had never seen a tower—much less an entire city—carved directly into a mountain. The rock was gneiss, with wavy bands of umber and taupe, beaver and bistre, and shades of wheat. Every wall and surface was rough-hewn but glittered in the light of the window holes and the few torches, as if the stone were perpetually wet.

After ascending a few stairways, they entered chambers above the throne room. The hallway was broad with several doors. As Eniri carefully opened one, Rildning was reminded of that feast night in Nalembalen, when she had first smuggled him into the Graparins' archive to let him glimpse the Cataclysm scroll. He thought about how she trusted him so easily even then and loved him before she really knew him.

And now, in this room, he knew a living symbol of their love lay safe and still. Walking silently with her to the crib-basket, he was overcome by joy. Tears welled and broke from his eyes as he looked upon his son for the first time.

Many times Rildning had dreamed of what his son would look like, and now he saw him sleeping in peace. His son had Eniri's hair and long eyelashes. Rildning had felt so much guilt at leaving her when his sword was required in the north, and he had buried the guilt until this moment. Eniri squeezed him. On their knees they watched the still child.

"His name is Enildir," she whispered to him. "Named as you wished, in the fashion of our people."

"Beautiful." His voice trembled as his hand lay steady on the babe's chest.

Eniri carefully picked Enildir from his wicker cradle and placed him in Rildning's arms. He grunted and wiggled but did not wake, and slept with Rildning's thumb in his grasp. Rildning realized he was not such a tiny infant as he had imagined, but a growing tot. There they sat on the floor until they grew tired. There was much to share but for now they drifted in the dream silently together.

❧

When Enildir awoke the next day, his sleepy eyes soon focused with a curious gaze on Rildning's face. Enildir was at ease with the new face, but he seemed to have many questions that he could not ask. They told Enildir the tale which Eniri had told him many times, about why Rildning had been absent. When Enildir was content, he scooted off Rildning's lap and played.

Servants brought Rildning a fresh tunic and he washed himself to the sound of babbles and squeals. There was no shouting of men's voices, no clash of steel and stone, no marching. Only the sounds of home.

"The cares of the world have not diminished in you, husband, nor in me I suppose. My dreams are still haunted by the burning city. The red snow and the arrows. Gratgofa and Pagdorat. That night and those that followed are a dark tree planted in the forest of my mind.

"Those memories will ever be there, but I don't allow them to grow and spread seed as you have with your burdens. We will address those cares as we must, but for now, take heart in our reunion and the health of our son, who will surely see better days than we have beheld."

"That is my prayer," Rildning said. "I have often imagined what he might look like, and you holding him. And I have wondered what will become of him when he is of age. Will he be forced to pick up my sword, or shall the world leave him in peace?"

"The sword is a certainty, for even Wurumnak's dawn of the electrum sword awaits. But I think Enildir will face his burdens as you have, with courage and justice. When he is ready, I have no doubt he will take his place defending what is good."

"Then I shall do all in my power to lessen his burden."

Eniri smiled. "Your Gali speech has improved, husband. Pagdorat would be proud."

Rildning nodded solemnly.

ɧ

That evening, after Enildir was again tucked into his warm crib, a feast was held to welcome the Vaynking and his warriors. Tirgranir and Sabani sat at the head of the table, with Rildning and Eniri taking their places with the other chieftains and their families. Each crowded table in the hall was laden with fresh trappings of game and autumn harvests.

"Why two empty chairs?" Rildning asked.

"To honor Umbyrking Erambrin and Goynking Odon," Eniri answered. "It's tradition, when others are out fighting."

"There could be many empty chairs, especially for the Umbyrs. Like your father. And men like Urgamdir, whose families perished before even the siege of Nalembalen."

"The Goyns have suffered the worst. Few are here in Gilgalem, despite the exodus. Even Rumban cannot easily count the many Gallerlander refugees who now live in the mountain."

"How long before Gilgalem cannot feed them all?" Rildning asked.

"Rumban says they've not yet had to tap into Gilgalem's vast food stores that Tirgranir had boasted about."

As he ate, Rildning noticed that the guards of Pindoarig were armed with spears of obsidian, black rippled and shiny like moonlit water. He was surprised that the only electrum in view was the rings of the chieftains and the ancient shield above the throne. He had imagined Gilgalem to be a glittering place, given the Maluram were said to mine vast quantities. Even faraway Nalembalen had many ornaments of electrum.

The spruce beer flowed, and the conversation of the tables grew louder. Tirgranir and his chiefs were merry, enjoying the comforts of home. But soon there was talk of politics, especially who would be the next high king. Rildning and Eniri were drawn in.

"The Gallerlanders have been headless for two years!" cried one of the Vaynking's supporters.

"All kings have fallen, all but one!" another yelled.

Tirgranir remained quiet when other chieftains of Odon and Erambrin clamored for their kings' claims. Owerdir leaned over amid the bickering.

"Tirgranir seems pleased with the debate," he whispered to Rildning and Eniri. "Comfortable in his position while the other two underkings walk the knife's edge of the Frontier Corps."

"He believes himself to be high king already," Eniri said. "Has he asked for your support yet, husband?"

"No," Rildning said. "He has not spoken to me about the high throne."

"He will," Owerdir said, "now that he isn't near a battlefield."

The debate around the tables became increasingly heated. Tirgranir smiled and chuckled.

"Surely he doesn't cherish the division of the Gallerlanders at such a time?" Rildning whispered to Eniri. "He's often decisive—if headstrong—on the battlefield, uncaring whether a Vayn or a Goyn or Umbyr leads a charge. He can muster any obstinate man to his side."

"But he can't unify anyone once off the battlefield," she replied.

Drunk tribesmen were now tossing insults around freely. Rildning could tell Eniri wanted to do or say something, but he knew, as a potential successor to the throne, she did not want to cause any harm.

Rildning pondered how to calm the Gallerlanders before a brawl erupted, then he noticed the Rahlampian. Mrigamad, the only one among his men permitted to join the feast, was visibly uncomfortable. Rildning also noted Mrigamad did not partake of the spruce beer. Rildning abruptly rose to his feet and spoke over the din.

"King Tirgranir, these tables have grown rowdy and unworthy of your audience. And it does not put our honored guest of Rahlampia at ease, nor would this meal persuade his people of our own peoples' unity in a quest for which we seek his help. Shall we clear the chairs until a new hour?"

Some of the Vaynking's ardent supporters remained indignant, using the pause before the king's answer to mutter about "the foreigner."

"Mrigamad of Castracane is no stranger to controversy, are you, son of Mearnsod the Floodbringer?" Tirgranir replied. "No, our guest should count himself fortunate to set foot in our sacred Gilgalem.

"As for the debate, let it be known I don't consider the claims of my brother-kings, Odon and Erambrin, to be forfeit simply because they are still joined in battle while we are now afforded respite. The Sage will decide our path, as it has always been in such cloudy times.

"Doubtless," he concluded with a glance toward Eniri, "High King Gratgofa would have wanted as much. Now, may the chiefs return to their meat and beer and merry talk."

Rildning could see a glint of flame in Eniri's eyes. Tirgranir clearly enjoyed publicly excluding Eniri as a potential successor to Gratgofa. Everyone knew she was once betrothed to Gratgofa's now-deceased son.

But this time, by evoking Gratgofa and his supposed wishes, Rildning new Tirgranir had provoked Eniri. She jumped to her feet and held her head high.

"As one who was closest to Gratgofa before he took his place among the heavenly Thuraniparin, I agree he would have wished the Gallerlanders to look to the Sage. But I know Gratgofa would frown on our divisions, for he tolerated no such evils while Nalembalen stood. Let us also remember the teachings of the Graparins. The great snake Demfrebra can only prevail at time's end if we are divided and do not seek the unity of Wurumnak's sacred sword."

Rildning saw the Umbyrs and many Goyns cheered her—with the exception of Arbardir and his ilk. He knew most were split in their support for Eniri or Erambrin or Odon, but only Vayns supported Tirgranir.

"Unity is the sword, 'tis true," Tirgranir said. His smile was smug and confident. "We will look to the Sage of Gilgalem."

Mrigamad, unimpressed, walked over to Rildning.

"How did these men ever claim the whole of Gallerlandia?" he asked. "They wouldn't agree on a single hill to walk up and would fight with one another on the crest."

"A good and unknowable question," Owerdir said.

"It is certain," Mrigamad continued, "that the power in these western woods is fading. The foreigners have taken your greatest cities and tossed about the armies of your kings. Their hounds, the Raffen, grow stronger by the day and threaten Rahlampia, while Vaynland holes up in a hollow mountain."

Urgamdir grew agitated. "Do you think the wet-footed Rahlampians could so easily supplant our greatness then?"

"Greatness?" Mrigamad scoffed. "You don't even see that the Frontier Corps has taken what greatness you may have had. We and the Gallerlanders are of shared blood from ancient time, but these new days will see us take a far different path. Domnitar Anfinnan will determine whether we wait for Gilgalem to fall before destroying the Raffen, or whether we will take Vaynland from you as a buffer now."

Mrigamad then looked upon Rildning. "And I remain puzzled by this green-painted foreigner. I cannot see how the

Gallerlanders have taken him in or how he could make a difference to the cause. Perhaps he is the cleverest of spies. Whatever the domnitar decides, we will be watching all of you."

Mrigamad departed from the hall, leaving the rest to weigh the truth in his words. Urgamdir pulled a mug of spruce beer to his nose, then pushed it away with a sour face.

15

HILSINGOR

Rachard, Bram Province
Frostfall, 2269

Hilsingor stood on the high rampart of his private chambers in the wooden castle. It was finally Frostfall, and he did not mind the cold. He had spent more winters in the field than beside a hearth fire at this point. As he had grown older, he had become content to trust his senior commanders to carry out his orders. Yet he still loved battle, and his keen mind was ever going over his plans for the spring conquest.

He looked down from the rampart to the first foundation stones of what would become his greatest fortress. The main keep would be completed by summer, but Hilsingor knew it would take years before his full design would be complete.

"Sir, a visitor for you," Arnolf said behind him. "Special messenger from the south."

Hilsingor turned to see a dark, tall man. He was one of the few equal to Hilsingor's own height. The man was dressed as he always was, in black leather-covered cuirass and greaves, weathered cloak, and hood. It was this garb that easily distinguished the Frontier Corps scouts from the regular soldiers. This man was his senior ranger-tracker and entrusted with duties hidden to everyone but Arnolf.

"Ah, yes. That will be all, Arnolf." The hooded man joined the marshal at the rampart. "It's been too long, Widsem," the marshal said. "But I know searching the vast wilds of Gallerlandia is not a quick or easy task."

"It is my honor, sir," Widsem replied, his voice hoarse with fatigue.

The ranger handed him a weathered bit of parchment, bound in rough-grass twine with green paint smeared on the knot in lieu of sealing wax. They went back inside so Hilsingor could read by the warmth of the fire. He sat in front of the hearth before pulling the string on the message.

> Gallerlanders reached Gilgalem.
> Rildning and Tirgranir with them.
> Much infighting.
> Will begin sabotage.

"Excellent," the marshal said. "Everything is going according to plan and now the little spy will soon make the heathens more desperate. Almost too easy. The Gallerlanders are too predictable. Please, have a seat, Widsem. Your road has been a weary one."

"There are no roads out there," the ranger said, sighing with relief upon taking his weight off his feet. "First big fire I have seen in months. The Gallerlanders use the deer paths and such, but their numbers have made them easy to follow, road or not."

"The roads are coming," Hilsingor said, then he paused for a moment. "I cannot help but wonder if they don't deserve the respect I have always been careful to hold for my enemies, whether back in Almeria or here, so as not to be surprised. The Gallerlanders are certainly not like the Arukans were—now there was a worthy foe.

"Emperor Olskeroth's father ordered me to end the Arukans' destructive rebellion," he continued. "He gave me eight legions to form the Rivercross Corps and, with pleasure, I brought the Arukans to their knees in the end. But it was a bitter challenge as they were defending their home realm. Only after the elimination of their royals and imprisoning thousands at Arcodum did they relent.

"That was before your time, Widsem, in a land your careful feet have never trekked. We were swift and unexpected, and the Arukans did not retreat. Ever. But these

Gallerlanders run as often as they fight. You have watched them up close. Why are they always so disorganized?"

"I cannot say more than you already know," Widsem said. "All they do now is run south. And Ferndeath will barely speak a word to me. He gives me these little letters, then scampers off without delay, running after them."

"He is odd, isn't he?"

Hilsingor recalled his first and only meeting with the little man who insisted on using that peculiar name for himself. Hilsingor could not even remember Ferndeath's real name.

"In his previous letter," the marshal continued, "Ferndeath said Vaynking Tirgranir desired face-to-face combat, but Rildning favored a careful rebellion from the bush and urged the Gallerlanders to adopt steel and horses. I surmise the Gallerlanders are divided over how to counter us, and Rildning is likely distrusted and even despised by many of the barbarians. I'd have many questions for our little Ferndeath if he were not so skittish."

"I could try giving him your letter again, or ask him myself."

"No, let us not attempt that again. We will let him be. He has kept his word for, what, six or seven seasons now? Though his messages are short and irregular, they are irreplaceable. He has provided hints of every major movement of Tirgranir's warriors and led us to Nalembalen, as you well know. I want to preserve him at all costs, including protecting him from my own curiosity. Has he asked for anything?"

"Nothing, sir."

"He was promised the world. His reward will be great indeed if they do not discover and kill him first."

"He looks—and smells—just like one of them," Widsem said. "More than once I've drawn my bow on him, uncertain if he was really a Gallerlander. He's lasted this long."

"Well, you know as well as I do there is one man among the Gallerlanders who could easily recognize Ferndeath if he opened his eyes."

"There are two that could, sir," the ranger said.

"Yes, but only one remains with the green-skins."

Arnolf opened the door to request entry, but a fuming red-faced Ravorglad pushed him out of the way. The knight glared at Widsem until the ranger got up and exited to find rest and nourishment before returning to his duty in the morning.

Hilsingor tossed Ferndeath's letter into the fire, then motioned for Ravorglad to sit with him. Ravorglad watched the message flare but did not ask questions, and Hilsingor offered no explanation.

"What troubles you now?" the marshal asked.

"Firkas." The crusader did not hide his disdain. "He's allowing his provincials—and worse, those Raffen and Bronhildi converts—to enter my crusaders' quarters and hall. And worse yet, his smithy—"

"How many times must I speak with the two of you?" Hilsingor groaned. "I have often said you both remind me of my own sons back in Almeria, and truly you act as children when you have not enough battle to busy yourselves. Must I seek a wet nurse for my knight-generals to get myself through the winter with my sanity? Depart from me at once, if you must complain further."

"Forgive me, sir. I only wish to retain the honor of my men so they may better serve you."

Hilsingor could see Ravorglad's irritation with Firkas continued to smolder.

"Why should your crusaders be dishonored by mingling with the provincial legions? Are they not the two arms of the Frontier Corps, as I have said before? Yes, winter quarters are tight this year, but you could use the situation wisely.

"There is much your soldiers could learn from the Raffen warriors, and it would be well for your men to know their ways. After the snow thaws, they will be marching shoulder to shoulder. You should be encouraging this, Ravorglad."

They sat in silence for a few moments, watching the fire pop and sizzle.

"In truth, the rivalry between yourself and Firkas is not unusual between commanders. Every general desires to be the best in his master's eyes. Your bravery is unmatched and your crusaders performed honorably in the north, especially at Nalembalen. However, your rashness has killed some of your best knights. The disaster in Ardfalm Forest is only one example, though certainly the worst.

"Firkas, on the other hand, has the patience of an hourglass, but he lacks your fire. His hottest ember is vengeance for his dead brothers, and he dreams of facing Rildning in battle. Worthy in itself, given Rildning's treachery, but misguided and all consuming. I don't believe Rildning murdered his brothers, based on my reading of the heretic's journal. Whatever the case, Firkas's aims are too narrow.

"So, between the two of you, I have unbridled bravery on the right hand and narrow steadiness on the left. But I won't see my right or left hand stray from the other."

Ravorglad nodded with sincere understanding.

"As I have told Firkas," Hilsingor continued, "focus on resting and readying your men over the next few months. Winter quarters are difficult for men bred to fight, but the spring will bring many opportunities here at the edge of the empire. We must be ready."

"How goes the empire's new capital in the west?" Ravorglad asked.

"The exarch has built a seat that honors our efforts," Hilsingor replied. "It is early days still, but the new imperial council will convene soon. In his latest letter, Bredahade said all the provinces and barbarian allies would soon meet to establish the emperor's new administration for Pemonia. We, of course, will continue to expand it as they decide how to best knit the pieces together."

"I'm glad to have the sword-end of the effort," Ravorglad said. Hilsingor nodded in agreement. "I could not bear the politics," the knight continued. "And all the petty bickering that comes with all those rival factions."

"I wish I could say I've avoided such bickering out here on the frontier," the marshal said wryly. "But I haven't."

16

BREDAHADE

Eglamour, Donovan Province
Frostfall, 2269

Exarch Bredahade was almost giddy to see the great carriage he had gifted to the Raffen king. He had been confident Genthus would persuade the heathen king to accept the invitation to attend the new imperial council in Eglamour.

The iron-studded wheels clicked across the new stone of the courtyard as the visitors were escorted by Bredahade's guards. Over his walls the exarch could see the five thousand Raffen warriors, which Genthus has mentioned in his letters, arrive at the timber barracks built for them on the outskirts of the city. The exarch had everything well prepared for Pendigied, the last of the barbarian kings to arrive.

Pendigied and Genthus stepped out of the carriage. Bredahade, Sarnaker, Ralmo, and other retainers of the imperial court greeted the Raffen king on the sweeping portico before the towering palace doors. The exarch noticed a Gallerlander, his hands bound and face sickly, being led away to the stables with the horses.

"Welcome, great king of the south," Bredahade said through Genthus's translation. "I'm glad to see your long journey brought you safely to me. I trust your travel was comfortable?"

"His Highness thanks you for the warm welcome and the many gifts, Your Eminence," Genthus said. "He has looked

83

forward to this day, but first wishes to thank the Messengian God for his safe arrival."

King Pendigied knelt to the ground with hands folded, head bowed, and eyes closed in prayer, as Genthus had tutored him. Bredahade noticed a pleasantly surprised look on Ralmo's face.

"Please tell the king we are most honored by his piety and we also gave thanks when we heard of his conversion," the exarch said. "Tomorrow he will be crowned with God's grace in full, but tonight he and his chieftains must dine at my table."

Genthus relayed his words. Pendigied stood and smiled boyishly. Bredahade recalled the words of Genthus's final rushed letter, delivered by his messenger mere hours before the Raffen king's arrival.

> You must know that I misjudged him. He harbors a brutally pragmatic character. The tales of his slaying of his father's chiefs are true. And I have witnessed a well-executed ploy wherein the Raffen king had some followers paint themselves to look like Gallerlanders. These false men attacked us on the road, resulting in the deaths of the last significant challengers to the king's rule. Only a few of the king's men knew of the scheme in advance.

Only two Raffen guards and Pendigied's wiseman followed him into the palace with Bredahade. The exarch was intrigued that the king did not fear a trap nor seemed interested in impressing his hosts by displaying a large retinue.

When they entered the great hall, Bredahade was pleased to see the Raffen king take in the view of the cavernous hall with a look of awe. The massive columns of beautiful white stone stood tall, the polished electrum animals and decorations gleamed, and the hearth fires burned bright and warm.

"The king says Your Eminence has built a worthy capital on the graves of the tree dwellers," Genthus translated.

"And with our friendship secured, we will do much more together," Bredahade replied. "Genthus, please show the king to his quarters so he can refresh himself before the welcome feast. He will overwinter in one of the villas with his own courtyard, stables, and every luxury and comfort the empire can provide. If there is anything he needs, he should merely say the word."

 споразум

When Genthus reported back to the exarch that Pendigied was settled into his chambers, Bredahade bade him to sit and talk.

"Who is the old man with him?" Bredahade asked. "I noticed you took great care to keep yourself between the king and his counselor."

"His name is Alda," Genthus said. "He opposed my visits to Woudenhod and has tried to convince Pendigied not to accept our friendship. Alda fears we will corrupt the young king. The king patiently listens to his arguments before rejecting them."

"Why does he keep a counselor whose recommendations he rejects?"

"When Pendigied's father was on his deathbed, he made Pendigied swear to keep Alda as his senior adviser. King Hrusthied hoped Alda would restrain Pendigied and prevent the loss of the realm. And so Pendigied swore to keep his counsel for as long as the old man lived, but he did not swear to heed his advice."

"Peculiar that a headstrong and tradition-weary king would abide by an oath made to the dead, or that he swore it in the first place," Bredahade mused.

"He is young."

"Ensure he knows, should the day come when he tires of Alda's gripes, that we can help relieve him of the burden."

"As you wish, Your Eminence."

17

PENDIGIED

Eglamour, Donovan Province
Frostfall, 2269

Pendigied, when walking into the exarch's palace, imagined himself as emperor of two realms, the foreigners' world and his. He was excited to overwinter amid such luxury, away from the stuffy talk and traditions of his fathers' dark fortress.

The villa Genthus led him to was itself immense. And the servants appointed to him were many. In his bedchamber, robes of silver fox and sable had been made for him. A hickory-framed mirror stood twice his height, and a steaming oversized bronze bath waited for him. Alda had a sour look on his face.

"You must not be fooled by these rich dressings, my king, for they are meant to buy your loyalty. All seems well now, but peril can lie beneath even the calmest waters."

Pendigied ignored the old man as he shed his weathered deer hide robe and mail. He climbed into the tub and the Donovard women scrubbed and massaged him. Pendigied breathed in the elderflower of the bath and the mint perfume of the women. He tried to savor the newness of it all, but Alda's pesky exhortations continued.

"Why do you think me so easily fooled, Alda?" he finally responded. "These foreigners have sought me as an ally against our shared enemies. And they will make me a great king and equal partner in their empire in return."

"You already have your father's empire. Your people and your lands need your attention—particularly the restive Nyden islands. They will soon rise again, it is said. Though they still fear the quicklime, they have built new ships and will again challenge you, mark my words. Your father would have—"

"Would have what?" Pendigied snapped. "He would have been a fool not to seek the treaty, if only for the horses. Look how our new riders have cleared so much of Vaynland, even with little training from the foreigners. I'm leading our people to a new destiny, one that the forgotten kings of old could not have attained. You always have warnings and cautions for me, but never have you encouraged the seizure of opportunity."

"I counseled your father during the greatest expansion of his empire," Alda said. "I know of opportunity. But I tell you, Pendigied, son of Hrusthied, you are neglecting what has already been won for you. A great realm was wrought, yet you look into the fire for more. Mark my words, if you don't tend to your realm, you will lose it."

"Leave me at once," the king said. His irritation with the persistent Alda had now melted into boredom. "I rule the Raffen and I know what is best for them. Go early now to your bedchamber and don't attend the feast. Do not speak to me until you have real wisdom to impart. If I receive nothing but endless doom from your lips throughout the winter then you will be sent back to Woudenhod on a mule, without my guard."

Dejected, Alda departed from him without another word. Pendigied enjoyed his bath and the beauty of the giggling women.

When Pendigied entered the exarch's dining hall, the soft evening light of torch flame and beeswax lamps glowed in all the electrum. He took his allotted place at one of the great tables, with Genthus at his side. With his new furs, the Raffen king felt distinctly part of something new. He looked about and saw chieftains of many tribes.

"Shall I point them out for Your Highness?" Genthus asked. "There is Highchief Harkarom of the Bronhildi. Golenrad, the half-Brintilian prince of the Ollohd, is to his right. Over there is Hunedorat, vassal-king of the Teshi Gallerlanders."

Pendigied saw that all three of the tribal leaders wore ornate crowns of electrum, each one uniquely incorporating their original native crowns within the electrum frame and set with red jewels.

"The rubies represent the blood-bond alliance," Genthus continued. "The use of your original crown symbolizes the realm that remains under your authority, with the electrum signifying the overarching benefits and responsibilities as part of the Brintilian Empire. Ralmo will crown you at the first meeting of the imperial council tomorrow."

Pendigied watched as the chieftains, imperial governors, and noble knights took their seats. Then his eyes fell upon a native king who quickly shifted his glance to avoid Pendigied's. The Raffen king took only a moment to recognize him as a Hral. This face grew dark as saw that he too wore an electrum crown over his tribe's traditional red-brown diadem of twisted jackal fur, dyed with the blood of battles. He turned to Genthus, but before he could find words, the drigoman sought to calm him.

"Don't worry, Your Highness. He is here at the exarch's invitation. But after your crowning, Shimga will be under your power."

"You cannot comprehend the enmity between his people and mine. The wars we have fought against the Hrals, the dying."

"Your Highness, the exarch is well aware. All of the tribes represented here have fought each other, but this is the new era. Shimga will be the only Hral chieftain you will see unbound in Eglamour, I promise you that. His clan was quelled by the legions in the Durgens, and we think he can eventually help persuade other Hrals to lay down their weapons.

"Shimga and his small band will accompany your warriors to help Marshal Hilsingor tame the Gallerlanders. If all goes well, the exarch will send you and Shimga to tame the Hrals.

Your Highness will be the most exalted king of the imperial council."

"Then I'm pleased to have the honor," Pendigied said. "But the surrender and cooperation of any Hral is suspect. If Shimga comes under my power, I cannot guarantee his success."

The exarch stood from his chair and raised an electrum chalice.

"Welcome, great kings and princes, to the table of Emperor Olskeroth. May God grant His Majesty long life. This feast is to honor you who have come from afar to join a great continental union. On this night we especially honor Pendigied, king of the Raffen, on the eve of his crowning."

The other kings, including Shimga, cheered Pendigied. He stood to accept the honor.

"And now," the exarch continued, "let us break bread together, as brothers in an alliance that will strengthen with the coming of spring."

Pendigied was amazed with the food of the feast. An entire elk was spit-roasted and wheeled into the hall on an iron-clad wagon, a bed of embers smoldering beneath it. Suckling pigs were on every table, resting on pickled onions and crowned with wreaths of apple and fig. Fishes of many varieties were also within easy reach of every king.

Lemons, limes, pomegranates, and other fruits entirely foreign to Pendigied were stacked into pyramids on cedar platters, with sprigs of mint and licorice sprouting from their tops. Every cup was filled with rich wines from Almeria and honeyed beers from Brewel Province.

"Your Highness, where is your wiseman, Alda?" Genthus asked when he had eaten through half his plate.

"Brooding in his chamber, no doubt," Pendigied replied.

"A great king like Your Highness has need of good counselors. I wonder, has old Alda served you well? I cannot but notice that you don't often seek his advice. And I overhear his mumblings," Genthus claimed. "Something about deals with the islanders, whoever they are."

Pendigied looked long at him. The envoy had the look of innocence, but even the young king could see it was false. The king continued eating, speaking between mouthfuls.

"Don't bother yourself, Genthus," he said. "I'm here in the exarch's palace, am I not? There is no need to denigrate Alda. You cannot plant in my mind what is already there. I have long wished to be rid of him, but he was my final promise to my father, as you know."

"Forgive me, Your Highness," Genthus said. "I only . . . It is my responsibility to see that you have everything you need and to guard you from distractions. Your time is precious to the imperial council."

"You will advise me on matters concerning the council, the exarch, and the empire, as you have. But let me deal with Alda as I see fit. He won't hinder me or threaten my position, I assure you."

"As you wish." Genthus refilled the king's cup. "Should I be of service to you on this or any other sensitive issue, my ear is ever bent to your words."

18

RILDNING

Gilgalem, Vaynland
Frostfall, 2269

Several days had passed and Rildning was growing anxious. White it was wonderful to see Eniri and Enildir, he wasn't content to wander the stony terraces and central yard of Gilgalem's great bowl for days on end. Eniri had told him the greatest wonders of the city lay deep within the rock.

"Have patience, dear husband," she had said. "The Sage will summon you soon, I know it."

"He has met with Tirgranir at least twice already," Rildning said. "Perhaps your wiseman has no use for a foreigner. I cannot say I blame him."

"The Sage is wise. I spoke often with him about you. He has long looked forward to your arrival, but I'm sure he has been preoccupied with Tirgranir's claim to the high throne. The Vaynking has undoubtedly pressed the Sage to support him."

"The Sage certainly has much to decide. The naming of Gratgofa's successor. Our strategy against the Frontier Corps. Whether we seek allies among the other tribes. How did so much power come into the hands of one old Gallerlander?"

"There has always been a sage," Eniri said, "and they have always dwelled here. You said Tirgranir told you the tale of the first Maluram miner and electrum smithy, how he was led to shelter here during a storm. But I think you only heard half the tale."

"Then do tell me the rest."

"The miner-smith stayed on the mountain as Wurumnak had commanded, but in time the priest from his village came searching for him. The priest was led here, as was also his destiny. When the priest came and found him, the smith told of what had happened. The priest believed him, but felt the miner-smith needed guidance and help for his great endeavor.

"And so the entire village moved to Gilgalem, where they labored together in the mountain and upon it. They built this secret refuge and harvested the shards of Wurumnak's electrum sword. The priest was the first sage, providing guidance to the people of the mountain and later all the Gallerlander kings who came to recognize Gilgalem as the center of the world as divined by Wurumnak.

"So while the high king has usually ruled all of Gallerlandia from his seat in Nalembalen, the Sage is the high priest and the Graparins his subordinate priests. And because Gilgalem lies within Vaynland, the Vaynkings have always ruled from here and protected the mountain."

Rildning loved Eniri's passion for the old tales and traditions. He knew she would serve the realm well if she became high queen.

"And no one knows the names of the founders of Gilgalem?" he asked.

"Perhaps they were written in stones that have been lost in the earth. This is why the Sage is known by the traditional titles, like the Knower of Change and Wind Seer, while his natural born name is forgotten. When the sages pass away, they are laid down in the heart of the mountain where few Gallerlanders are permitted to go."

"What names are etched in the headstones, to tell one resting place from another?" he asked.

"I cannot say. Perhaps in the eyes of Wurumnak they are all the same body, as they share a common destiny and breath of their creator."

"And how are the sages chosen?"

"They are not chosen but summoned by Wurumnak. They always come from outside Gilgalem, like the first sage.

They have simply arrived from the forests of Gallerlandia to answer the call of the Great One."

Days passed. Rildning walked the terraces with Eniri, waiting for his time with the Sage. The bitter mountain winds of Frostfall swirled above and around Gilgalem, but the city's bowl shape and the great spruces that girded the rim kept the wind out. The heat from the heart of the mountain prevented frost from forming on the stone terraces and walls. A faint fog often floated in the bowl.

As they returned to their quarters in the Pindoarig tower, a thin white trail of smoke seeped from short chimneys atop the tower.

"Look," Eniri said. "The forge fires are burning today." They watched as the smoke dissipated among the trees of the rim and dispersed among the clouds that floated among the peaks above. Rildning imagined the smoke would be well hidden to anyone looking up from the fields and valleys far below Gilgalem.

"The furnace lies deep within the mountain," Eniri continued, "and they only use the smelter when enough electrum ore has been harvested. The liberation of the holy metal and the peak-wispy clouds are good omens for today."

As they watched the smoking stones, Tirgranir's steward Rumban hurried around the terrace toward them.

"Rildning." He was panting through a smile. "The Sage will see you now, in the sanctuary." With excitement, Rildning and Eniri followed him back into Pindoarig.

The sanctuary was positioned directly below Tirgranir's throne room. Like the rest of the tower and terrace apartments, the walls were rough-hewn and lacked decoration. At the far end was a massive altar carved from the swirled, earthy colors of the gneiss rock of the mountain.

The altar was a large ring from floor to ceiling, with a giant stone sword set within it. The hilt of the sword formed the altar table. Torches lined the walls of the chamber. The only electrum in sight was the edge of the stony blade.

Eniri had come with Rildning to the door but could not enter, as she had not been summoned. Rumban pointed Rildning toward the altar, then departed. The rows of cracked pine benches on Rildning's right and left reminded him of a Messengian church. He stood before the altar, looking up at the apparent representation of Wurumnak's sword. The hilt-table of the altar was etched with old symbols similar to Gali, but Rildning could not read them.

"Those are the sayings of Agimdir," a gravelly voice said, "the last Seafather who journeyed to Cedelaebos and one of the few who returned alive." Rildning had not noticed a stunted little man with a crooked nose and crooked cane who was seated in the front row. The old man gestured for him to sit with him as he spoke.

"Most Gallerlanders simply know Agimdir as a great Thuraniparin, one of Wurumnak's chosen kings who are forever honored at his table in the White Forest. But most Gallerlanders cannot read the old symbols, so they don't know about his bitter voyage as you do," the old man said. "And that was Agimdir's intent."

Rildning recalled the smell of burning and mud as Nalembalen flashed through his mind. "I'm sorry the Graparins and their secret knowledge have perished."

"As am I. They were all my students. You are no more responsible for that than Agimdir was for the Cataclysm. Nevertheless, Agimdir preserved his wisdom, which now lives in you, Eniri, the three ivy-crowned kings, and me."

"Is there no great library of the ancient scrolls? Copies of the Graparins' tomes?"

The Sage shook his head. "The Graparins were the keepers of the secret knowledge, and that knowledge was carefully kept close to the high king in the tree city."

Rildning remembered the copy of the Cataclysm scroll he had made in his journal with Hegdir's help. "I must tell you that the eldest Graparin shared the Cataclysm scroll with me, shortly before the city fell. I copied it into my journal, which was lost when we fled. I cannot say what became of it. If it wasn't burned or swallowed by the mud, it's possible the enemy could have it."

"Eniri told me as much," the Sage said. "Don't be ashamed, for if it's destroyed, then the knowledge remains a secret. And if it has been revealed to the unpainted men, then it must be a sign that Wurumnak has chosen this time of upheaval to begin the revealing of the prophecy, in which the descendants of the Agnesci and the Almerics will populate both continents together and share the world in peace."

"I confess I'm skeptical about this prophecy, and I remember Gratgofa was as well. Hegdir had told me that the ancient voyage of the Agnesci across the seas and their encounter with the Almerics would one day spur the Almerics to cross the seas to come here, and that there would be peace. But the first colonies did not seek a lasting peace, and the Frontier Corps is daily expanding their empire. Gratgofa saw the aggression of the descendants of the Almerics—my people—and rightly vowed to defeat them."

"Gratgofa was a great leader but he could not read omens as I can. Eniri said Hegdir believed you were a sign of a new era, and that your coming was accompanied by good omens. From what Eniri has told me, I believe Hegdir was correct. The initial violence of the foreigners does not annul what will ultimately be a peaceful fulfillment of the prophecy.

"Tirgranir is also right to reject the use of the foreigners' metals and horse beasts," the Sage continued. "Although we must defend ourselves, we must not overreact to their coming with our own excessive violence, as the ancient Almerics did when they saw the Agnesci Seafathers on their shores."

"It is difficult for me to see peace at the point of the Frontier Corps' sword," Rildning said, "and impossible for me to see how the Gallerlanders can defend themselves against superior equipment, even if their own numbers and knowledge of the realm are superior. Alas, I won't speak to Tirgranir more about it, but the men who fight under me must heed my orders."

The Sage pushed up to his feet with help from his gnarled cane. "Come," he said. "It is time for you to see some of the depths of Gilgalem. Let us walk and talk together."

Rildning followed the Sage as he shuffled to a side door of the sanctuary. The Sage led him through several dimly lit halls and down a spiral staircase. At last they reached a junction where three doors were closed.

The Sage pivoted on his cane. "Do you know the way to the crypt?"

"No," Rildning said. "I have not been to this place."

The Sage rested on a stone bench. "Choose the crypt," he said with a smile.

Rildning paced in front of the doors. They were identical. Their archways were adorned with simple carvings, but no symbol was unique. He walked up to the left-hand door. It was cool to the touch and he could not detect sounds or movement of air. The middle door was warm, with the faint scent of smoke. The right-hand door was cool but in no way different from the first.

Rildning pointed to the door on the right. "This is the crypt."

"How do you know?"

"The middle door must be the forge and mines beyond, given its warmth and scented airs. I would guess the crypt could be either the left or right door, and the food store-rooms would be the remainder. But I remembered how the Gallerlanders always buried their dead with the palm of their right hand facing upward. And for chieftains, they would place their electrum ring in the open palm. I never thought to ask why, but clearly this was a sacred rite of death. So I chose the right-hand door as the crypt."

The Sage smiled warmly, a glint of satisfaction in his knowing eyes.

"Your choice is correct. The chieftains wear the rings to remind them of Wurumnak's calling. The rings symbolize service, to him and to each other. The placement of the electrum in the right hand after death is a sign of their dedication in life, and their readiness in death to pick up the sword in hopes of joining the Thuraniparin in the battle at the End of Days."

"I may not worship Wurumnak," Rildning said, "but I feel your god and mine may not be so different, especially if the Agnesci and Almerics were once brethren."

They entered the crypt. A chill breath of air greeted them from the dark. The torchlight behind them revealed a stairway inside the door. The walls gradually widened as they descended the stairs. The steps spiraled down to the right, broadening until twenty men could have stepped down shoulder to shoulder.

As they neared the bottom, their steps echoed into the cool darkness. Soon their eyes adjusted and focused on a faint light farther ahead. As they approached, Rildning could see a small flame sprouting from a dish of reddish-brown lumps on a pedestal waist high.

"It's amber resin," the old man said, "harvested from beneath the spruces or pulled up by their fallen trunks. The light of its fuel is short-reaching but long-burning and pleasant to inhale."

"Remarkable." Rildning recalled Yelgoram taking a bite of his candle, back when Rildning was his prisoner. He felt the same enchantment that Yelgoram and his men must have felt at seeing a new source of light. He wondered how Yelgoram was faring.

"Now," the Sage began, "don't be afraid. There are ancient things in this darkness that move. Great things that most never see. But they won't harm you, if you stay out of the way. Are you ready?"

Rildning nodded warily. The Sage shifted with his cane and took a half step toward the base of the pedestal. There arose a flapping sound from beneath the stone floor, then the scrape of wood and stone could be heard. Rildning sensed a shifting of great weight. The Sage looked up into the darkness above the amber resin flame, so Rildning followed his gaze.

There was a series of creaks and the sounds of sliding wood and turning stone all around them. Then, slowly, out of the darkness above them reached a thin black arm. At first sight it was a shadow that shimmered as it silently approached the small flame of the pedestal. The arm moved down and touched the resin light, then quickly disappeared back from where it had come with its own finger now alit.

They watched as the faint light nearly vanished high above them. The creaking and flapping sounds multiplied, so that the darkness above echoed with the sounds of a hundred workmen. Rildning saw the light grow, then explode into tiny pieces. These scattered lights also multiplied, like a starry night sky.

Rildning saw there were many arms that threw the light across the ceiling, like a great spider tossing its prey across a black web of wooden frames and stone gears. The contraption had by now lit many bowls of amber resin fastened to huge columns along the walls and hanging from bins affixed to the ceiling.

The darkness glimmered away as the walls were revealed to be solid panels of electrum, with sparkles of light dancing on their rough-forged faces. The irregular shape of the chamber showed it was originally a massive cave. The floor was also paved with broad electrum plates, which clearly hid more machinery beneath it. When the ancient contraption had done its work, it rested with a final shifting of weights and sliding of wood behind the walls and in the floor.

"It is named Napargaros, or Big Light-Bringer in your tongue," the Sage said. "Originally a plaything of the Agnesci, it now serves to shine the way to the resting place of the old sages. It's also proof of the lost handiwork of the ancient builders who made the great ships for the Seafathers."

"What a testament," Rildning said.

"Napargaros and the great ocean-crossing ships are but a sample of the machines our Agnesci forefathers built, to the doom of so many people. That is why their apparatuses and discoveries were destroyed, hidden from later generations, and ultimately forgotten. Few such relics still exist. Come."

The Sage led Rildning through the electrum-lit cavern. Rildning saw an arched tunnel at the far end, and on either side of its walls ran small troughs above their heads, filled with the red glow of burning amber resin. Every electrum panel in the winding tunnel was etched with ancient Gali symbols and bordered with designs resembling the empty rock veins and the body paint of the Gallerlanders.

At the end of the tunnel, they followed the amber flame into the next large cavern, its every surface plated with electrum. Great electrum columns fashioned like trees sprouted from the walls with branches. They gleamed with amber light at the top of the chamber where Napargaros had lit their boughs.

Rildning and the Sage soon reached a colossal cavity in the mountain, much larger than the first chamber. Around the walls stood a hammered electrum forest like those that had once stood at Nalembalen. At the center of the space stood a single, living willow tree, smaller than the rest and shod with a white metal that shone like the full moon. Its foliage was sparse but appeared metallic blue in color.

"This is the moonwood tree of Ubromynir. A cave willow, one of several living beneath the mountain. It represents Nawurihar, the White Forest of Heaven," the Sage explained. "This is the most sacred heart of Gallerlandia. Few beyond sages and high kings have trod here. Look over there, among the roots of Ubromynir."

Rildning approached the moonwood tree. There in the ground, to the right and left of his path, were long electrum panels inlaid with the same shining wood in the shape of bold symbols. He looked out and saw rows of these panels fanned out from the base of the tree in four directions, hundreds of them laid side by side in arcs.

"These are the sages of old, their names unknown but the number of their generation etched upon their slabs. The first high kings are buried here too, before their resting places were made outside Nalembalen." The Sage shuffled a few steps to stand on a plate with no inlay. "This grave will be mine," he said with a grin. "I am the four hundred and eighth generation of sages."

Rildning recalled his time with the old Graparin Hegdir when, poring over the Cataclysm scroll at Nalembalen, Hegdir explained his own generation was the 522nd.

"I know what you would ask," the Sage said. "Eniri wondered the same when I brought her here. The generations of the high kings are many more than those of the sages. Wars, disease, and infighting have made the ruling days of each king much shorter than the long lives of the sages, and so the kings' generations are more numerous and thus a poorer measure of time than your people would expect."

Rildning wondered why the Sage had shown Eniri and himself this sacred place. "I have so many questions, but I don't know where to begin."

"We have already begun, so you have only to listen." The Sage walked past him to a scuffed grave plate on the corner of the row nearest the white tree. "This is the first sage," he said. "When Wurumnak led this priest to Gilgalem, he did not have all the answers to his questions. But he followed the commands planted in his heart.

"Our civilization blossomed until its roots were nearly torn out during the Cataclysm, when the Agnesci Seafathers sailed to the continent of the Almerics and were destroyed. Yet those who did not sail survived that storm.

"But, with the coming of the Brintilian Empire, the Almerics' descendants have planted themselves within Gallerlandia. The old ways of burying our hurts and secret crafts, as we did by banning shipbuilding, will no longer provide a remedy. In fact, a remedy may not be necessary.

"As you can see, there are no tomb guardians on these graves, as there must be in the forests and valleys of the wild. These graves are protected simply by where they lie: in the heart of Gilgalem, the heart of Gallerlandia.

"You were told about the prophecy. Hegdir said the Almeric and Agnesci would one day rejoin as peaceful brothers yet remain loyal to Wurumnak. I believe that day fast approaches, and I may even live to see it before I rest under the limbs of Ubromynir."

Rildning could plainly see that the Sage's tired eyes were filled with hope as he looked upon the white tree, clutching his cane.

"I regret I cannot see the path as clearly as you," Rildning said, "for I know the minds of the men marching toward the mountain. They don't seek peace. At best they seek a corrupt, controlling form of it. And most of them would sooner seek the foul glory of looting and destroying, as they did in Nalembalen."

"For many years I've had a vision," the Sage replied, undaunted, "of Zebfargir and Gwarun, the first Agnesci man and woman created by Wurumnak. They are at peace, then they become troubled, then again they find peace. And during that interim trouble, they are preoccupied with mending relations between their quarreling sons.

"I believe this dream is an omen of your coming and joining with Eniri, that you will together mend the ancient bloodlines of the Almerics and Agnesci. Though it's difficult for you to see at this time, I believe you are the bringer of the change the prophecy has long foretold. Hegdir saw this too, otherwise he wouldn't have risked his life to show you the secret knowledge."

"I'm no high king," Rildning said, feeling unworthy of such a prophecy. "I'm merely a fallen knight who became a wilderman before being adopted by your people. I was a knight among your conquerors, cast out by my own shame and wanderlust. I could not be part of your wonderful dream. My coming has only been an omen of death."

"I have heard the tales of your surviving as Yelgoram's prisoner," the Sage insisted. "The snake pit and similar encounters in the deep woods. Was it mere luck that you, in the confused stupor of the original bite, drank from the spilled blood of the adder without knowing it would serve as both antidote and spiritual stimulant? Even most Gallerlanders remain ignorant of the powers of the adder blood, though it was well-known to the ancients.

"Today the Hrals drink it to focus their fury of *turserkgyn*. The Gallerlanders banned it long ago because of the blood's potential lethality. Of all the things you could have done, you drank the one thing that could save you and reinvigorate your own lifeblood. Do you not see that event as divinely guided?"

"Perhaps my god took pity and urged my mouth toward the red shimmer on the ground," Rildning said. He paused in thought. "But it was the glow of the electrum ring, which I took from the bony finger of Gofalnig in the Hral cave, that revealed the pool of adder's blood."

"Precisely. The sacred light guides us in the depths of the earth, so we may harvest the shards of Wurumnak's sword. Especially in the darkest of nights. Your story is not the first wherein electrum guided someone to life while facing death. A high king twenty generations before Gratgofa was said to have deterred a Welkar invasion after his son discovered the tracks of their scouts when he tripped over an electrum ore poking out of the ground."

"Will the Gallerlanders ever have a high king again?" Rildning asked. "I haven't met Erambrin and Odon, but I'm certain they must be fierce warriors like Tirgranir. And Eniri was favored by Gratgofa. Surely one of them is worthy of being high king."

"Tirgranir knows his men, knows the land," the Sage said. "He knows how to rule and how to fight, even to make peace when needed. He would have been a respectable high king had he been born in an earlier, darker era. But he lacks patience and self-restraint. And his pride is unmoving.

"Neither will Eniri rule as a high queen. She is from a respected clan but does not have enough support among the Vayns. And so long as the kings of Goynland and Umbyrland live, even if trapped by the enemy, her claim as widow to Gratgofa's heir is weaker than the claims of the three ivy crowns."

"So either Odon or Erambrin should be king?"

"The ivy-crowned kings of Gallerlandia are brave men and veteran warriors," the Sage answered, "but none of them understand the foreigners as you do, and they don't really understand the prophecy."

"Explain it to them," Rildning said. "They will come to understand. Surely they will seek the peace you speak of."

"They won't . . . they cannot. Even Gratgofa, who grasped the secret knowledge and lived alongside the Graparins in Nalembalen, did not believe the time of the prophecy's fulfillment had come. The three underkings who survive him are men of lesser minds. There is only one man who knows the Almeric and the Agnesci. You have lived as both, and your son is half one bloodline and half the other. With Eniri at your side, and Enildir as your heir, you will bring peace."

Rildning could not find it within himself to believe he was the next high king. Of all the people on the two continents, how could he be the one chosen to bring them together for the first time since creation? Could he even believe there was such a prophecy?

Rildning decided Wurumnak and his own Messengian god could be one in the same, especially after seeing the details of the Cataclysm scroll. But he wondered if the Agnesci could have gone astray in their belief in this prophecy. He was torn about what to believe, and he feared what his role would mean for Eniri and Enildir.

"I'm old as stone and frailer than dust, but my eyes see much," the Sage said. "I can understand your hesitance. It's not an easy thing to be told your arrival to this place is prophetic. Perhaps I shouldn't have told you of your burden, but I know in time you will accept it and succeed.

"We must summon an unprecedented alliance of the tribes," the Sage continued with a smile, "as you advised Tirgranir to do. He complained to me about your prodding, but I think you are just the person to bring the tribes together. I told him we must try your approach and he reluctantly agreed.

"All of the branches of the Agnesci that we can reach within reasonable time must be summoned to Gilgalem and be convinced to join together as one. Old divisions must be overcome, between the tribes and within them."

"A Rahlampian chieftain named Mrigamad accompanied us here," Rildning said. "Convincing his tribe would be a good first start."

"You see," the Sage said, "you were destined to take us beyond the wars and into peace. I will say no more of this, for the matter is in your hands, and you are in the hands of Wurumnak."

Rildning nodded his thanks. He was relieved to hear Tirgranir had agreed to seek allies. But he still believed the Sage was wrong about his destiny.

"Come," the Sage said. "Let us check the storerooms of Gilgalem. If a council is to be summoned and Gilgalem defended, you must inspect our provisions."

❧

Silent and deep in thought, Rildning and the Sage left the glittering tomb chambers and returned to the junction of the three doors. They entered through the other door that was cool to the touch. Downward stairs led to a large torchlit room with large doors in the ceiling above.

"Those doors open into the bottom of Pindoarig," the Sage said, "where men bring the supplies to lower them down into here. And these doors"—the Sage pointed to large circular doors of green-painted wood—"are the stores."

They entered and Rildning saw a honeycomb structure carved within the stone walls of a great cavern. Sparse torches flickered between large cells of the structure where wooden boxes and cloth bags were stacked. Ladders as tall as trees stood propped up against the walls. Their top ends narrowed to where wooden hooks steadied their balance. The storeroom was larger than any he had seen hoarded in the colonial forts. The Sage spoke with a special pride.

"There is wheat, rye, corn, oats, barley, spelt, flax, teff, and sesame. Gathered from fields across Vaynland and bartered from the Umbyrs and even the Raffen at one time. Dried grapes, currants, elderberries, persimmons, medlars, quince, and apples from the trees of Umbyrland. And potatoes, arrowroot, garlic, and onions from Goynland. Smoked meats of deer, boar, aurochs, and sheep. Many fishes and eels, salted or smoked. Brined turtles, pickled beets, peppered fowl, afban and hard breads. Aged meads, spruce beer, apple vinegar, nut oils, and spiced wines. Mustard, mallow, peppermint, rosemary, fennel, pecan, chestnut, and tabakat. The bowels of Gilgalem know no hunger, and neither will those that ever dwell here. Behold the Basket of Onitgora, the high king who first ordered its filling many generations ago."

The Sage walked Rildning toward the center of the chamber, where he saw a gaping pit. Rildning looked down into it. The chamber extended for a long drop, the honeycombed cells swelling with food all the way down. The Sage pointed out a wooden ramp spiraling to the bottom where the light was dim. The faint joggle of water could be heard as well.

"When the Maluram finished mining this area, they extended the natural spring-carved caverns. Then they harnessed the spring, weaving it around and through the storerooms to keep the caves cold and the air fresh."

Rildning saw the water was confined to a knee-deep masonry channel that ran along the walls and disappeared into the mountain behind the rock before it reappeared at the next level below. Roped buckets sat idle on stone stables built into the side of the spring pool where it funneled into the channel.

"So you see," the Sage continued. "Gilgalem can outlast any foe with these chambers, of which there are a dozen in use. These sacred mountains are our high wall, and its secret stores are nourishment for an age."

"The most impressive preparations I have ever seen," Rildning said, eyes looking down into the honeycombed well of food. "My mind is certainly more at ease knowing Gilgalem is so well protected and outfitted. But it's my hope we can persuade other tribes to join us, and that they bring more than stone blades for use against armored knights."

19

FERNDEATH

Gilgalem, Vaynland
Frostfall, 2269

As the voices faded away, Ferndeath relaxed again. It felt good to easily breathe the cool airs of the food stores again. He thought for sure he had been caught. How the old man and Rildning had not seen him crouching on the potato sack he could not guess. Perhaps they had been too busy feasting their eyes upon food that would never be eaten, by men at least.

He reminded himself it wasn't the first close call. Rildning had spotted him twice, but he was able to evade him both times. He worried Rildning would eventually be able to see through his green tattoos and realize who he was.

Ferndeath relished the idea of killing him, but Rildning was never alone so he never had the chance. He had to take extra care to avoid Rildning's evil, searching eyes if he was to continue the game.

Ferndeath crept out from one of the stone cells and lowered himself down a ladder. He had been here before and knew it well. Stealing a sack here and there for his own stash had been easy. The foolish Vayns never locked any doors. So trusting, so naive in their mountain haven.

Ferndeath slipped along the paths between the chambers, following the spring water channel as it weaved in and out of the mountain wall. After a while he came to where the flow pushed under a ledge and dove down into the black roots of

Gilgalem. The time had come to parch the roots, he told himself.

He closed the doors of the passage to the next chamber. Then his scrawny arms pulled down crates of vegetables, and he stacked them in front of the door. He took more crates and dumped their contents, then carefully dipped them into the flowing water ahead of the ledge. The cold water pinned them at the ledge, but still swirled around their parts and lashed at his dirty hands.

He submerged a line of crates and filled them with clay jars and pitchers and sacks of food. The water boiled and bulged, angry that its path was being blocked. As he repeated with more crates and debris further up the channel, the water finally broke free of the masonry and spilled down to the stone-hewn floor, searching for a crevasse or other escape. But it found none. His beady eyes watched merrily as the water welled up in the low places. Up the wall the water continued its search for lower ground.

Ferndeath's fur tunic was soaked and he shivered. He found a perch in a cell to watch a bit more. The water had now climbed the ramp to the door to the next chamber, but less water seeped under it than rose up its front. He smiled grimly as he admired his work, then bounded up the stairs to find a place to dry and hide for a while.

20

BREDAHADE

Eglamour, Donovan Province
Frostfall, 2269

This was the moment Exarch Bredahade had waited for: the convocation of the Imperial Council of Pemonia, and with it the crowning of the last king of the great tribes of the west. He looked out, seeing the faces of the emperor's subjects, peoples of the Old World and the New. His governors and barbarian kings were seated at the edge of an open, circular court before him. Behind them were risers for the knights, chieftains, wealthy merchants, and other courtiers.

The exarch sat upon a throne placed on a dais, also at the edge of the circle, with Ralmo seated to his right and Sarnaker on his left. Two coats-of-arms were affixed to the silk canopy above him. The white stallion on a blue field with a golden tower on the saddle was Bredahade's house. The crowned white lion on a purple field was the emperor's.

On Bredahade's head was a simpler crown that surpassed the electrum crowns of the kings and the purple shoulder sashes of the governors. It was a band of silver interlaced with myrtle, the sign of humility. Though he was master over all of imperial Pemonia, like all exarchs he was Emperor Olskeroth's representative and thus his foremost servant. Bredahade spoke with the voice of the emperor, but his presence, and his crown, reminded all subjects of the higher power back in Almeria.

He had thought much about this day during the long months aboard the ship to the New World. He did not fear the wide sea and its vicious storms, or the yawning whirlpools of the Edgewaters, or even the smoking seas of the Far East. He knew his mission to Pemonia was ordained by God, envisioned by the Martinus, and spoken through the lips of the emperor. No man or beast or the natural movements of the earth could disrupt what God had willed for the final years of his life.

"In the name of His Imperial Majesty the emperor, His Eminent Holiness the Martinus, and God Almighty, I hereby convoke the Imperial Council of Pemonia. Your loyalty to the emperor is through me, and every favor granted to you is by my hand from his. Every colony founded since the days of discovery and every native realm represented at this council, is hereby made a province of my government. All further settlement is at my command."

Bredahade and Chancellor Sarnaker continued to roll out the declarations and other formalities of administration, including the reading of proclamations from the emperor installing the exarch as supreme ruler. Common laws for the provinces were also established. The exarch knew most of the heathen kings would not understand their meaning, but he would depend on the drigomen to keep them from straying too far from his word.

When at last the pronouncements had concluded, each of the provincial governors and high knights reaffirmed their oaths of allegiance to Bredahade. He gave them gifts of electrum, livestock, trade rights, and lands in return. Following them were the heathen kings. Pendigied was the last to approach the dais.

"Welcome, again, great king of the Raffen," the exarch said. "Your crowning day has the special honor of sharing the occasions with the council's establishment. A fitting distinction given your contributions to the empire."

"Kneel to your master on earth, and bow your head to heaven above," Ralmo said, rising from his chair cradling an electrum crown.

Bredahade watched as the dark hammered iron crown all but disappeared behind the glow of the electrum. Genthus, kneeling beside the king, whispered a translation of Ralmo's consecrating words into his ear. He replied with the words of thanks and praise that Genthus had taught him, and offered the captive Yelgoram as a special gift to the exarch. Bredahade was pleased.

"You are hereby granted the lands known among the Gallerlanders as Vaynland," the exarch said. "That realm waits for you to conquer it alongside Marshal Hilsingor. You are young, but your bravery and desire to join the empire are well-known. Together we will build the New World. I have every expectation you will not fail in your duties, and you can always expect my favor in return."

Pendigied bowed deeply again, then departed from the dais.

When this was done, the exarch surveyed his court again. He was most pleased, but his mind was already turning to the next tasks. Much work lay ahead in taming the wild regions of the continent and building the provinces. And he knew the imperial council was rife with rivals, jealousies, and pure hatred.

Aside from the quarrels between the barbarians, Pemonia had long attracted men who sought their fortunes and glories. All of the governors were such men, even if they had been born in the New World. The unexplored wilderness was unknowably vast, yet many nobles already squabbled over lands and treasures, and friction between the provincials and the heathens was a constant headache. The chancellor would corral these wild stallions, he was sure, even as Hilsingor brought to heel new tribes for the mix.

"May I make a request?" Ralmo asked.

"Of course," Bredahade replied.

"It is my wish to have the Raffen king's special gift, the Gallerlander prisoner. I was told by Genthus that he is a respected chieftain. I believe his capture is a gift from God, and it's my prayer that he be tried and condemned by the church. Let him be an example to your new barbarian vassals. And the trial will consecrate God's justice in your new capital."

Bredahade pondered. He wasn't surprised by Ralmo's request, but wondered how many of the newly converted barbarian kings would have a dim view Yelgoram's trial, even if he did represent their rival Gallerlanders. Ultimately he believed Ralmo's suggestion that making an example of Yelgoram could strengthen his overall message.

"You may have him," the exarch said. "I don't want our new allies to entertain the idea of reneging on their new emperor or religion. But I also don't want you to make too much of a spectacle of the trial, so as not to alienate other potential allies."

"Of course." Ralmo grinned.

When the exarch's portion of the ceremonies had concluded, the council continued with each governor and tribal king making their pleas for Bredahade to intercede in matters of justice, trade, finance, noble succession, and innumerable other issues Bredahade was well accustomed to dealing with.

When he had tired of them for the day, he opened twenty days of celebrations in Eglamour with a great feast. Seventeen days were to commemorate the imperial council, and three were to honor the crowning of Pendigied, as had been done for the other tribes.

21

RILDNING

Gilgalem, Vaynland
Frostfall, 2269

Tirgranir's throne room was packed full of restless Gallerlander chiefs. Rildning knew the guards with obsidian spears would have no hope of quelling the crowd if it got ugly. He wondered whether a single chief from another tribe would even fit into the chamber if a grand council was summoned and convened.

The Vaynking looked tired, his woven ivy crown battered and brittle. Rildning knew the Gallerlanders viewed it as symbolic of the rule of the kings. If Tirgranir lived long enough, his ivy would be refreshed with new growth in the spring.

The Umbyrs, Goyns, and Vayns were no less rowdy and divided than in days past, but Tirgranir managed to quiet them enough to speak to them. Rildning and his captains, Owerdir and Urgamdir foremost among them, stood near the throne alongside Tirgranir's leading chiefs, including Arbardir. Mrigamad of the Rahlampians stood near Rildning.

"And so, when winter has passed, the war will resume in full," Tirgranir said. "We must take back Vaynland by defeating the Raffen. Then we will fight toward Umbyrking Erambrin and eventually Goynking Odon. But we cannot do this alone.

"Under favorable sky omens and the wise counsel of the Sage," he announced, "we will send envoys to the neighboring tribes. Travel through the snows will be slow and treacherous, but we must use this dark season to gain allies before the enemy awakens in the spring, as they always do."

"But we are safe in Gilgalem!" one of the chieftains cried. "What harm can come to us that requires help from those we count as enemies?" He glared at Mrigamad.

"Truly, this is a refuge that has never and will never fall in war," Tirgranir said. "However, if the foreigners continue their march southward, they will trap us here. What is Gallerlandia if the three kings are holed up in separate corners of the realm, while the enemy besieges us and claims our lands and forests for themselves?"

"It is time to bury the old rivalries," the Sage, seated next to the Vaynking's throne, added. "You, Brugmir, have too often crowed your complaints, and I don't think you speak for all your Goyn brethren. Here you sleep safe while your king is surrounded. You have berated the Vayns and never thanked them for your shelter.

"These sorts of divisions between you, and not merely the isolation of the clans at the hands of the enemy, have led to our defeat and flight. With the spring will come our chance to push back the enemy, rejoin the kings, and regain our lands. It cannot be done by ourselves. Help is needed from other tribes who are also threatened."

"We must convince them to meet us in council here before the spring," Tirgranir continued. "So envoys must depart as soon as possible if we have any hope of mustering their warriors alongside ours."

Rildning was impressed that Tirgranir genuinely supported the idea. He wondered whether the Sage had led the Vaynking to believe he would support his candidacy for the high crown. But what mattered to Rildning was that Tirgranir was true to his word in seeking allies if the Sage advised it. Rildning stepped forward.

"The snows are not the only peril," he said. "One of our Umbyr chiefs, Yelgoram, had been sent to the Raffen to broker peace with them and prevent their falling under the sway of the enemy. Yelgoram's son, Owerdir, has since learned he was taken captive by the Raffen. We don't know his fate, but the Raffen raids on Vaynland make clear which side they have chosen. So we must be cautious in choosing potential allies to approach."

"It is a risk," the Sage acknowledged. "But envoys must be sent to the Rahlampians, Welkars, Nake, and Naren-Dra. Even the Bronhildi, if there is even a remote chance of turning them away from their new alliance with the foreigners."

"The Bronhildi already ran us out of Umbyrland!" a chieftain shouted. "They are as much the enemy as the foreigners!"

"The Nake are stone-worshiping pagans!" cried another from the crowd.

"And the Naren-Dra are snake-eating cloud dwellers!" another yelled.

"The Welkars are defeated and scattered," Mrigamad mused to Rildning. "What help would they be?"

Tirgranir held up a hand to calm the chiefs.

"The Sage has spoken," the Vaynking said. "We cannot prevail if we remain scattered in the winds. Who will go?"

"I'll go," Rildning said. "Send me to your greatest rivals the Rahlampians, if you wish it." He stifled a smirk when he saw the shock on Mrigamad's face. Rildning knew no Gallerlander would volunteer to go east, and he was curious about these metal-wielding black-tattooed people.

"Done," Tirgranir said. "You shall seek out the Welkars also, since they dwell in the coastal swamps beyond Rahlampia. If you can find any of them alive, that is. Now, who will go to the Naren-Dra?"

"Send me," Owerdir said. "Let me continue the service that Yelgoram cannot." Rildning was proud of his friend but also disappointed. He had presumed Owerdir would come with him to the east.

"Done," Tirgranir said. "May you have better fortune than your father, for all our sakes. Who will go to the Nake?"

None answered. As the awkward silence dragged on, Rildning wondered if the Gallerlanders' inability to see the omens of the sky from inside the chamber froze their minds. Rildning could see the Vaynking squirm. He would be shamed if none of the Vayns volunteered and only Rildning's followers stepped forward.

Rildning had heard little about the mystical Nake people, and he wondered whether the Gallerlanders were afraid of them. He noticed Tirgranir stared at Arbardir, who simply stared back. He was Owerdir's half brother and no Vayn, but he was loyal to Tirgranir.

"You, Arbardir," the king said. "You will go to the Nake." The boar tusks in Arbardir's earlobes quivered with quiet rage. Rildning did not think the hot-tempered Umbyr would make a good envoy, though perhaps his desire to kill foreigners would drive him to be successful in his task.

"And the Bronhildi. Who will go?" Tirgranir looked around the assembly, not expecting a volunteer.

"Too dangerous!" a chieftain shouted.

"Impossible to turn them back against the foreigners!" another said.

"All true," Rildning said. "The Bronhildi have been thoroughly conquered and employed by the Frontier Corps, and the path is dangerous because it lies through territory held by the enemy. But the possibility of persuading the Bronhildi to strike at the heart of the corps—as only they can—is worth the risk to one envoy."

"A message to them must be attempted," Tirgranir chimed in. "Even if they merely agree not to help the foreigners press further into Gallerlandia, it would be worth the risk."

"I will go." It was a woman's voice, soft but firm. The chiefs parted to see Eniri standing boldly, her emerald eyes resolute. Tirgranir chuckled. Rildning felt his stomach turn but chewed his lip to avoid challenging her in front of the others.

"Highchief Harkarom might be persuaded by such a bold, beautiful messenger," considered the Sage aloud.

"No, I'll not allow it," Tirgranir said.

Rildning was relieved but also a bit surprised. It was an opportunity for the Vaynking to remove a contender for the high crown.

"Am I not worthy?" she asked, ignoring Rildning's worried eyes. "The women of Gallerlandia have long taken up the stonesword and spear in defense of the realm."

"The bravery of the Tamtur family of Balanland is well-known," Tirgranir said. "But Highchief Harkarom would hold you hostage. He would demand our surrender for your life. No, an Umbyr princess would not serve her people well as a hostage. Gratgofa would reach up and strike me down from his ashen grave if I allowed you to go to Bronhildia."

"I will go, in her honor and in memory of the high king," Urgamdir said.

Rildning turned to see him standing tall, his shoulder still bandaged from the wound received from saving Tirgranir's life at the Brambruk. "My mother's father was Bronhildi," Urgamdir said. "It will be safer if I go, for I know their customs and speech."

Rildning wondered if such a familial connection would help, but no other volunteer came forward. He noted Eniri's visible displeasure in having no support among the others.

"Then it's done," said Tirgranir with a solemn nod.

⚬

"Why did you offer to go to my people?" Mrigamad asked as the assembly dissolved.

"Because I trust you will be an able guide," Rildning answered with a smile. "You have proven yourself to be a clearheaded warrior. None of the Gallerlanders would go anyway. And I'm curious about your people."

"I'm curious about your loyalties," Mrigamad said with hard eyes.

"My loyalties are to my wife, our people, and the forests of Gallerlandia."

"I don't doubt your love for the beautiful woman. But how can a foreigner become a tribesman? You have the tattoos and the tongue, but you will never be a Gallerlander. Do you worship Wurumnak? Do you hold sacred the electrum, or look to the heavens for signs?"

"I suppose you are right," Rildning conceded. "But I—"

"You are not who you claim to be, are you?" Mrigamad stepped close, his dark eyes bounded by black lines across his face. "I saw you clutch the enemy's banner after the battle. You may have fooled these simple tree squirrels, hiding in their mountain, but you will not fool the Rahlampians. If Domnitar Anfinnan sends warriors to help them, it will be because I convince him of the need for a buffer land, not because of any web you spin with your words."

"I'm not a spy," Rildning said. "In time you will see."

"I suggest you go to your woman while you can," Mrigamad said. "The morning's path is perilous." With that, the Rahlampian departed from him.

"Don't let him scare you," Eniri said when Rildning found her in their chambers. "The Rahlampians are dark people, always scheming and fighting. Their minds are drawn to bloodletting and conspiracy."

"Perhaps Mrigamad is right." Rildning's face was sullen. "No amount of paint or speech will change the blood in my veins."

"Husband, how often must I counsel you against such thoughts? We have been apart for too long since Nalembalen, yet your smiles are few and your heart heavy. Does the sight and sound of Enildir not even lift your spirit?"

Rildning looked at the sleeping child. Even this young, the boy looked strongly built. He was of such a mild manner, always happy and observant. He had Rildning's patience, but his mother's dark hair and determination.

"You nearly dashed my spirits by volunteering to go to the Bronhildi," he said. "I admire your courage as ever, my love, but you should be a queen, not a captive. Tirgranir was right: they would have taken you as a hostage for certain. Think of Enildir."

Eniri flushed. "I've weathered plenty of dangers before you even came to Nalembalen. Don't think me to be the soft Brintilian wife of a settler, comfortable in one of their colonies."

"I'm sorry," Rildning said. "You must accept that I will worry for you. What's more, I wish you to remain here to help lead your people when they'll need you most. With the arrival of spring will come the Frontier Corps, waiting at the foot of the mountain, whether the envoys have arrived with allies or not."

Eniri shifted her eyes away. Rildning looked down at Enildir again, but his mind was pained by the coldness of the world. He sat down beside Eniri and told her of the Sage's words about the prophecy.

"I knew you were different," she said. "Wurumnak himself touched my heart when I first saw you. And I knew, while Enildir was in my belly, he was a special, peaceful joining of Almeric and Agnesci bloodlines. I am wife to a hidden high king and mother to his son." Rildning knew she could see the doubt in his eyes. "Rildning, you may have been born with the heart of a foreigner, but the blood flowing in your veins is now the green of Gallerlandia. The forests did change you."

She repeatedly urged him to accept the prophecy, but he could not find it within himself. It was hard enough to become a Gallerlander. How could he unite them all? He wanted to live with his family in peace.

"Rildning, you have told me before that you regret the necessity of fighting your former brethren, that you lament their deaths as much as their killing of our tribesmen." Rildning nodded. "I think that proves who you really are, what you really are, for both bloodlines."

"But I cannot see how coexistence is possible in Pemonia," Rildning said. "Either the empire will destroy the tribes, or the tribes must push the empire back into the sea. Neither side will relent."

"I remember the part of the Cataclysm scroll where the Almerics all but destroyed the Agnesci Seafathers before the last of the Seafathers escaped Cedelaebos. So we must push out or otherwise convince the foreigners to permanently return to Cedelaebos, but this is not the way of the prophecy."

"I do not wish for a cataclysm upon the people of the empire," Rildning said. "I don't know what the answer is, except to protect our people. And the only way is for the tribes to come together. I'm also worried about the envoys, even Arbardir. It was my idea to seek out allies among the tribes. I'm glad the Sage and Vaynking agreed to try, but if anything happens to them, as happened to Yelgoram . . ."

"Husband, is there no end to your worries? Owerdir, Urgamdir, and Arbardir are all hearty Umbyrs. I'm surprised Tirgranir allowed only Umbyrs and you. Perhaps the Vaynking is removing his obstacles."

"Now who is overly worried," Rildning smiled.

"My worry is you," Eniri said, "traveling alone with Mrigamad and his cursed-earth bladesmen. Please, Rildning, be careful."

22

YELGORAM

Eglamour, Donovan Province
Frostfall, 2269

It was growing cold but Yelgoram had not been offered any furs. His wolf pelts had been stripped off to show the crowd his many green tattoos during his trial. His green-streaked gray beard, once long and tied in a knot that rested on his chest, had been shorn and thrown to the crowd. His wolf claw moccasins and electrum circlet were confiscated, and even his electrum ring. Now they had come for him again. He was brought out into the cold light in chains and a loincloth.

He found himself back on the stone-hewn stage facing an even greater crowd of foreigners. The new city gleamed in front of him, with an imposing palace overlooking the square. Yelgoram squinted to see the powerful figure seated on the palace balcony, watching alongside the Raffen king Pendigied.

Yelgoram knew he had taken a great risk by going to Woudenhod on behalf of his people. But he had never expected he would be displayed for these foreigners. He hoped his sons and Rildning would forgive his failure to turn the Raffen into allies, and that they would be victorious where he had not been.

His thoughts were disturbed by the shouting of the man to whom he was delivered on the platform. He was as large as Arbardir and his face was shrouded by a black mask. His big hands, pocked with scars from disease, took custody of Yelgoram with a rough jerk.

Beside this man stood the priestly-looking man who had presided over his trial. He addressed the crowd in words Yelgoram could not understand, but they sounded ugly and whipped the crowd into a furor. Yelgoram looked up into the gray sky of coming winter, and there he saw an omen of peace: the distant glow of the sunlight searching for the ground, winds from the south, and two birds sailing silently abreast.

When the man's speech was finished, a wreath of thorn balls was hung around Yelgoram's neck. The masked man then paraded Yelgoram up and down the stage, driving him with a whip. Foul food, animal dung, and butchered cats were thrown at him. Next he was tied to a stake and made to endure stones and rubbish thrown at him. He cried out and wished to fall to the ground, but he hung there, bleeding and broken.

Finally, the pocked hands took hold of him. The stench of the man's heinous chuckle clouded Yelgoram's face. They unbound him from the stake and shoved his neck to the block. Then he felt no more.

23

BREDAHADE

Eglamour, Donovan Province
Frostfall, 2269

"You don't approve?" Ralmo asked. Bredahade rubbed his stubbled chin as he squinted at the archbishop. "Those found guilty of heresy endure far worse," Ralmo pointed out. "This heathen was spared much, and the mercy sword came quickly for him." Ralmo looked down into the square from the exarch's balcony. "The people saw the trial. The barbarians among them will recall the example we made of Yelgoram if they think of fighting the empire again."

"It was an unnecessary spectacle," Sarnaker said. "This isn't the best way to tame the barbarians."

"I agreed to your trial of the chieftain, but we had not agreed to this," the exarch said. "A trial and swift, clean execution would have been sufficient."

"What do you say, King of the Raffen?" Ralmo asked.

"I enjoyed the view," Pendigied said in rough Brintilian. Genthus translated the rest.

"Your Eminence, the king says the Gallerlanders are barbarians, as you say, and deserving of such a death. They have no place in the empire except as slaves. You must understand they have been crueler to other tribes over the years."

"Regardless," Sarnaker said, "I prefer to win the tribes with political charms and the benefits of the empire, not by fear alone."

"There is wisdom in both paths," Bredahade said. "I have seen many rebellions in the Old World and subsequent executions in my decades of service. Many alliances made, many broken. I have concluded that most men, regardless of origin, respond to two things: fear and desire.

"You, King Pendigied, have cast your lot with the empire because you desire to be part of a great alliance, enjoy its riches, and build a new world in Pemonia. The Ollohd also desired peace and trade. Alternatively, perhaps you feared a world dominated by the Gallerlander horde. The Arukans acted out of fear when they attacked Almeria long ago.

"However, say what you will about them, the Gallerlanders are a vast people. Even now, suffering many defeats and seeing their kings scattered, they greatly outnumber our own soldiers. We will bring Hilsingor's sword to their necks when needed, but otherwise we must try to convince them—or portions of them—that giving up the fight will not necessarily strip them of their honor. The manner of this chieftain's death destroys opportunities to bring them into the imperial council."

"You eminence," Ralmo began softly, "the Martinus has explicitly decreed that the crusade against the barbarians is an effort to overthrow the dominion of Memelos himself. There is no higher calling for any knight or ruler. The Martinus also authorized any means necessary to quell the heathens and punish them for their innumerable crimes.

"How many innocent women and children have perished during their raids on the colonies over the years? Many Brintilians and others have answered the call of the Martinus to cross the dangerous seas to join the crusade, so we must not pity the barbarians and forget the sacrifice of the holy and honorable knights."

Bredahade nodded solemnly. If there was anything that annoyed him more than Ralmo's incessant references to the Martinus, it was Ralmo reminding him of the purpose of the crusade. But he knew how to handle such churchmen.

"I'll be the first to acknowledge the truth of your words," the exarch said. "There is no crusade without the bountiful blessings of God and the Temple Father. True, the Martinus called the crusade, a beautiful thing that has united the Old

World—even the treasonous Arukans. And as ruler of this continent, I give thanks daily for the knights who have braved the rolling seas and wild forests to join us. I'll never value their sacrifice less than heathens who refuse to turn from the ways of Memelos.

"However, I'm sure you will agree we cannot treat every heathen as if they cannot be saved from the Depths. Our guest, the Raffen king, and the conversion of his people are the prime example."

"The emperor's representative is telling you that he will continue to rely on the support of the church as he, as exarch, decides how to prosecute the war and win the peace," Sarnaker said. "And as chancellor, I'm responsible for brokering the peace part. I'm sure that when word reaches the Martinus, he will be pleased to know the Raffen king and others have joined the empire and the church, and that our brave knights no longer fight their battles alone."

Bredahade could see the archbishop understood the message. After Ralmo excused himself from the balcony, the exarch felt the need to apologize to Pendigied.

"Genthus, tell him some Messengians have not yet gotten used to the changing times, but the emperor himself desires the Raffen and others as allies. Always strive to reassure him about the empire he has joined and the religion that he has accepted." Genthus relayed his words, and the king replied through him.

"Your Eminence, the king says not to worry for his sake. He does not blame the churchman or anyone else for their contempt of the Gallerlanders. The Raffen people are moving forward together with our people, and it will soon be easy even for ignorant ones to see the difference between the Raffen folk and the people of the woods. Lastly, King Pendigied insists that the Gallerlanders deserve to die as Yelgoram did, and that they will never join the empire."

As the balcony cleared, the exarch leaned to Sarnaker's ear.

"Odon of the Goyns is the Gallerlander king nearest to Eglamour. I want you to make sure he is hard pressed by the legions, then have a letter sent to him. Assure him that his surrender won't be greeted with an execution. Offer him collateral to guarantee your word. Even your own son, if you must."

Sarnaker nodded. "Certainly, Your Eminence."

24

HARSEN

Eglamour, Donovan Province
Frostfall, 2269

Among the people in the crowd who watched Yelgoram's execution was a man hooded in burlap and old sailcloth. A discerning eye would have noticed his beard was well kept and his face clean of dirt, however. He wasn't the pauper he pretended to be.

The spectacle of Yelgoram's death brought a tear to his eye while the people around him jeered for more blood. He knew he was the only one who had understood the chieftain's last words, spoken in Gali: *Wurumnak, father of all. Protect my sons. Protect Rildning and his son. And lead them to victory.*

Harsen did not know Rildning had a son. The woodsman recalled his final moments with his old friend, back among the burning giant trees. He had seen no other path for himself but to surrender to the soldiers, but he had not forgotten the pain in Rildning's face when he threw down his spear and fled into the soldiers' arms. As a rescued prisoner, he was treated well by the Frontier Corps.

But since that time, there was no bowl of soup or mug of beer he consumed without remembering Rildning's and his own hardships in the wilderness. Harsen's guilt had even softened his heart toward the Gallerlanders, whom he had grown to hate.

In spite of his rescue, when he made his way back to the cities he soon discovered he was a wanted man. The soldiers

126

who had toiled many months on the frontier were not aware, but after word spread of Rildning's treachery, Harsen was presumed to share his heresy. So Harsen avoided New Lorin and made his home in the new capital, where his face was not known. He continued trading but took precautions. He lived in fear of the day when soldiers would burst through his door. And haunted by Rildning's fire-lit face.

Yelgoram's fate now sharpened his guilt. He had dined with the chieftain many times in Nalembalen. Rildning had a close bond with the man he had called Chief Wolf. Harsen also heard the news from the front, that the crusaders had lately seen great success. Still, no one knew where the vastness of Gallerlandia ended. He heard the Frontier Corps had pushed farther into the wilderness, and was finally forced to stop and regroup by building forts and roads to keep up their supplies.

Harsen asked himself what he could do. Was there a way to help the friend he had abandoned? For weeks he would rack his brain as Yelgoram's piked head moldered on the wall overlooking the city square.

25

HILSINGOR

Rachard, Bram Province
Winterfall, 2269

The marshal paced along the foot of the wall. The fresh-cut stones and new mortar were speckled with the wetness of falling snow.

"Where is he?" Hilsingor grumbled to Arnolf. The marshal had come down to the builders' quarters expecting to find Bronderod, his chief engineer. Hilsingor wanted him to be working, but was now agitated by having to wait for him. The men said he was birthed on a battlefield, and thus he belonged there no matter the season. He certainly felt that way.

At last Bronderod arrived, huffing and rosy-cheeked from the cold. His beard was matted with bits of stone and mortar. Belted around his furs were several mallets and metal instruments that clanged with his quick stride. Hilsingor had always prized the engineer's tendency to get dirty alongside his builders, because he knew Bronderod would ensure the best work.

"Apologies, sir marshal, you know we don't even rest with the winter."

"Yes, Bronderod, but I have not had a report for some time," Hilsingor replied.

"Well, time spent reporting is not spent building, and you know where I'm best," the engineer said. "Sir, if you want this done quick and proper, there should be less talking and more backs breaking."

Few men dared to speak so gruffly to him, but the marshal knew that Bronderod knew his own value to the marshal. The master builder had always been there to advise him. There was the time he worked out the best way to mine under the Arukan citadels to help squash the rebellion.

And later when Hilsingor oversaw the rebuilding of the Arukan cities he had destroyed, Bronderod designed all of the new settlements and fortresses. Because Hilsingor judged there was no finer engineer in the Old World, he had not given Bronderod a choice about whether to come with him to Pemonia. Bronderod came, along with a grumpiness that amplified with age.

"Fair enough," Hilsingor conceded. "We are here together now, so show me."

Bronderod grumbled under his breath but led the way with a quick pace. "As you can see, the wall is only chest high. Progress is slow because the mortar freezes in this wind. We can't set enough fire barrels to keep the men and mortar warm. The early winter has bitten off the fingers of more than a few soldiers already."

As they rounded a bend, Hilsingor viewed the grounds before them where more complete walls stood waiting for refinement.

"These walls here and there will be the inner walls of the new keep," Bronderod continued. "The great hall will be large enough to enclose even your current wooden one, when everything is done. Over there will be the outer walls and towers with moat beyond. Those foundations were just set. The moat, curtain wall, and second moat and ditches will be over there. Toward those trees you can see the foundation for the barbican. Stables there, infantry quarters down that hill, cavalry grounds here."

"How long now?" Hilsingor asked.

"Winterfall work is slow. We'll have to stop at some point. Only so much we can do in the frozen earth. Much still to dig, and not enough stone to build as fast as I would like. The mines in those mountains are going well, but with the snows to snag the road . . ."

"Put every horse in service," Hilsingor said.

"Sir, your cavalry steeds are bred for rough danger, true. But they don't have the muscle and fortitude of my good draft horses. Your best destrier won't pull a sled of stone from there to here without a fierce fight, I'll wager, and even then how many would last the winter?"

"How long then?" Hilsingor demanded. The engineer pondered the question while picking at the mortar in his beard.

"At current rate of build, maybe ten or twelve years for the inner parts."

"That is several years longer than your first report."

"You added the second curtain wall and second barbican, and you enlarged the infantry quarters, sir. Digging and stoning the channel from the river to here for the moats will take much of the laborers at least six months alone, depending on the season."

"What about the central keep and first set of defenses?" Hilsingor asked.

"If the weather is merciful, stone is good quality, and if I get more heavy horse and workers, you can have the inner castle completed in two years, but you can sleep in it within a year," Bronderod answered. "If the supply from the new roads is not attacked by those damn barbarians, mind you. I lost five wagons last season on the Eglamour road."

"You leave them to me," the marshal said. "You will have your supplies and more heathen labor. But working this winter and next, I want the inner castle in eighteen months and I want a bed in it by the month of Midspring."

Bronderod shook his head and did not deign to reply. Hilsingor knew the ole ox was hard to push.

"We are not in the northern colonies," Hilsingor continued. "This is the frontier. You will transform this outpost into the greatest city east of Eglamour. The rise of Rachard will give the barbarians pause. Rachard will not only be the new capital of the emperor's most distant possession, it will be the seat of power that quells the wilderwood for a thousand marqs in every direction and perhaps a thousand years henceforth."

"It all starts with stone and mortar," Bronderod said. "I'll see what can be done." Hilsingor knew he wasn't a man who possessed great knowledge of the world, nor was he inspired by visions of grandeur. But he knew the engineer understood the aspirations of empire rested on his foundations.

～

"Sir, I cannot help but wonder if our efforts are too ambitious," Arnolf said as they walked back toward the wooden castle. "No one has ever built such a fortification anywhere in the world, much less on an uncertain frontier during winter and with our shortages."

"We have delays, not shortages," Hilsingor replied. "We sit upon a vast electrum treasury, amassed from all the hoards found from Nalembalen to here. Months ago I requested the exarch grant me the powers to melt down the electrum and mint them into imperial coins to fund this effort. And with the arrival of more soldiers, Raffen, and Bronhildi, we will have plenty of labor. Look there, what do you see?" The marshal pointed out into the southeastern wilderness, the dark forests graying with distant snows.

"The untamed Gallerlandia," the adjutant answered.

"Precisely. It is all around us. If the heathens had any strategic skill, they would realize Rachard is a pressure point for us. That heretic, if he knew of this feebly protected outpost, would surely muster the green-skins to overrun us.

"I meant what I said to Bronderod," Hilsingor continued. "Rachard will be unlike any other stronghold in its size and power. Our loss of an entire legion in the Ardfalm Forest is a failure that must not be repeated. The crusade will enter its third year with the coming of spring, yet we still don't know the vastness of this realm or its people—to say nothing of the continent. To swiftly move farther into the frontier requires a permanent anchor to solidify the gains we've made and to avoid another Ardfalm, which happened after the sabotage of our supply lines.

"What better use for all the electrum than to fund this master of all castles? I call it a *warcastle*, for it will not be used to house a king or noble family, or to govern feudal lands. Like the building of a warship, a warcastle is purely a platform for conquest. It must be utterly siege-proof to hold the frontier, and big enough to provide reliable quarters for several legions."

As they neared the wooden castle a horn called out from one of the watchtowers. The sentry raised a signal flag: friendly army approaching. Hilsingor hurried with Arnolf toward the opening gate. In came a Donovard scout riding ahead of the army.

"Marshal Hilsingor, sir. Five thousand Raffen warriors and cavalry, at your service."

PART II

ENVOYS

26

RILDNING

Gilgalem, Vaynland
Winterfall, 2269

The dim morning brought swirls of freezing rain and snow into the bowl of Gilgalem. It was the first time in living memory that a layer could accumulate on the stone warmed by the heart of the mountain. As the fur-bundled envoys gathered their packs and said their goodbyes, Rildning watched the Gallerlanders fret about the omens.

"I'm worried for you," Owerdir said. "Who will read the sky for you?"

Rildning chuckled. "Read it for me now, dear friend," he answered, "and I'll carry the message with me until we meet again." Owerdir gave him a hopeless look, then he squinted up into the gray sky.

"Spring will come early, just as winter's harshness has hastened," Owerdir said.

"I hope not," Rildning replied. "Time is already against us. Safe travels, my friend."

Owerdir was the first to depart. Tirgranir did not have anyone to send with him who knew the language of the Naren-Dra, but the Sage wrote a message with what little knowledge he had of their speech for him to carry. Tirgranir also provided two of his best climbers who were from the lands that approached the Naren-Dra's mountainous home.

Rildning was told no Gallerlander had ever scaled their peaks, and the old tales said the Naren-Dra had always lived

135

isolated from the other tribes high up in the clouds. As for Owerdir, he was eager to take up the journey in honor of his father. The fate of Yelgoram was ever at the forefront of his mind, even as he walked up the steps of the terraces.

Next to leave was Arbardir and a Vayn. He initially refused a companion until he was forced to admit he did not know the way to the northern peninsula where the Nake people dwelled. For the task, Tirgranir chose a rhymer named Gombir who had previously visited the Nake to learn their tales, as they were known to lack written words. Arbardir was incensed that he was made to travel with a mere entertainer, but he had no choice. The towering man departed with the rhymer with little ceremony.

Urgamdir was next. To relieve his loneliness on what would be the envoy's longest and most perilous journey to Bronhildia, the Sage pressed Brugmir into his service, the same Goyn who had complained the most and shouted the loudest during the councils. The choice was also a practical one. While Umbyrs like Urgamdir had long been rivals with the neighboring Bronhildi, the western Goyns had often played peacemaker between them after long periods of strife.

"I'm confident you will find it within yourself to be of use to Urgamdir," the Sage told Brugmir. "Otherwise he is at liberty to cast you off the trail to fend for yourself."

"The strength of my arm and will, and my knowledge of the Bronhildi tongue and customs, is all I require," Urgamdir said. "But I'll welcome Brugmir as my cook."

Rildning approached his friend before he left, patting his bandaged shoulder.

"Remember, you are not to seek out battle," Rildning told him. "You have the longest road by far, and through lands and woods long conquered by the Frontier Corps. You must hide your big self in the bush. Do not rush the task for our sake, as there is little hope in turning the Bronhildi. And we will have likely enlisted the other tribes and be on the march well before you even reach Highchief Harkarom."

"I understand," Urgamdir said. "I don't fear the foreigners or the Bronhildi. I fear I'll be unable to control my anger when I see what they have done to our forests."

"You must temper yourself," Tirgranir added. "Your task is that of messenger, not warrior. Think on the patient efforts of the Maluram deep within the mines. The electrum is hidden and must be searched for and picked with care. Your path demands careful steps. And I have not forgotten the bite your shoulder took from the metal blade in place of my head. I want you back in the ranks of our tribesmen. Finish this task, then return to us."

Urgamdir's bulky form departed from them in haste, with the portly Brugmir already struggling to keep up with his long gait.

Last was Rildning. The Sage approached him with final advice.

"May the winds carry you good omens and quiet paths. You will find the Rahlampians to be different in manner and custom." The Sage leaned in for a whisper. "But as you have seen with Mrigamad, they are intelligent, clever, and skilled with tools in ways the Gallerlanders have forgotten. The designer of the Napargaros light contraption was among the many Gallerlanders banished after the Cataclysm to what later became Rahlampia. Harness them, if you can."

Rildning kissed Eniri and Enildir goodbye. Tears laced Eniri's stoic eyes. She repeated her plea for him to be careful and glared at Mrigamad, who stood watching nearby. As Rildning walked away with the Rahlampian up the terraces, Tirgranir called out to Mrigamad.

"Honor my trust in you," he said. "Your domnitar and his warriors will be welcomed here, but if he does not come, return Rildning safely."

"Do not worry, great Vaynking," Mrigamad said. He stopped Rildning and reached inside his furs, jerking out the torn Frontier Corps banner. He tossed it down to them and shouted, "By spring, all loyalties will be revealed!" The starcross banner rippled through the snow and fell at Tirgranir's feet. Eniri picked it up and blinked with confusion. Rildning glanced back one more time as he stepped over the rim of the mountain, seeing her stare and Tirgranir's scowl.

27

ODON

Black Forest of Ondirhar
Winterfall, 2269

Goynking Odon quietly surveyed his tribesmen in the icy predawn light. He was a grizzled man with a matted beard and bag-swelled eyes. His tribesmen were cold and hungry but ready. Odon's frustration had grown as the months turned colder. He and his Goyns had not been able to help at Nalembalen, and he knew he could not expect help from the other clans. He was simply too far away, trapped by the foreigners and forced into the Black Forest of Ondirhar.

While the dark forest provided refuge from the horse beasts and steel blades, the disease and vicious animals they found there had gradually whittled down his tribesmen and their families. And there was not enough food to push through the depths of this forest toward Gilgalem.

He decided to bring them out. He knew from his scouts that the foreigners were waiting for him, camped on the plains and watching the forest edge. Odon had made up his mind. He told all of his people to ready themselves near the wood line. Warriors mingled with the old, women held babies in one arm and stoneswords in the other, and boys clutched two spears.

As dawn broke, he interpreted the clouds as favorable but then saw his birth star wink out behind high wisps. He glowered at the sky, then led his people on a walking march.

138

There were more soldiers waiting than he expected, but this did not deter him. Their march was steady and direct toward the enemy's main encampment. The foreigners formed up into their battle lines and waited for Odon to charge.

When the king was as close as he dared, he stopped the Goyns and held up his spear. Then he threw it down onto the ice-crusted grass in front of him. He drew his stonesword and cast it down as well.

One by one the Goyns did the same, until thousands upon thousands of weapons lay in a cold heap. When this was done, Odon carefully removed his ivy crown and laid it on the pile, then faced his enemy with chin held high. Many tears were shed behind him.

The commanding knight of the foreigners and a few of his attendants rode out to meet Odon.

"Pity," the knight said when he reached Odon, speaking through a drigoman. "I had hoped for a different end to this. But the exarch's orders were clear. Return his crown to him." An attendant dismounted and retrieved the ivy, and Odon accepted it.

"We will take the required hostages," continued the knight and drigoman, "to ensure your newfound loyalty. You will be sent to the capital for your oaths. Your people will be provided for, according to the exarch's orders."

28

HILSINGOR

Rachard, Bram Province
Winterfall, 2269

The marshal took the letter from Walpert's hand. The Raffen captain smiled broadly, exposing a mouth that was missing half its teeth. Hilsingor was not accustomed to receiving messages from barbarians, but his arrival with a half legion of warriors was most welcome.

"From the exarch, sir," explained the knight who had led Walpert's warriors to Rachard. Hilsingor had invited the distinguished knight and Walpert to dine with him and his commanders. "Walpert insisted he have the honor of giving you the letter, since he is King Pendigied's relative of some sort."

"Very well," Hilsingor said. He broke the purple wax and unfolded the lengthy parchment.

> Marshal Hilsingor,
> I am most pleased to send you the first half of the Raffen warriors you had requested. You will find a thousand light cavalry, three thousand foot, five hundred spearmen, three hundred archers, and two hundred supporters and craftsmen.
>
> The other half of this new legion will arrive with the spring as promised, led by King Pendigied himself. His five thousand will be similar, with his cohort of his best warriors. Take note that Walpert is essentially his cousin, though it is

difficult for our scholars to discern the complex family structures of the Raffen. Regardless, please see that your men treat him with respect, for the sake of the alliance.

The first meeting of the Imperial Council of Pemonia was a great success. There remain tensions among the tribes, and even some provinces, but they will settle themselves. The conversion of the heathens allows God to repair their hearts. Pendigied, Walpert, and their warriors are all Messengians now. With each new barbarian legion we will expand the empire. You are the sword edge, and my own heart is steadfast in the knowledge that you are God's most worthy tool for this honor.

I have received your letter about the warcastle, as you termed it. As marshal of the frontier and builder of our great city of the east, you are hereby granted authority to mint electrum into imperial coinage. Shipping the electrum by cart to Eglamour will decrease, and my stipends to you will cease as long as you keep finding electrum hoards. I want to hear that your new roads are filled with soldiers and settlements, not clogged with carts. I have entrusted Sir Wilsig with five minting stamps so he may set up your treasury.

May God continue to grant you victories worthy of our emperor.

Exarch Bredahade

When Hilsingor finished, he relayed the gist to his commanders. Wilsig produced a purple velvet bag and opened it on the table. "Congratulations, sir. I'm honored to serve as your knight-treasurer. My sword is yours."

"Very well," Hilsingor said, looking to his commanders Ravorglad and Firkas to welcome the young knight.

"Welcome," Firkas said.

Ravorglad glared back and forth between the velvet bag and the young face. Hilsingor knew they feared having their purse strings hampered by this newcomer.

"I'm sure your father does not wish you to stay in the treasury," Hilsingor continued. "Do not worry, you will gain much experience in battle here on the frontier. When the time comes, you will serve at the side of Firkas. I am also eager to hear of your travels with the Raffen from Eglamour to here. Can we depend on them in battle, as we have the others?"

"Yes, sir," Wilsig said. "We encountered small bands of Gallerlanders on the road. These Raffen don't flinch at a fight. I'd say you could trust them as much as the Raffen raiders your men have trained out here."

"Who is your father?" Firkas asked.

"The chancellor," Wilsig replied.

"Sarnaker sent word earlier in the year," Hilsingor said. "I'm not surprised he chose this opportunity to send you now. These are momentous times."

"It will be my honor to serve with you," Firkas said. "You must know that our duty out here is a difficult one. The Gallerlanders are still dangerous. Even if you were the emperor's own son, you must obey orders and consider the hazards of the frontier."

"Understood, sir," Wilsig replied.

"It is an honor to have Sarnaker's son among us," Hilsingor said to his commanders. "Like his father, Wilsig is a knight of the Harbor Thorns—"

"But not a true crusader," Ravorglad interrupted. "Did he fight in New Hovedollen? Or at Nalembalen? I think not."

"Silence!" snapped Hilsingor. "The title of crusader isn't for your knightly order alone. The Harbor Thorns were the first order created by Rin when he discovered the New World, and thus they are the oldest knights of Pemonia. These naval knights deserve no less respect than your Order of the Red Garland."

Hilsingor had expected Ravorglad to be irked by the arrival of more barbarians and the young Wilsig. The marshal would later tell Wilsig that Ravorglad and Firkas were honorable commanders of the corps, but that idleness in winter quarters so close to the enemy was deeply annoying for them. Though it seemed far away amid a deepening winter, the coming of spring was only a matter of time.

29

ENIRI

Gilgalem, Vaynland
Winterfall, 2269

Eniri was weeping softly, thinking of Rildning and the enemy's banner, when Rumban, the Vaynking's steward, came to her door.

"Lady Eniri," he breathed between gasps. "The stores . . . the food . . . destroyed. Some—"

She jolted up and settled his speech with her hands on his face. He gulped and steadied his breathing.

"What has happened?" she asked.

"They are flooded! The food stores are lost below. All of it—gone!"

"Take me there."

They walked out into the snow. It was now dusk and the wet winds lingered. She saw Gallerlanders crowded at the bottom of the courtyard. The great doors where provisions were lowered for storage in the mountain were flung open and everyone was looking down into the pit.

They made way for her, and she saw herself in the blurry mirror below. One of the tribesmen had been lowered down and was wading among the floating debris. The pool was ankle-deep but she knew that meant the lower chambers were submerged.

"We are already working to block water from entering the mines and tombs, with sacks filled with stones," Rumban said. "Oh, how could this happen?"

"Unless we find the source of this, it could continue," Eniri said. "Where is the king?"

"I sent for him, but he is on a hunt in the woods. I also sent word to the Sage, who—"

"We must act quickly," Eniri said. Images of starvation on the mountain flashed through her mind. "Your sack barriers won't be enough. Seal the doors with jars of wax, quickly!"

"It won't be enough," the Sage said as the crowd parted to let him through. "Something like this happened long ago, when the spring ran hot and gushed out of its channel. The lowest chamber was flooded for many years and finally walled off. Someone must go down."

Eniri looked back down into the watery pit. The thought of the cold water made her shiver. But she steeled herself, thinking of the perils Rildning and the others were already facing out in the cold.

"Two good swimmers will come with me," she declared.

"Lady Eniri, you cannot possibly—"

"Not another word, Rumban. I grew up in the trees of Nalembalen, but I also swam in the streams and pools that watered the giants' roots since I was a girl. I saw an omen after Rildning left: a bird flying with a twig in winter against a daylight moon. It hinted at my own burden to come."

The Sage placed a gnarled hand on her arm.

"Eniri, if the Vaynking—"

"You there," Eniri said, ignoring the Sage and calling down to the man wading in the pit. "Can you swim?"

"As good as any Goyn," he cried up.

"Who else will go?" she said to the crowd.

"A Vayn who once played in these storerooms must see to this," said one hearty-looking man. "I'll come with you." He stripped off his bulk furs and straw-stuffed moccasins, then followed her down the rope.

"Let them swim the hazards," Rumban said as they went down. "Rildning and Tirgranir will have my head as it is. Hearth fire and dry clothes will await all of you."

When Eniri plopped down, she saw the Goyn studying the sky. Fear was in his face. She guessed he had not agreed to drop into the pit for what she had in mind.

"What is your name, brave Goyn?"

"Girtimir," he said, handing her and the Vayn a stone knife each for their belts. Eniri looked at the door to the storeroom. Water squirted from around the bags and debris Girtimir had placed in front of it.

"And you?" she asked of the Vayn.

"I'm Wendon," he said as bundles of rope splashed down from above. His face was defiant, as if the water was an enemy he was determined to slay. Eniri looked up as a hoarse voice called down to her.

"Eniri, child," the Sage said. One of his attendants had appeared and tossed down several dirty leather bags. "Take these, you will need them."

She gathered the bags from the water and felt a tingle of consolation as she pulled the strings on one. She reached in a pulled out a perfectly round ball of electrum that fit snug in the palm of her hand.

"A delver's eye," Wendon marveled.

"Can it see?" Girtimir asked.

"No," Eniri said. "It is a mining sphere, fashioned by the Maluram to find their way through the dark rock toward the electrum veins under the mountain. They will be our light in the dark waters. Now, let us open that door."

Girtimir and Wendon unbarred it and kicked away the bags. When the door opened, a small wave rolled out. The water was rising, though slowly now. The two men entered into the dim, while Eniri looked up one last time.

"Send a runner after Rildning," she called out. "Perhaps the Rahlampians can send food."

She waded through the doorway and found the men staring up into the first chamber. The ceiling was high and packed with food, but not enough for the multitude that lived in Gilgalem now. She looked down into the inky depth, seeing the snuffed-out torches still in their sconces below the water.

"Maybe two weeks' worth of food is dry above the water," Wendon said.

"Not even that long," Girtimir said. "Should we light this chamber with the electrum? If we have any hope of seeing into the second chamber when we swim into it, we had better fill this chamber with light."

"We will multiply the torches, but we must not use the spheres yet," Eniri said. They waded around, taking torches to light the others. The deepness below slowly came into view. Everything had escaped the bags and crates and now floated through the water to obscure the view of the bottom.

"Girtimir, we will tie the ropes around our waists," Eniri said. "You tie them here. Pull hard if you feel a swift jerk."

"You don't want me to go with you?" the Goyn asked, half-relieved and half-worried.

"We need someone to pull us back if needed," she said. She pulled out two delver eyes and gave one to Wendon. "To light our swim down to the bottom," she said.

Eniri and Wendon found the spiral staircase and walked down, pushing away the vegetable flotsam as they went. She winced as icy fingers crept up her legs and back. The electrum sphere brightened when her hand dipped under the water. When the water reached her shoulders, she took a deep breath and ducked her head in, vanishing in the soup. Wendon unfurled the rope behind her, then watched it snake down.

She swam awkwardly at first, shivering and trying not to drop the delver's eye. The color of the stone and floating debris was like a darkened rainbow, with the glow of the electrum casting a warm light into the eerie gloom. All went well until she attempted to swim past a barrel. She dropped the little orb and watched as it sank toward the chamber floor, which she still could not see. She cursed herself as she returned up for air.

"It is crowded down there," she said.

"But you are getting used to the water?" Wendon asked. She nodded.

The second dive was easier. Eniri followed the now-familiar space. The barrel had floated away. As she passed her previous limit, a glowing spot smiled up at her from below, signaling the bottom of the chamber.

She swam for it, then twisted toward the doorway to the next chamber as it came into view. The passage was dark and Eniri could feel the push and pull of a current. It was like the gaping, breathing mouth of a stony fish. She became anxious, so she tossed down another sphere just inside the mouth. She heard the faint clink when it struck the stone, and watched as it rolled and settled in a corner. The passage glowed as the delver's eye shifted to and fro with the current.

She returned to Wendon and told him of the marked path. She would dive again and hopefully reach air in the next chamber. He was to follow the orbs if she did not return again.

The water felt colder as Eniri swam through the passage. The current pulled her into the stony mouth. The second chamber was blacker than night. Not a single ray of light from the first chamber could penetrate the depths of the second. Eniri could scarcely see anything beyond the glow of the electrum in her hand.

Eniri had walked through the stores before. She knew each chamber lay deeper in the mountain than the one that preceded it, and that the tops of each chamber overlapped a bit with the previous one. So she felt certain air existed at the tops of each chamber. But it was difficult to tell which way was up, and she again grew anxious as her lungs ached.

She closed her eyes to try and calm herself. Her eyelids felt faintly warm. When she opened them she saw two spheres tip out of her bag. They quickly disappeared into the cold darkness below, but at least she knew which way was up. Finally she reached the far wall of the chamber. Much of the food sacks were floating around her but not as many as had been pushed into the first chamber.

Eniri's lungs heaved again as she kicked for the top. Her teeth were grinding now, and she could feel the cold water trying to creep into her nostrils. The terrifying thought of no air pocket at the top flashed through her mind. The water seemed endless.

Her chest heaved again and she let out large gulps of air. Her brain sparked with the panic of realizing she could be going the wrong direction. More air lost. Then a tug on her legs and she swallowed a mouthful of water. She lashed at the water, but her legs were twisted in the rope. Her lungs were emptying now and her eyes grew wide.

She quickly loosed the knife from her belt and cut the rope. Kicking furiously, she tossed the bag of delver's eyes away. Her air was gone. Her light was gone. Eniri's mind pulsed with fear and her lungs called out to drink. Warmth touched the corners of her blind eyes. She kicked and reached and shoved swimming objects out of her path. Just as she pictured herself dead and floating among the debris, she lurched out of the water and into cold air.

Eniri's throat was too small a conduit for her sucking lungs, and she coughed and spat viciously. Her trembling hands grasped at anything that bobbed around her that would hold her weight for a brief moment. Her hands found the wall again, and then a ledge of a storage cell. She pulled herself into the cell and lay shivering on the cold rock. When she rolled over she noticed she had lost every bag of delver's eyes that were tied to her belt.

But she could not think on it. She felt only the urge to breathe, and the throb of her heart. She closed her eyes to the bitter darkness and prayed her thanks.

30

WENDON

Gilgalem, Vaynland
Winterfall, 2269

The rope fell limp in Wendon's hands. There had been a brief tugging but when he attempted to reel it in there was no tension. He yelled to Girtimir and tied his own rope snug.

Before diving in after Eniri, he found a set of stoneware jugs. He dropped his sole delver's eye in one and tied the handle to his belt. Two other jugs he pushed into the water upside down and corked the air inside with a turnip each. These he also fastened to his belt. He took two other jugs into his hands and filled them with water.

He waded into the water up to his waist. The jugs of air floated but remained tethered. He took a breath, then stepped off the spiral ramp. To his delight, his weights pulled him down through the debris. He closed his eyes and waited until his feet touched cold stone.

When Wendon opened his eyes he saw the glow of the electrum markers left by Eniri. He let go of the water-filled jugs and swam for the passage to the second chamber. He saw no sign of Eniri when he passed through, so he continued downward. He exhaled and sipped the air from an turnip-stoppered jug. Next he picked up a heavy sack of something that lay on the stone ramp. He relaxed himself again and stepped off into the dark.

For a while Wendon's only light was the electrum shining upward from the mouth of the jug at his waist. When his rope became rigid, he cut it, imagining Girtimir's surprise and worry. Eventually specks of light came into view below.

He saw delver's eyes scattered on the chamber floor, as well as several leather bags that glowed faintly, but no sign of Eniri herself. After taking another swig of air, he carefully made his way around the chamber walls but found nothing except the next passage, which was blocked by several heavy ladders that had fallen across the path to the third chamber.

Wendon looked up into the dim. He tried to think as his limbs were beginning to stiffen and numb. Eniri had not come this way, he thought, unless she cut her rope loose and wiggled through the ladders. He reasoned this was unlikely without air jugs, which he had not even considered until his time came to enter the water.

Deciding she was at the top, Wendon took a long gulp of air and discarded all the jugs except the remaining air jug. With his delver's eye in hand, he kicked off the floor and sped upward.

31

ENIRI

Gilgalem, Vaynland
Winterfall, 2269

niri was startled by the sound of bubbles bursting on the surface of the water. She peered into the darkness, hoping to catch a glimpse of light, and there it was. Beautiful green-golden warmth.

"Wendon!" she cried. She could hear him sputtering and thrashing in the water. "Breathe! Breathe!" She would never forget the fear that gripped her, of hitting the top of the chamber to find it airless. Eniri continued to encourage him until he recovered. She could now see him clutching the electrum sphere.

"I'm sorry, I failed," she said after he had safely crawled up into the cell.

"You did not fail," Wendon said as he piled burlap sacks and bits of wool on himself as she had. "You lit the way. But we will need to find a way to unblock the next passage. Ladders have fallen across it."

The delver's eye glowed on the stone between them. In the dim light she could see his muscles jerk uncontrollably.

"I cannot feel my fingers and toes," he said with a smile.

"It will pass," Eniri said. "When it does, you can eat. Everything up here is old and dry but edible. And there is plenty of it. When you burst up from the water I saw at least two levels of storage cells above us."

"So plenty of air then," Wendon said.

"Is that what you have in the jar?" She pointed to the turnip still stoppered in the mouth of the jug at his waist. He nodded.

"This is why you needed a Vayn for this task." He smiled.

They stared at the glowing orb for a time, pondering what to do next. Soon their cold, aching bodies demanded sleep. And so they did, under bags and vegetables with only the heat of their bodies to warm each other. When they awoke, the chamber looked as they had left it. No dawn to welcome them, no omens to be viewed in the sky. But the electrum beckoned them with a fresh gleam.

"They won't come for us, will they?" Wendon asked.

"We cannot wait for them to," Eniri answered.

"I wonder if the Maluram will mine a drain tunnel," Wendon said.

"It would take a long time."

"Will we ever find the source of this tragedy?" he asked. "There are so many chambers . . . dozens, though not all in use."

"We must try."

"The old tales say miners followed the spring and expanded the caves in search of the electrum. When they found little on this side of the mountain, they worked the other, where the mines are today. My uncle was once the keeper of the stores, which is why I came down here as a child. I've not seen every chamber, but I know the main spring dives under the mountain from the third chamber on the other side of those fallen ladders. From that chamber, many passages were hewn, so many chambers connect to the third.

"They carved the caves this way because, my uncle said, the Maluram feared to delve too deeply here. They say one tunnel below here opened into the top of a great dome, and inside far below was a lake of hot water beneath the mountain's roots. Two miners fell in, but the others could not even hear the splash because it was so far down. That tunnel was sealed long ago."

Eniri shivered at the thought of the hidden and dangerous depths of the mountain. The idea of being lost to a secret boiling lake was awful. She suddenly longed for the strong trees of Nalembalen, the open sunny spaces and green everywhere. The tree-root tunnels had been the deepest she had ever been underground. She thought of Rildning and her son.

"Could the lake have flooded these stores?" she asked.

"No," Wendon said. "It is too deep, and this water would be too hot to swim. Something must have happened to the spring. We must move those ladders and have a look at where the spring dives under the mountain."

"Should we use your air jugs? We have plenty of jugs and vegetables to cork them," Eniri said.

"Yes, that could work. We could fasten them to the ladders and raise them out of the way. The delver's eyes you dropped down there will be more than enough to work by."

They gathered all the clay and stoneware vessels from their cell and the one above them. One by one they plugged them with carrots and turnips. Wendon figured that every air jug could be tied to two other jugs full of stones, pottery pieces, and water to weigh it down to the bottom. They tossed them into the water and watched them disappear. The idea had lifted their spirits, though they dreaded to leave the scratch of the burlap for the cold of the water.

When they had sunk enough air jugs, they ate a quick meal of bone-dry venison, stiff carrots, and handfuls of raw oats. Then they gathered more twine from bags and tethered weighted jugs to their belts to bring themselves speedily to the bottom. They stuffed their ears with garlic cloves on Wendon's recommendation, as he knew the weight of the water on their heads was heavier down below than it had been elsewhere. With Wendon's lone electrum sphere in hand, they stepped off together into the black water.

When they arrived at the bottom, they found all the jars waiting for them, like stony plants swaying in the current. They set to work by the light of the scattered delver's eyes, refastening the air jugs from their weights to the ladders. They succeeded in partially moving one of them, but there was much still to do.

After a while they returned to their cell to rest and gather more air jugs. On their second dive they noticed the water at the mouth of the passage was different. The normal back-

and-forth motion was replaced by a gentle, constant pull. Vegetables and wood bits that floated into the passage disappeared.

The pull from the passage became stronger after the last ladder was lifted out of the way. When they returned to their dry cell for one last rest, they were alarmed to find the cell was now higher above the waterline.

"Should we wait?" Eniri asked. "Perhaps it will drain."

They watched the water for a moment.

"Comes and goes," Wendon said. "We should press on."

On their final dive, they retrieved the bags of electrum spheres and entered the passage. They were laden with many air bottles and enough weight that they could walk along the floor. They entered the third chamber and looked down into the yawning darkness. Although they were deep already, Eniri still could not shake the look of the depths.

They took a breath from their jugs and stepped into the dark. Their heads soon ached as they sunk down. Eniri lost a garlic clove from her ear and winced, plugging it with her finger. She could feel her lungs twinge. As they floated down they noticed bits of debris rush past them. They could feel an invisible tug on their toes.

Eniri motioned for them to go back up, but Wendon shook his head. As they debated without words, they felt the water pull at their legs like a great swirling tongue. Eniri felt her long hair pull down her back. Abruptly the pull reversed, pulling her hair upward. They looked at each other with excited realization.

They cut loose a weighted jug each and kicked upward. They saw the spiral ramp near them and swam toward it, feeling the current pull them toward the wall. When they reached the ramp, they could see the spring's channel along the wall. Eniri dropped a delver's eye into the channel. It lit up a crate in the channel. They looked at each other with worry.

She dumped a bag of the spheres along the channel, illuminating all the sack-filled crates neatly stacked within it. Her eyes widened as she realized it was blocking the exit for the spring water. One of the spheres disappeared near a ledge on the wall where the water still tried to escape under the mountain. They felt a strong but intermittent current pulling them toward the ledge. Eniri deposited one of the bags of electrum next to the channel, leaving one tied to her waist, and they both left a few air jugs at the same spot. Then they cut loose their weight and swam for the top, which they found to be dry.

"Sabotage!" screamed Wendon as they broke the surface. They coughed and sputtered as they crawled up into a cell. Eniri clenched her teeth and stared down into the dark water.

"All the food," she muttered. "Who would do such a thing? Are there no guards for the storerooms?"

"This was the safest place in Gilgalem," Wendon said. "No one ever comes down here, except those tasked with filling the cells, and they have no need to come into the deep chambers that are already filled with food." His curses echoed loudly. They watched nervously as the debris floating in the water churned. Then it ceased.

"Perhaps I can shout it down," Wendon jested.

"Maybe the spring is trying to free itself," Eniri said. "Maybe the weight of the water has become too great."

"Or maybe the mountain will spew out more. We should lift the crates blocking the channel as we did the ladders."

"This is more dangerous," Eniri said. "When the blockage is moved, it will pull us down into the mountain. We'll be like those ancient miners, drowned under the roots of the mountain."

They looked around their cell, finding that they had the same materials to work with. Wendon stood, picked up a crate, and dumped it. Then he refilled it with empty jars.

"We'll pull the blockage, then lift ourselves with a crate-worth of air jugs. All the weight jugs will be tied to the air crate with one tether, so when the drain clears, one swipe of a knife will cut the air crate loose so we can escape the mountain's drink."

"If we get close to that drain under the ledge it will grab us," Eniri said.

"Yes, but its pull comes and goes, as if trying to clear the blockage itself. We can pull the last blockage when we're on our way up. In fact, we can make air crates for the blockage.

This will work. We can always block the drain again if it's too strong." Eniri nodded warily.

They filled two crates with air jars for the blockage, and one crate each for themselves. They tested them and saw that they floated well and needed much weight to pull them under the water. When everything was ready, they stepped into the black with the crates for the blockage.

When they reached the channel, they found the drain had stopped its pull, allowing them to work more easily. But several delver's eyes had disappeared, so Eniri opened another bag and distributed them. They cleared some of the blockage by hand, then fastened the air crates to the rest before returning to the surface.

"Now we take our air crates down and I'll take hold of the twine we used to secure the weights of the blockage air crates," Wendon said. "When we cut our weights, I'll pull the twine, and everything will rise up together as the water goes down. At worst, if the drain is still too strong, we can swim to the spiral ramp and hold on until the water recedes past us."

Eniri thought it was a good plan, and his confidence put her at ease. Wendon knew these chambers better than she did, after all, and the people of Gilgalem were counting on them to save what food was left. But she still wished for a sky omen.

They reentered the cold blackness one last time. They found the water pulling and swirling again. They each took their air crates in one hand and their stone knife in the other. Their heads and lungs ached, and their bodies and fingers were growing numb. They reached the channel and Wendon fished the twine out from the blockage crates where it had become entangled. They nodded to each other.

They cut their air crates loose of the weight and sped upward. A moment later Eniri saw the twine in Wendon's hand tighten and then snap. They watched in horror as the twine flagged in his grip and the electrum light faded from view.

Wendon let go of the broken twine and his air crate and swam down. Eniri gurgled a yell but it was no use. She let go of hers to follow after him, but before she did all of the glowing light below suddenly vanished. A crunching, crashing sound rippled through the water.

The water plucked the new garlic from her ears and tried to pull the breath out of her. Vegetables and debris slashed down her body and forced her eyes closed. She could not tell if she was still rising or falling. The crashing and ripping sounds continued, along with a groan from within the stone walls.

Just as it felt her lungs would burst, her air crate burst out of the water and she crashed into it. The jars shattered and the weight fell upon her, but she thrashed and kicked until she had hold of the lip of the spiral ramp.

The water snarled and tore at her legs but it quickly receded. She pulled herself up over the ledge and lay upon the ramp in the cold dark. She could hear the shove and crackle of all the barrels, food, and debris in the soup below as everything fought for a place atop the swirling water. She wept as she heard the sounds of the mountain swallowing its great meal.

When she heard a waterfall, she sat up and pulled a delver's eye from her last pouch, tossing it down into the dark. The water from the chambers above was pushing through the passage down to the drain, where the water level had settled. There was no sign of Wendon.

The waterfall continued as she slept under burlap and wool. That was how Girtimir found her, with bones stiff and lips blue amid the stench of water-logged food. The blood from her lashed body dribbled down the ramp and into the water below.

She would later recall their efforts to everyone, telling of how the mountain reclaimed the electrum mined from it, and how Wendon became the third brave Gallerlander to perish in the secret sea beneath it.

32

RILDNING

Eastern Wilderness of Vaynland
Winterfall, 2269

"I don't judge you," Rildning said. "I'm an adopted Gallerlander, remember? I harbor no ancient quarrels with your people. I only seek to unite and guide the tribes against the enemy."

"Don't forget," Mrigamad replied dismissively, "you are guided by me now, and will become my prisoner, should I wish it."

Rildning was not about to remind Mrigamad that Tirgranir had trusted him to guarantee Rildning's safe passage into Rahlampia. He did not fear Mrigamad, judging he was more bluster than genuine threat, but felt compelled to win him over to ensure his tribe would ally with the Gallerlanders.

"As I explained to you," Rildning continued, "I'm not a spy for the Frontier Corps. I took the banner on a whim as a memento, a reminder of my own religion. I have no loyalty to them or any colony."

"Perhaps your Gallerlander woman will feel differently, if you ever see her again."

Rildning stopped in the middle of the snow-covered path. Mrigamad snapped around and sneered at him. Rildning wondered if this Rahlampian wanted a go at him. They had been on the path for several days. The walk through the frozen river valleys east of Gilgalem had been slow but uneventful, with Raffen raiders probably hunkered down by firesides further west.

Yet Mrigamad had daily grown more annoyed with Rildning, as if his presence was a pestilence. And now he was becoming belligerent. Rildning had tried to be friendly, but Mrigamad's tribesmen paid little attention to Rildning and the chieftain insisted on picking fights with him.

"Mrigamad, I'm not your enemy. You know this, otherwise you wouldn't have agreed to take me to your lands. You've seen me fight the Frontier Corps and make peace between you and Tirgranir. And you saved the Gallerlanders—and me—on the field of battle, when we would have been lost to the Raffen. Yet you freely threaten me. If you intend to poison this chance for the Gallerlanders and Rahlampians to align, then it's better if you left me to find my own way to the domnitar."

Mrigamad scoffed. "You would never make it. The snows would lock your legs and the Pernadun would drown you. Denildon of Swaleshil, the Riverkeeper, would kill you. Or you would lose yourself in the thorn swamps of the Usodimare. There are so many ways for a weak foreigner to perish in the realm beyond Vaynland." By now some of the Rahlampians halted their march to watch the two men.

"So it's pity then?" Rildning asked. "You help me because you couldn't bear my death on your shoulders?" Mrigamad walked up and stared him in the face. The black-painted lines on the chieftain's cheeks and brow wrinkled with disgust.

"Your death would mean nothing to me," he scowled. "Even less than the scores of foreign sailors I have slain on our shores."

"What about the innocents crouching in Gilgalem?" Rildning asked. "Perhaps you like to see women, children, and old men die?"

Mrigamad struck Rildning across the jaw. He fell to the ground, having not expected the chieftain to become violent. Rildning rubbed his jowl as he stood. By now all the Rahlampians had stopped to watch.

"I came with you in good faith," Rildning said. "If this is the peace of your people, perhaps the Gallerlanders were right about—"

This time when Mrigamad lashed out, Rildning dodged and struck his own blow to Mrigamad's face. The chieftain bounded up from the snow and charged him. They tumbled down together. A few more blows were exchanged before Rildning locked Mrigamad's head in his arms, and Mrigamad held a knife at his ribs. They both froze, panting in the cold air for a moment. Finally Rildning spoke.

"What sailors?"

Mrigamad was puzzled at the question, then he grew angry again. Rildning let go of his head and shoved the knife away from his ribs. They sat in the snow glaring at each other.

"Do you really not know?" Mrigamad asked. "Have you so quickly forgotten what your own Gallerlander council had said about the Welkars?"

"I've not forgotten," he replied. "They were defeated and scattered by the colonists' ships."

"A large fleet, more than fifty ships," Mrigamad said, wiping blood from his chin. Pain was in his face, but not from the blow. "I helped lead the Rahlampians sent to help the Welkars, but it was too late, as both sides had nearly destroyed the other. When we returned to our own land, we saw the remaining ships catapult flame into our coastal cities as they departed. The fire—"

Mrigamad's voice broke and Rildning understood.

"They burned your city of Castracane," Rildning said.

Mrigamad's fury returned. He jumped to his feet and swept out his long, thin blade. Rildning stayed where he was, easily within striking distance of the weapon, but Mrigamad kept its point skyward. The chieftain gnashed his teeth and blinked tears away, wrestling with himself.

"I have also lost to fire," Rildning said. "You know of Nalembalen, and I've lost many more to war. Perhaps your sword could sate your loss with this foreigner's blood, but I'm not those men. And I don't judge you. My preference is to live and help the tribes take back what they have lost."

"Can the savior of Gallerlandia return the dead to life?" Mrigamad mocked.

"I'm no high king. But I know this enemy. I know what is required. Unity is merely the first step."

Rildning stood and put out his hand. Mrigamad wavered with indecision as his men circled about and watched anxiously. Rildning's gaze was steady and resolute. Finally, the chieftain loosened his grip and let his sword point rest on the snow. Mrigamad quickly stepped forward and snatched Rildning's hand without letting go.

"You pledge your life to this? To shed the blood of your own people?"

"They are not my people," Rildning answered. "I will fight for Gallerlandia and her allies for as long as I have breath."

"We will see."

§

Mrigamad's men grew more at ease as they continued eastward, though Mrigamad was quiet. Rildning was relieved to have finally broken through to the chieftain. Throughout his journey he would learn bits and pieces from the other Rahlampians about Mrigamad's past.

His entire family, and the families of the men who went to help the Welkars, was killed by the fire from the ships. Mrigamad and the others had returned to find the coastal towns transformed into smoldering ruins. They sailed after their enemy in their own ships. Only one of the ships was caught, and the brutal vengeance visited upon its crew had not filled the void in their hearts.

It became clear to Rildning that many of the Rahlampians still fostered an ancient, bitter rivalry with the Gallerlanders, or even pure hatred. But most seemed to understand that times had changed, that a new common foe was upon them. Rildning hoped the domnitar would feel the same way.

§

The lowlands of eastern Vaynland were cracked with numerous fertile river valleys now blanketed in snow.

"We'll reach Rahlampia after crossing the Pernadun River," Mrigamad said when they had camped. "It's a mighty, broad river that drains the great mountain ranges of the north, including many of the cloud-shrouded peak dwellings of the Naren-Dra peoples."

"How will we cross it?" Rildning asked. He recalled the monstrous Glombruk that had proven to be a fatal obstacle for his original expedition from New Lorin.

"Unlike the Gallerlanders," Mrigamad said, "we have not forgotten how to sail sea or river. The riverboats of Denildon the Riverkeeper will ferry us across."

"They haven't been attacked by the Raffen?" Rildning asked.

"They have. The Raffen are skilled with the sail and oar, but their numbers are fewer the closer we get to the Pernadun. And Denildon is the chief of the borderlands, and brother of the domnitar. We will have little or no trouble."

Rildning looked into the campfire. It was as good a time as any to press Mrigamad about his tribe.

"The Sage of Gilgalem told me the Rahlampians were descended from ancient Gallerlanders who were skilled with tools but banished after the Cataclysm. Do you know this tale?" Rildning asked.

Rildning noticed the Rahlampians shifted uneasily around the fire. But they continued eating their pickleweed and shrimp loaves without complaint. After several days with them, Rildning judged these men to be generally quiet. They were not prone to the jovial banter and raucousness of the Gallerlanders. He wondered if their womenfolk were similar, and whether they too were warriors like the Gallerlander women.

"We call it the Tarborchast, or the Solemn Journey," Mrigamad said, trying to appear unsurprised with his question. "We were the Agnesci families who were banished for building the great ships used by the Seafathers to sail to Almeria, resulting in the Cataclysm.

"The Tarborchast was a new beginning for our people. We were driven eastward out of what became Gallerlandia and soon displaced the Welkars, who became dwellers of the tidal marshes. We still warred with them and our former Gallerlander brethren. Our Gali language changed over the years and we became a confederation of clans, since we had no high king.

"Soon the wisest and more respected elder among the clans became the figurehead of the councils, and he was called the domnitar. Anfinnan of Bodamweym is the domnitar of our day, and the councils have bestowed new powers to him since we have faced this new enemy.

"After the Tarborchast, did the Rahlampians continue to observe the old religion?" Rildning asked.

"Yes and no. Wurumnak remains our god, but we long ago abandoned the sacred electrum myths. In truth, worship is a private matter for Rahlampians and is rarely discussed publicly. The faith of our ancestors was irreparably weakened after the Tarborchast, and we no longer believed lumps of shiny metal in the earth would save us at the End Times.

"Unlike the Gallerlanders, the Rahlampians refused to forget the machine arts. Since we believe our own ingenuity will contribute more to the Last Battle than the electrum, we have no use for the Gallerlander ways and don't care for their ancient secrets."

"And I see you allowed yourselves other metals," Rildning noted.

"Freed from the electrum," Mrigamad continued, "our forefathers pursued the powers of joining wood and metal. We have used catapults and ships and other machines, while the Gallerlanders played in the trees and dug in their sacred mines. They view iron as evil, even more so now that the foreigners cut them with it. I must admit, the foreigners' iron is stronger than ours."

"It's steel," Rildning said. "Purified iron, made harder and sharper by smiths. I've seen your swords in battle and wonder how it can be so long and thin. Surely it has great strength like steel." He gestured to Mrigamad's open-ended scabbard with the blade stretched out behind him where it disappeared into his fireside shadow. Mrigamad stood and carefully unlatched it. He pointed it high above the fire.

"We call them windrazors," Mrigamad said. "Often twice as long as he who wields it. It is born in bog iron, then finished in the forge with anchiclade, a special ore mined from the Anchiclade Mountains of our realm. It is folded into the iron over many days and beaten thin."

After hesitating, Mrigamad offered the blade to Rildning to hold. He accepted the offer, finding the hilt exceptionally heavy. But once Rildning adjusted to the sword's balance it was like brandishing the breeze. He could almost feel the blade split the smoke of the fire.

"How would this be practical for battles not on the open plains?"

Mrigamad smirked. "Windrazors can take down small trees, and we use shorter blades while aboard ship. But we avoid fighting in the woods, if we can help it. In the old days, the Gallerlanders would always rush out of their forests and over the fields because they were confident their greater numbers would prevail. It was the same with the Welkars. But they feared our windrazors and cursed us for using the metal.

"None of them should be surprised when the foreigners' iron shatters even their best obsidian blades and granite hammers. We have been breaking their stone weaponry since the Tarborchast."

"A people of the plains, of strong forges, and keepers of ships and machines," Rildning observed. "Why did the Rahlampians not sail to new lands?"

"I suppose our forefathers never felt the need, especially after the Cataclysm. We've conquered all the plains and hills from the Pernadun to the Peridod in the east. We have settled lands south toward Aggarwal and as far north as Harmengaud, past the Usodimare. Although we sailed the seas to trade with the Raffen, Bronhildi, Velps, Nyden, Caribani, and others, the arrival of the foreigners have changed everything."

"Velps and Caribani?" Rildning said with excitement. "Just when I begin to think I have encountered or heard of the farthest reaches of this continent, I receive news of something beyond."

Mrigamad gave him a strange look but smiled. "The world is large, but small is man," he said. "I've never seen most of these tribes myself. I suppose we lack the foreigners' reach and wants." Rildning nodded in agreement.

"It helps to have horses," he said. "The Gallerlanders won't use them, but they are a great advantage. Your people use what is necessary. Would you use them, if you had them?"

"I will confess they are odd beasts," Mrigamad answered. "Spindly, kicking legs and odd teeth, but swift and powerful. I would ride one as long as my windrazor could be used."

"Knights use swords and lances on horseback," Rildning said. "You must help me persuade the domnitar. If the Rahlampians can learn the skill of cavalry, the tribes will have a chance."

Mrigamad nodded. "I have seen the foreigners' cavalry, as you call it. The domnitar will listen to what we have to say about it. It will be easier to persuade him of this than of allying with the Gallerlanders."

As they prepared to settle in their bedrolls for the night, a shout was heard from the path behind them. They stood and Mrigamad yelled out to the sentries posted around the camp.

"Someone is coming," he said to Rildning.

A few moments later two sentries came to the fire clutching a Gallerlander between them. They had knifepoints resting on his neck and belly. As they brought him up he fainted.

"Bring him closer to the fire," Rildning said. He made a place for them to lay him. "You won't need your weapons," he said, pushing away a knife.

"The sentries said he was running up the path," Mrigamad said, crouching down with Rildning over the man.

"Perhaps a messenger," Rildning said. Mrigamad said something to one of his tribesmen. He produced a small stone jar and slid off the cap. Mrigamad dipped a finger in and slathered the bluish-gray paste on the Gallerlander's upper lip. Rildning recoiled at the smell. The Gallerlander jolted up, fear widening his eyes and quickening his breath.

"It's all right, you are with Rildning," he assured the man.

"Gil—Gilgalem," the Gallerlander said as he regained his wits. "The food is drowned. Gone!"

"Settle down now," Rildning said. "Tell me what has happened."

"A flood! The storerooms are flooded."

"How did this happen?"

The runner shook his head. "Lady Eniri sent me as soon as we found the water."

"Should you return?" Mrigamad asked Rildning. Rildning thought for a moment.

"Rest now," he said to the messenger. Rildning stood and looked out into the darkness that settled over the path behind them. "I must continue," he said, shaking his head. "Unfortunately I will have yet another request for your domnitar."

33

OWERDIR

Northeastern Wilderness of Vaynland
Winterfall, 2269

The deepening winter brought a growing dread to Owerdir. He did not mind the cold, as his wolf skins kept him warm and his mind nimble. As a child he pictured himself as half-wolf, half-man when he stalked game in the forest. He thought back to those times when he felt danger about him. This time it was the prospect of the snowy mountains, looming like giants in the distance, that gave him chills.

"I'm a man of the forests, like Yelgoram and my forefathers," he said when his guides chuckled at him. "I miss those lands . . ."

"Can you return?" Birnin asked.

"Those forests were overrun by the foreigners. The last time I saw my father's village was when we traveled to Nalembalen with Rildning as our prisoner. Later, when we were on the path back home, we saw the foreigners and turned back to Nalembalen. The tree city was already burning by then, but we found Rildning and the others before everyone escaped south."

"Living in the mountains is better," Felbanir said. "Harder for the foreigners to reach."

Owerdir gave a nod. Gilgalem had been tolerable, but he would never understand how the Vayns could live in the empty head of a mountain, surrounded with fields instead of thick forests. He wondered how they had come to live that way and still consider themselves Gallerlanders.

Despite the gloomy mountains that waited for him in the distance, Owerdir was glad to have two Vayns for company. The brothers whom Tirgranir had sent to lead Owerdir to the Naren-Dra people were born climbers, talkative, and in good spirits. But this did little to allay his dread as he listened to them discuss the Naren-Dra around their campfire.

"That is not why the cloud dwellers won't come down from their mountains," Birnin said. "It's because the mountains have trapped them there. The first true mountains begin after the foothills. We call them Hesid's Teeth. Those peaks have chewed and spat out many climbers.

"Then there is the Cloud Hollows, a basin that forces you back down from your earlier efforts, then forces you back up again. No Vayn has gone farther than the Hollows, but beyond that can be seen the Earthgate, where—"

"Wait." Owerdir held up his hand. The fire was warm but he was still chilled. "You told me your clan lived near the foothills and climbed the mountains. All the way up. You did not say the Vayns never got beyond . . . whatever it's called."

"Why would we go that high?" Felbanir was puzzled. "It's too dangerous. Not just the peaks, but that is getting into the territory of the Naren-Dra."

Owerdir shook his head in disbelief. "Why didn't you say so at the council?" he asked.

"We are not like you and the foreigner Rildning," Birnin answered. "None among our clan would deny anything to our ivy-crowned king."

"Yes, but proper knowledge of the dangers may have led the council to avoid sending us to the Naren-Dra," Owerdir said.

"We are good climbers," Birnin said.

"We have the knowledge," Felbanir said.

"We know where the Earthgate sits. Once we pass through it, the path will become harder," Birnin conceded.

"We have heard the tales since we were young," Felbanir continued. "The mountain roads are secret thereafter, hidden by the clouds that the peaks gather up to keep the Naren-Dra up there and outsiders down here. But the mountains are said to reward the bravery and patience of the pure hearted who seek out the hidden ways.

"This was how the Naren-Dra came to settle up there. The mountains lured them with mystery and beauty. The pure hearted made the summits and settled in the rocky vales, because they were prevented from following their steps back down. So there they live among the clouds."

"We have always wondered if they can see the sky omens better than we can," Birnin said. "They must be able to easily look down upon even the tree-crowned heights of Gilgalem."

"Have you ever met the Naren-Dra?" Owerdir asked.

"Never," Birnin said. "But our clansmen once did, near the Cloud Hollows. He said it was a clear day on the ridges but the Naren-Dra man disappeared in a misty cloud as they approached him. The tales say they sometimes climb down no lower than the Hollows to hunt for special stones for their magic."

"Magic?" Owerdir scoffed. "Are you saying they know the dark whispers of Ominchar?"

"How else did that man disappear in his own cloud?"

None of this sounded good to Owerdir. He reminded himself that Rildning and the other envoys faced their own dangers. He would put his fears aside the best he could, place his faith in the two eager brothers, and look skyward often.

34

URGAMDIR

Northwestern Wilderness of Vaynland
Winterfall, 2269

"You call this food?" Urgamdir spooned up the chunks of a raw root he could not identify. They clumped together at the bottom of the reeking broth in his bowl. Bits of feather floated on top.

"Well, I haven't got the proper materials!" protested Brugmir. "If you wanted a wintertime feast in the middle of nowhere then you should have stayed in Gilgalem with the real cooks. If they had asked me, we wouldn't be out here going to Bronhildia. We'll never make it. I've never been so—"

Urgamdir stared at the grumbling Goyn, not listening to his latest rant. Urgamdir recalled the Sage's words that Brugmir would be a good travel companion on the long road to the far north. The wiseman also wanted the Goyn to learn some humbleness and take on tasks, like that of camp cook. But Urgamdir, staring at Brugmir, was already fed up after three days. He flung the foul soup at Brugmir. The Goyn sat in silent shock, his furs dripping.

"Your task is food, not talking," Urgamdir said. "They didn't ask your opinion because you are crankier than a mangy old squirrel that has lost his stash. I didn't ask your opinion either. I asked for a meal.

"Now, we'll take only one more dinner from our supplies, as we have a long road ahead of us and food may be scarce in places. Tomorrow you will gather and hunt as we walk. And if you make me hungry under the next moon, I'll send you back home through those Raffen patrols we passed, but this time you won't have my ax to save your mangy hide."

Urgamdir could see the Goyn was digesting this with difficulty. He knew the last thing Brugmir wanted was to go back to Gilgalem. The Goyn hated the Vayns and their caverns more than being a camp cook. At least Brugmir was no coward.

"You know I'd die fighting beside my Goynking Odon before spending another day in that place," Brugmir had told him repeatedly. Urgamdir knew he meant it, but he didn't have that option.

While he was glad Brugmir was not afraid to fight, Urgamdir regularly reminded himself of the words of Rildning and Tirgranir. He was to avoid fighting and creep through the bush, especially once he reached the lands conquered by the foreigners. He told himself he would obey this command if nothing else, no matter what he saw or heard. The exception had been a small Raffen patrol he and Brugmir obliterated when they were still within view of Gilgalem. He had just started the journey, and they had it coming.

"Perhaps a tale, as you unpack us a plate of something," Urgamdir suggested as he tried to calm his anger. "Surely a good story from the good Goyns will warm the night for us."

Brugmir grumbled under his breath as he fiddled with the leather ties of a food satchel.

"The Sage said I was to be your cook, not your grand-mother," he quipped. Urgamdir glared at him. When Brugmir saw the smoked venison, afban, and dried medlars he softened and relented to Urgamdir's request. "So be it," the Goyn began as he handed Urgamdir a plate. "How about the Ghost of Elmbud?"

"Truly, every Umbyrchild learns that yarn from their grandmother," Urgamdir said. "Come now, think of a tale for men."

"A tale . . . a tale . . ." pondered the Goyn. "All right, I have it. It all started back before the Gallerlanders came into Goynland long, long ago. Well before the dark omens that scared away the woodsprites who charmed the roots of the trees and enchanted their fallen branches. The kerchinfolk still lived in Goynland in secret places, hiding from the sprites and their enchantments.

"Among the kerchinfolk were the brothers Rustbeard and Dustbeard, who stumbled upon a waterfall when out looking for melonberries. Behind the falls they could see a faint light. They were drawn toward it and found a secret water garden. There were fishes that changed color as they swam, and stones of solid nacre, like giant misshapen pearls. But what caught their eyes was the abundant sneezeweed, long known by the kerchinfolk to ward off the woodsprites. More grew in the secret garden than had ever been seen before.

"They left the garden behind the waterfall and came to elder Gustbeard with news of their discovery. Gustbeard charged them with harvesting and bundling the sneezeweed and taking it in secret to Slimethorn Forest. It was a moss-woven knot of a place where the woodsprites often gathered and where no kerchinfolk dared to go. All hope of ridding the realm of the sprites was placed on the shoulders of Rustbeard and Dustbeard.

"The brothers were afraid but did as they were told. When they returned to the waterfall they found the rainbow fish floating lifeless. Every pearly stone had darkened to soot. And the sneezeweeds had all been picked, with petals strewn about.

"Dustbeard wanted to turn back and tell their elder what had happened, but Rustbeard was determined to finish their quest. So they followed the sneezeweed petals out of the falls and down the far bank of the stream. There the petal trail entered the woods toward Slimethorn. Soon whole stems of sneezeweed were lying among the petals, as if someone had dropped them from a bundle one by one. So the brothers picked them up as they walked, happily bundling them as they had been told.

"When at last they reached the stunted mossy trees of Slimethorn, they could feel a peculiar chill in the air. It was the same creeping cold that told the kerchinfolk when the woodsprites were near. The brothers clutched their sneezeweed bundles and continued on. They tried to lay the bundles here and there, but it was too late: every petal had already fallen from the stems. The air grew colder and colder. The last thing they heard was the raspy echo of the woodsprites drawing near . . .”

Brugmir’s voice faded awkwardly. Urgamdir shook his head. “On the eve of our dangerous journey you choose a parable about fools’ errands?”

Brugmir shrugged.

“Well,” Urgamdir said, “you botched the soup and the tale, but the venison was good.”

35

ENIRI

Gilgalem, Vaynland
Winterfall, 2269

Eniri could see the anger and frustration in Tirgranir's face. He had honored Eniri and Girtimir and paid homage to Wendon's sacrifice for ending the flood of the food stores. It had been a solemn ceremony with no sign of the jolly feasts the Gallerlanders were accustomed to. The assessment from Rumban, who had handled the rationing even before Wendon drowned, was only two or three weeks' worth of food remained in the once-vast stores. This sent the Vaynking into a rage.

Eniri knew Tirgranir was one to depend more on his weapon than on prayers. But there was no foe to strike down. He had organized hunting parties to bring a steady, if meager, supply of game. Foragers and skirmishers were also sent out to look for edibles and steal food from Raffen camps. But the deepening winter had pushed even the Raffen raiders into fortified quarters. All of these efforts might extend the rations for another week or so, Eniri thought.

The Vaynking shifted uneasily on his throne as the Sage spoke.

"The Gallerlanders have survived greater trials than this," the Sage said. "Just this morning I saw an owl still up with the bright and clear dawn, a rare omen suggesting the merciful Wurumnak will deliver us from hunger and the cold."

Tirgranir ignored the Sage and turned to Rumban, who had slept little the past few days as he organized the gathering and rationing. He had also corralled trusted chiefs to determine who sabotaged the stores.

"What news of the effort to find the criminals?" Tirgranir asked.

"Still nothing," Rumban replied. "And no sky omens to point out a clue."

Eniri watched as Tirgranir's eyes searched the faces of the council, then met hers. She had avoided spending too much time in his presence, but she had been summoned with the others. She had prepared herself for the ridicule she knew was bubbling in his mind.

"It is a pity we can't ask Rildning," he finally said to her. His tone was accusatory and his face grim. "Perhaps he secretly kept too many Frontier Corps banners and wished to wash them down into the waters of the mountain to hide his true loyalties."

Eniri took a deep breath to keep calm. She had burned the banner Mrigamad had thrown down to them. The look of surprise and concern on Rildning's face, her last view of him, had troubled her since that snowy day. But she knew him and refused to believe he had strayed from his adopted tribe.

"Can any of you truly doubt Rildning's loyalty? My husband sacrificed all he knew to become one of us. He has fought bravely on our behalf, and led our warriors well. Now he faces the blizzards and the hostile Rahlampians so we don't have to fight the enemy alone. The banner was no more than a token for him. He has never abandoned his religion, nor should he. But it does not mean he is still with the foreigners. He will always be one of us."

"I agree with Eniri," the Sage said. "Rildning has a special purpose we may not fully comprehend, but his loyalty shouldn't be in doubt." He cast a knowing glance at Eniri.

"Perhaps his arrival wasn't properly aligned with the omens," Tirgranir said. "Look what happened to Nalembalen after he arrived there. He led the enemy to the tree city, and perhaps he has done the same to us. He left before the flood was discovered."

"There is no authority on this mountain that can divine the sky as correctly as I can, great Vaynking," the Sage said. "If your focus is the safety of Gilgalem and its people, I will provide you wisest counsel. But I'll not look skyward to confirm your conspiracies."

Tirgranir had had enough and ended the gathering but asked Eniri to stay behind. She had expected this more personal intimidation as well.

"Why must you protect him, even now?" he sneered. "If you wanted to take my throne and be the high queen, you would disown him for his treachery."

"Why are you so quick to condemn him? You've not spoken to Rildning for an explanation. And what makes you think I would seek to overthrow you? I have as much claim to the high seat as you, but I don't covet that honor in these dire times, nor should you. I regret Gratgofa cannot be here to lead the Gallerlanders. Even Odon or Erambrin would lead better than you."

"Gratgofa?" Tirgranir snorted. "He lost our greatest city to flame, forfeiting his place among the Thuraniparin of Wurumnak for all eternity! Odon and Erambrin are like saplings bent in the winds of our foes. No one has done more to save our people than me."

"Even now, as starvation creeps up the mountainside with the hardening of winter, you think only of yourself," she countered. "You did not even volunteer to go to the tribes yourself, where you might have persuaded great men where lesser men would fail. But no, you sent Rildning and his men on those hard paths. To find hope, Tirgranir? Or to protect yourself?"

"Careful, Eniri. I'm still the Vaynking and you are princess of nothing but an ash field. Do not too hastily confirm yourself to be the enemy I have come to suspect you—and Rildning—to be, or I'll—"

"You'll what, kill the princess of the Umbyrs? The clans will further divide, more than you have already allowed them to. They would destroy themselves even with the mountain walls of this refuge long before the foreigners arrive."

Tirgranir gripped the stone armrests of his cold throne. Eniri stood steadfast before him, the strength of her fathers bright in her eyes. Eniri waited for him to throw her out of his hall or perhaps banish her from Gilgalem. But he did not break the silence or his gaze. Before one of them could end the standoff, Rumban cleared his throat down at the end of the hall.

"My king, I'm told the last of the floodwaters have drained, if you wish to tour the stores."

Tirgranir looked at Eniri with hard eyes but spoke softly. "When I've defeated the foreigners and become high king, I will demand either your firm loyalty or your exile."

She glared at him. "When Rildning defeats the foreigners and reunites the clans, I will demand your humble apology."

❧

Later that evening, after meager rations, Eniri found herself walking with Rumban on the margin of the throne room. The chiefs had gathered to smoke tabakat and reminisce about better times. She knew Rumban had overheard her argument with Tirgranir.

"I apologize, as steward I prefer to be privy to all of the Vaynking's concerns. It pains me to see the conflict between the two of you. I'm devoted to serving Tirgranir, but I agree with you. Gratgofa—or any high king—would not have allowed such divisions between the clans in such dark days. Spring is a time of renewal, yet it hangs above our heads like the evil metal blades of the foreigners. We must do all we can to prepare and strengthen ourselves, but I fear we are not doing enough."

"I agree, Rumban. You are an honored servant of the Vaynking and you serve well. What would you ask of me?"

"I'm no sage, just a humble keeper of this stone house. I have no wisdom worthy of a princess of the great Umbyrs."

"A princess in name only, and only because the rightful heirs are dead," Eniri said. She thought about Nalembalen, their escape, and the birth of Enildir. She knew her son depended on her, but she felt an intense responsibility to do more for the people, for Gallerlandia. She was praised for clearing the flood, but it did not feel like a victory, since the damage had been done. She wanted a better future for Enildir than the perpetual threat of the foreigners.

"He will do you no harm, you know," Rumban continued. "The Vaynking is a passionate man, but he isn't a schemer or murderer. He may never trust Rildning, and he isn't alone. Many of the chiefs still wonder about him, myself included. And your half-blood child, poor thing, has your spirit and the look of his father. No harm will come to your family from Tirgranir's hands, I'm sure of that. But you must not give him further cause to accuse or offend."

Eniri wanted to counter but she was working to regain her calmness and patience. Her thoughts dwelled on what she should do besides pace the cold halls and terraces of Gilgalem. Then an idea struck her.

"I'll go," she said.

"Go where?" Rumban was puzzled. "What do you mean?"

"I'll go as an envoy. To the Nyden. I must do my part."

"Princess Eniri, think of your small child. And your people who need you here. It is winter and—"

"I'm thinking of my child and my people. The Nyden are the natural enemy of the Raffen. The Nyden could help distract the Raffen and tear them away from their alliance with the foreigners. I don't know why we didn't consider sending an envoy to them earlier."

"The Nyden are across the southern sea. Too perilous."

"If they can distract the Raffen, maybe we'll have a hope of defending Gilgalem. They might also send provisions. Rildning and the others are not here to object to my sailing to the Nyden lands, and Tirgranir will be glad to be rid of me."

"Princess, this is not a task for you to attempt. Nydenland is far away and they are more divided than the Gallerlanders. They are a conquered people, long part of the Raffen Empire despite many attempts to break from it. This idea is too dangerous and is certain to fail. Stay here and—"

"If you do not arrange the ship, then I'll find one myself," she insisted. "In the meantime, please watch over Enildir. I know Vaynqueen Sabani will provide for him."

He breathed a heavy sigh. "If you must do this, please at least wait until morning. And I'll send Tegmad with you. He is from the Aggarwal clan and will take you to that coast to find a suitable ship. But if Rildning returns before you do, I will deny ever helping you. I hope you will understand."

Eniri nodded.

36

RILDNING

Pernadun River, Rahlampia
Winterfall, 2269

The Pernadun was wider than any river Rildning had ever seen. It was more like a long lake, its gray surface lumbering southward with swift currents along its middle. The far shore was scarcely visible through banks of fog.

"This has long been our best wall," Mrigamad said as they approached the river. "Now the Raffen ships sail up the river from the sea at night. The river is deeper and narrower farther north where there Gallerlanders used to cross over to raid our lands, but the Raffen don't know those paths through the Ibdahar Forest there."

Mrigamad turned to his men and spoke in his native tongue, after which a dozen of them stood in a line facing the river. With windrazors held out in front, they slowly brought the blade points skyward, then twisted their grip side to side before sweeping the blades in a slow arc. Rildning watched as they repeated the apparent signal twice. Moments later a faint conch horn sounded in the fog bank on the far side. A boat pushed through the river clouds toward them.

Rildning marveled at the first native-built watercraft he had seen since he met the Ollohds long ago. This was a single-mast boat with a broad black band in the middle of the sail with three thinner bands above and below, not unlike the tattoos on the Rahlampians' faces. The vessel was painted black. At the prow was the carved head of a long-billed crow, with eyes that shone with silver. At the stern was a small hut-like structure.

The ship turned and docked a short distance downriver. There a small berth was half-hidden behind the hedges. Rildning boarded with Mrigamad, who was all smiles.

"A Rahlampian is as much at home on the small waters as on the vast, flat plains," he said. "It is good to be home."

"Small waters?" Rildning was puzzled. "This river is anything but small."

"These are the wet stretches of Rahlampia," Mrigamad said. "Known for river-ribboned lakes, channel towns, and stilted cities. The swamps of the Usodimare and the salty tidal marshes farther north are my own home, but here on the plains the waters are fresh and moving. So the big waters are the seas themselves."

Once they were ferried across, the ship returned for more of Mrigamad's men. He and Rildning walked toward a small set of sod-brick hovels that guarded the landing site. A large, muscular man appeared from one of the homes.

Rildning could see Denildon's left eye was milky gray. The way Denildon tilted his gaze confirmed the eye was blind. Otherwise he appeared to be a hulk of health and well armored in reed plates and iron, with spikes on his reed greaves and gauntlets. He wore the usual Rahlampian tattoos but the top portion of his face was painted black, while the bottom half was decorated with narrow lines.

"Denildon? Why are you, chief of the Pernadun lands, down here on the bankside?" Mrigamad spoke in Gali so Rildning could follow.

"Troubles," the big man grumbled, glancing suspiciously at Rildning.

"Don't worry. Rildning is . . . a friend. What about these troubles?"

"The domnitar," Denildon replied haltingly.

"Is he in danger?" Mrigamad asked.

"Methinks. Unpainted men," he said, holding up three fingers.

"We will go at once," Mrigamad said, taking Rildning by the arm. As they walked past Denildon the big man held up a scarred hand.

"No, there." Denildon pointed south.

"To Cadentod?" Mrigamad asked. The big man nodded. "Why? It was destroyed by the Raffen."

"Domnitar camp."

"So Anfinnan has come to the border and camped near the ruined city?"

"Troubles . . . Three . . . Camp," Denildon repeated.

"Come, Rildning," Mrigamad said.

"Why does he speak that way?" Rildning asked when they were on the path.

"Denildon is a warrior, not a talker. He's chief of these borderlands. People call him the Blade of the River. He is one among only a few men I've seen who can wield a windrazor in each hand."

The path to Cadentod was short. Within an hour they came into view of the ruins.

"Like our northern coastal towns, the Raffen ships sailed up the Pernadun and sacked Cadentod and nearby villages," Mrigamad said. "But that was before Anfinnan appointed Denildon to be the Riverkeeper. The Raffen have not repeated those raids since.

"But Cadentod was burned by the Raffen's new fire," Mrigamad continued. "This foul-smelling fire was unquenchable and even burned on the waves of the sea. We had heard tales of it from the Nyden, who lost their great fleets to the Raffen. The Raffen used the same fire here, after they looted the city and took hostages for ransom, including the nephew of the domnitar."

They walked toward a cluster of reed-wall tents erected on the outskirts of the ruins. When they neared the largest tent they were surprised to see three horses with imperial saddles waiting outside, their reins held by Rahlampian servants. In the distance by the river they could see two ships anchored near the ruins.

The guards nodded to Mrigamad as they approached the tent. Inside three imperials stood before the domnitar. He was seated with several small chests piled in front of him. He was a fat man, with a wisp of a beard that could not hide his flabby chins. His face was pale with a few thin-painted lines of black on his forehead.

Draped from his shoulders was a peculiar cloak with many symbols and tokens sewn onto it. Under this he wore fine reed-plate armor and a helmet with black feathered plumes. He was not the elder wiseman Rildning had expected, nor did he appear to be a warrior despite his armor.

Two of the imperial men were fully armored knights wearing the garb of the Frontier Corps, their swords sheathed. The third man was richly robed and handing an electrum necklace to the domnitar as they walked in. An open bag in his hand revealed the shimmer of electrum. An open parchment sat on Anfinnan's lap.

Anfinnan's voice was gruff and grunting, but he greeted Mrigamad warmly enough. Rildning watched the foreigners as Mrigamad spoke to him in Rahlampian. The imperial envoy was peeved and growing increasingly flustered.

The conversation between the Rahlampians grew heated. Anfinnan showed Mrigamad the parchment, and Rildning saw his face sour as he read it. Mrigamad pointed to Rildning and spoke while the domnitar studied Rildning. Mrigamad motioned for Rildning to step forward, displacing the envoy, and they switched into Gali.

". . . and then he wed a Gallerlander princess and became one of their great warriors," Mrigamad said. "I fought alongside Rildning against the unpainted men, and I believe that he can help. Gilgalem also requires food." Mrigamad looked at Rildning.

Rildning glanced at the imperials, whose eyes widened when they heard his name. They looked as if they had seen a ghost.

"The unpainted men are fools," Anfinnan said in Gali. "They don't know our people. They sent me this letter written in crude Gali, and this messenger of theirs speaks neither my language nor the tongue of the tree dwellers. But, I'm not ignorant of what has happened in Gallerlandia. I want no more of this war and will go to their assembly of tribes."

Rildning was surprised but kept his composure. "May I see the letter?" Anfinnan gave it to him freely. The imperial envoy shuffled with agitation, so Rildning read quickly.

Esteemed Domnitar of Rahlampia,

Thank you for considering our offer. As mentioned in my previous letter, I will guarantee your personal security, as instructed by His Eminence the exarch.

I urge you to join with us by attending the assembly in our capital. Peace will be assured between our peoples by your attendance. Drigoman Trelnaf will have a ship ready at your command. If there is anything else you need, you have only to ask.

Sir Hilsingor of Ned Gollen
Marshal, Imperial Frontier Corps

"This is a trap," Rildning said, "regardless of the terms these men have offered you."

"I did not ask for your advice," the domnitar huffed.

"Rildning is probably right," Mrigamad warned. "The foreigners will try to divide and weaken us as they have the Gallerlanders. When they conquer Gallerlandia, they will turn their eyes upon our lands."

"I'm not afraid of the foreigners," Anfinnan said. "I have stopped the unpainted men and their Raffen filth, and they dare not cross the Pernadun now except to offer me terms. We have proven our courage, and now they sue for peace. In making a treaty with them, I would ensure our common enemies fall, trade blooms with the unpainted empire, and our own people prosper. On top of it all, they will return my nephew to me, without ransom."

Rildning pointed to the sacks and chests of electrum. "How much stolen wealth did it take to sway your mind? I'm glad no true Gallerlander came with us to see this."

"These unpainted men have all but destroyed our Gallerlander enemies, and yet you ask me to send food to them?"

At this point drigoman Trelnaf confronted Rildning in awkward broken Gali.

"Stand there . . . stand back, Rildning," he stammered. "Do not poison the great mind with your stinking mouth. The domnitar to be . . . hatted . . . king of this provinces. And you as gift . . . I will now requested with the treaty . . .”

Rildning looked at him threateningly. He wanted to break this man and his knights. He chose not to upset the peace under which Anfinnan had welcomed these visitors, but he stepped up close to the envoy’s face and spoke calmly in Brintilian while Mrigamad and Anfinnan continued to talk.

“Listen to me. Your scheme will not work and your hopes of conquering these lands have small chance. The tribes know what you have done to Nalembalen and countless other places, and it has only strengthened their resolve.”

“You should have burned in Nalembalen,” Trelnaf sneered. “One thing is certain, seeing you now with your green-painted skin and living among the heathens. The wretched heresy in you is far greater than even the tales say. The stench of Memelos fills my nostrils. God has numbered your days, and were I not on a mission of peace, I would be honored to deliver your head to the marshal myself.”

Rildning again wished to take the envoy’s scrawny neck in his hands but felt a touch on his shoulder.

“The domnitar will take more time to consider your requests.” Mrigamad’s face was morose.

“Tell this fool messenger he will sleep tonight in one of my tents to await my answer in the morning,” Anfinnan said.

Rildning was happy to relay the command.

37

OWERDIR

Naren-Dra Mountains
Winterfall, 2269

Owerdir clutched at his chest. Even through the layered wolf-skin tunics, he could feel the little parchment was still in there. The swift, icy winds of the mountains swept down into the foothills.

Now the fingers of the wind were searching him, trying to lift every corner and prod every seam of his furs. But it was still there, safe in a deep chest pocket. Owerdir protected the Sage's letter as if his life depended on it. In fact, many lives of Gilgalem might well depend on his success.

The Sage had consulted his scroll chamber to fashion a crude message to the Naren-Dra in that tribe's own language. No one at Gilgalem spoke the cloud dweller's tongue, but the folded parchment was the best that could be done to try and secure an alliance with them.

The snow-dusted foothills had not been an easy climb. Craggy and littered with stones that threatened to roll down upon the travelers, their progress was slow and cautious. Owerdir imagined the great stones to be the weapons of the mountains, ready to plow over any army that threatened to charge up their shrouded slopes. He believed the mountains allowed them to pass as an initial test.

Owerdir believed what his guides told him about the living mountains and tried to be pure hearted in his thoughts and steps. Just as he would never rip up a sapling in his home forests, he avoided needlessly turning any stone underfoot.

The brothers were quiet and focused on the meandering paths during the march, then jolly and talkative around the campfires. As the days passed and they reached the low ridges, the foothills far behind them looked like an easy stroll. Finally, on a clear day, they passed around a bend. Looming directly ahead was a vicious sight.

"There it is," Birnin said.

"Are those the Teeth?" Owerdir was in awe. The ridge they walked on abruptly ended in what appeared to be a sheer wall of stone. Along the top of the wall was another ridge of broken stone, sheared by time to resemble a nightmarish saw-toothed beast. The stone was black and foreboding, and there was no mysterious cloud or mist to hide its hard, brutal grin.

"Hesid's Teeth," confirmed Felbanir. "We have made it at last."

Owerdir looked to the sky. Clear and sun bright. But his chills of dread would not leave him. They approached the sheer wall, which turned out to be sharply sloped with many overhangs and dead ends.

At this point the brothers' large packs were opened and their equipment was laid out. They brought long, thin bundles of flax rope, which they tied about their waists and to each other. They showed Owerdir how to fasten his wolf-skin moccasins into a special shoe consisting of a wooden pad with sharp stones hammered through like spikes.

Similar devices were strapped to their knees and elbows, and everyone was provided a gleaming obsidian pick. Then they brought out separate ropes that were knotted every arm length and had stone weights tied at the ends.

Birnin began the ascent by throwing the weighted rope up into the cliff nooks above. Once the weight was properly wedged, he hauled, spiked, and picked his way up. When he reached the top it was easier for the others to follow with his help. Birnin and Felbanir leapfrogged in this manner, helping Owerdir along the way. It would be days before Owerdir would have the know-how and confidence to try going first.

After several nights camped precariously on the toothy ridges, Owerdir insisted they spend part of the next day resting. They had consumed their food slower than planned and could afford to rest. And so they slept well into the next morning. When they awoke, a thick cloud had veiled their view of above and the path below them.

"We had been lucky so far," Birnin said. "Now the mountains grow weary of our plodding."

"How far until we reach the Cloud Hollows?" Owerdir was eager to move on.

"We must be close. Maybe two, three days."

"We should not move under this heavy cloud," Felbanir said. "We could fall on the teeth if we can't see them."

"Don't be so afraid," Birnin chided. "Normally we would have seen many more shrouded days. Down here it slows our path but does not stop our feet. We should continue."

"We still have much food. Owerdir will decide."

Owerdir looked upward but couldn't read any sky omens. The mist got heavier with their every breath.

"Let's be cautious," he said. "One slip and we fail. We'll camp here again tonight."

The following morning was scarcely better. The wind would swiftly clear the clingy clouds, then new ones would soon settle lazily around them. Their march was slowed, then hastened over and again. As the day passed, the black teeth around them became more blunted. When they camped, the clouds faded and the sky sparkled with countless stars. The moon rose brighter than Owerdir had ever remembered seeing it. The world below the mountains was gray and distant.

"We must take it as a good omen, don't you think?" Birnin asked.

Felbanir cut in. "Climbing at night is too dangerous, even if the teeth are more rounded here. Moon shadows can hide teeth and pitfalls even more than the mists. The omens are good for deeds upon the earth, but up here omens on such nights are only for the eyes of the wise."

"But the winds are growing stronger," Birnin said. "We are certainly nearing the breath of the Cloud Hollows. We could gain back some time and camp on its edge, ready to rise fresh for the descent into the Hollows by morning."

They looked to Owerdir for direction. His eyes returned to the crisp moon. He looked down into the cloaked earth, then again at the moon. A streak of light appeared above the crescent. They all saw it.

"If a flying star isn't a sign to go up, I don't know what is," Birnin said.

"I agree," Owerdir said. "Rare to see one this time of year. Let's go up, staying out of the moon shadows as much as we can." Felbanir relented without another word.

They had no difficulty seeing the ropes and catching crevasses with their weights. Owerdir felt the moon watching them climb up as it slid down its own path. When the moonlight dwindled behind clouds on the horizon, they discussed whether to continue. The moonlight withered away.

They looked toward the peaks above them and saw smoky clouds gathering. Snow soon swirled on violent winds that winked out even the light of the stars. In a short time they were hurrying to stow their equipment and trying to light a fire in the nook of a stone tooth. But it was no use; the faststicks would not light. They erected their tent and huddled together as the cold bit hard. Few words were spoken. They were shaken by the quick onset of the storm. Rumbling could be heard in the distance.

Owerdir palmed the wolf skin on his chest as he had grown accustomed to doing. The gentle scratch of the parchment corners was not there. He tore open the tunics to expose the inner pouch. The pocket was empty.

"The fingers of the wind!" he shrieked. The brothers watched in shock as he tore through the tent flap. It was dark and snow was piling up. They joined him in searching along the dim rocks and snow, finding nothing with their numbing fingers.

"Our effort is wasted without the Sage's words," Owerdir shouted over the wind and rumble. "We must find it!"

"It is lost!" Felbanir cried. "The mountains have won. The storm is the laugh, the letter is the prize."

Birnin rushed back to the tent and emerged with his pack. "The winds are fast but low to the ground here," he said. "They slide on the rocks like snakes on their bellies. The parchment could be below us, jabbed in a tooth."

"Too dangerous!" Felbanir cried. Birnin ignored him, walking toward the ridge from which they had come. Owerdir rushed to him.

"I'll do it," he said, pulling the pack off him. The rumblings in the peaks above them grew stronger.

"But I'm the climb—"

"My decision," Owerdir insisted. "I was entrusted with the letter. Stay up here and look around." He snagged his weighted rope and hopped down. He looked up and saw their faces peeking over the edge, watching and trying not to be pushed off. When he looked up again their faces were lost in the snowfall.

When he reached the rocky platform below, he searched around the teeth as Birnin had suggested. He felt sharp desperation as he flicked aside the new snow and found nothing but cold rock. The winds could have carried the parchment days away and buried it.

Owerdir scrambled around a cluster of bare-branched shrubs. He was about to move on when more rumblings sent him a chill. He hesitated as a flutter caught his eye. There in the bony scrub, wedged inside a crack in the stone, was a small square nearly the same color as the snow. He pressed his body into the stabbing branches and reached for it. His fingers edged closer, the branches dug further into his neck and face, and the winds rushed.

He thought he heard shouting, but couldn't be sure it wasn't the howl of the wind. The rumbling in the peaks was now a deep booming. Then it was a constant roar. The scrub and snow around him darkened. He felt warm blood stream on his cheek and neck as the frozen branches pierced his skin. The parchment fluttered as it tried to escape, but he caught it. He wrenched it into his fist as he pulled up from the scrub.

The rumbling became a deafening roar. The rope around his waist fell slack. Owerdir looked up and saw white. He sprinted toward the cliff overhang, shedding the rope and throwing himself against the rock wall. He ducked his head as snow rushed over his head.

When he felt the press of the snow toward him, he pushed into the scraggly branches along the wall, breaking them to make a space for himself. Then he turned and watched the snow pile up like a wall, all the way up to the lip of the overhang. Then the white wall darkened as it thickened, shutting out the light. It was fully dark long before the roaring ceased. Then all was silent.

Owerdir leaned against the bush and rock. He loosened his grip on the parchment. He chuckled to himself, knowing he had saved it but condemned himself to a tomb of ice. He knew his friends had fared no better, probably swept off the mountainside. He wondered if they had seen the avalanche coming and had tried to shout a warning to him.

He listened to the snow as the weight of the new wall settled. He wondered how long it would be before the arched portion that had formed at the lip would collapse and crush him. Or how many days of starvation would pass. He let the parchment fall from his fingers, and then closed his eyes to the cold darkness. He prayed Rildning and the others would be more successful than he had been.

38

ENIRI

Gilgalem, Vaynland
Winterfall, 2269

Tegmad was waiting for Eniri where Rumban had said he would be, out in the ancient boulder field where the electrum shield was forged long ago. Eniri's every step out of the terraced bowl of Gilgalem was heavier than the last. She wondered if she had done the right thing by leaving Enildir with Sabani.

She reminded herself that Enildir had grown attached to Sabani's young children and would be among friends. She told herself no harm would come to him, but she already felt like she had abandoned him. Sabani had not judged Eniri's motivations, nor had she criticized her for leaving Enildir. Eniri knew Sabani was a patient, understanding woman, not least because she wed Tirgranir.

Eniri hoped that if Rildning did return sooner than she did, he would forgive her. But her resolve remained strong. She would do what she could to enlist the Nyden in the fight against the foreigners. She would do her part to ensure they would not do to Gilgalem as they had done to Nalembalen.

She had robed herself in simple, warm fur cloaks before departing, casting off her high clan winter garb so as not to alert anyone. Tegmad was also heavily furred. He had a food pack, as Rumban had promised, and walking sticks to help them trudge through the snow.

"It will take us the remainder of the day and tomorrow to reach the river boat," Tegmad said. "Thereafter, we will paddle to the sea and follow the coast a bit to the tip of Aggarwal. There we will find a ship to take you to the Nyden islands."

"You won't be accompanying me on the voyage?" she asked.

"No, Princess. The steward of the mountain gave me strict orders to ensure your safe travel to the port at Amlon to find a ship, then I'm to return to Gilgalem."

Eniri wasn't pleased to be dumped at the port. She had assumed Tegmad would escort her, but she would have to be satisfied with the extent of Rumban's help, given her situation. For a moment she could not help but wonder if the steward was getting rid of her on the Vaynking's behalf. But she told herself Rumban had initially resisted the idea, and he had been genuine throughout.

Eniri was soon reminded that she was unaccustomed to these lands. The cold slopes of Gilgalem were caked in layers of snow and ice, and the snowfields below were difficult to push through. Not only were the winters less frigid in the north, but the great canopy of the tree city had always prevented much of the snowfall from reaching the dwellings and the forest floor, knee-deep at most. But here, Tegmad was pushing through waist-deep drifts in places, making a narrow path for her to follow.

As they struggled through the snow, doubt started to creep in. Had she been too rash? She did not speak the language of the Nyden, and, because her voyage was a secret one, she didn't carry a parchment written by the Sage as Owerdir did. When Tegmad halted for a midday rest, she asked him about the port.

"Amlon is the greatest of the three ports of Vaynland," he said. "All of them are controlled by the Aggarwal clan. Amlon is an ancient place full of markets where the Raffen, Nyden, Caribani, and many others used to come to trade. But since the coming of the foreigners, the Raffen have only caused trouble at the ports. The Nyden must visit with their Raffen overlords now, and the Caribani demand such high prices for their goods that the Gallerlanders cannot buy them. So the only ships we are likely to see are the enemy Raffen, the hindered Nyden, and the arrogant Caribani."

"Do the Gallerlanders of Amlon not build their own trade ships to sail to the other tribes?" Eniri asked. Tegmad looked at her incredulously. As soon as she spoke, she realized her slip.

"Shipbuilding is forbidden." His face was grave. "As the Sage and the Graparins have taught, the seas are not for the Gallerlanders. We don't need ships anyhow, since the traders come to us."

Sometimes Eniri wished she knew nothing of the Cataclysm and the secret histories. For a moment she wondered if the changing of the times would finally reveal the ancient prophecy, and whether, with peace between the Almeric and Agnesci bloodlines, the histories would be known by all. Then she had a sudden realization.

"Whose ship will take me to the Nyden?"

Tegmad shrugged. "I don't know, Princess. We might be able to persuade a Nyden captain, or perhaps a Caribani on his way to the Nyden ports." There was a long, cold pause between them. "Do you wish to return to Gilgalem?"

"No," she sighed, "I will find a way." She was sure he thought she was mad, but she was determined not to turn back.

The second day was easier. The mountains were behind them and the wind was not as fierce. Eniri felt more at ease moving among the tall larches and birches of the foothills.

By midday they found unfrozen ground. It became boggy as they neared a pair of intertwining streams. The water was warm and bubbled up from hidden seeps. Its gentle steam frosted nearby rocks and plants.

"The furnaces and underlying heat of Gilgalem touch even these waters," Tegmad said. "The roots of the mountains grow far and their warmth touches many unseen places."

They continued following the streams until they merged one last time into a single, swift river. Soon they came to a grove of hazel and mulberry trees with brambles and dead vines skirting their trunks. Tegmad walked back and forth examining the contours of the brush until finally he smiled.

"Here is the way," he said. He pushed a few snow-dusted branches aside to reveal a little wicker door. "See, the

Gallerlanders of the south have not forgotten the old ways of our northern tree-dwelling cousins."

They entered the door to the little grove. Eniri felt at home. It was a ring of bramble-walled trees, with sunlight streaming down into the middle. It was as spacious as any modest Umbyr hovel. The tree limbs and brambles on the inside, protected from foraging deer, were still dotted with frozen berries and nuts, from which they took.

When they were ready, Tegmad guided them to four long mounds that appeared to be graves. He dusted the snow, stick, and leaf layers off one of them to reveal the tar-coated hull of a small boat, just big enough for the two of them.

"The next step is up to you, Princess. We can sleep here in the safety of the grove and leave with the dawn, or we can ride the river without delay and paddle during the night. If we paddle, we could reach Amlon by the following night if there is no ice and the river is still deep enough."

"Let us leave at once."

They carried the boat end to end out of the secret grove and to the river. Tegmad steadied it for her to step in, but she felt dizzy and uncertain.

"What is it?" he asked.

"I've never been in a boat . . ."

"Princess!" He laughed. "You boasted of swimming the forest pools, and lived in the great houses of Nalembalen that sailed on the breeze, and you drained the flood of Gilgalem."

She glared at him. "I can swim, I just haven't swam on the surface of water on a thing."

"Perhaps this isn't a good idea," Tegmad said. He moved to pull the boat from the water, but she leaped in and clutched the sides.

"Get into the boat," she insisted.

"All right. But I must be in the back to steer."

She carefully scooted forward. Tegmad shrugged, pushed the boat from the bank, and hopped in.

After a basic lesson on how to paddle, they set off down the small river. She ran them aground on sand bars more than once, despite his best efforts. But she improved quickly, and they were traveling unhindered before too long.

39

URGAMDIR

Frontier of Bram Province
Winterfall, 2269

The path out of Vaynland into the areas conquered by the foreigners in Umbyrland had been cold and slow for Urgamdir and Brugmir. Not too many months ago they had fled south through these same lands toward Gilgalem, but it was different to Urgamdir now. He had mentally noted landmarks of great trees and rock outcroppings as they fought their way south, but now some were cut down or picked away to make roads through the forests.

The snows had mostly covered these new stone-paved roads, but Urgamdir recognized the straight, treeless lengths from his time in the far north, before his clan fled to Nalembalen. No matter where the foreigners stepped, he thought, their iron-clad feet wished to walk upon stone roads. Or perhaps it was their horse beasts that preferred the stone.

"Look at the wheel ruts and foot tracks," Urgamdir said.

"Active road." Brugmir nodded. "More than the others we've passed."

"We should stay away from them. They'll just as easily see our tracks."

"We will get to Bronhildia quicker if we use the roads with caution," Brugmir said. "If you are concerned the dim-witted foreigners will see our feet, we can sweep them away with a branch."

"They'll see a swath of disturbed snow," Urgamdir said. "They'll still track us."

Brugmir became frustrated. "Why didn't those damn Vayns give us those wide-footed moccasins, the snow-walking ones? They sent us on this journey without the proper gear."

"No one thought about the roads. We had forgotten how the foreigners change the forests. We must keep moving."

"Well, we could make the snow moccasins," Brugmir said. "Take a good hide and stretch it over a rack of sticks, fur-side down. Then tie the—"

"Forget the moccasins," snapped Urgamdir. "We can't trouble ourselves with that now. Winter is deepening and we'll need the fur on our bodies, and no amount of fur and sticks is going to hold my weight or soften my footfall anyhow."

"Then let's use the road," Brugmir said. "We'll hear the hoofs of their beasts long before they see us."

Urgamdir wanted to move on but he considered carefully whether to take the road. He knew the journey to Bronhildia was long. And Rildning was right. Even if he made it, and if he was given the opportunity to talk with Highchief Harkarom, he was unlikely to return to Gilgalem with help before the foreigners attacked the mountain.

He looked down at the road. The snow had started again and he watched how the flakes soon filled their tracks. He gazed into the edge of the forest on the far side of the road. White snow drifts slanted up against the trunks and branches hung low under their white burdens. Brambles and bush were thickly grown and snow cloaked. He returned to the road, tracing the paths northward with his eyes.

"We are a people of the forest," he finally said. Brugmir nodded in agreement, then sighed.

"But this forest has changed. I don't like their stone paths, but . . ."

"Let us take the foreigners' road, but no talking. Any hoof sound at all and we go to the woods."

∾

The walk on the snow-blanketed road was much quicker but they took their steps warily. The day passed without incident. When night came they abandoned the road to make camp in the forest, choosing a spot hidden by a low, snowy hedge that was a comfortable distance away.

"We've gained a good bit of distance today, but the road offered no hunt or berry forage," came Brugmir's preemptive statement.

"I don't want a cooking fire this close to the road anyhow," Urgamdir conceded. "Use the supplies, but we will run out much sooner than planned." He chuckled. "Perhaps our gain today will be our loss later, when we spend more time picking and hunting."

It felt good to be back in the woods again. As they lay in the fur-heaped bedrolls, Urgamdir looked up at the clear winter sky, thinking of how Rildning and the others were faring. The icy darkness soon melted with the golden sun, and leaves and stems of new green curled up from the ground. He saw himself walking alone in an ancient forest, the woodland columns spreading out under a green sky above. Birds flittered about and the smells of earth and fungus and sweet fruits swirled around him as he walked.

Then darkness gripped the distant reaches of his dream. Faraway trees faded and a sooty burning smell overcame the familiar scents. A woman was running from the darkness, a swaddled baby clutched to her chest, four other children running behind. He feared for them, but he could not take a step. He struggled, seeing his feet sink into ashes.

He continued to struggle but they were gone. The darkness was near him now. His lungs tightened and tears streaked the soot on his face. He became frozen, unbreathing and unseeing.

When his eyes jolted open, Brugmir's face was close, wrinkled with worry. The Goyn was whispering but Urgamdir's ears were still full of the screams from the dream. Brugmir gestured toward the road with his stonesword. Urgamdir lunged up and Brugmir shushed him.

"They've stopped," he heard Brugmir whisper. "Didn't you hear me?"

"How many?" Urgamdir asked, reaching for his ax and trying to peer through the hedge.

"Dozens maybe," the Goyn whispered. "They've not followed our tracks straight in. Men are walking into the forest this way and that." He pointed the knife in his other hand toward their flanks.

Urgamdir cursed under his breath, turning to look out into the forest behind them. He remembered his orders to evade the foreigners, not fight them. But if they tried to escape now, they would be seen. And if they stayed, they could be caught. Brugmir read his mind.

"We could take to the trees," the Goyn said.

"They'll see the snow falling."

"Maybe your big self will shake the snow, but . . ."

"We're trapped if we try that now."

"We're trapped anyway."

They could hear the clink of metal and the men's voices coming closer. Urgamdir and Brugmir exchanged desperate looks.

"Our effort is lost," Urgamdir said.

"You should run. I'll distract them."

"I'm not fast enough"

"Then hide in this hedge and I'll run. When they catch me you continue onward."

"They'll see the two bedrolls and our two sets of prints."

"You always have something to . . . If you don't run now and finish the task, then I will," Brugmir said. "We are both dead otherwise. But you have a drip of the Bronhildi blood in you, so you should at least try." Urgamdir remained silent. "Then I've decided," the Goyn said. Urgamdir could see Brugmir was, for once, done talking. He stood from his crouch and spoke his last words to him. "Take flight now!"

Brugmir took off running toward the left flank of the searching men, knife and sword in hand. Angered hot, Urgamdir clutched his ax and slung a food satchel over his shoulder as he stood. He ran as fast as he could deeper into the forest.

He heard the foreigners burst into shouts. He didn't slow when he heard Brugmir's screams. He didn't relent even when his heavy legs begged for rest. He stomped through brambles and hedges and snowdrifts. He crushed through frozen streams and ripped through low branches and brush.

When he finally tripped, he coughed out the snow and frozen dirt and wiped his eyes. Amid the shouting behind him, he bent over to vomit and sucked in more air. Then he ran again, abandoning his dropped ax.

He was slower now, and the cold air ripped at his gasping throat. Through the throb in his ears he could hear a man gaining on him. When the footsteps drew close, he dove to the ground and rolled away from the sweep of a blade. As the man recovered his reach, Urgamdir lurched over and grabbed him. He lifted him off his feet and bashed him into a tree trunk.

Urgamdir stooped to pick up the shining steel sword. He hesitated for a moment, but the sight of the next man running toward him forced his hand. The man screamed as he charged Urgamdir with a spear. He deflected the stab and swept a heavy fist across the man's face. When the man fell, Urgamdir stomped on his neck and took his spear. This he threw at a third man, with good effect. More were coming.

Urgamdir hid behind a tree that shadowed enough of his girth. He raised the gray-metal blade up to his face. It was much thinner and perhaps twice as long as the stoneswords he was used to. He remembered the words of the Graparins, that the evil metal was the profane gift of Ominchar meant to distract from the holy quest for the electrum.

Splinters of bark and wood burst into the left side of his face as a spear narrowly missed his head. He ducked and spun around the tree to meet his foe, crushing the man's helm with the sword. An archer in the distance took aim on him. He flung the sword at him and started running again.

Urgamdir's experience fighting the foreigners in the far north of Umbyrland returned to him. He swerved left and right as he ran, watching the arrows fly ahead of him. He wondered how many had gathered behind him. He felt the bite of metal in his shoulder, felt his legs weaken. Ahead of him an older forest loomed, with large strong-armed larches that buttressed grand silver firs and hemlocks in a darker wood.

He reached up and yanked the arrow out, feeling the flesh tear and a surge of blood. He heard his own scream echo off the trees. A large oak was ahead, so he summoned his strength and ran straight for it and leaped as his people had learned to do.

The flat of his moccasined foot struck the trunk and he swung his arms upward, bringing the next foot up as he hacked at the sides of the tree with his hands. He took another step, then another and another. He rappelled from the tree, clutching a knob and pulling, then another, until the low branches were within reach. He heard the *plunk* of arrowheads burying themselves into the wood below him. He scratched with feet and hugged with his arms and pulled with every muscle.

At last he stepped around to the back of the tree and paced carefully along a great limb. Arrows continued to fly up through the bare branches, and the shouts of the men merged below. The snow-cloaked branches of the evergreens were just ahead. With a breath he leaped into the closest firs, grabbing hold and pulling himself inside. The men below disappeared from view, but he did not rest. Urgamdir moved from one to the next, hearing the foreigners fan out on the forest floor. Occasional arrows shot up through the needles, but these soon ceased. He rested for brief moments before moving again.

He stopped when the sky glowed gray with the coming of dawn. Finding a three-armed crook hidden high in an ancient fir, he packed bits of fur into his wounds and covered himself with a heap of needled boughs. Then he slept.

40

HILSINGOR

Rachard, Bram Province
Winterfall, 2269

Hilsingor decided it was time to visit the dungeon. He had intended to use the hastily dug and leaky chamber as his cellar until the stone keep was built. But the requirements of the Frontier Corps demanded more space for all the prisoners, including a new captive who had caught Hilsingor's interest. It was time to visit this heathen because he knew Ravorglad would enjoy beating the man a little too much.

When he and Arnolf arrived at the bottom of the steps, they found the Gallerlander bloody and unconscious. But that was not stopping Ravorglad.

"Enough," the marshal said. "If he hasn't told us anything useful, he certainly won't in that condition."

"Nothing useful," puffed Ravorglad, wiping sweat and specks of blood from his brow. Hilsingor looked around the room. It was only Ravorglad, a soldier who had led the patrol that captured the heathen, and a jailer who looked bored.

"Do any you speak Gali?" Hilsingor asked them.

"No, sir marshal."

"Then how do you expect to understand if he has said anything useful?"

"They never have anything useful," the jailer replied.

"Go get someone," Hilsingor said to Arnolf. The adjutant bounded up the stairs. "As for you, Ravorglad, go see to something more befitting of your rank and honor."

Ravorglad did not respond. He looked at the heathen slumped on the floor, sniffed, then departed.

"Leave his ring," Hilsingor added. Ravorglad clutched the electrum. Hilsingor glared at him until he dropped it. Then the marshal turned to the soldier. "Tell me how you found him."

"It was just off the new road toward the south, sir. We were taking a new load of stone and fresh laborers to continue the work toward the Raffen country, sir. It was night but our scout saw tracks. When we came up on them, they ran. This one killed one of my men. We would have killed him on the spot, but I thought it best to bring him to Rachard, since we thought that area was abandoned by the barbarians."

"You did well," Hilsingor said. "Arnolf mentioned there was a second one?"

"He escaped, sir. Killed three of my men, badly injured a fourth. I didn't see him myself, but they said he ran up into a tree, as we saw them do farther north."

"Yes," Hilsingor replied as he tapped his chin in thought. "This heathen sounds like a northerner. But why would he be coming up our road, especially if he took refuge with the others in the southern mountains?"

The man on the floor moaned. They turned to look at him as he struggled to wake. Then Arnolf reappeared with a Donovard scribe.

"Calm him," Hilsingor ordered. "You may leave us," he said to the soldier and jailer. Then he took a stool and waited. The trembling man finally sat up, but it was evident he could not see through his swollen face.

"Tell him I've sent them away," Hilsingor told the scribe. The scribe spoke the words in Gali, but the heathen continued to tremble. The marshal glared at the scribe. "Tell him exactly what I say, or you'll find yourself in a similar situation."

"Yes, sir marshal."

"I am Marshal Hilsingor, commander of the Frontier Corps. You know of us?"

The man nodded after the translation.

"What is your name and where are you from?"

"He says his name is Brugmir and he is a Goyn," the scribe said.

"Goynland then. Far north and west of here." Brugmir nodded.

"Your situation is, of course, dire," Hilsingor continued. "We don't keep prisoners long in winter. The food is rationed, and farmland not accosted by the forests is rare on the frontier. Is there any reason you can give me to let you live?"

He nodded but did not speak.

"Brugmir, must I take your silence as proof that you no longer wish to speak to me?"

He remained silent. Hilsingor retrieved the electrum ring and placed it in Brugmir's hands. The Gallerlander clutched it close, then restored it to his own finger.

"You are a chieftain, aren't you?"

He nodded.

"Why is a Goynland chieftain from southern Gallerlandia traveling north? Surely you do not hope to reach faraway Goynking Odon?"

"He says he is a messenger," the scribe said.

"To whom?"

"The Bronhildi."

"They are my ally and firmly against the Gallerlanders," Hilsingor said. "What hope do you have?"

"None," relayed the scribe.

"Gilgalem. You were there?" the marshal asked. Brugmir nodded. "What message demanded this risk?"

Brugmir remained still. Hilsingor pondered.

"Tell him . . ." the marshal began, "tell him we have his companion. He already told us about Gilgalem. Tell him that." Hilsingor watched Brugmir's reaction closely. Brugmir remained still. "And tell him his companion, the one who tried to run, we know he is a messenger also."

Brugmir hung his head. Tears mingled with blood and dripped from his chin. Hilsingor was happy with his bluff.

"Tell him, this messenger saved himself. You can too."

Now sobbing with difficult breaths, Brugmir spoke slow and coarse to the scribe. It was explained to Hilsingor that the Gallerlanders holed up in the mountains sent messengers to every neighboring tribe in a last effort to build alliances against the Frontier Corps. When Hilsingor demanded their names and the tribes to which they were sent, Brugmir wanted assurances that Urgamdir would not be killed.

"Ask him who this Urgamdir is," Hilsingor said. "Wait!" he said, but it was too late. The scribe translated just as Hilsingor thought better of it. He saw that Brugmir realized he had been tricked. The Goyn lashed out blindly at the marshal. They backed away from him and let him fall back to the floor. He pawed over to the wall and hid his face to weep. Arnolf went to fetch the jailer.

"Sir marshal, did he strike you?" the jailer asked when he returned.

"No, but we are done." Hilsingor glanced at the pitiful Brugmir before walking to the stairs.

Arnolf was waiting anxiously at the top. "Sir, an urgent message for you. From the south."

They walked back up into the light. Widsem was with Arnolf. He handed Hilsingor the tiny fold of green-painted parchment the marshal had come to expect from Ferndeath. He quickly opened it.

> Their food is drowned.
> The mountain is barren and cold.
> They have sent word to the tribes.
> Only Tirgranir remains.

"I'm sorry, Widsem," the marshal said, "but there will be no rest for you in Rachard this time. Times are difficult for the enemy in the mountain, and we must ensure their difficulties persist until the spring. You will go south again, but not toward Gilgalem. A patrol took a prisoner on the road to the Raffen. There is a second heathen named Urgamdir who escaped. He is one of the messengers who are seeking help from the Bronhildi and other tribes. That provincial knight over there will show you where to begin your search for this Urgamdir. Bring him back if you can, kill him if you must." Widsem nodded as Hilsingor turned to Arnolf.

"We must send word to Eglamour about the heathen envoys. I want to make sure the allied tribes are still loyal to us, whether the Gallerlander beggars have reached them or not, especially the Raffen. Draft a letter at once."

"And Brugmir?" Arnolf asked.

"Get rid of him."

41

RILDNING

Pernadun River, Rahlampia
Winterfall, 2269

"I know this enemy," Rildning insisted. "They will be your ally until they have disarmed and splintered your people, and then you will be their slaves." Rildning was glad the domnitar had granted him another meeting, but he was frustrated that the new day had not brought Anfinnan clarity. He was willing to be blunt to convince the domnitar not to join the empire.

"Careful, Rildning," Anfinnan said. "You are a traitor to your own people and adopted by my enemy the Gallerlanders. You are unfit to counsel me in such a tone. I know what is best for my people. The unpainted men offered terms that leave my lands intact and my enemies—"

"They offer you a crown that is already yours," Rildning interrupted.

"What if there was another way?" Mrigamad asked the domnitar. "You could put me on this envoy's boat and send me to their capital in your stead. I could attend their assembly as your representative and learn what they intend to do. I could speak with the other tribes and attempt to persuade them to abandon their alliances."

"You would effectively be their hostage," Rildning said, "until the domnitar arrived. They won't be satisfied until the tribal leaders are in their grasp."

"I will go," Anfinnan said, glaring at Rildning, "not to be in their grasp, but to do what I must. Rildning, you are right: the unpainted men are not to be trusted. There is no such thing as a true or permanent ally, but I'll take what I can get for Rahlampia. If I don't like what I see, I will abandon the effort and try to persuade the other tribes to do the same. If I learn anything of use to the Gallerlanders, I'll sell it for a price. But I make no promises. I'll secure my own realm using any means.

"As for your request to allay Gilgalem's food problem, my heart is not hardened to the hunger of children, even those of my enemy. During the night, Denildon's men gathered what food could be spared from his borderlands to send back with you. Tell Tirgranir it's a gift from me, and if I join the empire, I'll expect him to consider surrendering to the empire through me.

"And as for you, Mrigamad, you will come with me on their seaship to Eglamour, since you have fought the unpainted men and the Raffen in lands across the Pernadun. I will require your counsel, but not Rildning's. We will leave with the unpainted men shortly, so take Rildning to Denildon. A landship should be ready for him."

Rildning wasn't completely satisfied with the domnitar's decision, and Mrigamad wasn't either, especially with the prospect of going to Eglamour. But Rildning considered it a partial victory because of the food and because Anfinnan retained some distrust of the imperials, despite their bribes to him. Rildning also held out hope that Anfinnan would send information useful for the defense of Gilgalem.

Rildning said his goodbyes as respectfully as he could. He wished to see the imperial drigoman once more, but he was eager to return to Gilgalem and his family. The winter was deepening and he knew the hunger would be great.

Mrigamad led Rildning back to Denildon's docks. Rildning expected to see a few small boats or a modest ship with grain sacks. But what he saw stunned him. There on the riverbank was a ship set upon six great wheels. Each wheel was easily the height of four men, with iron spikes studded around the rims, which were partly caked with bits of frozen loam and snow.

The sides of the ship were banded with iron. Two tree trunk masts had their sails carefully stowed away from the wind. As they neared the ship, Rildning could see that the men hurrying to finish stocking it with food could easily pass under the ship's belly without bumping their heads.

"You never mentioned this to me," he gasped to Mrigamad.

"I said the Rahlampians had not forgotten how to build the ancient machines. This one is named the *Earthark*, one of many landship designs. It will speed your journey back to Gilgalem, and the food should last a while."

"Quite a rare breed of ship." Rildning remained in awe. "Now I'm not so sure the Rahlampians need horses." Mrigamad chuckled.

"Well, like our windrazors, the landships are best on the open plains and rolling hills. Though with these winds, you should have no problem with the snowdrifts, rivers, and lakes between here and Gilgalem. And I still think we could use horses. The battles that lie ahead won't always be on favorable land."

Rildning shook Mrigamad's hand. "The Gallerlanders will be most grateful for the generosity of the domnitar, even if the domnitar intended for his gift to sway the mind of Tirgranir."

"You don't have to relay that part of the message, about surrender," Mrigamad said.

"I won't." Rildning grinned. "I count you as a friend, Mrigamad. Thank you for your trust. I wish you a safe voyage to Eglamour, and I hope to hear from you and Anfinnan. If not, may we meet on a victorious field of battle. Whatever happens, don't let your guard down in the imperial capital."

Mrigamad nodded. "I worry our journey will ultimately lead to a ceremony welcoming the Rahlampians into the empire. And that the unpainted men will keep us beyond the spring so that my people will be of no help to Gilgalem when the Frontier Corps besieges it. I'll not cease pressing Anfinnan to send word or aid."

42

WIDSEM

Forests of Bram Province
Winterfall, 2269

Widsem had tracked down the brute quickly and had gotten close several times. He could smell the venison and salted fish on the Gallerlander's breath. The ranger wondered how a wolf had not taken interest in the stinking savage during the night.

The marshal had said dead or alive. Widsem knew alive would fetch an extra stack of coins for him, but he also knew this mark would not go easily. If he could get close enough while the Gallerlander slept, he could knock him out and bind his hands. Then he could set him on a drag sled and take the road until a wagon came by. It was a good plan, but this native, Urgamdir they called him, kept stuffing his big body under the brambles and hedges. It was easy for the master ranger to creep up on him while he slept, but impossible to reach him without entangling himself.

Frustrated night after night, Widsem now perched in a tree a small distance away. His bow was bent, the string taut in the notch of his arrow. One eye looked down the shaft, aiming at the rising and falling barrel chest. The ranger slowly let out half his breath to steady himself. But the arrow remained still. He opened his eye and watched Urgamdir's slumber. Widsem frowned and lowered the bow. This was not a hunt.

When Widsem awoke from his night nap, his prey was gone. He had overslept in his fatigue. Cursing but glad for the sport, he jumped down to examine the place where the barbarian had camped. The footprints in the snow continued east, as they had for days. Widsem thought this was odd for a messenger who was supposedly going to Bronhildia. He trotted silently ahead, dagger drawn and scanning the snow. Broken twigs by the bushes. He paused to smell the chill air.

The tracks disappeared around midday at the foot of a cluster of firs. Widsem studied the freshly compacted moss on one of the trunks and knew Urgamdir had gone up. He hoisted himself up with his grappling hook, then followed the branches with disturbed snow.

Widsem thought about what it would be like to track the Gallerlanders in the summer. Following the Hrals on the mountainous western coast had been easy, regardless of the season. But he was glad to be back with Hilsingor here in Gallerlandia. The marshal paid well and he enjoyed hunting on this frontier.

Widsem stopped and refocused his thoughts. The markings on the shoulders of the trees had changed abruptly. He pressed his back into a tree trunk and remained still, searching with his eyes and ears. Had Urgamdir jumped to the next tree? Something was different.

In the corner of his eye to the right he caught a movement. A fir bough shimmied. He could not see past the thick curtain of needles. Another movement. A slight breeze, as if the tree had let out half a breath to steady itself. Then there it was: a gray slit amid the needles. Widsem kicked off his perch and fell through the tree just as the stone knife bit into the trunk where his head had been.

He slapped his left hand, the glove with the small steel pricks, against a nearby branch, digging into the bark as he fell. He caught hold of the next branch and found a hold for his boot. But he allowed his momentum to carry him so that he was already running when he hit the ground.

The firs tapered out, so he knew the Gallerlander would come down to the ground to run. Salty breath hung in the air here and Widsem soon found the tracks. His dagger was at the ready as he ran.

The tracks led to a snow-cloaked thicket of thorn and brush. These brambles grew tall with arching, draping arms that formed brown-ribbed tunnels half the height of a man. Widsem could see where his prey's knees had dropped to the ground to plunge inside, and so he followed.

It was a labyrinth. Urgamdir's tracks were mingled with those of wolves, rabbits, and bear, but it was easy enough to discern the brute's fresh, sweeping form even in the dim light. As he crawled, Widsem told himself he would have to kill this heathen. This prey would not be taken captive, and Widsem would not risk his life over it. Unlike some rangers, he took pride in not coveting every possible coin to be made—so long as the marshal saved the best hunts for him.

Widsem came to a long corridor of brambles that Urgamdir had clearly entered. The smell was different here and he hesitated for a moment. There was little room to maneuver if a wild animal was hiding ahead. But Widsem kept on.

The scent of bear became unmistakable as he crept forward. He also noticed Urgamdir's tracks were now spoiled, perhaps intentionally. There were large gaps in the bramble ribs. The snow was muddied and deeply scooped, as if something had rolled on it. Widsem peered ahead into a gloomy spot.

As he drew closer he saw a fur satchel with hints of Urgamdir's food. Perhaps his prey had been killed by a bear, he thought. Widsem knew he was nearing a den, but he did not hear heavy breathing or feel the thud of heavy paws. If Urgamdir had been killed, he would have to confirm it.

Widsem crept closer. A bend in the tunnel obscured his view, but the smell of bear was strong. He reached out for the satchel and heard heavy footsteps break into a run ahead of him outside the tunnel. When Widsem glanced back, he saw a brown bear sniffing at the entrance to the tunnel. It entered slowly, filling the corridor like a cork in a bottle.

Widsem scrambled back to where the gaps in the brambles had been. He had been hidden in the darkness but now the bear saw what he had smelled. It roared in protest and clawed the muddy snow, sending a chill through Widsem. He steeled himself as he wiggled toward a gap.

"You should be asleep!" Widsem roared back.

The ranger rolled onto his back as the bear charged down the tunnel. He popped his head into the gap and gripped the thorny ribs, then kicked his legs upward and curled his body up over his head. With a snap, he flipped up onto his feet and was outside the brambles.

Widsem ran around to where he had heard the footsteps. Seeing no one, he sheathed his dagger and readied his bow as the bear came crashing up out of the brambles. The animal roared as thorns tore at its fur. It stood at its full height to look out over the brush for the ranger.

Widsem fitted an arrow to the bowstring and ran with it. When the bear pursued him he repeatedly swung around a tree and shot into the beast, then ran a bit farther.

Each new arrow angered the bear further. As it finally closed the distance it reared up on its hind legs again. Widsem shot as fast as he could into its exposed neck with veteran accuracy, puncturing its jugular with three arrows. The bear swiped at him, shredding part of his shoulder and casting the ranger and his bow aside. He was smacked again when he tried to stand.

By now Widsem was sprayed red with blood. He rolled away, regained his feet, and backed away from the struggling animal. The ranger looked into the eyes of the bear and unsheathed his dagger. The animal was nearly standing on his bow, which he feared would break it.

The bear wavered but was intent on a last try. It fell onto all fours and Widsem skipped around to its rear. The bear menaced him but was too pained to turn. The ranger leaped onto its back and shoved the dagger into the base of its skull with his palm. The bear tossed Widsem off, but not before the ranger wrenched the dagger with a popping twist.

Widsem crawled back to the bear and leaned against its furry warmth. He smiled and allowed himself a half chuckle. His prey had briefly made him the prey. He guessed Urgamdir wouldn't get too far. The heathen had abandoned his food satchel, whereas Widsem would eat his fill of fresh meat tonight.

43

ENIRI

Port of Amlon, Aggarwal
Winterfall, 2269

Eniri had heard the tales of the ship cities of the Aggarwal clan, but even those had not prepared her for Amlon. Huge hulls and broad sails filled the docks around the city. Tegmad had been glad to return to his home, but as their little boat neared the mouth of the river he grew unsettled.

"Too many gray sails," he said.

"The ones with the foxes?" Eniri asked.

"Those are brown wolves. Raffen ships."

The view was stunning. Every berth and quay was jammed with ships, mostly gray sails, and teemed with men and supplies and the flash of steel.

"What are they doing?" she asked.

"I don't know," Tegmad answered. "We should go back, truly this time." He held up his paddle to coast, but she paddled harder in response.

"Wait, wait," he insisted. "Amlon may belong to them now. We can't just—"

"Look." She pointed. "Those are not wolf ships." He saw she was right.

"The blue stripes of the Nyden. But remember, the Raffen conquered them, and most of the Nyden fleets were burned. Just because it's a Nyden ship does not mean—"

"Enough," Eniri said. "Do you speak Raffen or Nyden?"

"Very little Raffen," he replied. "But they will know we are Gallerlanders."

"You must help me find a ship to the islands," Eniri said. "Then you return to Gilgalem and tell Tirgranir the Raffen are here in such numbers. You must warn him they could be planning to approach from the south as the foreigners approach from their northern camps. But find me a ship first."

Eniri's boldness was now scaring even herself. She had fought during the last clan war. She had faced the foreigners and burning forests. She had even faced down wolves as a newly tattooed girl. But nothing compared to feeling the river pushing her tiny boat into the enemy's harbor and the stretch of the empty sea beyond.

"We cannot do it like this," Tegmad insisted. He shook his head as she turned around. "If we try to dock we will be taken. To survive this, we will have to sneak you aboard a ship at night before it sails. I could listen to the Raffen to identify which ship is going to the islands, but even then it is risky because they may go elsewhere first. You would be alone to find a hiding place and food. I cannot believe you want to risk this."

"What if Rildning and the other messengers fail to secure help from other tribes?" she asked. "The Bronhildi are already against us and the eastern tribes are too small, too weak, or too hostile to the Gallerlanders. I must try the Nyden. I'm not asking you to come with me, but you must get me aboard."

He guided the boat into the frost-crusted reed beds along the riverbank, where they shivered hidden until sundown. Patches of thin fog formed at the river's mouth and crept toward the nearby ships. Tegmad pushed their boat away from the snowy reeds and they quietly paddled toward a ship with blue-striped sails.

"I watched them load that one," Tegmad whispered. "It's a Nyden ship, but Raffen are also aboard. It will surely sail soon, but hard to tell where to."

"Should we try?"

"The Raffen believe their own ships are superior for fighting, so there is a chance it will sail back to the islands.

The ship also flies the banner of Toredwoak, a Nyden family openly allied with the Raffen. So it could be a trade ship or a slaver."

"Slaver?"

Tegmad shushed her as a man with a lamp appeared on the deck of the ship they were passing. They held their breath and Eniri's eyes flicked up at the moon. It was a small sliver, like a curved fang of Demfrebra the Black Snake. It also appeared in the dark shimmering water in which they floated. She did not like these omens, but she knew if the moon had been full and good, they would be easily seen by the ship guards despite the patchy fog.

When the man with the lamp strolled toward the far side of his ship, they carefully moved forward. Tegmad maneuvered them under a pier, where they whispered.

"You want to put me on a slave ship?" she scoffed.

"You can hide in one, if you still want to do this."

"Wouldn't all the slaves want to hide away as well? It can't be that simple."

"It's not," he said. "As I said, I think we should go back and focus on warning the Vaynking. Your efforts thus far were not wasted. We've learned with our own eyes that the Raffen have amassed a fleet here and Amlon is likely no longer a Gallerlander port." It wasn't enough for Eniri, however.

"You tell Gilgalem about it," she said. "I will go aboard." Tegmad shook his head.

"If—Wurumnak forbid—they find you, they will know you are a Gallerlander. Tell them these words: *ibeles agd setbroner*. That will tell the Raffen you are a princess and they would likely try to ransom you back to Tirgranir vice enslave you. That's if the right sort finds you. If any other sort—"

"I understand," Eniri said. "How do I get on?"

"We go up onto the pier from here. Once aboard, head toward the galley, which is where they keep the food. Hide in a sack or cabinet or something. But you must be careful, as the galley is usually near cabins, where the sailors sleep."

Tegmad tethered the boat to a pier post and led the climb up the framework. Eniri was reminded of climbing in the trees of Umbyrland. But as she neared the edge of the enemy, she could only think of Rildning and Enildir.

Tegmad peeked above the dark pier. Much of it was shaded from the moon's light by the gray sails of a great ship. No one was about, so Tegmad climbed over the edge and Eniri came after. He led them across the pier and over the gangplank where she set foot upon her first ship. For a fleeting instant she was relieved the ship's size hid the fact that it was floating.

They found a hatch in the deck that had plump sacks and crates of chickens stacked around it. Tegmad motioned for her to go down. She hugged him and descended the ladder into the darkness, feeling her way.

She could hear her heart throb. She looked up but there was no sky to be seen, no light. She closed her eyes and tiptoed forward, touching more sacks and crates and the cold, shoulder-smoothed wood of the corridor. A finger prodded an unsuspecting chicken, startling the hen and herself. She steadied her breathing and continued, repeating *ibeles agd setbroner* in her head.

When the clucking subsided, she heard shouting above deck. Tiny beams of lamplight poked through a few cracks in the planks above, then went away. She heard Tegmad's voice. He was struggling. She could hear several voices in the scuffle. Two she recognized as Raffen, and the third she guessed to be Nyden. She froze in the dark.

There was a thumping of heavy boots coming down a distant ladder and more shouting. Tegmad was shouting curses and attempting to speak Raffen, but his speech was cut short. Eniri could feel tears well in her blind eyes as she neared the wall to listen. There was the sound of metal clanking and clasping. Then silence.

44

OWERDIR

Naren-Dra Mountains
Winterfall, 2269

Owerdir was awakened by his nose. His eyes were too cold to open, and he could no longer feel his limbs. He could hear his slow breathing, weak heartbeat. Then there was the smell. It brushed warmth into his mind, reminding him of tabakat. And yet, also similar to the smell of electrum. He thought perhaps his senses were starting to fail him, mingling with his memories before dying off. He wished his mind had let death take him in his sleep.

As Owerdir leaned against the bush he realized the scent was growing stronger. Perhaps his senses were not dying after all. He forced his eyelids open, breaking the thin ice that had glazed his face.

Owerdir saw the faintest glow in the snow wall, just enough to cast a ghostly light inside his frosty tomb. He guessed that the night had passed and the storm along with it. He broke his right arm free of the frozen snow that clung to the rock. He held his hand up to his face and breathed on it. His fingers were unfeeling but he could feel his breath on his palm. He lifted his left hand where it had lain on his lap. The heat of his body and his tunic had protected his thumb and most fingers well enough.

He slowly worked his arms back and forth to gather strength. Then he rubbed his fur-covered legs for a time, flexed his neck, and bent his knees and ankles. When Owerdir finally brought himself up to his feet, pain shot through his body. He guessed some of his fingers were already dead.

Owerdir touched the snow wall with the back of his hand. It was smooth and slick, melted then refrozen. He broke a stick from the bush with his palms and good fingers, but it would barely scratch the ice. It was solid, yet he could feel the movement of air from somewhere. And the smell that woke him persisted. It was metallic, spicy, earthy.

He stomped another large stick off the bush and gathered smaller ones that had been thawed by his body. He scraped some of them to make tinder. After much effort and pain, using his palms and a few half-frozen fingers, he found the faststicks method of his home forest worked. The small fire lifted his spirit. He could see the chamber in which he was entombed was not small. Felbanir and Birnin could have survived in here with him.

In the light, Owerdir could see the fingers of his right hand were bluish and waxy, though the thumb still moved. His left hand had two blue fingers. He considered prying off the deadness with the sticks and burning the wound with the flame, but to what end?

He also considered creating a second fire at the base of the snow wall, but in trying to melt a hole he risked collapsing the arch and burying himself. Even if he escaped, he had no provisions to return to Gilgalem or finish the climb, and he did not know the way.

Owerdir returned to the bush to harvest more wood. He would at least try to make himself comfortable. His nose met with the stronger scent when he reached into the bush. He broke off more twigs and held them up to his nostrils, but they were not strong.

He pushed his head into the bush and sniffed deeply, finding the scent again. He retrieved a burning stick from the fire and squinted into the bush. Its bony shadow played across the rock wall behind it, everywhere except one patch directly behind its stem. There it remained dark.

He flicked the flaming stick at the darkness and was surprised when it bounced through the rock wall and echoed. He took a bundle from the fire and fashioned a torch, then filled his tunic with sticks from the bush. He glanced at the crinkled, frosted parchment as he worked. There was a chance, he told himself. He stuffed the parchment back in his pocket with a pat, happy to have hope renewed.

Owerdir pushed his body through the bush, uncaring of the scraping and clawing as it tried to keep him out. He found himself lying in a small tunnel. The scent was now strong and he could feel the movement of air.

Owerdir did not know where the cave would lead him, but his hope grew with every step. At least, he told himself, the cave should have drinkable water. And soon he did find frozen puddles with liquid beneath the crust. He drank deeply, then moved onward.

He noticed the stone inside the mountain was similar to the gneiss of Gilgalem and the small mountains of Umbyrland and Goynland, but banded with carmine and quartz among the browns and grays.

As he walked, Owerdir recalled Felbanir's words about the Naren-Dra climbing down from their heights to visit the Cloud Hollows, supposedly to gather magical stones. Owerdir did not believe that these people, though mysterious, had harnessed some dark art of Ominchar.

Back home, the rhymers told many tales of far-off peoples who had forsaken Wurumnak and hastened the End of Days, but he wondered how many of those tale-tellers had visited those places and those people to see for themselves. As he gazed upon the cave walls, he doubted the Naren-Dra would climb this far down into the Hollows just to look for stones. He also wondered if they used the caves at all.

After hours of walking and crawling and squeezing though the passages, he rested. He was getting hungry but tried not to think about food. He filled his belly from a cold pool before lying down on the cold ground. He placed his faststicks in his pocket to keep them dry and warm. Then he dreamed of the cozy green forests of home.

45

URGAMDIR

Forests of Bram Province
Winterfall, 2269

Urgamdir had stayed in the trees for as long as the dense firs would carry him. It had been two days of limb jumping and his feet were sore. When the great trees finally gave way to younger trunks, he climbed down while watching the woods from where he had come.

He lamented Brugmir's death but resolved to honor his sacrifice by continuing his journey as fast as he could. His own wound was minor to him. He had scraped golden resin from a tree and warmed it in his mouth to make a salve and bandage. He also applied this to his thorn-scraped legs and splintered face.

He found a few hibernating squirrels that he consumed raw to satisfy his belly, and he filled his tunic pouches with nuts from their dens. Sure that the black-cloaked foreigner had given up his search of him, he camped early with a rejuvenating fire and slept deeply.

After another two days of travel, Urgamdir again returned to the trees when he heard marching. When he determined the army wasn't close, he climbed as high as he could. From his perch he witnessed a great battle between shining armor and bristling spears held by probable Gallerlanders.

He watched in sorrow as the tribesmen were overrun by the glint of metal. He saw some attempt to flee but they were run down by what Rildning had called cavalry. Urgamdir wondered if he would reach Bronhildia too late, and whether Highking Harkarom would even listen to his message.

He continued on in a somber mood. Cold and lonely, he now understood why the Sage insisted the messengers—particularly him—not travel alone. He enjoyed company. His mind wandered, thinking about the feasts of home, the jolly banter and dark wine. He missed Rildning, Owerdir, and his other companions. He thought about them walking in the wetlands of the east or in the snowy mountains. At least he could walk freely in the forests, even if the foreigners had changed them.

A few days after leaving the treetops, Urgamdir more than once thought he heard someone behind him. But when he turned, he saw only a scavenging bird or windblown branches. He told himself that he was being too skittish. Once he was certain he heard a snow-muffled stick break underfoot. That night he decided not to make a campfire. Under the thorn hedges he listened while gripping his stone knife and feigning sleep.

46

HILSINGOR

Rachard, Bram Province
Winterfall, 2269

Hilsingor had gotten into bed and closed his eyes, savoring the warmth of the hearth stones placed under the bed. He slept less nowadays, preferring to sit by the fire and read every available dispatch from other corners of the frontier while snacking on delicate cheeses from his large supply.

And if there were no dispatches, which were slower to arrive in winter, he would reread one of his books. He had brought many to Pemonia, mostly treatises of war written by Wilhargant and other great rulers of ancient times. He had also written several works of strategy and tactics himself, but still enjoyed the old tomes.

On this night he had contributed more ink to his own memoirs of the campaigns against the Arukan rebellion in the Old World. It was a fine war that cemented his place at the emperor's right hand, even back then. He never doubted his destiny of establishing the New World as the jewel of all imperial possessions.

Hilsingor's eyes snapped open at the panicked entry of Arnolf into his chamber.

"Sir marshal!" came the adjutant's frantic panting. "We're overrun! Sir! We have word—"

"Calm yourself," Hilsingor ordered as he swung his legs out of bed. "What has happened?"

"Sir, beg your pardon. The eastern outposts have been overrun. A heathen army now threatens to enter Bram, if they haven't already. Word just—"

Hilsingor snatched the parchment from him.

> Sir Marshal,
>
> At dawn we were awakened by a raid from the east, undoubtedly Erambrin's tribesmen. They were a mix of Gallerlanders and Nake from the peninsula. They overran all our posts and the farmsteads. Surviving soldiers fled to Fort Arbuth, but we were unable to hold the fort. We escaped west to Fort Rommested, where we remain hard-pressed. A few of my lead knights from the other forts have fled here as well, meaning the eastern flank has collapsed. Reinforcements or alternate orders requested.
>
> Sir Vinfrad

"Marshal," Arnolf began meekly, "Vinfrad is already dead, according to the rider."

"No matter, we will push them back. Wake Firkas and Ravorglad. We won't wait until spring to destroy Erambrin."

Under a high moon Hilsingor watched his commanders assemble three legions of the Frontier Corps. He and Ravorglad would each lead ten thousand crusaders, while Firkas led a provincial legion along with the Raffen cavalry.

"They'll be expecting us to march down the east road," Firkas said.

"Let them lie in wait for us then," Ravorglad said. "We will crush them wherever they slither out from."

"The road is the quickest route," Hilsingor said. "We will march double-time to reach the Plains of Ambrist before they do. There we will unleash the cavalry."

"And if the heathens have already taken the plains?" Firkas asked.

"If they beat us to the plains then the legions will dismount and flood the woods at the edge of Bram until the heathens run," Hilsingor said. "Then we'll run them down and retake the outposts. Thereafter, Ravorglad, you will garrison Fort Rommested until we find Erambrin. Onward!"

47

WIDSEM

Forests of Bram Province
Winterfall, 2269

Widsem cursed himself for being so clumsy. The moon was snuggled behind clouds that night and he had not seen the twigs. He halted as he stepped on them, but the damage was done. He heard Urgamdir stop walking. They listened to the dark, searching for one another. The ranger could not see his prey, but he could sense Urgamdir wasn't sure of Widsem's position either.

These woods were webbed in thick strangling vines nearly as big around as the great elms and white oaks on which they hung. The snows had been heavy here, filling the gaps in the canopy and vines until little of the night sky shone through. The faint grayness of the snow was the only light.

Widsem held his breath for the longest time. He was rewarded with the slight movement of a bulky shadow, perhaps behind a tree. Widsem gingerly moved off the twigs without taking his eyes from where he saw his prey. He silently drew his dagger and crept forward. As he neared the place he heard distant shouting toward the north and east. He remained still as the shouting was overcome by the raucous, but still distant, noise of a battle that had begun.

There was a step of crushed snow to his right. Widsem turned, black dagger forward, and quietly paced the shadows. More far-off shouting, possibly closer. Widsem paused, looked left, then felt a small breeze just prior to feeling a great fist cave into his face. The ranger fell, rolled, and swiped up defensively with his dagger. A man unseen yelled out and recoiled. Widsem could hear Urgamdir take to the trees again as he regained his feet.

Widsem could feel the blood gush from his nose and mouth. He followed the Gallerlander on the ground. He could hear the brute clomp along the branches and jump from one tree to the next. He could hear the snow fall beneath, and occasionally glimpse his shadow. Widsem shot a few careful arrows without luck, but kept his focus on following the big squirrel. He would come down eventually.

Widsem heard the distant battle coming closer and realized they were running toward it. He could again make out the shouts of men. He heard Brintilian and Gali and guessed it was the heathens who still held out in the east. He knew they regularly harassed the Bram frontier.

As the chase continued, the ranger worried Urgamdir was intentionally running toward the battle to make his escape. He tried to shoot more arrows, but it was no use. Soon enough the torchlights ahead ruined Widsem's night eyes, and the shouting concealed the sound of Urgamdir's steps.

Widsem knew from the shouting that he was nearing the heathen side of the battle. He slowed to a trot and listened to the last thuds of the tree runner as his prey disappeared above the fray. Ever patient, the ranger hid himself and rested until the battle waned.

48

URGAMDIR

Forests of Bram Province
Winterfall, 2269

"If I had a few more surprises like yours, we might turn every battle between here and Hilsingor's city." Erambrin smiled at Urgamdir and then shook his head, knowing further help would not come.

Urgamdir felt honored by the Umbyrking's compliment, but he knew Erambrin was trying to hide a sullen mood. His king was different from the last time he had seen him after Nalembalen. Back then, Gratgofa ordered Erambrin to lead a large group of warriors to seek aid from the Bronhildi who had also fought the foreigners. Urgamdir never learned what became of the Umbyrking's efforts, only that he and his warriors were eventually isolated in eastern Umbyrland, where many other refugees flocked to him.

"And if our Bronhildi flank had not so easily folded, that might also have made a difference," Erambrin added.

"How did you come to have all these Bronhildi and Nake warriors among your men?" Urgamdir asked. He glanced at the short, strange-looking men who walked around with a luminescent rub on their faces. "And if Highking Harkarom is now with the foreigners, why do some Bronhildi still fight alongside you?"

Arbardir, who was seated on a log beside Erambrin, harrumphed and spat into the campfire at the mention of the other tribesmen. Urgamdir noticed Gombir the rhymer, whom the Sage had sent with Arbardir when he left

229

Gilgalem, was not with him. Urgamdir was seated across from Arbardir and Erambrin.

"It's a long story, one that cannot be told without more wine," Erambrin said, motioning to his servants.

Several of Erambrin's other chiefs joined them around the fire, all of them northern clansmen Urgamdir had not seen since they had fled to the tree city together. Urgamdir, over the past two days retreating with Erambrin's men, had had the chance to talk with them. But this was his first opportunity to sit with the Umbyrking directly.

"Fine wine, very fine," the king said after a long gulp. "Only the cold winters properly bring out the murkyberry of this spiced wine. Now, Urgamdir, you asked about the patchwork of my army. Truly, it has been one disaster after another since Nalembalen.

"Gratgofa had not known the foreigners had already whispered to the Bronhildi, nor did I. I was surprised to find Harkarom hostile and we had to fight our way back to Gallerlandia. Even knowing what the foreigners had done to Nalembalen, and experiencing it to some extent themselves, the minds of the Bronhildi could not be swayed. Except one chieftain.

"Isberen, whose villages were decimated by foreigners raiding from ships, could not so easily forgive Harkarom's new allies. He brought his clan with us into Gallerlandia, but unfortunately he was killed soon thereafter. Keeping his clansmen together has been near impossible. They dwindle away during the night to walk back home. Several of our folk speak Bronhildi, as your family does. But still, there is nothing we can do, short of fighting, to persuade them to stay.

"As for the Nake, they joined us later when the foreigners pushed us farther east. I was desperate for help anywhere I could find it, even from the illiterate stone worshipers. Bidagdir here was chief of the Umbyr village closest to the Nake lands. If it wasn't for his knowing a bit of their weird speech, we might never have received their help. The Nake have not been bothered much by the foreigners, as far as we could tell, but they understood what was coming.

"Even with this help from the unreliable Bronhildi and the few Nake, we were always outnumbered and outmaneuvered by the foreigners. Our supplies have also been persistently low, and we are not crafting enough new stoneswords and spears to replace our losses."

"Use the foreigner's metal," Urgamdir blurted out. Confused stares around the fire prompted him to explain. "I confess I have used the forbidden metal. And if I hadn't, I would have been killed like my companion."

"You have no shame for this?" one of the Umbyr chieftains asked.

"Only a little," Urgamdir replied. "I did not keep it, but I used it when I needed it. It was lighter and sharper than stone."

"I'll hear no more of it," Erambrin said. "If the Graparins had survived, they would surely make an example out of you. I'm glad Tirgranir sent you and Arbardir here to help me, but do not stray to the path of Ominchar."

"Great king," he began with a weak voice. "Tirgranir did not send me to—"

"You came on your own then? Missed the companionship of your own Umbyrs, I'm sure. Well, I don't blame you. Those Vayns have leaned on the strength of the Umbyrs for so many generations of the high kings. I can't recall a single tale about any Vayn who became high king that was strong enough to—"

"I was sent to go north, to the Bronhildi." Urgamdir saw the faces around the campfire scowl at the revelation, even more so than the news that he had laid hands on the evil metal of the enemy. Arbardir could not resist a chuckle.

"Who sent you on such a foolish errand?" gasped the Umbyrking.

"We met in council. The Vaynking, the Sage, and Rildning made the decision. Envoys like me have been sent to the tribes."

"So I heard from Arbardir, but I did not think we would try the Bronhildi again. As for Arbardir's task, he found it already completed when he found them alongside me. But his efforts won't be as useless as yours will be." Erambrin sighed and shook his head again. "As if Gilgalem did not think I would have tried to persuade Harkarom again if it was possible? Fool's errand, Urgamdir."

"I must try," he said after a pause.

"You will be killed," the Umbyrking replied with certainty. "I doubt you will make it that far, given—why do you keep turning to look behind you?" Urgamdir had not realized he had been glancing over his shoulder. The woods behind them were dark and still.

"A foreigner has been hunting me. I came upon your battle by chance and lost him. Or so I hope."

"One man?" Arbardir scoffed. He slapped his thigh and roared with laughter.

"This one is different," Urgamdir said, glaring at Arbardir. "He ran the trees with me. He is quiet as a breeze and clothed black as night."

"Then you best stay with us," Erambrin offered with a grin. "Give up the errand and fight with us. You are still one of my Umbyr chieftains of the north. Here in the heart of Umbyrland you will find a task worthy of your talents. First, we will continue the retreat back to the borderlands of the Nake realm. There we will resupply and recruit. With the coming of spring we will give the foreigners a battle as they've not yet tasted." Reluctantly, Urgamdir shook his head.

"I cannot, great king. The greening of the grass will undoubtedly bring the foreigners to Gilgalem."

"The Vaynking is a fool, as he always has been," Erambrin said. "I have the best warriors, he has the children and old men. What hope do they have?"

"Little," Urgamdir replied, "but it's placed in me and the other envoys. So I must try, as I'm sure Arbardir has done."

"I forbade Arbardir from asking the Nake to send help to Gilgalem," the Umbyrking said. "I need those stone worshipers here with me, fighting to win back the realm, not overwintering in the mountains. I'll not stop you from going to the Bronhildi, because I respect your courage and dedication—hallmarks of the Umbyr warriors. But you will die there."

49

ENIRI

Aggarwal Sea
Winterfall, 2269

Eniri had learned the rhythm of the ship. Even from inside her sack of apples she could hear the grumble of the men rising in the morning. The clang of their plates, the shouting of repetitive orders, and at night, the paces of the watchmen. The entry of unseen people into the narrow pantry where she hid was also predictable.

She had wisely chosen the back of the room where they seldom went. With this knowledge she knew when she could emerge to walk about and look out the little porthole. A sky of gray and a sea of darker gray greeted her the same every morning.

Eniri had wept knowing Tegmad had been imprisoned, possibly enslaved. She also lamented not being able to warn Gilgalem about the Raffen fleet at Amlon. But she no longer thought of whether she should have turned back, even for Tegmad's sake.

She tried to busy her mind with how to free Tegmad, or at least take him food. She wasn't sure where to go, because she could no longer hear him or his chains. But she thought he must be alive, because if they had wanted to kill him, they would have done so on sight.

Every day Eniri became bolder, tiptoeing closer and closer to the ladder during the quiet times. She had repeatedly checked the other door, which she had learned was the kitchen, but it was always locked. One night she crept up the ladder and lifted the lid of the hatch. She couldn't see anyone but even so she couldn't bring herself to leave the safety of the pantry.

One day, she grew careless. A boy entered the pantry from the hatch during what was normally a quiet time in midafternoon. She had come out of hiding to warm up her legs, when the boy entered. She instinctively dove into the nearest pile of sacks and hanging dried meats. The chickens were aflutter with the sudden action. Eniri watched the boy, whom she had never seen before. He sniffed around until he found something to his liking and ate as he pleased.

This boy repeated his trespass for several days straight around the same time. But then came a day when he was caught in the act. The thief fell to his knees and the man who had caught him raised a hand to strike him. The man glanced behind him toward the ladder and open hatch.

Seeing no one, he lowered his hand and lifted the boy's chin. With a stern glare the man scolded him until the boy nodded, then he released him. The bow scurried up the ladder, leaving the man alone in the pantry. The man shook his head and smiled to himself.

Eniri watched with great interest. The man reminded her of Rildning, tall and powerfully built, but his eyes were gray like the water and his straw-colored hair was gathered in a small ponytail. He had a short beard and a long mustache that curved upward like horns. This, she thought, must be a Nyden, for the Raffen were dark haired like the Rahlampians. And no tribe she knew of had that distinctive mustache or lacked tattoos and paints as he did.

The kindness the man had shown the thieving boy also reminded her of Rildning, balancing discipline with mercy and never rushing to inflict punishment on friends or enemies. She felt an overwhelming desire to come out of hiding, as if she could embrace Rildning himself. She wondered if this man would help her. But a quiet voice inside her urged caution.

She watched as the man looked around the storeroom in a puzzled manner. He walked up and down, surveying the provisions. Then he came over to her apple sack. She held her breath, watching as he discovered a smaller bag where she had hidden apple cores and other refuse. She cursed herself for not tossing it out the porthole earlier, as she did every morning.

He held the bag for a moment before returning to the spot where the boy had been eating. There were bits of dried meat and bread lying about. Eniri could see the confusion building in his face. He picked up the boy's scraps and tossed them and her little bag out the porthole. He gave the shelves one last glance before going back up the ladder. Eniri exhaled but it was a while before she could bring herself to move. When she did, she found a new hiding sack.

The following day the boy did not return, but the man did. He came back in the late morning, after the cook had finished and locked the door to the kitchen. The man glanced around but promptly left. He reappeared that night and sat on the ladder with the hatch open.

When the clouds grew dark with rain, he closed the hatch and lit a lamp with flint and a knife from his pocket. Eniri did not like the look of the shining metal. But there was something about this man's patience, and the mercy he had shown the boy, that drew her to him. She battled with herself on whether to reach out for help.

The man set the lamp in a fixture on the wall, folded his arms, and leaned back on the ladder. Eniri waited until his eyes closed before she shifted her feet. He had kept her frozen, and her legs and back cramped. He was motionless, but she fought to keep awake. And for a while she did.

When she awoke during the night there was no lamplight. She held her breath again, listening to the rolling creak of the ship, the flutter of the sails above deck, and the occasional peep of the sleeping chickens. When she was satisfied, she moved the sack and peered out. The man was gone and the hatch was closed.

The next night the man appeared again. He fastened the lamp to the wall.

"I've spoken to your friend," he said in rough Gali. Eniri was shocked and fearful. "He is fine. He would not admit you were aboard, but I know the boy wasn't alone in his crimes. He could not eat all that the cook said was missing."

Eniri watched the man sit on the ladder, looking around the room, clearly unsure of where she was. She could not bring herself to respond. She told herself he could be lying and Tegmad could be dead. But the man seemed patient and genuine.

"You are fine as well," he continued after a pause. "It's better I found you than the others. We are merely two days away from the islands. You will need a plan." After more silence he stood and put his hand on the ladder. "Then I'll go," he said, leaning over to pluck the lamp.

Her heart raced as she slowly stepped out from behind the food sacks, ten paces from him. He was startled and held out the lamp.

"You are a woman?"

She watched him carefully, to see if his hand went to the knife in his belt. When it did not, she spoke.

"You speak Gali?"

"My father traded with the Vayns his whole life," he said. "This was his ship. I've sailed to the Aggarwal ports since I was a boy. Now, why are you eating my food?"

"I need to see the Nyden."

"Here I am." The man's blond-tusked smile had an awkward charm. For the first time since setting sail, Eniri felt comforted.

"My friend," she began, "is he all right?"

"In chains," he answered. "It would have been worse, but I persuaded the Raffen to take him as a slave."

"How is that not worse?" she snapped, forgetting herself.

"I'll let you think on that. You want to see the Nyden? You will see a broken people. Half-enslaved, the other half profiting from that enslavement."

"And which are you?" she asked.

He looked down at the wooden planks. "I'm surviving, neither slave nor profiting. Nor free."

"Yet my friend is now captive on your father's slaver ship."

"This is not a slaver, it's a trade ship. And it belongs to my uncle now. My father perished in the last war against the Raffen. I'm his only surviving son. My uncle has cast his lot with the Raffen, not that we had much choice. We help the others when we can, like that thieving boy. My father would have gladly died twice before seeing Raffen set foot on his decks."

Eniri calmed herself. She had heard tales of the wars between the Raffen and the Nyden, and the wars among the Nyden themselves. She could see this man represented those caught in the middle of all the conflict. He was, perhaps, her only hope.

"I'm Eniri of the Tamtur clan, once a princess of the Umbyrs of Gallerlandia," she said with pride. She knew the names meant nothing to him, but she wanted him to know. "I've come in secret to speak with the Nyden chieftains on behalf of our people, who face dangers as grave as your people have doubtless seen. I have come to seek help."

"That is a task." The man could not help but smile at the notion. "My name is Bothrobim. I must tell you now there are only two men who will be able to help you, if they chose to. One is my uncle Toredwoak, but as I said, he made his peace with the Raffen and is a vassal of their king.

"The other man is Belordoos, Toredwoak's twin. After the death of my father, who was their elder brother, Belordoos lost a duel with Toredwoak over submitting to the Raffen. My father had prevented the twins from dividing the Nyden between those willing to fight or submit to the Raffen. But after the Raffen killed him, well, the gale winds split the sails, as we say."

Eniri sat on a keg. "So there is no hope, for your people or mine . . ."

"Nearly," Bothrobim conceded. "My good uncle Belordoos lost to his brother but he's not done completely. Toredwoak is protecting him from the Raffen, giving him—and his men—time to join with him. But I know, like my father did, that Belordoos will never join with the Raffen. Toredwoak must know this too, but I'm sure he hopes most of the Nyden chiefs will stand with him. So it's a matter of time before Belordoos is exiled or killed."

Eniri felt sick, helpless, foolish, and afraid. She wept softly, then felt Bothrobim's hand on her shoulder.

"All is not lost. How can a face so beautiful be so sad?" He smiled, but she looked at him warily. "Don't worry," he said, "you are safe with me. I've heard tales at the wine halls in Amlon about what has happened in Gallerlandia. My uncles know little of it, but perhaps they will be curious about your message. I can't promise they will help, but I will take you to them. The Raffen must not discover you, however. Stay in hiding here and I'll come for you."

"Thank you," Eniri said. "And my friend?"

"I'll try, but cannot promise anything. He belongs to the Raffen now."

50

RILDNING

East of the Pernadun, Rahlampia
Winterfall, 2269

Crossing the Pernadun River in the food-laden landship had been calm, and misleading. Once they were sailing over land, Rildning's awe for the huge *Earthark* was displaced by unescapable discomfort of all the senses.

The bone-jarring shaking and popping of the hull was constant as the landship crashed over streams and rocks and hedges, its sails full with winter winds. Forced belowdecks by the cold and lacking any tasks aboard ship, Rildning crawled from one food sack to another, searching for a cushion to soften the blows. He feared the landship would rip open or the massive wheels would splinter apart.

Then there was the smell. The scents of cooked meats, breads, and sugared fruits were soon overpowered by dusty grease. When he boarded, Rildning had seen the black gobs of tallow oozing from the wheel shafts and axle holes of the hull, helping to keep the wood from rubbing away. But inside it smelled as if whole pigs were mushed along the working parts.

Most penetrating was the bitter wind, which blasted down through every opened door. There was one small furnace in the quarters, but the three Rahlampian crewmen, who worked in shifts day and night to steer the landship, were finicky about anyone using it. Minimal space was reserved for firewood.

It was difficult to become friendly with the crew. Two spoke little Gali and the third spoke none at all and always glared at Rildning. Denildon the Riverkeeper had also provided no instruction for how Rildning could be of assistance, simply telling him to "ride."

Rildning tried to occupy his mind with what needed to be done once he reached Gilgalem. He wondered if any of the other envoys were having better success or would arrive back to Gilgalem before he would.

51

OWERDIR

Naren-Dra Mountains
Winterfall, 2269

Owerdir was again awakened by the strange smell, now stronger than ever this far into the cave. In the dark he used his palms and good fingers to rekindle his torch with faststicks. He gulped water from a pool to staunch his hunger and continued down the tunnel. More than once his path split into multiple passages. Each time he chose the cave with the strongest odor.

Before long Owerdir's nose and eyes watered with the heaviness of the smell. He considered returning to one of the side shafts but was pushed onward by curiosity. In time he was rewarded with signs that someone, or something, had been digging into the walls of the cave.

Some of the dug-out areas were shallow clefts in the stone, with sooty burn marks in their center. Others were arm-deep alcoves where veins of an apparently prized stone were harvested. In the torchlight he could make out vague footprints in the rubble and dust on the tunnel floor.

Owerdir's mind wandered as he followed the prints. Would the Naren-Dra welcome him and offer him food and warmth? Or would they view him as a trespasser and deal harshly with him? He wished the brothers were still with him, or that he had taken the time to ask more questions of them.

Owerdir's hand soon felt the heat of his shortening torch. He had come to the last of his sticks. He considered tearing off strips of his wolf-skin tunic, but he knew it would purchase him little time, and he would need the clothing. He waited until the embers singed his thumb before flinging the low light ahead of him.

His pace slowed as he felt along the wall and shuffled forward with his moccasined feet. He finally closed his eyes to the darkness and let his other senses lead him farther into the mountain.

Owerdir eventually tripped over rubble. He could feel that he tore one of his blackened fingers from his hand and bent another. There was no pain but the putrid ooze was worrying. Only when he stood to get a closer look did he realize he could see. The light was dim ahead. He continued cautiously and soon found the source of the light.

A small fire burned among a heap of ashes. A shallow metal bowl was nestled in the embers, with bluish-pink dust glowing inside. Near the fire were hand-sized stones that looked like colored ice, but they did not appear to be melting. The flames reflected in their many facets.

On two logs lay a few hammers and a set of thick leather gloves. Iron rings were sewn into leather at the knuckles and the fingertips were capped with iron. On the back of the gloves was a disk of bone with dust-filled cracks.

There was no sight or sound of anyone, but Owerdir guessed whoever owned these things was nearby. He looked around the chamber, seeing many dug-out places in the walls hidden by shadows. Several of these gaps had small wooden fixtures hanging in the darkness at eye level.

Owerdir spotted several leather sacks behind one of the log benches. Hoping for food, he quickly untied each one. The first and second contained more glassy stones. The third held spiny green rocks, like peach pits. And the fourth held lacy leaves that were terribly bitter but soon vanished when he tried them on his tongue. There was also a small bundle of molted snake skins.

Frustrated, he shoved the bag away. Then he saw movement out of the corner of his eye. One of the wooden fixtures leaped out of the darkness. Then many others came from all directions. They flew at him like birds and calling out. When they were close he saw black slits in the wooden masks and felt the vise grip of iron-fingered hands.

Owerdir felt pain in his head as all became dark.

52

HILSINGOR

Fort Rommested, Bram Province
Winterfall, 2269

Hilsingor looked out from the wooden rampart of the bailey. The moat below was red with the blood of the fallen. He was proud of his men. They had rallied to the road quickly in Rachard and marched swiftly.

They found the Gallerlanders on the Plains of Ambrist, disorganized and disheartened. But retaking the eastern outposts had not been easy because the Gallerlanders defended them like their own villages. Most stood their ground and perished.

Hilsingor ordered his legions to take a good night's rest with a portion of extra beer for every man. Tomorrow they would continue to the last Gallerlander-held fort at Arbuth.

"Will you reconsider?" Ravorglad asked.

"No," the marshal said. "I chose you to stay here and hold Rommested until the frontier defenses are restored."

"Crusaders are not accustomed to serving as a garrison. Sitting behind wooden gates while victory awaits out on the field . . ."

"Was the taking of this hill not a victory?"

"Minor enough," the knight replied.

"All great victories are built upon smaller ones," Hilsingor retorted. "I want Firkas to use his new Raffen troops against the Gallerlanders at Arbuth. The scouts say a Gallerlander king, Erambrin of the Umbyrs, haunts a wood not two days' march east of here. Firkas and I will go, and you will follow when your legion has rested and the supplies have arrived. Do not disobey me. Winter campaigns end badly when grain and meat are not secured for the men."

"So my crusaders are to miss the battle with the heathen king?"

"Not if the supplies arrive in time, as they should. Do not worry, there are still many heathen kings yet."

"Sir marshal," Arnolf interrupted, trotting up behind them. "A letter from Eglamour, sir."

Hilsingor broke the purple seal and unfolded the parchment. An electrum ring accompanied the message.

> Marshal Hilsingor,
> It is with great gladness and thanks to God that I inform you that Odon, King of the Goyns, has surrendered.
>
> We decided to use his capitulation to our advantage by making him an ally. He now sits in the Imperial Council of Pemonia with the other heathen lords, a fine example to the other Gallerlander clans that their resistance is wasteful, while their potential alliance with the empire can be enriching and honorable.
>
> Enclosed you will find Odon's ring. He willingly gave it up to you as proof to his tribesmen of his surrender. He hopes it will help the others negotiate their own submission.
>
> May God continue to grant us the strength to shoulder the mighty burden that is transforming this continent of barbarians into a Messengian realm of the holy empire.
>
> Exarch Bredahade

Ravorglad was visibly disgusted when Hilsingor relayed the contents of the letter.

"Odon should have been executed. Only then would his barbarian brethren submit. Let us not give Erambrin the opportunity to surrender. If the Gallerlander underkings live, their followers will always put their minds to a revolt."

"Indeed, there are risks to courting or killing them," Hilsingor acknowledged. "If we bring them all under our banner, then they can strike us on the inside when we least expect it. I remember there was an Arukan leader I made commander of a mixed army of friendly Arukans and Mordheyri peoples. He had been against the original Arukan rebellion and served me well in the campaign, on the field, and in offering terms to the other Arukan lords.

"But before the campaign ended he turned against me. He murdered my deputy, torched my camp, and gave the Arukans all the intelligence they would need to effectively resist me. To this day I'm uncertain what changed his mind."

"What did you do to this traitor?" Ravorglad asked.

"I wish I could say he met his death on my sword. But he was simply discovered in a ditch not far from our camp with his throat slit."

"Doesn't the exarch fear similar treachery from the barbarians we now call allies? And why won't he let you do to Gallerlandia what you did in Arukia?"

Hilsingor gave him a hard glance. "I have not asked for such methods because they are not necessary. The exarch wishes to harness the tribes as subjects of the empire and converts to Messengianism, not perpetual enemies. But don't worry, the tribes will never unite themselves enough to truly pose the threat the Arukans and their allies did.

"The Arukans had positioned themselves to politically and militarily upend the balance of power among the ruling kingdoms, therefore challenging the empire itself. But these New World savages will never aspire to such heights. They will never give up their petty tribal affairs, so they will always be conquered and reconquered. Thus, it's a matter of time, not of methods."

Hilsingor noticed Arnolf remained with them, clutching another folded parchment.

"Something else, Arnolf?"

"Yes, marshal. A letter from the archbishop as well."

Hilsingor sighed and reluctantly held out his hand. "Give it to me then," he grumbled. "What does this meddling churchman want this time?"

Sir Marshal,

God's grace is showered on the faithful, and he smiles on those for whom the task is winning souls from the Depths of Memelos into his own hand. As a faithful knight who fights for even the most wretched and unwinnable souls, you are surely his favored tool. It is my hourly prayer that your victories continue.

Given that you have the power of God in your sword, I sincerely doubt you have any use for the vile tome written by that foulest of heretics, Rildning. As the highest holy judge of the emperor's New World possessions, however, it will be of great use to me in planning the trial against Rildning and other relevant enemies as they are captured. Send the book to me at your earliest convenience, and God will reward you for assisting my onerous but holy task.

May God continue to bless your legions. Your triumph is ever on my mind, and, with Rildning's journal in my hand, the trial of the heretics will be a bright plume on your helm.

Archbishop Ralmo

Hilsingor chuckled.

"Sir," the adjutant continued, "the archbishop's personal messenger awaits your answer before he returns to Eglamour."

"Does he? Tell the messenger to tell Ralmo he will receive both the journal and Rildning when I capture him. Only then will I send both back together for trial."

Arnolf nodded and disappeared.

"What is so special about a heretic's miserable little scribblings?" Ravorglad asked.

"Ralmo is jealous," Hilsingor answered. "He has heard about the journal and thinks it contains writings inspired by Memelos."

"Does it?"

"Since you believe, as Ralmo does, that all heathens speak the tongues of Memelos, then yes. But for me, the journal is a window into the heart and mind of a formidable enemy. Of course, Rildning is a heretic, the most notorious since Regnarul the Bound during the Age of Calming Winds. But Rildning is also probably the only man who can cobble together these tribes and make our task more costly."

"Buy you said the tribes would never unite," Ravorglad said.

"No, I said they would never unite by themselves. Rildning transcends their hierarchies and cultures. He is of Brintilian blood, a New Loriner, and will never be one of them. That means he can sit down and talk with any of them and they will listen. It has been some time since I consulted his journal, but I should reexamine it. And there is something else." Hilsingor looked down in thought.

"What is it?" Ravorglad pried.

"I think Rildning stumbled onto much more than he expected."

"Such as?"

Hilsingor studied Ravorglad. He knew this knight would know nothing of the ancient tales, the Brintilian version of the Cataclysm described by Rildning in his journal. There was no use trying to explain it to Ravorglad. But he had been thinking hard on certain passages of the book, trying to understand.

"Suffice it to say the Gallerlanders may not be as primitive as they seem," Hilsingor said. "Rildning appears to have discovered a hidden past, a mastery of machines. Perhaps even flying."

Ravorglad roared with laughter. "They have mastered only face painting and the retreat. They never built anything more sophisticated than rickety watermills farther north. I torched every one we found."

"Perhaps you are right," Hilsingor said.

5 3

FIRKAS

East of Fort Rommested, Bram Province
Winterfall, 2269

Firkas had waited a long time for this moment. Best of all, the marshal had not arrived yet, and Firkas would not wait any longer.

He pulled up his sword and spurred his horse forward. His men followed and the trees swept past in a blur. They charged out of the wood line and made for the center of the Gallerlander camp. His plan had worked. The heathens were clearly caught off guard by Firkas's small unit. The rest of his legion would follow as soon as they heard the battle begin.

Firkas led his men through the camp, hacking left and right as heads rose from bedrolls and tents. He heard the sound of horns behind him and knew the timing was right.

As he approached the camp's center, he saw the ivy-crowned head of Erambrin. The Gallerlanders around him were all large but nimble. Firkas learned early in the campaign that the acrobatics of the northern Gallerlanders was no trick. He had seen knights chase down a Gallerlander only to see the heathen run up a tree, somersault behind their pursuer, then strike the knight down from behind. The veterans of Firkas's provincial legions—particularly the one he led today—and all the Raffen took great care to avoid such traps.

Firkas had once been jealous of the specialized training of Ravorglad's crusaders. Two crusaders on foot and back to back could hold their own against a mob of heathens. But his provincial troops soon found that the shoulder-to-shoulder line tactics, especially fronted by a line of shield men, was effective in intimidating and breaking a charging horde. And the Raffen, wild and risky on their newfound horses, were a prized asset in field or forest. But this time, Firkas caught the Gallerlanders in a long, open glade. For this, he chose to lead the charge himself.

Firkas could see Erambrin was rallying the Gallerlanders quicker than he could get to the king. Stoneswords and spears flocked to Erambrin, encircling the ivy crown with a large protective force. But Firkas did not slow his horse. He and his men soon crashed into Erambrin's circle.

Firkas was among the few knights not unhorsed by the spear wall. He charged forward, then reared around, back and forth, trying to reach Erambrin. But the Gallerlanders were vicious. His men fought bravely but were greatly out-numbered, and Firkas worried their bravery wouldn't be enough.

Firkas looked to the woods from which his mounted raid came. There was the sound of the second horn, but it came from the woods on his flank. He called to his men to fall back. Erambrin's circle held fast where they stood, with a few impatient pursuers breaking off to join the general melee.

Firkas watched as the Raffen cavalry burst out, sweeping over the flank of the camp. He held up his sword and called to them, and they charged right through Erambrin's circle. Firkas watched with delight as the Umbyrking's stonesword broke in half when he buried it in the chest of a Raffen horse. Erambrin next took up a great ax and continued the fight.

By now the entire camp seethed with battle. Firkas and the knights who took up the initial charge found themselves pushed away from Erambrin's circle and increasingly isolated from the Raffen and the rest of the legion. He could see the Raffen were turning to charge at Erambrin again, but he was beset by luminescent-faced Nake wielding stone clubs and blowing darts through river cane. The darts were deadly accurate and instantly lethal for those knights not wearing helmets with full visors. He felt several bounce harmlessly off his own armor, and saw one lodge in his visor.

The red snow on the glade soon turned to muddy slush as the battle churned. After another Raffen charge and the arrival of more of Firkas's provincials, the camp's defenses crumbled and Firkas rejoined the main body of his men. Erambrin's circle had thinned.

Within minutes the Umbyrking's protectors were decimated. By the time Firkas and his knights approached, he was protected by two hulking brutes and one swift spearman. The rest of the Gallerlanders were fighting for their own lives or running.

One of the big men employed a stone ax the size of a wagon wheel. Any knight or footman who was brave enough to confront him had armor and chest cleaved open. The ax was badly notched but served its purpose, often catching a weapon or rim of armor that allowed him to crush the unfortunate to the ground before following up with another cleaving blow. This Gallerlander finally fell when they filled his tunic and face with arrows.

The second man was even taller than the first, with boar tusks in his earlobes. He fought with a simple strong pole that vaulted his huge form into his enemies, crushing them against trees or into the mud where they were easily killed by others. He could also disarm the knights with a quick stab of the pole. Breaking necks with this pole jab was a specialty for him.

Only knights and provincial troops with heavy gorgets and helmets were saved, but all were disoriented. This man endured more slashes than Firkas could count. With a great loss of blood and flesh gaping on every limb, he finally fell.

The last of Erambrin's protectors kept Firkas from engaging the Umbyrking directly, while Erambrin cut down any who evaded the spearman. It was only the sacrificial charge of a determined mounted Raffen that distracted the spearman long enough for the Raffen commander, Walpert, to kill him.

Firkas took the opportunity to charge Erambrin. The king spun to avoid his sword, then flicked his ax around to take off Firkas's horse's front legs at the knees. Firkas was thrown forward. The animal thrashed about, nearly squishing him down into the mud. The provincials pulled him to safety and restored his sword, but they too were cut down by Gallerlanders or bashed by the flailing horse. Firkas regained his feet and wiped the mud that covered half his visor. He saw the ivy crown come for him.

Firkas parried the ax over and over again, then Erambrin's strokes slowed. The knight saw a broken arrow shaft protruding from his ribs. Firkas ducked the next ax swing, then Erambrin spewed blood and struggled for air. Firkas raised his sword high and brought it down on the Umbyrking's unarmored fur-cloaked chest, sending him to his knees. Erambrin squinted up at Firkas, who raised his visor. The knight took off his head.

54

URGAMDIR

North of Fort Rommested, Bram Province
Winterfall, 2269

"Well, there is something else I should tell you," Urgamdir said. "There is a master hunter of the foreigners who follows me. He has undoubtedly seen me with you, and will think you are my helpers. So you've no choice but to help me, since you will now be hunted as well."

The Bronhildi looked at one another. Urgamdir was glad their hostility had faded. His Bronhildi speech was stale, but they understood him well enough. All but one of them seemed convinced.

"But our people are allied with the foreigners," the woman said. "We have no reason to fear your hunter. We intend to return to our own realm and will offer no further help to the feeble Gallerlanders."

"Do you think this hunter cares about what you intend to do?" Urgamdir retorted. "He only knows what he sees, which is this messenger running northward with Bronhildi."

"We were in no danger until you followed us," she scowled, shaking her spear. "You have put this on us!"

"You were in danger the moment your chief broke from Harkarom and came with Erambrin to Gallerlandia. All I ask is that you help me travel safely to Harkarom, then what he does with me is my own fate. This is a small burden for you, since your feet already point toward Bronhildia."

"We owe nothing to the Gallerlanders," she insisted. Then a less stubborn Bronhildi stepped in.

"This Gallerlander may be a lucky thing for us, despite the hunter behind him. If we deliver him to Highchief Harkarom as a gift, then we will have earned a welcome back into the tribe."

The woman warrior seemed to acquiesce to this plan, but Urgamdir was wary of their hushed tones. He knew he could fend off the four of them if they tried to attack, but he knew the Bronhildi often favored conspiring and planning over taking action.

"I would not oppose your plan," Urgamdir said, trying to move their decision along, "so long as you deliver your gift safely and with haste."

"It's agreed then," the enterprising one said. "I'm called Danyhad. These are my brothers, Dombrad and Kemet."

"And I'm Yoriksa," the skeptical one said. "We know who you are from the camp. It was said by your kin that you fought bravely in the north and in the ruined tree city. But to me, you, like the others, are foolish. Just as our chieftain Isberen was. He was my brother."

Urgamdir had initially believed he needed no guide through these lands. Umbyrland had been his home, vast and beautiful. But it was his home no longer. His Bronhildi companions clearly knew better than he which trackways were safe and which were regularly patrolled by the foreigners or watched by their tribal allies.

Their progress was measured and slow, but Urgamdir was satisfied to be moving closer to his objective. He was constantly haunted by his memories, feeling severe guilt for turning his back on the Umbyrking. He had been within earshot of the foreigners' attack and fled north, where he encountered the Bronhildi who had brought news of what had happened.

The guilt ripped at him, but he knew if he had even a small chance of peeling the Bronhildi away from the foreigners, accomplishing that would be better than even a thousand strokes of his own sword.

Night and day they journeyed northward, stopping for short periods to rest or forage. The winter fruits were more plentiful in these forests, especially the melonberries and yew arils, frozen on the vine and bough but quickly thawed. The Bronhildi, being master marksmen, supplemented these fruits with fresh game.

"Why risk such a dangerous journey?" Danyhad asked during one of their stops.

"My people are in great need, as you have seen," Urgamdir replied. "You would do the same."

"Our people were in great need, so we allied with the foreigners instead of continuing a futile fight," Yoriksa said. "Do you realize you're effectively our prisoner now?"

"So be it," he said, "as long as you take me to Harkarom."

The day finally came when they found a newly built road to the north. They walked it to give their feet a rest from the wilds. The Bronhildi also wanted to find a group of their own tribe, so as to have safety in numbers before crossing into Bronhildi as returnees. And soon they found some.

Ahead was a squat shack next to the road. New timbered walls framed a single door, and its roof was covered with fresh snow. As they approached, a Bronhildi came out, a leather pouch tied to his belt. Several others with bows were seen standing alert in the woods nearby.

"Halt! Pay the toll," the man demanded from the shack.

"What is a toll?" Urgamdir asked.

"We are your Bronhildi brothers," Danyhad said. "We return from fighting in the south."

"You must pay the toll . . . the road tax," the man insisted. "If you walk the road, you pay the toll." He jutted his hand out.

"We have no money!" blurted one of Danyhad's cousins.

"Is this not Bronhildi territory now?" Yoriksa asked. "Why would a Bronhildi pay another to walk a road that they share?"

"Beyond this shack is the Imperial Province of Barres," the man said. "Part of the imperial realm of Highchief Harkarom, vassal-king of the Brintilian emperor. Pay the toll."

"Vassal-king?" Danyhad was puzzled. The man of the shack gave them a curious look.

"If you had been away, fighting in the south, you would know this. The highchief traveled to Eglamour to take up his new crown and is now seated here, in his new dominion of Barres. The throne of Harkarom is in the new city of Gradhild. If, however, you were with the Gallerlanders, you would not have heard all of this. Will you pay the toll?"

Urgamdir steamed when he realized what had happened to his home forests.

"Gradhild is not a new city," he said to the toll man. "It was once called Gradumbyr, before the foreigners sacked it. Clearly the Bronhildi have been given the scraps from the foreigners' table. Perhaps you already have your filthy hands on my villages too, with our electrum wrapped around your filthy necks!"

The toll man drew a long steel sword. Another sentry appeared in the doorway of the shack, his fine steel breastplate unmistakably imperial.

"I see you have been bought as well," Urgamdir scoffed. Danyhad jerked on his arm.

"This is how you intend to turn the mind of Harkarom?" he asked. "You were better suited to die in the battle you fled from. Better that than to be skewered on the envoy's road."

"This Gallerlander is a gift to the highchief," Yoriksa said to the Bronhildi guarding the road. "We once passed this way when it was free of demands for payment. And we must pass through again to deliver a gift to Harkarom he will surely want."

"A hostage of the northern Umbyrs," Danyhad added. "His king will pay handsomely for his return. Also, he carries a message for the highchief." Yoriksa glared at him for his indiscretion.

"You were astray with the Gallerlanders," said the breastplated man, strutting toward them. "Fighting your own blood. And now you wish to return with only this prisoner as payment. Not a clever trick, but certainly a tall request."

Urgamdir's face reddened. He didn't like this man. But before anyone could speak, a voice came from the woods behind them.

"You can give him to me."

The Bronhildi archers turned their arrow points toward the voice, looking this way and that, flustered that they had not detected the person earlier.

"No need to shoot," the dark-clothed man said as he stepped out of the forest and onto the road. "I'm your ally, after all." He was speaking rough Gali. Urgamdir and a few of the Bronhildi could understand him. When he drew closer Urgamdir realized who he was.

"Stop there!" said the senior guard with the breastplate.

"I'm a ranger, sent by Marshal Hilsingor of the Frontier Corps to fetch this man," the man continued.

"Don't give him up to this foreigner," Danyhad pleaded. "We have fought alongside the Gallerlanders, it is true. But so have many Bronhildi, and many have returned. We wish to purchase forgiveness with this Umbyr chieftain. And he carries—"

"Enough," the senior guard said. He turned to the ranger. "You imperials are so fond of paper, so show me your orders."

"My orders are direct from the mouth of the marshal," the ranger said. "That should be enough for a toll taker."

"No papers, no chieftain. So I'll claim him for myself."

"What is your name, keeper of the toll?" the ranger asked. "I will report your disregard for imperial authority."

"I'm no toll keeper. I am Premarom, chief of the Emodony Forest and brother of Harkarom, Highchief of the Bronhildi. Speak my name well when you use it, little ranger. But be wary of how you use it. Now, what is your name, so I may report you?"

The ranger looked about him. The Bronhildi archers had followed him out to the road, their bowstrings at the ready. He remained still and silent.

"No name?" taunted Premarom. "Then I'll call you the Great Uninvited. Go home, little ranger."

Urgamdir could not resist taking this opportunity. He walked up to the ranger and spoke into his hooded face.

"I don't need your name, imperial. Next time you follow me, I'll kill you."

"I have let you live as well, more than once, but only for sport and coin," the ranger said. "Enjoy your time in the north. If you find the courage to come see Gilgalem burn, I will meet you once more in the night."

Urgamdir's heavy first crunched into his face, too quick and unexpected for even the ranger to evade. The ranger picked himself up and drew his dagger, but Danyhad and the others pulled Urgamdir away as the ranger encountered five arrow tips pointed at his face.

The ranger stood still, breathing fiercely and gritting his teeth as blood spilled out between them. Urgamdir looked back at him as he filed past the toll shack with the others. Premarom mounted a horse hidden behind the shack. He rode up to the ranger and looked down on him.

"Go. You can tell your marshal that this Gallerlander chieftain is dead, as he undoubtedly will be. And you can tell your marshal that I hit you, as I certainly would have."

Urgamdir stopped to watch the ranger sheath his dagger and wipe his mouth with his arm. He flit the snow from his black cloak and, without another word, turned and walked back down the road. Urgamdir smiled to himself, but the watchful eyes of Premarom reminded him he was far from escaping the dangers around him.

55

OWERDIR

Naren-Dra Mountains
Winterfall, 2269

Owerdir awoke sitting at the mouth of the cave with his hands bound in front of him, surrounded by large sacks. It was his first good look at his hands. The fingers on the right were beginning to turn black, mangled and puss filled. The left was better, having only two fingers that were decaying.

The snow-dusted glade of junipers was busy with the activity of his captors. Most had their wooden masks slipped up over their heads like hats, enjoying the bright sun on their unpainted faces. Their furs were an eclectic patchwork of rabbit, wolf, bear, and mountain lion. They wore wooden shoes with rounded tips and iron-spiked soles that allowed them to walk effortlessly on the icy terrain.

None of these people, whom Owerdir presumed to be the Naren-Dra, appeared to carry weapons. Their hammers, chisels, picks, and iron-ringed gloves could be used as such, but these appeared to be reserved for work. They labored in silence, using elaborate nods and hand gestures to communicate. Owerdir was curious about the masks. They were solid single pieces of juniper wood carved to curve around their entire face and ears, with narrow eye slits breaking their smooth surfaces.

Finally, one of the Naren-Dra noticed Owerdir's gaze. He rushed over and raised a hand to strike the Gallerlander, but a grunt from another man stopped him. This second man was tall and arrived with a pair of mountain goats nearly the size of the foreigners' horse beasts and with shaggy taupe hair. They were bulky rams harnessed together, sure footed and tame. They sniffed curiously in Owerdir's direction.

The tall man reached his gloved hand toward Owerdir. He braced himself, but the man merely pulled out a tether hidden by the bag in front of him. This he latched onto the rams' yoke and they pulled. Owerdir realized he and the sacks around him were the load. Other teams of rams pulled supplies loaded into giant tortoise shells upturned like boats. The rams did not need to be steered. A few jerking nods from their masters and they were off, one following another.

It was windier on this side of the cave. All the Naren-Dra were wearing their wooden masks but Owerdir was forced to bury his head between his knees. Inside the bags he could hear clinking of stones, the swish of sand, and the crinkle of dried leaves. The sway of the shell soon lulled him back to sleep.

ॐ

The slowing of the mountain goats' pace woke Owerdir. In a spacious glen fenced by ancient junipers was a large stone building with a fire glowing in every window. The rams brought his shell sled up to the oval door, which was emblazoned with a large blue symbol above the handle. It looked like a sliver of moon lying on its back, with a plant sprouting up from the middle and its flower appearing as a radiant sun. He looked toward the clear sky above to discern any omens but was quickly hoisted from the tortoise shell.

Owerdir was weak from cold and hunger. When the door of the hut opened, masked Naren-Dra came out and picked him up. He was ushered to a table in the middle of the hut. The tall man who had prevented him from being slapped sat across from Owerdir and slid his mask up over his head. The others busied themselves bringing all the sacks and equipment into the hut.

"This is your home?" attempted Owerdir in Gali. He tried to smile at the tall man, but he was certain his own fear showed through. "Any food?" he continued, but the man remained silent and stared at him. He did not appear hostile, so Owerdir rested his frostbitten hands on the table and looked around.

Any wall space not used for windows or hearths was lined with wooden shelves from top to bottom. They were filled with little leather bags, mushrooms, small pots of glistening powders, little boughs laden with dried berries, bits of fur, feathers of every color, baskets of blotched and dappled eggs, and many kinds of glassy stones that Owerdir had seen in the cave.

The floor was smooth stone tile littered with wood shavings and fragrant pine needles. Owerdir smelled food in the pots hanging in the hearths and remained hopeful he would be fed.

In the middle of the table was a candle. He had not seen once since marching Rildning as a captive to Nalembalen, and seeing him write in his journal by candlelight. Owerdir and the other Gallerlanders had been fascinated by it, and it was the first time he hoped the high king would spare Rildning.

A plump, old woman waddled over. She directed the men to put sacks here and there. There was no elaborate nodding or hand gestures as there had been outside. Inside the hut they all seemed to speak normally, but in their own tongue.

When all the workers had left, the old woman came and sat across from Owerdir with the tall man. Her eyes were wide and her face was weathered. Owerdir was put at ease by her grandmotherly gaze and bright green eyes. But when she spoke again the man pulled from his furs a parchment Owerdir recognized as the one he had been entrusted by the Sage to carry.

The old woman opened it and read with some difficulty. An eyebrow lifted when she was done deciphering, then she hummed and stared at Owerdir. He wondered whether the correct message had gotten through.

Owerdir's fears flared when the old woman spoke to the tall man and he retrieved a large knife from a shelf. He slid the blade back and forth over the candle flame as the old woman watched Owerdir. Owerdir's eyes went back and forth between her and the heating of the knife.

She took the knife from the man and gave him orders. Owerdir watched as she slid the knife into the hot coals of the hearth fire, not noticing the man circling behind him until he had taken hold of Owerdir.

The tall man clamped down on Owerdir's wrists, pushing them to the table with his iron-ringed gloves. The old woman returned with the knife, now red-hot. Owerdir yelled out as she approached, but she ignored him. With quick action she cleaved off his frostbitten fingers. He screamed though his hands had become numb with rottenness—the sight of loss was more painful than the severing. Owerdir passed out as the hot blade sealed the wounds shut.

When he woke, his finger stubs were bandaged. The old woman was pinching brown powder from a cup and sprinkling it over the candle. Satisfied that he was awake, she brought him a bowl of stew from the cooking pot and a stone mug of herbal brew. She carefully spooned it to his mouth.

Owerdir was exhausted but he consumed every morsel. He gritted his teeth, trying to comprehend the loss of so many fingers. He looked across the table at the tall man and old woman and found empathy in their faces.

The man pulled the mask off the top of his head and turned his head side to side, revealing shriveled fins where the cold had eaten his ears. Then he removed a glove, showing the loss of two fingers. Silently, the old woman showed scarred forearms, then pointed to her foot and held up three fingers.

"I see," Owerdir said. He nodded and they smiled. Despite his loss, he was beginning to feel optimistic. The old woman pointed to his bowl. He nodded and she refilled it twice more. When Owerdir was finally satisfied, she set aside the bowl, then unfolded his parchment on the table and pointed to it. She spoke in her own language but gestured with her arms and hands like mountains and then ram horns.

"You're telling me I must travel farther up?" Owerdir's tone was one of displeasure, which they clearly understood.

"When do we leave?" he said, looking at the door. The old woman got up and rustled around on her shelves and in her bags. She returned with a sack of food, a cup of salve, spiked wooden shoes, and a wooden mask. The inside of the mask was lined with soft fur. She also provided a fur coat, the same patchwork snow robe that the others wore.

Owerdir wished to show his gratitude, but he also did not wish to travel without rest. The tall man got up and stood by the door and put his gloves and mask back on, indicating to Owerdir there was no time for rest. He fumbled with the snow robe, so the woman helped, replacing his tattered thin furs with new ones and then the patchwork robe.

She situated the mask on his face and showed him how to pull it down and up again. She gave him a left glove of bear fur, and a covering for his right stump. Lastly, she put his food back on his shoulder and secured his parchment in a leather pouch that hung about his neck.

The old woman led him to the oval door and spoke a few words. Owerdir, clutching his bag and tucking his right nub close, tried to say his thanks. Then they were out in the snow.

The tall man led him to a larger sled and two rams that were tethered independently. The sled was two tortoise shells, one spooned within the other, and iron handholds lined the rim of the inner one. Inside the shell were several leather bundles of supplies.

The tall man pointed to himself and said what sounded like "Urikimesh," then slid his mask down. He pointed to Owerdir, and the Gallerlander responded with his name. "Owentheer," Urikimesh repeated. They climbed into the sled and the rams sped them off.

56

HILSINGOR

Fort Rommested, Bram Province
Midwinter, 2269

"There will be seven days of feasting in the capital to celebrate our victory," announced Hilsingor with great pride. Firkas beamed despite his bruised face and missing front teeth.

"I'm jealous also," Hilsingor continued with a smile. "I did not expect the Umbyrking to be where he was. Otherwise I would have taken the honor for myself. As it was, Firkas led his legion swift and well."

"You already have the golden helm of Gratgofa on your wall," Ravorglad said, "and he has Erambrin's broken stone-sword. Odon surrendered, and the Raffen may get Tirgranir before I have the honor of taking even a single swipe at an ivy-crowned head."

"Are you forgetting you killed Erambrin's predecessor, Woridam, shortly after the fall of Nalembalen? And who killed Odon's son, the red-haired chieftain of Yoredgoyn? And which knight tamed the Hangodir clan? The nobles of Eglamour have feasted more than once in your honor, my forgetful commander."

"Woridam wasn't wearing the ivy crown at the moment I killed him," Ravorglad said. "Still, I should like the honor of killing Tirgranir."

"This cannot be promised to you," Hilsingor replied. "We will see what becomes of Gilgalem in the spring."

"In the meantime," persisted Ravorglad, "let me take my crusaders to the peninsula of the Nake. We should punish them for fighting alongside the Gallerlanders."

"Have you not heard of the evil Memelos magic in that land?" Firkas asked. "The Gallerlanders and the Raffen call the Nake stone worshipers for good reason."

"Your provincial knights and heathen expendables may believe in that rubbish, but my crusaders fear no Nake spirits. We will slay Memelos in any of his forms, whether will-o'-the-wisp or barbarian spawn."

"Perhaps neither of you has heard of Admiral Arnasbirg's efforts on the Nake peninsula," Hilsingor said. "Arnasbirg wrote this to me himself. The Nake had constructed no docks of any sort, so Arnasbirg's ships had searched along the coasts of the peninsula for some time, but they could not find a suitable natural harbor. The coastlines are rocky and high cliffed, with white waters all around, too treacherous even for rowboats to pull in. When they had nearly given up, they found a low rocky shore. The admiral sent a landing boat with a few well-armored naval knights and crew.

"As they drew up to the shore, they felt as though a strong wind was pulling them inland, but there was unusual movement of the bushes among the rocks. There was no one on the shore but they felt the need to draw swords.

"In an instant, their swords were ripped from their hands and flew onto the rocks. When they tried to retrieve them, the knights fell and were unable to rise, as if invisible hands held them down. They screamed for help but the crew was afraid. One of them went ashore with his spear, but this too was eaten by the rocks. Being without armor, the crewman leaped back into the surf to return to the boat.

"When the rest of the crew saw this, they pushed off from the shore as quick as they could, leaving the naval knights to squirm and shout on the rocks. When they returned to the admiral's ship, fear gripping their faces like a stroke, they reported the knights had been killed. But when it got out that no Nake people had been encountered and no fighting had occurred, the crewmen were forced to tell their improbable tale. The admiral ordered twenty lashes for those men for abandoning his knights, a light sentence. But by then all of his men had heard the frightening story and feared the evil of the Nake lands.

"The admiral did not say whether he returned to that shore to retrieve his knights, but I suspect he avoided doing so to keep his men from mutinying. I'm uncertain what to make of the crew's story myself, but it apparently was enough to make Arnasbirg abandon plans to raid the peninsula."

"A good bedside story for your grandchildren." Ravorglad chuckled. "For a people who worship oddly shaped boulders, the Nake have some trickery that effectively scared off the empire's most honored seaman and his veteran fleet."

"Nevertheless," the marshal continued, "the scouts say the Nake have fully retreated and are sealing off the approaches to their peninsula with boulders and traps. As long as they don't return to the interior, and the Gallerlanders remain scattered, the Nake won't be a threat. So we will not waste any more time with them."

"We will march south to Gilgalem then?" Firkas asked.

"Not yet. We have done enough campaigning this winter, none of which I had planned. The men need rest. When spring arrives we'll be relentless in the march. That time draws near. Let us return to Rachard to prepare."

57

MRIGAMAD

Calbrian Sea
Midwinter, 2269

The wind was cold but Mrigamad and Anfinnan stood at the prow of the imperial ship to take some fresh air. Mrigamad felt naked without his windrazor latched to his side. He resented being ordered by Trelnaf, the drigoman, to stow his sword below; the crew was not accustomed to having long blades in their way, Trelnaf had explained.

Mrigamad intensely disliked the pompous, big-nosed drigoman. Mrigamad thought him an odd choice for an emissary, except that his Rahlampian speech was good enough to understand, even if the domnitar complained about it. Trelnaf said his father had taken a Rahlampian wife upon the death of his mother, so he had learned the speech from her as a young boy.

Mrigamad had little time to speak privately with Anfinnan since they had left Rahlampia via the Pernadun River. The drigoman constantly accompanied Anfinnan, telling him all about the empire and Eglamour. What's more, Anfinnan brought his adult son, Morlbeag, who always looked sickly and was said to be infirm. Mrigamad couldn't guess why the domnitar brought him, but finally Mrigamad and Anfinnan were above deck alone.

"How do you plan to convince the other tribal leaders in Eglamour to leave the empire?" Mrigamad asked.

"I don't," Anfinnan said.

267

"But I thought . . . You told Rildning—"

"I told that fool what he wanted to hear," Anfinnan said. "And what Tirgranir wanted to hear."

"The Gallerlanders are depending on our help," Mrigamad fumed. "Your gift of an entire landship of food will be seen by them as a sign of trust."

"When have the Gallerlanders and Rahlampians ever trusted each other? I sent the food to get Rildning out of our realm and lull the Gallerlanders. I don't want the empire to think we are aiding them; they'll always be our enemy. And unlike them, I know a stronger foe when I see one. We will ally with the empire against the Gallerlanders."

"Rildning trusted me far earlier than I trusted him," Mrigamad protested.

"He's not a Gallerlander. He's a liability for them and a traitor to his own race. The only reason I didn't send his head to the Frontier Corps was because I wanted him to provide Tirgranir a reason to believe we would help them or help negotiate their surrender. We will have peace and a new ally before they suspect otherwise."

"You cannot use the cloak of the domnitar in this way. How can you—"

"Hold your tongue! I'm the domnitar, and I'll do what is best for the Rahlampians."

"Do our chiefs know?"

Anfinnan gave him a hard stare. "You are like your father, which is why you—despite being the chief of your clan—will never wear the domnitar cloak. Of course some of the chieftains know the reason for my voyage. The others don't want to know the details of such things. I go to win peace for our people. All of the chiefs will welcome it when I return with an agreement in hand."

"I don't want to serve the empire," Mrigamad said. "Just being here on their ship makes me feel . . . corrupted. I won't be part of your scheme."

"Yes, you will. You can speak to the empire's naval attacks and the Raffen attacks on our lands. I will depend on you to help me win concessions from them. I want the boldness of your father, Mearnsod the Floodbringer, in my entourage. Your father was a fool, but a brave fool. Follow me, and we can build a new kingdom."

"Kingdom?" Mrigamad scoffed. "There is no such thing in Rahlampia, unless you intend to make yourself a king. Is that why you brought your son? Is Morlbeag meant to show the exarch you have a legitimate heir? When they see his stunted mind, they—"

Anfinnan backhanded him. When Mrigamad moved to spring upon him, his arms were arrested by Trelnaf's two knights. He struggled but they had him firmly.

"You will help my effort," the domnitar said calmly, "then you will return with me to Rahlampia to help convince the chieftains to accept the new era. You are senior and well respected, and they will listen to your words. But if at any time I have cause to doubt your loyalty—not just to me but to the future of Rahlampia—then I'll have the unfortunate task of telling the chiefs of your accidental death at sea. Is that clear?"

Mrigamad knew he would do no good for Rahlampia if he got himself killed. He would have to be patient. He turned and looked out at the sea.

"That's better," Anfinnan said. "It's not all about me, of course. The tales will call you 'Mrigamad the Kingbringer' for many years to come."

58

RILDNING

Eastern Wilderness of Vaynland
Midwinter, 2269

Rildning watched the snow rush by below. From the stern of the *Earthark* he had a clear view of the massive tracks left on the land behind them. The ruts of the six giant wheels snaked through the snow and mud, the hull still too high to even scrape the top of the drifts.

The landscape was different from when he and Mrigamad walked from Gilgalem. They had taken a different route as the *Earthark* forced them to go around the wooded and mountainous areas. Otherwise there was no snowy rockfield, hill, frozen marsh, lake, or river they could not cross with ease.

He was sure the Rahlampian crew of the *Earthark* had been instructed to return the landship to Rahlampia once the food was offloaded, but he hoped that, in time, Anfinnan would decide to help the Gallerlanders by sending more landships. No imperial cavalry would be able to defeat such a craft, though any ship was vulnerable to fire.

Rildning tried to be friendly with the crew despite not knowing their language, but they disliked or distrusted him. So the days passed slowly for him. He made himself as comfortable as possible, thinking much about Eniri and Enildir. He also wondered about the other envoys. He would not be returning to Gilgalem with a solid new ally for the Gallerlanders, but he hoped Anfinnan would see the other enslaved kings at Eglamour and change his mind.

Turning to leave the stern, Rildning caught sight of a black blur on the distant plain from which they had come. It soon took the form of a rider. Rildning tried to hail one of the crewmen, but they ignored him. He watched as the dot became two, then tree distinct riders. They were clearly riding hard, using the wheel ruts made by the *Earthark* for their path.

Rildning again hailed the crew. Finally one of them bothered to look and relayed his concern to the others. By then the three riders became five. Rildning drew his sword, prompting the crew to do the same.

The crew donned reed-plate armor and readied their shorter windrazors, adapted to fighting aboard ship. There were no bows but each had belt bags of black throwing stones carved with crisscrossing rings for gripping. A crewman with a scarred cheek handed a bag to Rildning.

The riders were closing the distance quickly. Rildning saw eight of them now, heavily cloaked, and they were not Rahlampians. Rildning surmised that whoever they were, they were not friendly.

Rildning and two ringstone-throwers waited at the stern, while the third crewman steered the landship. When the riders split into two groups, Rildning motioned for the throwers to post themselves on either side of the *Earthark*. He would wait at the stern to protect the steering crewman.

The riders were close enough now for Rildning to make out the splotchy blue face paint of the Raffen. They flung their cloaks up, revealing their weapons and one steel-clad knight. A banner fluttered open, showing the starcross of the Frontier Corps. The riders bristled with swords and spears, and the single mounted archer took aim at the steering crewman. Rildning jumped behind the wooden battlement that protected the steering deck as an arrow sunk into the battlement. Then the riders fanned out around the *Earthark*.

The steering crewman turned the wheel side to side, causing the landship to weave back and forth, trying to crush the riders, but they maneuvered away and still kept up with the landship. The Raffen who had gone under the belly fared worse. Rildning felt a slight bump before seeing the rider and his horse thrown up behind a wheel with red snow.

Rildning could not see the archer, so he jumped out and joined the crewmen in pelting the raiders. The lightly armored Raffen took care to avoid the ringstones or parry them. The heavily armored knight seemed unconcerned until a well-aimed stone struck his helmet and he wavered. The riders' spears broke like twigs in the spokes of the wheels.

Rildning saw the archer reappear from the other side and motioned to a nearby crewman. When the archer brought up his shield, they targeted the head of his horse. Tired from the chase and now bleeding, the animal relented.

The rest of the raiders circled the ship, looking up and down its hull. The knight, despite the continued weaving of the steering crewman, ventured close enough to give a frustrated hack at the belly. With a few of the riders and horses now suffering from bloody welts, they slowed their pace and let the *Earthark* pull away from them.

Rildning and the crewman cheered. The thrower who had been on the other side of the ship did not even realize an arrow had cut right through his furred cloak. He wiggled a few fingers in the hole and laughed heartily.

Rildning now understood why the crew did not bother with bows. The *Earthark* was untouchable and just as fast as a ship on the sea. But he could not help picturing a landship decked with archers as a new bulwark against the cavalry of the Frontier Corps. He wondered whether the Rahlampians would supply a fleet of landships, or if he could convince the Gallerlanders to build them.

59

OWERDIR

Naren-Dra Mountains
Midwinter, 2269

Owerdir and Urikimesh traveled for several days through howling wind and rugged terrain. Through the slits in his mask, Owerdir could see steep slopes of white snow on dark rock that jutted up from the valley floors. Twisted junipers grew anywhere they could gain a root hold, stunted by decades of steady wind. The peaks of the ridges were usually cloaked with clouds, but today they were clear. Their summits shone brilliant in the sun.

Though it was bitterly cold, the snowfall wasn't as deep as it had been below the ridges. The two mountain rams were undaunted, pulling the double tortoise shell with relative ease and stopping to rest when they needed to. Owerdir was still surprised Urikimesh did not guide or control them in any way.

Urikimesh would forget it was a Gallerlander behind the mask, sometimes launching into elaborate hand signals and head nods. When Owerdir shrugged in response, Urikimesh simply pointed and grunted.

Making camp was hard work. At dusk they would unharness the rams and pull the inner shell out. When the rams had grazed their fill of sparse twigs or the food from Urikimesh's hand, the rams would lie down in the snow. Urikimesh would flip the shells over the rams. There, with the tortoise neck hole for breathing, they would sleep sheltered from the wind.

For their own shelter, Urikimesh chose a stout broad-limbed juniper with deep snow drifts around the trunk. They dug out the snow and packed it into a wall and cut boughs to form a roof leaning from the trunk to the wall. They slept curled around the trunk and did not make a fire. But they were out of the wind and safe from night hunters.

One night Owerdir was awoken by the sound of fierce scratching and vicious screams as an animal tried to get the rams, which stayed in their armor-like shells. Urikimesh did not name these animals, but Owerdir understood the need to stay quiet. Urikimesh relaxed after hanging a sachet of bitter-smelling material from the boughs. The following morning Owerdir examined the shells, but he could not discern claw marks from the gashes and scrapes caused by sliding over ice and rock.

&

In the afternoon of the following day, the rams brought them to the foot of a jagged slope. Its loose boulders and sharp spires fended off the snow and glared defiant in the sunlight. The rams stopped and waited patiently. Owerdir presumed they were lost.

Urikimesh pointed for Owerdir to exit the sled, then he fiddled with the iron holds on either side of the rim. Next, he got out and removed the inner shell, flipped it, and together they placed it over the first like a roof. They crawled back in using the aligned neck holes. When they were again seated, Urikimesh lifted the shell to align the rims before locking them in place with the iron fasteners, making a fully covered sled, while the neck holes still allowed a forward view. The rams seemed satisfied and began their ascent.

Owerdir found the experience most unsettling. The enclosed sled crashed along the rocks carelessly. Over and again they would dangle in the air, pressed against the back of the shell as the rams mounted some precipice. Owerdir tried to remember how thickly woven the tethers were, or whether the yokes were cracked. He removed his mask to breathe air into his queasy insides. At one point Urikimesh looked back to find Owerdir at the back of the sled with arms and legs splayed out. Owerdir heard Urikimesh chuckle but felt no shame for his fear.

By day's end the crashing mountainside rapids gave way to smooth slopes and ice-filled ravines. The clouds faded and the snowfall thinned until the sky above was deep blue and cloudless. The air was fresh but Owerdir labored to breathe. His head felt as if he'd drunk too much of the Vayns' spruce beer. He sat down in the snow while Urikimesh converted the covered sled back into an open double hull, then they continued onward.

At last they came to a huge black stone gate with no wall on either side. Its great columns formed a fortress with empty windows and balconies. Only a pair of wood-masked guards stood in the great arch. Like the first settlement with the old woman, the guards did not possess any visible weapons. Urikimesh exchanged a few nods with the guards, and then the rams continued through the gate without stopping.

Once past the gate, Owerdir saw large stone huts, built in the same oval fashion as the old woman's. Black smoke rose from crooked chimneys, and warm light flooded from their windows. Around the huts and lining the paths were stunted trees and knotty hedges. Scarf-like banners hung from wooden poles at the entrances of the stone huts, each one embroidered with unique designs and colors.

The rams finally halted in front of a large stone house perched on a crag. It was tall and roundish, but much too broad and kinked to be called a tower. Its walls were a mix of raw stone and cut blocks, and the top was domed with layers of shale plates. It was half building and half mountain, with doors and windows woven between natural outcroppings. At the top was a spire with three scarf banners of white and sky blue.

After exiting their tortoise shell, Owerdir collapsed and found himself lying faceup on the ground with Urikimesh's mask looking over him. Urikimesh pulled him up and Owerdir felt the dizziness spin his eyes. Urikimesh spoke a few words before leaving him to rest a moment. He watched as Urikimesh retrieved three bells from a supply sack. He tied one around the neck of each ram then set them loose.

He stuffed the third bell into the pouch of his snow robe as the rams trotted off to graze among the hedges.

Urikimesh helped Owerdir regain his feet. He stood still for a moment, his head swimming and his lungs heaving. He saw the purple and crimson sunset, an omen for a night of revelations. The sky was so big and round up here. For a moment Owerdir forgot his troubles. He allowed his eyes to take in the view until Urikimesh tugged him forward.

Together they climbed the steps of the great house and approached the great oval door. The guards, who once again lacked weaponry of any kind, exchanged nods with Urikimesh. Owerdir recalled how his own people had thoroughly searched Rildning and the other foreigners before taking them to see the high king. The Naren-Dra had no similar procedure or simply did not fear him.

Painted on the great door was the same moon-flower-sun symbol Owerdir had seen on the old woman's door. It creaked open enough for them to file in.

Pushing up his mask, Owerdir saw a hall of polished stones of every color and pattern, similar to the patchwork furs of their snow robes. Columns of stone with the same Naren-Dra symbol reached up to the vaulted roof. Between the columns wandered giant tortoises. Their wrinkly skin was blue-gray and their shells were adorned with hat-like furs trimmed with silver thread.

Owerdir watched them as they walked, his every step crushing dried herbs underfoot that calmed his dizziness and eased his breathing. There were many people in the great hall, all still wearing their snow robes despite the hearth fires.

They walked the length of the hall toward a dais of six thrones arranged in a half circle. Urikimesh bowed low as they approached, so Owerdir did the same. The men and women who occupied the thrones stared at Owerdir. Urikimesh spoke and they listened.

After a few moments Owerdir thought it would be a good time to bring out the Sage's parchment. As he reached into his robe, redness clouded his face and he fell to the floor, coughing and spitting furiously. His eyes filled with tears and he panicked when he could no longer see and could barely breathe.

Urikimesh came to him, shouting. Then there was more shouting. Ice-cold water wet Owerdir's lips and face, and he drank the burning down. They wiped his eyes with a sweet-smelling cloth and made him eat spongy bits of something flavorless.

He was still blinded when they pulled him to his feet. The speaking continued, more urgent but not shouting. Another voice was near, deeper and angry. Owerdir heard this man say what sounded like "Nalembalen." He tried to calm his breathing to listen for more. The men took him by the arms and lowered him into a chair. A cup was placed in his good hand and he was made to drink more cold water.

Owerdir now heard many voices. It was like a debate, but as his sight returned he noticed that one of the chairs was now vacant. He looked about him, finding Urikimesh, an attendant with a pitcher of water, and the deep-voiced man who was stooping to look at him.

Through watery eyes Owerdir saw this man's sullen expression quickly change to a smile when he looked upon him. He was silver bearded with pale gray eyes and gapped teeth. This man stood tall again, patted Owerdir on the shoulder, and then retook his place on the empty throne.

The debate continued as Owerdir's eyesight improved. He did not make any sudden movements, for fear of again attracting the strange magic of the Naren-Dra. As he waited, Owerdir wondered if he had done the right thing in volunteering to come to these mountains. Perhaps a Vayn more familiar with the lower reaches would have been a better choice. Perhaps the brothers could have been entrusted with the task without Owerdir slowing them down.

"Come forward," the deep voice said. Owerdir thought he was imagining the words. "Come forward, I say." He was stunned to hear the Gali language spoken so clearly by the silver-bearded man. "Well?" the man said. Owerdir stood and presented himself to the six.

"You speak the language of my people?" Owerdir asked. His own voice sounded strained, with the burning and soreness of his throat not quite quenched by the water.

"Yes, but only me," the man said. "Now, Urikimesh says you have a letter. In your pocket?"

Owerdir nodded but hesitated as he glanced at the guards.

The man spoke loudly to the guards near the dais, then turned back to Owerdir. "Go on then."

Still wary, Owerdir closed his eyes as he slowly reached into his robe with his good hand. He pulled out the parchment and held it away from his body with two fingers, wary of another sudden burst of cough and burn. A guard fetched it for the silver-bearded man. He read it carefully once to himself, then read it aloud to the other thrones.

There was much gasping and whispering from the thrones and the people in the hall. Everyone except a white-haired grumpy-looking man whose face hardened before the debate resumed. This man railed against the letter more than anyone else. Again, Owerdir hoped the right message had been written by the Sage. He watched a tortoise wander across the dais as the debate continued.

After the silver-bearded man argued back at the old man, all six of the thrones erupted angrily and their courtiers joined in. Despite the foreignness of the Naren-Dra language and their abode, Owerdir could not help but be reminded of the divisions among the Gallerlanders. He wondered if any of the envoys had found a unified ally willing to help.

60

ENIRI

Chadwoid, Nydenland
Midwinter, 2269

Their bickering was incessant. Eniri had never seen a more unusual arrangement among rulers. She was relieved to not understand the angry shouts of the twin kings of the Nyden, sitting upon their ugly thrones.

She had told them, through Bothrobim, of the defeats of the Gallerlanders, the march of the foreigners and the Raffen, and the dire situation at Gilgalem. She trusted Bothrobim enough to translate her words in full, and, as he had predicted while aboard ship, the twin kings did not agree on how to respond.

"I warn you again," Bothrobim had said as they made their way through the harbor to the hilltop fortress. "Toredwoak and Belordoos have had dueling knives at each other's throats for the past four years, and Belordoos has the scars to prove his losses. They are more likely to be merely entertained by your story than they are to sympathize with you, despite the similar hardships of the Nyden. Only Belordoos may consider sending aid of some sort, but he isn't truly in command. Toredwoak is." But Eniri had insisted.

Bothrobim had kept her safe and hidden in the ship until they arrived at the harbor. When the time came to bring her out, he claimed she was a common Vayn woman, captured in Amlon and kept as his personal slave. She had hoped to be smuggled off the ship in secret, perhaps in a barrel or crate, but Bothrobim insisted the Raffen would look in every container before allowing anything to come ashore, and they did.

The Raffen at first seemed no different from the raiders that had swept across Vaynland. They were only concerned with what they could loot. But she soon discovered the Raffen in Nydenland looked different in one important way: they wore more electrum ornaments than she had ever seen on a person.

Her heart broke when she stepped off the ship with Bothrobim, her tears undoubtedly reinforcing the ruse that she was his new slave. She noticed some Raffen had melted down the electrum to fashion their own designs. Part of her wanted to rip the jewelry from them, and part of her wanted to return to the ship. But she tried to center her thoughts on Gilgalem and her family.

The Nyden harbor of Chadwoid looked much like Amlon. The harbor was blanketed with snow that was refreshed daily with flurries. The docks were crowded with Raffen and dour Nyden who wore many scars on their faces. Bothrobim explained that they were face flogged by the Raffen after the latest uprising, but they were the ones the Raffen let live.

Not far inland from Chadwoid harbor was the seat of power for the twin kings, a great fortress of octagonal basalt stone scared by many wars. It overlooked the harbor and the surrounding sea from its windy perch on the craggy edge of dwarf tree forests.

“These days,” Bothrobim told Eniri as they climbed up, “the twin kings’ court is as packed with Raffen as the harbor, but I’m one of the few who can ask my uncles for a private meeting. There you will plead your case.”

It did not turn out to be that easy. The uncles refused to dismiss their courtiers. They showed their nephew Bothrobim much less respect than Eniri expected. She had pictured two brother kings sharing power, with one holding the dominant influence over the other. But it was Toredwoak, the one who had become cozy with the Raffen, who gave the orders. Belordoos ranted but had little sway. Bothrobim did his best to relay Eniri’s verbal message requesting help for Gilgalem, but he was constantly interrupted.

"They are arguing about what we have told them," Bothrobim said.

"I can see that," Eniri replied.

At length, Belordoos ignored his brother and spoke to Bothrobim.

"My good uncle says he is impressed with your courage, though this task should not have been given to a princess."

"Tell him I came on my own. Vaynking Tirgranir did not send me, but I speak for all the Gallerlanders."

"Are you sure you want to say that?" Bothrobim asked. She eyed him sternly, so he translated. It drew a chuckle from both kings, followed by rowdy laughter from courtiers within earshot. "Uncle Toredwoak says in that case you are a prisoner of the Nyden and will be ransomed back to Tirgranir." Bothrobim's face was dark. "He is serious, Eniri."

"Tell him I refuse to be his prisoner. I'll not play games while my people starve. But I will accept—"

"Eniri, you—"

"And tell them the electrum hanging around Toredwoak's neck will be going back with me regardless," she said.

"You don't want to say that."

"Tell him." Her face burned with anger.

She knew if Gratgofa were alive to see what she had, he would have killed Toredwoak. She did not fear the Nyden. Bothrobim's translation caused great laugher from the bad uncle and most courtiers. Oddly, Belordoos sat silently.

"Uncle Toredwoak says if you love your people so much, he will send a ship of food. He said your boldness has purchased that. But the ship will only sail if . . ."

"If what?" she demanded.

"If you give yourself to him. And he will also consider further help. Eniri, he wants to enslave you in return for aid. You have been reckless. He won't let you leave now."

Eniri was speechless. Her mind was clouded with visions of a starving Gilgalem, a starving Enildir, or herself in chains in this fortress. She saw Toredwoak summon an attendant who promptly left the hall after a whisper from him. Then he spoke to Bothrobim.

"My uncle says he has summoned his Raffen commander so your decision can be made easier. He says if you do not choose well, he will tell the Raffen about the situation at Gilgalem, a weakness they will surely want to know, he says."

Eniri's anger returned. "I braved the sea and my enemies to come here seeking your help in good faith. If you won't help us, at least do not hinder me."

Toredwoak laughed again.

"My uncle asks, when have the Gallerlanders ever helped the Nyden?" Bothrobim said. "The Gallerlanders have always thought themselves to be the greatest of the tribes, he says, yet now you come begging when Gallerlandia is on its knees. The Nyden have found peace with the Raffen and will not bow to demands from a defeated people. Eniri, I'm sorry—"

"Don't!" She brushed his hand away and struggled against tears. "I'll be leaving now."

She turned toward the door but found it blocked by face-flogged Nyden guards. There was no pity in their torn faces. She could hear Toredwoak's commanding tone behind her.

"Uncle has ordered that you be taken to his private chambers, to dress and prepare for tonight's feast," he said.

"I want to leave, Bothrobim."

"We have no choice," he said as she shook her head. "Please, Eniri, you must listen to me now. Do not fight him. I'll think of something."

61

URGAMDIR

Gradhild, Barres Province
Midwinter, 2269

Despite his situation, Urgamdir felt fortunate that Premarom was not far from his brother Highchief Harkarom. The Bronhildi king was camped outside his new capital of Gradhild, only a few days away from where the Bronhildi captured Urgamdir at their toll shack. It was evening when they reached the tents.

Harkarom was seated on a chair that had legs carved to resemble eagle wings uplifted. The highchief was a tall man with a slender face. His black hair was cut short to the skull, almost shaven, and he had a thin band of a beard without a mustache. His breastplate was filled with ornate etchings of eagles.

Premarom placed his hand on his heart to greet his brother, then explained the situation.

Harkarom listened carefully before speaking. "Yet he is not restrained by ropes or chains?"

"None needed," Danyhad said. "The Gallerlander came willingly."

"May I speak?" Urgamdir asked. His Bronhildi speech had steadily improved since traveling with his captors. Harkarom nodded.

"Vaynking Tirgranir sent me as an envoy, not an enemy. I carry a message for you from our council at Gilgalem."

"Speak your message then," Harkarom said.

"The Gallerlanders are scattered and hard-pressed by the foreigners. Our three kings still fight but we are increasingly desperate. Your people and ours have had alliances in the past, bound, then broken again by the tides of time. But the foreigners are different.

"We must not ally with them, but rather rekindle our old bonds. The father of my mother was Bronhildi, so I'm living proof of those former bonds of friendship. In the name of Vaynking Tirgranir, and on behalf of the Umbyrking and Goynking, I ask you to lay aside your treaty with the foreigners and instead fight alongside us to rid our realms of them."

"You risked your life in winter through lands held by me and the empire, just to deliver these words?" Harkarom asked.

"My companion gave his life, and others may have as well," the Umbyr replied. "The Gallerlanders, young and old, who shelter at Gilgalem depend on your help. You must—"

"With your message now complete, don't presume to tell me what I must do," Harkarom said. "Listen well, Urgamdir the odd-blooded. While it's true alliances between the Gallerlanders and the Bronhildi have come and gone through the generations, your passion reminds me of the reckless and uncompromising nature of so many of your brethren chieftains who, in times past, found it easier to take Bronhildi lands than make peace.

"High King Gratgofa was truly the last of the great lords of your people," Harkarom continued. "Were he still alive today, the situation might be different. But now you are left with men like Tirgranir, since, you should know, Odon has surrendered and will be a vassal of the empire, as I am.

"Gilgalem will fall, as sure as spring will come. Only then, it seems, will the Gallerlanders see that their dominance has ended and a new era has begun. Gallerlandia may have been great, but the foolishness of its people and its kings will ensure your tribe is humbled and remade into the least.

"Even so, your blood won't be on my hands. As an uninvited envoy of the enemy, you will be ransomed to Marshal Hilsingor of the Frontier Corps. You call them 'foreigners,' but their proper names should become familiar to you. You shall remain imprisoned in Gradhild, where you may recognize cells once used by the Gallerlanders to jail Bronhildi. When a price is agreed upon, you will be sent to the marshal."

Kemet, one of Danyhad's brothers who had remained the quietest Bronhildi during their travel from the south, stepped forward to stand with Urgamdir.

"His coming was in good faith," Kemet said to the highchief, "and his plea is genuine. War and peace have been between our peoples like rain and sunshine, but surely they are our closer brothers than the men from across the sea. I believe chieftain Isberen was right to join the Gallerlanders, and I'm now ashamed to have abandoned them."

"Then I will offer you for sale to the marshal as well," Harkarom said. "And if he won't buy you, we'll kill you. As for the rest of you, your errant ways are forgiven as you were misled by Isberen, whom I wish could be killed again for his treachery. But as a price for your welcome, you must take the steel sword in your hand and the horse beast as your seat against the Gallerlanders you once served."

62

RILDNING

Gilgalem, Vaynland
Midwinter, 2269

Rildning received a cold welcome upon returning to Gilgalem, even as he helped unload and carry the Rahlampian food up the mountainside. Tirgranir did not speak to him at all. In the evening Rumban came to Rildning.

"The king will not see you because of the Frontier Corps banner he saw Mrigamad pull from your tunic as you left," Rumban explained.

"Why must he be so suspicious of me? Have I not repeatedly proven my loyalty to the Gallerlanders?"

"It was a peculiar thing to see, Rildning. Eniri defended you well, but when a king sees his enemy's symbols hidden in the clothes of one of his commanders, he naturally questions the reason. Many others suspect you as well and think you unworthy of returning to Gilgalem."

"It was merely a token, a memory."

"Tirgranir hasn't banished you, so it should pass," Rumban said. "The Rahlampian gift of so much food is most unexpected and will help. I noticed, by the way, that the food also tastes . . . peculiar."

"It's the salt," Rildning said. "As a coastal and marshland people, the Rahlampians are farmers of saltwater plants and tenders of brackish shrimp ponds. You will find pickleweed, shrimp loaves, mallow seedmeal cakes, and whelks. Quite good when you get used it."

"Even so, you have satisfied our people's hunger for a while longer," Rumban said. "I hope your journey was without much peril. Unfortunately, none of the other envoys have returned."

"Not even Owerdir?" Rildning asked. "I had thought he or Arbardir would have returned sooner, given their shorter journeys."

"Owerdir faces the dangers of high mountains and the cloud dwellers. Arbardir must find a way to convince the stone-worshiping Nake mystics. The Rahlampians have long been an enemy, but your path was guided and known. Come, you must rest."

They walked in silence toward Pindoarig tower.

"What happened to the food stores?" Rildning asked.

"It is still a mystery," the steward replied. "Signs of sabotage were found and—"

"Sabotage? How could that be? Only the Gallerlanders walk within Gilgalem."

"Except you," Rumban said.

"I see," Rildning said. "And what of the enemy, have they approached the mountain at all?"

"The Raffen riders go here and there, but none have dared to venture up. Also, another envoy was sent. Or rather, we learned she departed by her own will."

"She? Where?"

"Brace yourself, Rildning. Eniri went to the Nyden."

Rildning stopped walking.

"I tried to dissuade her, but—"

"You and Tirgranir let her go there?"

"Who are we to stop the Umbyrqueen?" he said.

Rildning noticed Rumban's normally helpful manner had darkened since he was away. From the terrace Rildning looked down into the bowl of Gilgalem, where the lamplights glowed warmly. The ancient place was at first a welcome sight to him, then it seemed distant and cold.

"And Enildir?" he asked.

"He is safe with Tirgranir's queen, Sabani. Like his mother, Enildir is an intelligent, independent little soul. He has been well cared for."

"Please take me to him."

"It is night and the Vaynking's household sleeps," Rumban answered. "Your old chambers are empty. Go and rest tonight, and you will be reunited with your son in the morning."

Rildning wanted to hold Enildir, but he was too exhausted to argue with the steward. He knew Sabani would continue to watch over him. He knew Tirgranir wanted the high kingship, and to be rid of Eniri and Rildning. But unlike the imperials, everything Rildning had learned about the Gallerlanders told him they would not murder one another for the high offices or riches.

They acted as a large family would. Though prone to constant squabbles, even in the face of destruction, they did not resort to bloodshed among themselves. Rildning had been frustrated many times in his efforts to unify the Gallerlanders, but their avoidance of internal bloodshed helped keep his hope alive that they would eventually come together to defeat the Frontier Corps. For the same reason, Rildning believed that in the end the Vaynking would choose to keep him as an ally.

There were many matters to attend to, but Rildning allowed his mind to drift to Eniri as he lay down for the night. He longed for her and hoped she would be safe. His last thoughts before sleep finally took him were of her emerald eyes.

63

OWERDIR

Sipadshur, Naren-Dra Mountains
Midwinter, 2269

Owerdir was awakened by Urikimesh. The sun had already risen. Their travel to the Naren-Dra's mountaintop settlement had completely exhausted him. Owerdir was offered goat cheese, raw mushrooms, and an odd fruit that was black dappled and scaly like a lizard. Urikimesh sat with him in the stone-walled apartment they had provided to him for the night. They sipped snow melt, looking at the last embers of the night's fire.

The Naren-Dra did not burn wood, as trees were scarce. Instead they burned black crumbly stones that smelled oily and gave off thick smoke. He heard them call the burning stones "kowl." Even with the fire, Owerdir had slept in the snow robe the old woman had given him.

When Owerdir had finished eating, Urikimesh led him back to the main hall where the six thrones were again locked in debate. One of them, a beautiful woman with pale eyes and golden hair, mediated between the silver-bearded man and the portly white-haired grump. The latter's pale face reddened when he saw Owerdir, whereas the former smiled warmly.

The woman appeared to issue orders to both men, and then their discussion ended. The silver-bearded man stepped down from the dais to greet Owerdir and Urikimesh.

"Bright morning to you," he said. "Please excuse our rudeness, we are simply preoccupied with the business of your letter. I'm Ankarmesh, the Seneschal of Sarbondibum and elder brother of Urikimesh. He has told me all about your troubles, at least the ones he has witnessed. No doubt your entire journey has been difficult."

"Yes, but still less difficult than what the people of Gilgalem face. I cannot read the contents of our Sage's letter, but I hope the words provide a hint of the plight of the Gallerlanders."

"Your Sage has told us well, but we will speak more on that later. First, you should know my people are not in agreement on whether to help or not. You and I must spend time together so I can better understand what has happened. And there are things I want you to see. Then we will see what can be done."

Urikimesh quietly departed from them, and Ankarmesh led Owerdir out of the great hall. Owerdir could not contain his curiosity as they walked down a window-lit corridor that looked out over the lower mountain peaks.

"How did you come to speak Gali so well?" he asked.

"That is a long story," Ankarmesh said. He chuckled but said no more.

Owerdir kept silent as they walked. From the windows he could make out that they were walking a narrow path along a cliff side. The drop was steep but he could see they were approaching a bend and a large outcropping beyond. The corridor soon ended at a door painted with the moon-flower-sun symbol.

Beyond the door was a circular room with a thick stone column in the middle. Ankarmesh led him to a large window set in the curved wall. In the distance they could see the black crags jutting up from the thick snows. The vast snowfall smoothed the contours of the ridges and valleys.

"They think because you trespassed the sacred mountains that we should not help you," Ankarmesh began.

"I did not know. The Sage did not—"

"Of course not. In truth, they wouldn't be keen to help you anyway. The Naren-Dra have no use for the affairs of the dwellers of the Low Earth."

"And yet, the old woman and your brother helped me get here," Owerdir said. "And you speak Gali."

Ankarmesh looked at him with a thoughtful nod. "My people want to remain isolated from the world," he said, "but that does not mean all Naren-Dra are ignorant of it."

"Does that mean the Naren-Dra could be persuaded to help?" Owerdir asked.

"No one here will help," Ankarmesh said. He seemed to share Owerdir's frustration.

"I've lost two friends and nearly my own life to your mountains," Owerdir said. "If I survive long enough to return to Gilgalem, I'll be of less use as a stub-fingered cripple. My sole task, my life itself has come down to securing the help of the Naren-Dra against a foe that will surely threaten even your high mountains."

Ankarmesh nodded knowingly. "I believe what you say. In fact, I saw the smoke rise from your greatest forest city. I've watched the foreign armies and their many ships. I've even seen the Raffen clans swirl around the plains below Gilgalem."

Owerdir was puzzled. "You mean you have heard tales?"

"No, I have seen. Put on your mask and follow me."

Owerdir followed him around to the far side of the column in the center of the room, which hid a spiral staircase. They climbed up several levels until they emerged on a narrow tower that stood in the center of a broad, flat roof. The sun was bright and the wind frigid.

On the western rim of the platform was a giant wooden wheel that loomed over them. A long wooden tube, like a hollowed-out tree trunk, extended from the center of his wheel and tapered down toward them. It rested within a smaller wheel that rode the rim of their tower. Both wheels rolled easily along grease-caked tracks. Owerdir could not imagine the purpose of this strange contraption. Ankarmesh put his masked face to the small wheel hub, then waved Owerdir over to have a look.

As his face neared the wheel hub, Owerdir caught a glint of light from it, as if a silver gem was embedded in the hub. But as his eyes came closer, the silver glimmer became a blurry landscape that grew larger as he moved closer. Startled, he jerked back from the wheel and clutched the rim of the tower, afraid that by some Naren-Dra magic he was falling into the broken clouds below.

Ankarmesh smiled. "This is called an eyepiece. Try again."

Slower and with more caution, Owerdir returned to the eyepiece. Again the landscape came into view, as if he were looking through a tiny window. He watched blurry black shapes move across the white. The picture changed when he moved from side to side, but he could make out mountains near the moving shapes. From the heights of the Naren-Dra, he could see one of the mountains was hollow at the top.

"Gilgalem," confirmed Ankarmesh when Owerdir gasped. "I have watched the Raffen swirl around it, as I told you. Gilgalem's plight is no mystery to me."

Owerdir withdrew from the wheel hub and looked out into the landscape. Gilgalem had disappeared. He looked out along the side of the wooden pipe, then returned to the hub and found Gilgalem again.

"What sort of magic is this?"

"There is no magic," Ankarmesh said with a polite grin, "only the inventiveness of the mind, despite what your people and other Low Earth dwellers may believe. It is called Kalbum-Nuna. In Gali it would mean the Wheeled Window of the World."

"What makes such a far-seeing eye possible?" Owerdir asked, still amazed.

"Only wood and crystal, originally crafted by hands long dead."

"What is crystal?"

"You must have seen them in the mine you snuck into, when you encountered the gatherers of Rimushira. She is the old woman who tends to the cave harvests and farms the crystals, only the finest to craft my lenses for Kalbum-Nuna." Ankarmesh could see Owerdir was thoroughly puzzled.

"Here, look," Ankarmesh continued. He removed his glove and pinched his fingers into a slit at the top of the small wheel. He pulled up and out came a round glassy disk. "This is a lens. Pure shulmel crystal."

"Ah, like quartz," Owerdir said. "Gallerlanders use it as children's toys, chipped from stones."

"It is not a toy. It is found only in our sacred mountains. We mine them in the caves, then grind them down. We heat the powder until it becomes crimson then white-hot, removing all impurities. We pour it into a mold where it cools clear, like ice. The larger lens in the big wheel down there required many shell loads, many days of forging by my father's father, Tizkarmesh. He was an alchemist as well as a seneschal and was viewed as an oddity, as am I. Do you know of the alchemists?"

"Are they great mountain warriors?"

"They are the interpreters of the sacred mountains and everything in them. Since the first dawn, the Naren-Dra have known what to pick, what to crush, what to mix, and what to fire. They are harvesters and planters, mist-makers and sun-breakers, and refiners of metals and airs. They are the alchemists."

"So they make your lenses, but you don't practice the craft of the alchemists yourself?"

"Not anymore," Ankarmesh said with a tone betraying regret. "As one of the six seneschals, I must devote myself to representing my people here in Sipadshur. While some of them still make time to pinch and stir, I set my eyes to the Wheeled Window of the World. My aging mind and hands are now better suited to the wheel vice the mortar and pestle. That is why I know of Nalembalen, Gilgalem, and your burdens. Perhaps I even know more than you."

Ankarmesh lifted a small wooden flap in the tower rim. Inside were two iron rings tied with gray twine. He pulled on one and the large wheel lurched to the right. Owerdir heard the faint grunt of men below. Ankarmesh watched through the lens, then pulled the second iron ring. Kalbum-Nuna jolted to a stop. Ankarmesh motioned for Owerdir to have a look as he spoke.

"There, you will see the new great city of your enemy. They have been busy, even through the winter. The clouds and snow have often obscured my view, but they are obviously clearing woodland and building much with stone. Farms and walls and such. The beasts they ride and the glint of their metal has multiplied."

"I can even see their flags," Owerdir said. "How can the Naren-Dra be unconcerned when you can watch all of this with the far-seeing eye?"

"Come," Ankarmesh said, "let us get out of the wind." They went back down the spiral stairs and removed their masks in the circular room. "I asked all the seneschals to come see the smoke of Nalembalen when the tree city fell," he continued. "Most came, but their hearts were unstirred. You must understand. The Naren-Dra care nothing for the Low Earth world, except to preserve their isolation from it."

"But you are different," Owerdir said. "You know so much about the world, yet you keep your knowledge to yourself?"

"There are a few reasons. Firstly, our realm is a confederation of clans. There is no high king as there is among the Gallerlanders. Not since the Gray Summers. Each seneschal travels here to Sipadshur, the Mountain Mast, to sit in council. Once in midwinter and once in midsummer. The current gathering is the Snowshelling, and the next will be the Sunstepping.

"Decisions are made by consensus only, or otherwise deferred to the next council. This is the fifth council where I've urged them to take seriously the world viewed through my grandfather's Wheeled Window. It is my hope—faint as it is—that your timing will prove fortunate."

"Why have you taken an interest in helping us, if you know they will favor isolation?" Owerdir asked. "Why have you continued urging them for so long?"

"The burning of Nalembalen was barbarous," Ankarmesh said. "It plucked my anger and stirred up . . . old memories." His gaze sank for a moment.

"Memories of what?" Owerdir asked.

"My younger days. Never mind that for now. I want you to address the council of the seneschals. They need to hear it from the mouth of a Gallerlander, not just an old man peering through a lens."

"I will," Owerdir said.

64

ODON

Odon had heard about Yelgoram's execution since coming to Eglamour. He guessed the open-air stone-hewn stage that he stood upon was the same platform they had used for his execution. Although some in the crowded square below him heckled the Goynking, he hoped this ceremony would be different.

Instead of sitting in his balcony above the square, the exarch himself stood beside Odon, as did the Goynking's drigoman. Chancellor Sarnaker was addressing the people, while the drigoman translated for Odon.

"And so, with this declaration of fealty," the chancellor concluded, "the Gallerlander tribe of Goyns is hereby admitted into the Brintilian Empire as a vassal people and ally. Let no man doubt their loyalty so long as the declaration rests in the hand of the emperor, and as long as a Goyn sits on the Imperial Council of Pemonia.

"As every people of the empire are respected, so let the Goyns be respected. As every people are taxed for the good of the empire, so let the Goyns be taxed. As every people are defended, so let them be defended. As every people enjoy peace, so let them enjoy peace. As every people demand justice, so let them have justice. And as every people are called to serve the empire, so let the Goyns serve when they are called.

"These are the five sacred pledges made between the emperor and every province of every realm of the empire."

A light snow drifted down as Odon listened to the translation echo after Sarnaker's words. When the speech ended, the exarch turned to him and grasped both of his hands, the way the Gallerlanders greeted one another. Odon bowed to the exarch, as he had been instructed to do. The crowd cheered and the long procession to Ralmo's cathedral began.

Odon followed the exarch and his retinue. Odon learned from the drigoman that no one walked ahead of the exarch, because he was the emperor's representative. The other government functionaries, important Goyn tribesmen, and musicians and jugglers followed the Goynking. At the end was a rearguard of Eglamour soldiers. Then the common folk of the city and some Goyns wandered behind them.

At the cathedral, the designated place for coronations, Odon saw the other members of the imperial council were seated and waiting. The great electrum ornaments of the place stunned him. He was ashamed, remembering what he had left behind, but many eyes were upon him and his choice had been made.

Odon saw Golenrad of the Ollohd and Hunedorat of the Teshi. Nathom, a younger brother of Highking Harkarom, represented the Bronhildi. And there was Pendigied of the Raffen. Electrum crowns adorned their heads, or in the case of Nathom a circlet. Odon looked away from them and knelt where the churchmen motioned. Ralmo approached him, while the exarch and Sarnaker looked on.

"Kneel to your master on earth," the archbishop said, "and bow under the command of our holy God in heaven." Ralmo placed a gaudy electrum crown over the ivy. It lay heavy on his brow, as if the wrathful eyes of Wurumnak were pressing upon it. He whispered a prayer begging forgiveness, which Ralmo mistook for a Messengian prayer. He saw the archbishop smile at Odon's supposed conversion.

But in his heart, Odon did not abandon his god or his beliefs. He simply compelled himself for the survival of his people. He paid little attention to the translation of the consecrating words of Ralmo, but repeated his beg for Wurumnak's pardon.

"You are hereby granted kingship over the lands known as Goynland," the exarch told him, "and any other lands of the enemy that you may gain in service to the empire, as confirmed by the council. Now stand and be recognized as an imperial vassal-king. You shall be celebrated with three days of feasting."

Odon arose and turned to face the throng of clapping hands. He did his best to appear happy and honored, but to those Goyns closest to him, his shame hung about him like a lasting fog.

65

HARSEN

Eglamour, Donovan Province
Midwinter, 2269

There was another man back at the city square that could read the shame in Goynking Odon's face. Harsen was glad Odon had not suffered the same fate as he had witnessed for Yelgoram. Harsen glanced up at the chieftain's withered head still on the pike on the wall. Harsen had not known Odon as he had Yelgoram, but Harsen's guilt of abandoning Rildning grew sharper at the sight of the Goynking being paraded like a trophy.

Harsen had been considering ways to journey to Rachard, where he heard the Frontier Corps had now based its campaigns. But he was still in hiding, wary that some traveler or soldier from New Lorin would recognize him in Eglamour and be the cause of his arrest.

After the exarch led Odon out of the square toward the cathedral, Harsen noticed soldiers had set up a table to gain new recruits inspired by seeing the heathen chieftain. Many men were crowding around to hear about the pay and tales of the exploits of the Frontier Corps. Harsen walked across the square to listen in.

"Archers, footmen, swords for hire, all are called to join the corps!" the recruiter shouted amid the flurries. "Smaller tax now for the wagon merchants as well. Smiths, carpenters, all types of camp followers needed for the spring campaigns! Archers and foot! Smiths and merchants!"

Harsen drew closer, inadvertently attracting the recruiter's attention.

"You there, hooded beard!" Harsen froze. "You look better fed than your tatters suggest. What skill do you have?"

"Ah, well—"

"Do your duty, go to the frontier! If you're not a freeman, perhaps your lord can spare you?"

"I'm a freeman," Harsen said, pulling his hood down further over his face.

"What's wrong, you got the pox?" The recruiter flipped the burlap hood open. "There now, what skill do you have?"

"Merchant," Harsen replied. "Seen better times."

"Join the corps! We need reliable camp followers. The soldiers need to buy and trade their wages. Otherwise, pick up a sword as a footman and fight those mongrel Memelos kin! What say you?"

"As a merchant, can I take my wagon where I wish?"

"Stick to the roads. You'll be part of the march to Rachard, come Thawtide," the recruiter said. "Whole convoy of wagons will go with the army. You must supply your own cart and pay the tax. Any gouging of the men on your wares, and you'll be run out into the wild woods to die."

"Fair enough," Harsen said.

"Put your mark here." The soldier jutted his dirty finger onto a dirty parchment. It was full of the names of new soldiers and craftsmen. Harsen feared his name would be recognized, so he made a little squiggle like the illiterate men did. The soldier looked at him funny.

"How does a merchant who can't read or write make coin?"

Harsen smiled. "Not lately. But I know quality, even if I don't know letters," he pretended. "Do the soldiers care about my wares or whether I can write a treaty?" The soldier nodded smartly and moved on to the next recruit.

Harsen walked away as the other men pushed in. Plans formed in his head as he strolled across the snow-flecked square. First he would go to where he had hid his money, then he'd buy a new wagon and supplies. Before long, it would be time to go.

66

ENIRI

Chadwoid, Nydenland
Midwinter, 2269

The old woman who was waiting for Eniri in King Toredwoak's private chambers was pleasant enough. Eniri couldn't understand a word of her constant chatter, but thankfully Bothrobim was permitted to stay with her. The woman opened a trunk of dresses.

"She's going to help prepare you for Toredwoak," Bothrobim said.

Eniri glared at him. In a short time she was dressed in fine woolens and sea silk. The old woman stroked her hair with a fishbone comb and rubbed in a sweet-smelling perfume. Then Bothrobim led her out and toward the banqueting chamber.

"Don't worry, I'll get you out of this," he said.

"Yes, you will."

"When they're all drunk we'll have our chance. Until then, just act the part of a guest and try not to anger him."

A flog-faced guard opened the door to the chamber. Eniri immediately saw the empty seat to the left of Toredwoak. He welcomed Bothrobim with a scheming grin, then turned his sour breath toward her. His words were mere sounds but not as threatening as when she asked him to help Gilgalem.

"My uncle welcomes you and says he is delighted to see you in his late wife's feasting gown," Bothrobim said.

Eniri cringed and tried not to look at Toredwoak. "Get me out of this," she said as she looked around the room at all the

300

blond tusk mustaches. Toredwoak gently urged her into the chair beside him.

"Don't worry, I'll be right here beside you," Bothrobim said as she sat.

She looked at him to plead again but was interrupted by servants setting a large platter on the table. It was a great fish with a spear-like snout and a back as broad as the sail of a ship. She was stunned by its size and beauty. Around it was piled every color of potato along with turnips, radishes, and cress.

Toredwoak looked at her with greasy eyes and gestured toward the big fish, sweeping his hands out across the bounty of the table.

"My uncle says all of this can be yours, and more."

Toredwoak held his hand out to her. She tactfully looked away. Undaunted, he cupped a few curls of her long dark hair and smelled deeply. She did her best not to notice.

"Eat," Bothrobim said. "This will go faster and you'll avoid irritating him."

Eniri allowed herself to eat a little from the plate she was given. The food was piled high and smelled delicious, especially after the rations of Gilgalem and the apples she had stolen as a stowaway. But she tasted guilt in every bite and wept.

"Don't," Bothrobim whispered. "You'll just . . ."

It was too late. Toredwoak leaned over to speak softly in her ear, his blond tusks flapping against her cheek as he chewed. Again he held out his hand to her, and again she turned her gaze to Bothrobim, where it hardened.

As she considered returning to her plate there was a commotion across the table. Toredwoak's brother, King Belordoos, stood up. His cup of cyser fell from his hand and the golden liquid dribbled from his mouth. His eyes were fixed on the stone ceiling as he attempted to suck in a breath. Then he hunched over the table with rapid convulsions.

The woman beside him screamed. Bothrobim and other Nyden chiefs jumped from their chairs. After a short burst of coughing and heaving, Belordoos fell still on the table. Eniri stood, horrified and confused. Toredwoak didn't stop eating but slowly pulled her back into her chair.

The banquet hall erupted with shouting, breaking dishes, and swords unsheathing. The doors of the hall were flung open. Eniri tried to remain calm, gripping the chair and focusing on the mad flicker of the disturbed candle in front of her.

Bothrobim shouted as the Nyden lunged at each other's throats. Several of the chiefs who had been seated near Belordoos had their necks slit before they too were thrown on the table. Raffen fanned out everywhere, swords and knives in hand. Bothrobim turned to her but seemed lost for words. His eyes betrayed a helplessness that drained her hope of escaping Toredwoak.

The Raffen commander seated at Toredwoak's right hand stood and shouted an announcement over the din. The remaining Nyden chiefs who initially protested the death of Belordoos gave up their struggle. Then the king of the Nyden sipped his cup, stood calmly, and gave a short speech.

Bothrobim swallowed hard before translating. "He says it's unfortunate Belordoos had a stroke in the middle of his cyser. And that his brother has had problems for a long time. But he assured the chiefs that he will continue to lead the kingdom. Now he's thanking them for their loyalty and for the assistance of the Raffen."

Toredwoak returned to his plate and winked at Eniri.

"Do something!" Eniri snapped.

Bothrobim shook his head slowly, red-faced and with eyes fixed on Toredwoak. "Nothing can be done," he muttered. "Not like this. It would mean another clan war."

Eniri watched as the bodies were lifted off the table. A Raffen man by the door spat on the corpse of Belordoos as it was ushered through. None of the Nyden reacted.

Bothrobim finally addressed Toredwoak in the Nyden language. His uncle replied through a mouthful of fish, spewing bits onto Eniri. Bothrobim shouted angrily. Then the king calmly spoke a few words. Enraged, Bothrobim bolted from his chair toward the door and some Nyden chiefs followed him. Eniri gasped.

"Don't worry," Bothrobim called over his shoulder. "Just entertain him."

Eniri's eyes boiled as he disappeared. She worked to calm her breathing as she turned toward the king. She looked on in disgust and fear as Toredwoak and his top Raffen commander returned to their plates. There seemed to be no limit to the tragic drama of this place. Everything was violent and unpredictable.

It was clear to Eniri that only those loyal to Toredwoak, or those who cowered under him, remained in the banquet hall. She felt abandoned but found herself worried for Bothrobim at the same time.

Toredwoak held out his hand to Eniri for the third time. She could only stare at him with sharp eyes. He chuckled and withdrew his hand, speaking again to the Raffen commander. This man leaned forward and spoke across to her in rough Gali.

"A princess? You are no wise enough still."

"What is happening?" she asked with more fear than she intended.

The commander smiled. "My brothers defeat you peoples outta there. You be defeated here too still. It is normal."

There was something evil in his voice. She looked at the gray metal breastplate that bobbed on his chest as he laughed. Three massive electrum medallions, hastily cast but circular, were set in the ugly iron. The image of a wolf head had been pressed into each medallion. Toredwoak spoke to the Raffen commander and the latter smiled.

"The king say I take you outta thisa room. Follow me still."

Eniri eagerly complied, leaving Toredwoak to finish his meal with the death of his brother still lingering on the table. The passageways back to the king's private chambers were eerily empty and silent. She heard only the occasional echo of a distant shout. She feared for Bothrobim, and herself.

The old woman was waiting at the door for her, smiling as if nothing was happening. As Eniri entered, the Raffen commander bid her farewell.

"Foolish princess do not be. Be wise an maybes king let you peoples live some time longer still."

The old woman changed Eniri in a gray-laced gown, then left her to wait alone in Toredwoak's bedchamber. Eniri stifled a sob as the door was shut and locked.

"Escape," she said aloud to herself. "Get out, Eniri."

The windows were small and barred. She tried the far door but it was locked tight. Then she saw an old, ceremonial sword leaning in a corner. She grabbed it and cast off the sheath, thinking of Rildning. She would sooner fall on the blade than let this king have her. But then Rildning would never know what had happened to her. Enildir would not even remember her. She would not do this. She would fight.

Eniri looked at the cold iron blade. It was typical of the seafaring Nyden, short and broad, but with many small gems and frills. She felt unclean holding the evil-earth metal. Gathering her courage, she held the sword aloft and flanked the door. Toredwoak would likely kill her but not before she took a swipe at him. She knew his death would plunge the Nyden back into civil war, even if Belordoos's poisoning failed to. But maybe the Raffen would be robbed of their control over the Nyden, thus removing another potential enemy for the Gallerlanders.

After a while the blade grew heavy. Not hearing a sound, she rested. But she grew anxious and paced the room with the sword. She went to the window where she could see the lights of the harbor below. It was overly active for this time of the night, with many ships' sails unfurled as if preparing to go to sea.

The sound of footsteps jolted her from the window. She raised the sword and sprinted to the door. Silence. The latch slowly lifted and the door crept open. Her heart pounded in her throat and her muscles twitched for the right time to strike. The door was then kicked open and she pulled the sword downward with all her strength.

Perhaps it was her shadow from the window or lamplight, or the flicker of the blade. The man at the door recoiled at the last moment and she struck the wooden frame of the door. He rushed in as she raised the sword for a second attempt, but by now he had overcome her.

His sword disarmed her and she stumbled backward and fell. Eniri scrambled up the bedside but he was instantly upon her, shouting her name. She screamed and fought and kicked, but his grasp was strong.

"It is me, Bothrobim," the voice said. Through her anger she allowed herself a glimpse of the face, then collapsed in tears. "It's me," he repeated as quiet as he could. He lifted her from the bed and carried her to the door. It was then she noticed he was dressed and armored like a Raffen warrior. Confused and ashamed, she wrestled away from him and stood on her own.

"It's me, Bothrobim," he repeated. "We must leave at once. We have ships ready. We must—"

"Are you with them?" She glared at his garb.

He shook his head. "I needed these clothes to sneak back for you. I was never with the Raffen. I was allied with my uncle Belordoos. He's dead now, so we must leave. Now, Eniri." He reached out his hand and she took it.

They hurried through the darkened passages, turning when shouts ahead came closer. More than once they ducked into side chambers and held their breath. Bothrobim knew every step, but it was not enough. Finding themselves cornered by the guards, they raised their swords to prepare their final defense. A familiar shout from behind the guards froze their advance. It was Toredwoak's Raffen commander.

He came forward, sword left in his belt. He spoke to Bothrobim in the Nyden language, never losing his sneering grin. Eniri guessed he was trying to negotiate their surrender, but the Raffen looked like he preferred to kill them. A moment after Bothrobim lowered his sword, the Raffen sprang upon him and cracked an iron gauntlet across his head. Bothrobim collapsed unconscious.

Eniri wasted no time. She leaped over his body and bounded off the wall, like it was a tree trunk in Umbyrland. She swiped at the Raffen's head as she sped past him, but he dodged. Turning, he disarmed her with his sword. She sent two guards to the floor as she passed by them like a shadow, but there were too many. She was captured, and a hood was placed over her head.

67

URGAMDIR

Gradhild, Barres Province
Midwinter, 2269

"Harkarom spoke of the foreigners' empire as if he enjoyed being part of it," Urgamdir scoffed. He paced about the stone-wall cell he shared with his new companion. The guards did not bother to shackle them.

"I suppose he does enjoy it," Kemet said. "My dead chieftain Isberen was there when the foreigners' ambassador came to the highchief. The Bronhildi had been defeated over and over again on every coast of our realm.

"Then the armored horsemen came into the interior of Bronhildia. Isberen urged Harkarom to unite the clans and reach out to the Umbyrs, but Isberen said the foreigners gifted Harkarom more gold and lands than he could refuse and promised that he would remain highchief of the Bronhildi."

"The Gallerlanders were never offered such terms," Urgamdir said, "not that we would have taken them. Perhaps because it was our electrum that bought the other tribal kings, and our lands that were easiest to carve off, being so near the foreigners' settlements. If only we had understood what was upon us. And what of Odon? Do you know why Harkarom said the Goynking was now a vassal of the empire?"

"I don't know," Kemet answered. "Was Odon a great warrior of the Goyns?"

306

"In earlier days, yes," Urgamdir said. "The people of his realm became trapped, isolated after Nalembalen fell. Perhaps Harkarom spoke true and Odon has given up. The news will sadden everyone at Gilgalem if they hear of it."

"What will happen to the Umbyrs, now that Erambrin is dead?"

"Some will fight on. They know the land. But I . . . I don't know . . . What about you, why have you taken such a risk by siding with me? You should be with the Bronhildi, enjoying the fat of the empire."

"It's as simple as I told Harkarom," Kemet said. "Isberen was right to join with the Gallerlanders, and the Bronhildi were wrong to turn their backs on the Gallerlanders. After he died, many of the clansmen Isberen brought into Gallerlandia wanted to turn back. A minority wanted to stay. But, like the Umbyrs, we could not easily run back north given the advance of the Frontier Corps.

"Bronhildi warriors leaked back in drips for months, but the shattering of Erambrin's main camp forced the rest of us to risk it. Isberen would be ashamed. I would rather share your fate than bear that burden of shame."

The sound of steps outside the cell door quieted them. Urgamdir could not make out the hushed Bronhildi speech, but Kemet could.

"My brother, Dombrad," he said, rising to his feet. The door opened and Dombrad entered, along with Premarom. The two brothers embraced.

"Premarom has interceded with the highchief to let me see you," Dombrad said. "Are you well? It was a foolish thing you did. You must turn away from your error and come back to our people. Abandon the Gallerlanders; their fight is not ours. Premarom can arrange—"

"No," Kemet said. "I don't want to be part of the empire. Isberen did not wish to see us enslaved. We must not forget his example."

"The Bronhildi are not slaves," Premarom said. "We are allies."

"Why do the foreigners need the tribes?" Urgamdir asked. "It can only be our lands and everything in them. And what do the tribes need from the foreigners?" He looked upon

Premarom's shining steel breastplate. "Did we need to trade our lands for the evil metal? I have gripped the sword of steel in my hand, but I don't seek to trade the freedom of our people for its power."

"Sharp tongue for a blunt oaf," Premarom said. "I will make no intercession for you." He turned to Kemet with a stern eye. "As for you, rejoin your own people. I won't offer my hand to you again."

Kemet took Dombrad's hand in his. "It is for our people that I'll continue to fight," Kemet said. "If our greatest warriors will not lead me, then I'll walk in the path of those tribes that will."

"Then you have made your choice," Premarom said. "If the sense in your head were as strong as the bravery in your heart, you would have made a fine warrior. Instead, you are made into a fine fool, and soon a corpse. Come, Dombrad."

Dombrad dropped Kemet's hand and walked out of the cell with Premarom. Dombrad looked back at Kemet with frightened eyes as the door was slammed.

68

RILDNING

Gilgalem, Vaynland
Midwinter, 2269

Enildir bounced and wiggled until Rildning finally let him loose. The boy was so happy to see his father that he had not left his side all day. But now Enildir had grown anxious, or perhaps simply wanted to explore the sanctuary. Rildning found it difficult to pay attention to what the Sage was saying, so he let Enildir roam among the columns and pews.

"But my belief," the Sage concluded, "is that Rumban or one of his men helped her find a ship to cross the sea."

"Eniri . . ." Rildning grumbled under his breath. "Then I'll follow after her. It will be some time before we hear back from the Rahlampians, if at all. The least I could do is go and help her."

"The most you could do is stay and prepare our people for the foreigners who will soon be gathering in the foothills below us. Eniri did what she thought was best, and perhaps some good will come of it. But you must focus on Gilgalem, especially since Owerdir, Urgamdir, and Arbardir have not returned with allies yet."

"What about Tirgranir?" Rildning asked. "He is the Vaynking. These stone walls are his house and his fortress."

"Gilgalem is for all the Gallerlanders," the Sage replied. "And you already know what I think about your place among our people. You must stay. Give Eniri time to carry out her task, as you have done yours. Your greatest task is yet to come, and it does not involve crossing the sea."

Rildning shook his head. "You still think me a high king? I could not even secure much help from the Rahlampians. A high king wouldn't fail in such things."

"Our salvation from this enemy does not lie in whether one alliance succeeds or fails. It lies within us, particularly in you." Seeing Rildning was unconvinced, the Sage continued. "I want to show you something. Remember the third door down below? You had found the door to the mines without having been there. I want you to see what most Gallerlanders never do. Let us go there."

They left Enildir with Sabani and descended the steps.

"The Maluram," the Sage began, "are quite different from the other clans, as you have heard. They are considered at once untouchable because of their status as diggers of the earth, while also holy for their gathering of the electrum. They are the enablers of the tools of victory at the End of Days. But they are also misunderstood by Gallerlanders who look down upon them because the Maluram cannot look to the sky omens. The Maluram don't need to consult the heavens to derive Wurumnak's path for them, as we must, because their path is already chosen."

They approached the door and the Sage opened it. The warm air smelled of earth and hot metal. Faint steam collected in the tunnel ahead, which spiraled downward.

"The furnaces have been blazing steadily for seven days," the Sage continued. "The Maluram have found a new great vein of electrum in the bowels of the mountain. They had labored to free the electrum from the rock in which it has been entombed since Wurumnak's sword was broken, eager to be remade for the End Times."

"How long have the Maluram mined?" Rildning asked.

"Since the early beginning," the Sage replied. "They have toiled throughout all of Gallerlandia, but especially here."

At last the tunnel leveled off and emptied at another door flanked by great columns carved like trees. Stony branches arched over the door, and set in the boughs was a large electrum ring pierced by a sword, like the sanctuary altar.

In the trunk of the left tree was carved a rising sun, and in the right trunk was a waxing moon. Their exposed roots were blanketed with a heavy dark moss, with sprigs of seed heads poking up here and there like stray hairs. The moss grew along the edges of the door and upon its steps like a carpet. Inside, a hidden world opened before them.

The cavern was the largest Rildning had yet seen. Innumerable houses were built into the walls a dozen high, similar to the terrace of Gilgalem's bowl. The dark moss covered every walking path, step, and terrace. Every door shimmered with electrum, and all the windows looked down into a central courtyard where a stream-fed pool glimmered with electrum bricks beneath the water and lamps at intervals around it. An ancient cave willow with gleaming moonwood and blue foliage grew in the middle. Electrum ornaments hung on the ends of every sagging bough.

As the Sage led Rildning to the pool, they were approached by a blue-eyed Maluram woman who offered them black shoes. They were crafted from rough and porous stone but were light as wood.

"It is their custom," the Sage said. "These shoes are made from what we call cinder, one of two special rocks often found alongside the electrum. The other is obsidian, used to fashion the swords and spears for Tirgranir's guards. The cinder protects the Maluram from the heat of the furnace. You will see that those not directly involved in mining or smithing will gather living moss in the holes of these shoes. So like the grass-filled moccasins of their forest-dwelling cousins, they walk silently."

Rildning and the Sage put on the cinder shoes and approached the cave willow pool. They looked up into the tree.

"How do they grow beneath the earth, without the sun to warm them?" Rildning asked.

"The purest water and the warmth of the furnaces perhaps, but its growth is slow. It is said this tree has grown here for as long as the Maluram have mined here, though it isn't as old as the one that grows at the tombs. No one knows for sure how it came to root in this place, though there are many tales."

"It's beautiful," Rildning said. "And all the electrum . . . the Maluram are permitted to build and decorate with it, unlike other Gallerlanders."

"The life of the Maluram revolves entirely around the electrum. They are the gatherers and protectors. They use it how they wish, so long as it stays at Gilgalem, ready for the End Times. Come, let us go to the furnaces."

Leaving the courtyard, they came to an archway and another wide-mouthed tunnel that burrowed deeper toward a red glow. Steam condensed and dripped from the walls and ceiling. The noise of hammering and squelching water echoed toward them. The chamber beyond was carved like a grand cathedral of the colonies. Worktables were clustered around rows of massive columns. Cinder-footed Maluram smiths and their apprentices beat and shaped electrum into many forms. Cooling wells and hearth fires were built into the walls between every stall.

As they walked, Rildning could see the greatest glow came from the big smelter and forge ahead. The heat increased with every step along the Gali symbols carved into the tiles of the floor. Wheelbarrows full of raw electrum ore waited to be fed into several hatches of the large domed smelter. A large Maluram with heavy leather and cinder gauntlets poured the glowing liquid into ingots.

The Sage led him over to a collection of baskets.

"Electrum ore, saved from the hidden places of the earth. Shards of Wurumnak's holy sword. And this," the Sage said, holding up a black stone, "is the raw cinder which clings to the electrum like a crust. The Maluram say it gained its many holes from the holy heat of the electrum's fierce glow."

Rildning held the stones, one light and rough, the other heavy and glimmering. Then he watched the steam rise up into the shafts in the ceiling.

"Saved from the dark depths," the Sage continued, "just as we will be at the End Times."

"What heats the furnace?" Rildning asked. "I see no supply of wood big enough."

"You will see," the Sage said. "Come."

They walked toward a set of doorways hewn straight into the mountain around the furnace. Miners with iron picks and wooden shovels in their belts rushed in and out with wheelbarrows.

"They are allowed to use iron tools?" Rildning asked.

"There is no other way to pry the electrum from the clutches of the depths," the Sage said. "But this is why the Maluram are untouchable in the eyes of the other clans. They sacrifice their own cleanliness so Wurumnak's people may be defended when Demfrebra opens his jaws."

They entered one of the passages to look at the mines. It was not the hollowed-out tunnels Rildning expected. Narrow passages were cut to follow the electrum veins. The iron picks were clearly used sparingly.

The Sage pressed him forward as far as he could fit. The light from the furnace behind them grew dimmer. Up ahead in the stony darkness was a faint glow Rildning had not seen since wearing Gofalnig's ring in the black forest of Ondirhar.

The electrum vein was like a bolt of lightning, streaking up through the rock. Rildning touched the vein. There was no coldness in it.

"This is no ordinary mountain," the Sage said. "The electrum can be found throughout Gallerlandia, but none more pure and plentiful than at Gilgalem. Beneath this mountain and the boiling lake at its roots sleeps fire like a hidden sun. A fierce heat made by Wurumnak's sword piercing deep into the earth. It keeps the forge alive and keeps the mountain from freezing, even in the harshest winters."

"A volcano?" Rildning murmured.

"Is that what the foreigners call it?" the Sage asked.

"I've heard the bards' tales about the fire mountains of the Far East, but never imagined one could be this close," Rildning said. "They also exist back in the Old World, and on the spice islands between the continents."

"There is surely no mountain like Gilgalem in the world," the Sage said. "The heart of the electrum. Come."

They wiggled their way out of the narrow maze and returned to the furnace. There they entered another door made of solid electrum and etched with sword forms of every shape. The room was dark except for a single slow-burning torch. The Sage took it from the sconce and dipped its flame into a trough. Like the amber resin that lit the tomb chambers, the soft fire quickly spread through narrow channels cut into the rock.

The light arose up the walls and into torches set high in columns. The growing light revealed tall ladders leaning on electrum ingots stacked up to the ceiling. The Sage stooped to light a central resin bowl in the floor. It burned down a long pathway between the columns of stone and ingots, extending further and further away until the darkness of the cavern strangled their view. It was an electrum hoard too large for even the greediest Brintilian noble to imagine.

"Incredible," Rildning said.

"The labors of the Maluram have been long and fruitful," the Sage said with pride. "Wurumnak will reward them." Rildning stifled a chuckle.

"My apologies, I'm sure they will be rewarded. I was just remembering something I told a captured Frontier Corps soldier back in Nalembalen. Siglef was his name. He had claimed the Gallerlanders had a hoard of electrum, which I denied because I had never seen the secrets of Gilgalem."

"Well, Nalembalen and most other great cities of the north did have much electrum hidden in tree root tunnels and other such places. I'm afraid what does not melt back down into the ground from their fires will be found by the foreigners."

"We won't allow them to come here," Rildning said.

"I brought you to see the Maluram and their work not because I doubt your resolve or dedication to protecting the mountain and the people in it, but because I want you to see the heart of our world. This refuge is a city, storehouse, tomb, forge, and mine. It is the safest, holiest place in all Gallerlandia.

"More electrum is here than anywhere else, and here is where Wurumnak's great sword will be reforged when the time comes. Gilgalem is the center of life for the Gallerlanders, and the ladder to the next life."

"I understand," Rildning said, "and will do all I can to defend it."

As they walked back through to the furnace, one young Maluram smithy caught Rildning's attention. It was a woman, standing alone in her own forge nook, hammering away at some undefined lump. It appeared to be electrum at first, but then Rildning noticed a brownish glint in it. Rildning stopped to watch, seeing there were sacks of many powders and ores around her worktables. The Sage smiled knowingly.

"She is Niberi, but the Maluram call her Crooked Hammer. She took special interest, even as a young girl, in the oddities that crumbled out of the face of the mines. Even metals, though they tend to frown upon it. She would scurry over, pluck out interesting ores, and hide them away like a mouse until she could tinker with them. No one could prevent her, so she now labors alone and out of the way of the others."

"Has she made anything good?" Rildning asked.

"I prefer not to know what blasphemy is worked up in that child's hands."

As they turned to leave, Rildning caught the Sage winking at Niberi. Rildning started to ask the Sage what he was hiding, but then caught sight of another Gallerlander. The man was watching him. It was the thin, ragged man Rildning had seen after the battle at Fenthugren River and upon approaching Gilgalem.

Rildning trotted away from the Sage to pursue the man, but he disappeared behind columns and was gone. The Sage, who had not seen the man, looked at Rildning strangely.

"Are you all right?"

"Yes, I . . ." Rildning continued to look about. "I just thought I saw someone familiar to me."

The Sage chuckled. "There is no one familiar to you down here in the bowels of Gilgalem."

"A suspicious Gallerlander. I've seen him before, twice now, and he's always watching me."

"Well, you are a bit different from the rest. What do your instincts tell you?"

"I'm not sure . . ."

"Only the Maluram and a few Vayns who bring provisions come down here. Perhaps you simply saw a Vayn veiled in a bit of steam and shadow."

"Perhaps."

69

OWERDIR

Sipadshur, Naren-Dra Mountains
Midwinter, 2269

"For my part, I simply told the seneschals that I have watched the armies of the foreigners march and burn across the lands, and I fear for the future serenity of our realm," Ankarmesh said. "Their eyes have not been convinced by the Kalbum-Nuna, so maybe their ears will be enlightened by hearing from one who has been where the lens sees. And I told them I would translate for you."

Owerdir looked up at the dais of thrones. Ankarmesh did not take his seat but stood alongside Owerdir. The Gallerlander took a deep breath.

"Great seneschals of Naren-Dra," Owerdir began. "Thank you for the hospitality you have shown a stranger, even one who had unwittingly trespassed on your sacred mountains. It speaks, I think, to the friendliness and patience of your people."

Owerdir paused while Ankarmesh translated and noticed all five of the faces remained cold.

"As one who has fought the foreigners since Nalembalen," he continued, "I can say they have no such kindness or respect for places and things held sacred by the tribes, nor do they seek forgiveness as I do. It's because of their brutal march upon our lands that our council in Gilgalem sent me to seek an alliance with you. As a Gallerlander of the faraway northern clan of Umbyr, I confess to being ignorant of your ways and the conflicts of days past, but I'm faithful to my people's wish to seek peace between us and a common defense of our lands."

Owerdir realized he had said too much too fast. Ankarmesh was struggling to keep up. Owerdir paused and studied the faces of the seneschals while he waited. They remained cold and unfeeling. Ankarmesh gave him a nod.

"Please don't think the foreigners cannot touch you," he continued. "The foreigners' greed is boundless, and their reach grows ever longer. Even we once thought we could prevent their march, that they would not dare move from the coasts into the great forests of Gallerlandia. But we were wrong, and you have seen the result through Ankarmesh's far-seeing eye. All of us will perish or submit. We have won some victories, but nothing has slowed their march for long."

Owerdir heard some pretentious snorts from the white-haired seneschal and watched the doubting head shakes from the others, but he continued on.

"There is one among the Gallerlanders who many believe will lead us to a final victory. Rildning was a foreigner, lost and alone in the forests before Nalembalen fell. Our forests tested him and changed him. He later came to my father's village, where he risked his life to warn us of an attack by the foreigners, previously his people. We even tested him again, and he survived.

"Our high king saw something in him, as does our Sage, and he received a pardon and was welcomed into our tribe. He wed an Umbyr princess, and she bore him a son who must see better days. Rildning, myself, and others now travel to seek help from the tribes. Rildning knows how to defeat this foe, we simply need help to do so. Will you join us before we are gone and you stand alone against their march?"

"Trusting Gallerlanders is one thing," said the woman seneschal via Ankarmesh. "But you would have us trust Rildning—a foreigner? How can you ask this of us?"

"A foul mix," bellowed the white-haired seneschal. "If the sky-watching Gallerlanders had looked up to our mountains for peace in earlier days, perhaps they would not be wondering at the moon now. Take your feeble pleas back to the Low Earth!"

"We do not share the burdens of the Low Earth peoples," said the youngest seneschal. "This council wouldn't send an army even if the strange folk from the seas had toppled every tribe. The sacred mountains are high and will protect us."

Owerdir held up his stub-fingered hands.

"You must understand," he cried. "I wouldn't risk life and limb to climb your mountains while my people are besieged if our times—and yours—were not dire. The foreigners will come for you, just as they are coming for us upon our sacred mountain. Maybe a generation from now, and maybe you'll be the last to fall. But they will come."

"Then let us be the last!" cried the white-haired seneschal. The other seneschals scowled and waved Owerdir away. Ankarmesh was grim.

"I'm sorry," he said. "I was afraid they wouldn't listen. And now they have revoked your welcome. You must depart this hall. You are free to walk about while I rejoin the council. I'll find you after."

Owerdir wanted to give the seneschals a final plea, but he knew they would not be persuaded. He walked as quickly as he could out of the chamber, head held high.

He burned with anger. How could he return to Gilgalem like this, with less than he left with? He paced quickly through the corridors, his thoughts racing. His heart ached as he thought of the people of Gilgalem. Part of him hoped he would perish on the way back down the mountains so he wouldn't have to tell Rildning of his failure. His friend and everyone else had trusted him with a task he could not fulfill.

Owerdir sat alone on a cold bench, wooden mask in hand. He stared out one of the windows looking out on the world below, wondering how the Naren-Dra could have hidden themselves from the world for so long. They were never seen below the mountains. What an odd, cruel people, he thought. They believed they could live above the clouds and all the problems below were irrelevant. At most they watched from a distance through their lenses and masks, mixing and doing whatever alchemists did.

Owerdir threw his mask to the floor as hard as he could, but the wood did not split. Ankarmesh appeared and picked it up.

"I'm sorry, Owerdir. Perhaps I allowed us to have too much hope. There was never much chance for the mixture to come out right, as we say. But not all is lost. I still have some ingredients we can use." He smiled and patted Owerdir's back. "Follow me."

They walked in silence until they came to the corridor that led to the Wheeled Window of the World, but instead of going up they went down a stairwell into the mountain. Above them hung lenses, set in wooden frames bolted to the stone ceiling of the tunnel. Owerdir could see the lenses focused and shifted the sunlight further inside the mountain.

Ankarmesh noticed the look of wonder on his face. "Older lenses, put to good use," he said. "These were among the first to be made by my grandfather."

"How did you, and your forefathers, become so different from the rest of the Naren-Dra? So much more . . . interested in the world."

Ankarmesh seemed nervous. "Well, as I said before, it's a long story. It has not always been this way."

The seneschal did not speak further, so Owerdir didn't prod. The corridor soon ended at a door with the moon-flower-sun symbol.

"The symbol of your lands?" Owerdir asked.

"Yes. It is a glyph for sipad, the flower of the caves."

"A glyph?"

"Our writing is quite different from yours. We convey even complex ideas with single glyphs. The sipad symbolizes the warmth of life even in the darkest climes."

"And kindness, surely. Your brother, the old woman, and you. I see now that you are of the same clan."

"You may not always think we are so kind."

They entered a large domed chamber where lenses and sheets of silver metal mingled in the light above. Many people worked inside. Some were at tables in front of a throne, while others busily mixed or boiled things in an adjacent workroom separated by widely spaced columns.

Urikimesh greeted them and led them to a table where a few others drank from stone mugs. Ankarmesh spoke to them in their own language. Owerdir knew from the disappointed looks on their faces that the seneschal told them of the council's meeting.

Urikimesh pushed a freshly poured foaming mug toward Owerdir. It tasted of chicory and wattleseed. Urikimesh then cleared everyone from the table so they could talk alone.

"Now, Owerdir," Ankarmesh began. "The time has come to talk of grave matters."

"Have we not been talking of grave matters since my arrival? Perhaps you can let me enjoy another mug before you send me back down the mountain in a shell with goats."

"You won't be leaving," Ankarmesh said. "Not yet. Not until the rest of winter has passed. The sacred mountains have been merciful by nibbling your fingers but sparing your life. The mountains would surely finish you if I send you home now."

"I cannot stay over the winter," Owerdir said. "The foreigners will attack Gilgalem in the spring. I must be there to help."

"To fight with crippled hands? No, if this Rildning you speak of is the high king of your people, as you have described, then you can wait. There is much for you to learn here, which will be of great help when you return to them. Winter passes too soon for what I want to teach you."

"I don't—"

Before Owerdir could protest further, Ankarmesh vanished, leaving behind a dark cloud of shining dust that reflected bits of red from the hearth fires. Owerdir's hand disappeared into the cloud as he reached out. He jumped when he felt a hand on his shoulder.

"Do I have your attention now?" the seneschal asked.

Owerdir nodded as Ankarmesh returned to his seat. The cloud had gone, leaving a faint smell like browned bread.

"Vanishing is among many things I want to teach you while you overwinter here," Ankarmesh said. "I want to share our craft of alchemy, which your people believe is magic. Your days of wielding stoneswords in the face of steel-clad foreigners are over. You will see our teachings are not magic, but simply the wisdom of mind and mountain."

"Why would you share your craft with me?"

"I feel I owe it to you, for reasons I must take time to explain."

"But the other seneschals. Won't they oppose your plan?"

"They certainly will oppose it, once they hear of it, yes. But, as I said, the seneschals rule their own realms independently. I'll do as I wish, so long as my people support it. And you have already seen the quality of my people. As for this place, the land of Sarbondibum and this fortress of Sipadshur are part of my domain. The seneschals traditionally flock here for councils because it was the seat of the ancient overlords, before the Gray Summers.

"If you succeed in learning what we teach you, you will also win a group of my men, led by Urikimesh, to travel back with you. I'm too old and must remain seneschal, but they will safely escort you down in the spring and be at your command thereafter."

Owerdir looked at Ankarmesh in surprise. The seneschal nodded with a proud smile.

"You must first learn some of our Nari speech as well," he added. "This isn't the alliance or the army you came for, but it's all I can offer."

"I accept and will always be grateful."

"Wait, you must hear the rest of what I have to say before you accept, partly for your own understanding and partly to cleanse my own guilt."

"Go on," Owerdir said warily.

"You asked me how my forefathers and I became different from the others who preferred isolation from the world. I discovered things too late in my life to be different. My father never had this realization. I know this is confusing, so let me begin by asking, what do the Gallerlander tales say of the Naren-Dra?"

"Not much," Owerdir answered. "Only that your people have long kept to themselves. Some name you as cloud dwellers and casters of dark magics, gifts from Ominchar. But I see now there is no magic, but concoctions of alchemy, as you call it."

"Precisely," Ankarmesh said. "But we've always been glad to let the myth persist because it warns people away from our sacred mountains. There is another great myth that says the Naren-Dra have kept to themselves."

"I don't understand. You are the most isolated of any tribe I've ever heard of."

"There once was a king of the Naren-Dra, Overlord Zimberdet, who feared the mountains would be overrun by the powerful Welkars. This was a long time ago, when the Welkars under King Thigor dominated the lowlands east and south of here.

"The Welkars were at the height of their power and a menace to our people. Zimberdet's fears were justified after the Welkars besieged our realm and he was killed along with many others. His last surviving son, Zimudar, was an outcast, preferring to practice medicine and artistry rather than warfare.

"But when the moment came for Zimudar to rally his people against the Welkar invasion, he did so with great courage and skill. He used his knowledge of medicines, poisons, plants, and powders to trick the Welkars. In one moment a Welkar chieftain would be walking past a copse of stunted trees, and the next moment the trees would spring to life and kill him. Or a boulder crouched along the path would unfurl and stab at the heart. It was the same for walls and clouds and animals, even doors and the waters of rivers. Death came to the Welkars like the wind, unseen, unheard, and unstoppable. The invaders fled the mountains, never to return.

"Although the Welkar threat was gone, the Naren-Dra remained fearful. They crowned Zimudar as the new overlord, and the greatest warriors were recognized as those who had mastered his new art of shroud alchemy. There had always been alchemists among the Naren-Dra, but Zimudar's knowledge was now the focus of alchemists' efforts.

"We do not burden ourselves with large and heavy weapons. We prefer the small, hidden in the hand or pocket or sleeve. No armor can protect against many of our best methods."

"Like the red coughing cloud that was cast upon me?" Owerdir asked.

"Yes. You did not even see the guard throw the tiny pod, did you? Your surprise and confusion were as potent as the mixed powder that produced it.

"Now, when Zimudar became overlord," Ankarmesh continued, "he fostered a group of orphans whom he trained in his alchemy of the shroud. Zimudar then sent them down into the many realms of the Low Earth, where they hid and watched for potential enemies.

"As time passed, subsequent overlords used these watchers, who became known as the Clan of the Hidden Eyes, to not merely watch but to sabotage or kill the leaders of other tribes deemed hostile to the Naren-Dra. Their actions long passed unknown to the world because they used poisons or arranged blame to fall on the rivals of the dead. In this way, the Naren-Dra preserved their isolation.

"Gallerlandia was an early target for these alchemist-warriors. Over the years, attempts were made to kill even high kings, though I'm aware of only one Umbyrking who was killed by them. Petty Gallerlander chieftains nearer to our mountains were easier.

"The shroud alchemist who killed the Umbyrking returned to the sacred mountains an honored hero. But he wished only for isolation for himself. He left the Hidden Eyes and became a hermit. This was my grandfather.

"My father, also a Hidden Eye, was ashamed of my grandfather. My father hid him from me and my siblings. Later we learned of him, though by then I was a Hidden Eye as well. I must confess that chiefs of Gallerlandia, Rahlampia, and other realms perished at my hand. I learned the Gali tongue to better blend in, as all shroud alchemists do.

"When I learned of my grandfather and his guilt, I sought answers in his writings and inventions, as he was long deceased. He spent many years studying the world through the Wheeled Window, a world he had long walked as a fatal shadow but never truly seen. I dropped the cloak of the Hidden Eyes and devoted myself to his studies and eventually the care of my people as seneschal.

"And so that is why I'm different. I want to help the Gallerlanders, perhaps as some small penance for my own ill deeds and those of my forefathers. Now that you know who and what we are, you are not obliged to accept my help. But I hope you do."

Owerdir studied Ankarmesh's face. He wished someone with more experience had come. He was unsure if he could read sincerity in the seneschal's voice. Owerdir was wary of being used by the Naren-Dra for some dark purpose.

"Why have you told me all of this?" he asked. "Don't you fear the other seneschals will hear of it?"

"I fully expect they will," Ankarmesh answered. "And they will try to stop you, not because they believe the foreigners cannot touch them, but because they want the foreigners to eliminate our enemies. If you accept the shroud alchemists I send back with you, only Urikimesh is to be trusted."

Owerdir reasoned that if Ankarmesh had meant him harm, he wouldn't have gone to the trouble of explaining his tale. Owerdir also remembered Rildning and the risks the envoys had taken. He didn't have much choice.

"I accept your help, and I'm grateful for it," he said at last. "It seems many things can change with time. Most of the Gallerlanders forgave Rildning's past, and he has proven more loyal and brave than some of our own. But I cannot offer you forgiveness on behalf of Gallerlandia for what the Hidden Eyes and their masters have done. That is beyond my power as an envoy, but if we all share a future without the foreigners marching over us, then perhaps an understanding can be reached between our peoples."

"I'm glad to help you, and could not expect one man to offer forgiveness on behalf of generations of people," Ankarmesh said. "Together, let us seek a future without the foreigners. I also hope to meet this Rildning one day, and would join the adventure if my bones were young enough. Shall we begin your training?"

"Today?" Owerdir asked.

"The days of winter are dwindling. There is much to do."

70

HILSINGOR

Rachard, Bram Province
Thawtide, 2269

Hilsingor nodded with satisfaction. His eyes pored over the newly drawn map, the first of its kind. On one large sheet of stitched vellum panels he could see Rachard and his surrounding provinces, roughly surveyed by his scouts. The Gilgalem Mountains were also there to the south. Paths and rough distances as described by Raffen and imperial commanders were annotated.

"How swiftly can we march that distance?" the marshal asked.

"Hard to say, sir," the mapmaker answered. "The scouts who drew this part travel light. We don't know about those forests and plains during the month of Raingreening, which would slow the march of the men. And, of course, the road south is not more than a few days in length, since the workers have focused the winter work on your castle."

"Warcastle," Hilsingor corrected him.

Arnolf and Widsem walked in as the marshal was pondering the march.

"Leave us," Hilsingor said to the mapmaker and his apprentice. Arnolf escorted them out as the marshal and Widsem sat down in front of the hearth fire.

"I'm certain you could draw me a map of all Umbyrland and Bronhildia by now." Hilsingor smiled. "You have trod more wild paths than any other. Do you have good news about the Gallerlander envoy, what was his name?"

"Urgamdir," Widsem said, his voice tired. "Not the news I wanted to give you, sir. I was unable to capture him, close as I got more than once. The Bronhildi have him now."

"Did they hear his plea on behalf of Gilgalem?"

"I cannot say. They stopped me on the road to Harkarom. Urgamdir was within my reach, and I had given up on catching him alive. But Harkarom's own brother forbade me to enter their new territory of Barres. He protected Urgamdir and the others for his own purposes."

"What others?"

"Urgamdir joined up with a few Bronhildi who escaped the fighting in the east. They took him to the north and he appeared to be their captive. They would not give him up."

"I see." Hilsingor stroked his beard. "Harkarom is greedy. He will undoubtedly ask for a ransom for Urgamdir."

"Do we still need him?" Widsem asked.

Hilsingor knew Widsem was frustrated. It was rare for the ranger not to get his mark and he probably dreaded making another long trek into Bronhildia.

"We know of the envoys," Widsem continued, "thanks to the capture of his companion Brugmir, but what good are they? The snows are thawing quickly."

"If Harkarom offers, then I'll buy him," Hilsingor said. "This Urgamdir will have knowledge of Gilgalem. But not to worry, I wouldn't send you to deal with a ransom. I have a new task for you. After you have rested here, you will go south to seek out Ferndeath again.

"I'm anxious to know how the Gallerlanders fared over the winter, and what he is up to next. Ferndeath should be told we are preparing the campaign, so he can tell us what we need to know. You will accompany a troop of Raffen cavalry that will separately be tasked with taking a letter to Gilgalem."

"You wish to give a message to the Gallerlanders?"

"I want to tell them about the crumbling of Gallerlandia, if they don't already know it. The death of their envoy Yelgoram. The surrender of Odon and the death of Erambrin. The capture of Urgamdir. The solid alliances we have with the Raffen and Bronhildi. And our new truce with the Nake.

While we ready the corps, I want Gilgalem to see how dire their situation is.

"If they have been short of food, as Ferndeath designed, and short of friends, due to the failure of their envoys, then they will be divided and vulnerable to such a message. Lead Walpert and his cavalry to Gilgalem, but let them deliver the message. I want Gilgalem to see my message coming through the Raffen."

After Widsem departed, Hilsingor thumbed through Rildning's journal, as had become his bedtime habit. He had read it twice already since acquiring it and felt he had a good measure of the man. But he still liked to flip through the pages for new nuggets of Rildning's personality, fears, desires—anything the marshal thought could be used against him and the heathens. Arnolf appeared at his door as Hilsingor set the journal aside.

"Sir, beg your pardon for disturbing you. But good news: scouts from King Pendigied's half legion have arrived. We expect the Raffen to arrive by midday tomorrow."

"Very well, thank you, Arnolf."

Hilsingor blew out the candle as the adjutant closed the door. Then his tired mind sparked.

"Wait one minute, Arnolf!" He waited for the adjutant to return. "Do you recall the men who first set off with Rildning, back on their original expedition from New Lorin Colony?"

"Yes, sir. There were four in total."

"There was a forester who survived until the end of the journal. Do we know what ever happened to him?"

"Not that I recall, sir. What was his name?"

"Harsen. The heretic wrote that he tried to flee after we sacked Nalembalen."

"Ah yes, I remember," Arnolf said. "He was rescued, said he had been imprisoned by the savages. As far as I heard, he returned home, sir."

Hilsingor pondered for a moment, propped up on his pillows in the dark. He considered sending Widsem to New Lorin to find Harsen. But the ranger was busy with other tasks and more valuable on the frontier in general.

"Shall I send someone to fetch him?" Arnolf asked.

"Perhaps not," Hilsingor murmured. "We've certainly had plenty of time to find him before now. And if found, he would arrive too late to be of any use. Our campaign is near, Arnolf." Hilsingor considered the situation for a moment more, then waved a hand to dismiss the idea from his sleepy mind. "Arnolf, when Pendigied's cavalry arrives, I want you to take stock of their readiness and needs. See that every smith and tanner of Rachard is at their disposal."

With that, Hilsingor fell into his pillows.

71

HARSEN

On the Road to Rachard
Thawtide, 2269

arsen bought a new covered wagon and outfitted it with extra canvas for warmth, spare wheels, and two stout draft horses. To look the part of a merchant, he stocked it with all the things he knew soldiers on campaign wanted: choice foods like hickory-smoked capons and custard yams, tobacco imported from Almeria, game dice, new boots and other essential garments, kegs of clove-spiced beer, gin jugs, and plenty of coin to buy their booty. He had been a camp follower in his younger years before trading with the Ollohds and Gallerlanders.

Most of the other camp followers had sons, wives, apprentices, or servants that accompanied them, but Harsen traveled alone. He hoped to avoid scrutiny and reach Rachard without incident. He reasoned that he would hear of Rildning's general whereabouts when he arrived, but he had not yet determined how he would break away from the Frontier Corps to reunite with him.

Harsen was impressed with the new road built between Eglamour and Rachard. Even with the snow and rock-splitting ice that attacked it during the winter, it was reasonably smooth for a path cut through a long stretch of wilderness. There were already toll stations set alongside it, with stone towers standing at two-hundred-marq intervals. The soldiers who manned them had warm quarters and their own stocks of corn and wheat. Raffen King Pendigied also slept in them when not using his great bed carriage.

Harsen was curious about the Raffen. Their king was more like a Brintilian noble than a native of the continent.

"And it's said his father was half dog," said one long-nosed camp follower named Seef during a fireside chat. "Or maybe it was half wolf."

"No, you've been drinking too much of your juniper jug," said a lumpy-faced carpenter named Garonig. "He's a man, same as you and me. I've been trading with the Raffen for near five years now. Never seen anything in the Durgens that would suggest somethin' queer about 'em. But I tell you this, they are fierce in going after the other barbarians with us."

"I heard that, too," Seef said with a quick nod. "They say the Raffen have been on the decline for centuries before we got here and made somethin' out of 'em. They're lucky, I say." Garonig shook his head again.

"You've got the juniper juice running out of your nose now, Seef. Here's how it is. The Raffen have their own empire. Their realm in the far south, the islands in the west, the Nyden islands in the southern sea, even islands and places we ain't never seen yet. That was before we got here, see? True, they welcomed us at the Durgens, and we helped 'em against the filthy Hrals. But heck, they don't need us no more than a pigeon needs a velvet cape."

"Yeah, that's right," Seef said. "What I meant was they're lucky to have friends like us."

"Let me tell you," Garonig continued, "that young king of theirs, he likes our people, see? Wants to be like us. But they don't need horses and such. They'll take 'em, sure, and they'll march with us. But I tell you, sooner or later they won't bother. When those other barbarians are quelled or dead, well, we best watch our backs."

"You're saying our ally will turn on us when their rivals are gone?" Harsen asked.

"Mark it down," Garonig said with a nod. "I've spent time enough with 'em in the Durgens, see? I know 'em."

"You may be right," Harsen said. "Their king is said to love us, but all of them surely don't. I heard some of them harassed the road builders?"

"Yes indeedy," Garonig said. "One particularly stubborn clan, apparently a rival of the king, is the primary reason the road from the Durgens to Eglamour has taken so long. That and the terrain, rocky with hanging cliffs. And behind it the mountains are like a tumbled stack of bricks, shifty and prone to quakes, see? I'm glad to be out of that damned place."

"Why did the Raffen settle there?" Harsen asked. "And why did we settle there with them?"

"Perhaps the view?" Seef said, gin bubbling from the side of his mouth.

"There's a view, all right," Garonig said. "After years of living there I still couldn't tell you what draws them there, since the cradle of their people is farther south. Maybe it's some heathen religion thing or a crossroads if they ever traded with the Hrals—which I doubt. Maybe the earth didn't always shake there. God knows."

72

ENIRI

Chadwoid, Nydenland
Thawtide, 2269

Eniri awoke in darkness. Her body was stiff. She felt wet straw on the floor. Then something furry brushed her hand and she recoiled and kicked. There was a screech and a scurrying of tiny claws. Then silence as she leaned up against the cold wall.

Eniri drew her knees up to her chin and felt along her legs, arms, and body. She was cold but there were no injuries other than the bump on her head. She did not know where she was or how she had gotten there. She touched the wall behind her and felt along it to find the corners.

The cell was small with the facing walls just out of reach of her outstretched fingertips. She felt the slime of moldy wood, clearly the door. She soon found the keyhole. The rust of the lock brushed off like sand onto her fingers.

She wanted to call out for help but feared what might come. She leaned down until her ear captured the small waft of air through the keyhole and listened. She could hear a faint shuffling, then silence.

"Hello?" she heard herself say in a timid whisper. More shifting of something on the straw outside the door. "Hello?" she repeated. Growing braver, she put her lips near the keyhole. "Is someone there?"

"Yes," came a whispering voice.

"Where am I?" Her voice was a tremble.

"We are where even light goes to die," the whispering voice said. It was unfamiliar and had come closer.

"Is that you, Bothrobim?" she asked.

"No, child."

"Can you help me?"

"Yes." The whisperer was very close now. Eniri backed away from the keyhole.

"Who are you?" she muttered. "Please help me."

Even in the flooded storerooms of Gilgalem she had never felt so trapped and alone. She instinctively looked up toward the sky.

"Are you afraid?" came the voice, now speaking through the keyhole.

"Yes," she whispered. She was now standing against the back wall.

"Do not be afraid. When you remove your eyes, it will be better. You will no longer seek the light. Come closer."

"No," she said in her smallest voice. She felt her cheek warm with tears.

"Please help me," mocked the voice. "Help me!" he shrieked. She screamed and cowered in a corner, praying Wurumnak would free her. The voice did not resume and all was silent.

When Eniri awoke again, she had grown hungry. She tried to think of Enildir's smile but the cold darkness made it difficult to focus. She could feel her stomach and see it rippling impatiently in her mind's eye. She wondered how long she had been in the cell.

Eniri heard a scratching noise as she drifted away again. She stood and looked toward the door, but the sound was coming from the wall to her right. She turned her head this way and that until she found the spot, just above her head. She was startled when bits of rock fell from the wall. She could hear a faint voice on the other side.

Gathering courage, she slid her fingers over the rocks, feeling more bits fall onto her. She reached higher, then recoiled when her fingers found flesh. The muffled voice in the wall grew excited.

It was a few moments before she could reach up again. There were two fingers protruding from the wall, warm and strong, but they did not grab at hers. She kept still, and the fingers patted hers before withdrawing. A faint voice tried to speak through the hole, but it was no use. Then there was a thudding, like blows against the wall, and more stone bits fell. She backed away as larger chunks of wet, crumbling stone crashed down into her cell.

"Eniri, are you all right?" came the voice from the wall. "It's Bothrobim. I'm in the next cell. Are you all right?"

"Yes, but . . ." She feared drawing the attention of the man behind the door. "There is something out there."

"Stay away from—" The rest was muffled.

"What?" she clamored, reaching for his hand.

"He has a—"

The broken stone she stood on shifted.

"What?"

"Escape," Bothrobim said. "I'll think on it."

She squeezed his hand, then he withdrew. She wept when she awoke again. The darkness demanded her sleep. She wanted to know if it was night or day, whether food or water would come. She tried to speak through the wall to Bothrobim, but there was no reply.

Eniri searched the straw on the floor for the largest stone he had broken from the wall. Finding it, she rapped on the wall, but still nothing. After a few moments she heard a shuffle outside her door, and a thin metallic sliding sound, but the lock did not turn and the door did not open. The sliding sound seemed to be inside her cell.

Curious, she crept toward the door. She touched the slimy wood but heard nothing more. She wanted to put her ear to the keyhole but explored the lock with her fingers first. Where the keyhole had been there was now metal. With a metallic sliding sound it withdrew back out of the keyhole, cutting her finger. She gasped and the voice behind the door returned.

"Please, let me help you take your eyes."

She leaped to the back wall, sucking her finger and stifling a scream. The man behind the door violently thrust the slender blade in and out of the keyhole.

"Help me help you!" he shrieked in a raspy voice. "No eyes will help, you will see. No eyes will help!"

The blade would not cease its screeching. She pawed at the straw until she found the big stone again. When he thrust the blade in again, she bashed the rock toward the sound, leaning on the blade with all her weight. It snapped and she hit the far wall and fell onto the floor.

After the cruel man shuffled away, Eniri used the broken blade to chip at the soft rock between her and Bothrobim.

"They will come for you soon," Bothrobim said.

Eniri could hear him better. She reached up to take hold of his hand. "What is that creature?" she asked.

"The blind jailer. He was a nobleman but committed grave crimes. My father spared his life because he pitied him, so here he has remained for years. I thought he had long since died, but perhaps he has survived on torturing others. Eniri, you will not bring down this wall, so do not further dull the blade. You must prepare yourself."

Bothrobim was right. Soon footsteps returned, and with them came a golden light. She waited, standing with her back to the wall opposite the door, clutching the broken stone in one hand and the blade fragment in the other. The dim light appeared like rays of sun through the keyhole and around the door, forcing her to squint.

The footsteps stopped at her door. There was a hushed muttering of voices, and the keyhole blackened. There was a tumble in the lock, then the door's rusted hinges creaked open.

"Come quietly," a new voice began. "You won't be harmed if—"

Eniri sprang off the back wall and crashed into the opening door, catching the man in the face. Then she jerked the door back open, closing her eyes to the blinding lamplight but not before seeing where the two forms were. They did not have time to shout.

She bashed the rock into the already bleeding face of the tall man and slashed out at the hunched man behind him. She forced herself out between them as they fell wailing. She opened her eyes to see them rising.

Again she pounced upon the tall man, stabbing viciously into his leather armor. One blow of his heavy fist met her ribs, then he slumped to the floor in a gurgling heap. His garments, wet with blood and lamp oil, caught and encouraged the flame.

Then Eniri saw the blind jailer. His clothes were ragged and moldered, white wisps of torn beard patched his scarred face. His eyelids had sunken into his sockets and were blotched with bruises.

"I can hear you breathing, child. I can smell your fear," he said. He raised a terrible instrument as he spoke. It was a large-toothed blade with thin spines along its back. "If you had embraced the darkness, as I have, the darkness would have welcomed you with peace . . ." She remained still as he twisted his head side to side and sniffed. She could see the brass keys glimmer in the light of the flames as they ate into the tall man's tunic.

The blind man felt with his bare, gnarled feet until he kicked the keys. He jiggled them with his festering toes. "Is this why you have not fled? You wish to save Bothrobim?" The blind man kicked the keys again. "Take them!" Eniri remained frozen. "I feel the heat. You must take them before they are warped by the flame."

The dank corridor became hazy with smoke. The blind man stepped toward her. He lurched forward and slashed at the wall, forcing her back. Her little blade fragment could not block his. He lurched and swiped again. As he grew tired she rolled under the next swipe, buried the fragment in his thigh, and reached for the tall man's short sword.

The hot pommel burned into the cuts on her fingers and palms, but she lifted it in time to deflect his stroke. Reduced to fighting on one knee, the old jailer would not relent. She held the sword aloft and brought it crashing down onto his evil blade. Then she did the same upon his head.

Eniri dropped the steel and reached for the keys just as the flames began to lick them. She quickly tried them in Bothrobim's cell door. When at last the lock turned, he rushed out and hugged her. He picked up the short sword and led them out.

After several days in the cells their bodies had been weakened, so their escape to the harbor took time. Fortunately for them, the Nyden had already started to fight each other again, causing such a distraction that they reached the harbor without much incident, hopping from castle corner to roadside bush as the night waned. There they found Bothrobim's men faithfully waiting for him, fighting off Raffen warriors that had come down to foil them.

Bothrobim's men pushed back the Raffen, most of whom fled to a nearby ship. When Eniri was safely aboard Bothrobim's ship, she looked toward the Raffen ship as it readied sail in pursuit. She heard a familiar shouting from their deck and saw Tegmad struggling as the Raffen led him down into the hold.

"They have him," she cried to Bothrobim. He came alongside her and saw them drag Tegmad belowdecks.

"They will try to catch us, but my ship is faster."

"Can we save him?" Her eyes were pleading but he shook his head.

"We will see . . ."

They set sail under a full moon and unshaded stars. Eniri was glad to see the good omens of the cold night sky but wondered if it meant Tegmad could be helped. As Bothrobim predicted, the Raffen ship pursued them out of the harbor, though a bit behind them. The Raffen would shoot an arrow at Bothrobim's crew every hour or so, but his ship sped onward.

"Will we return to Aggarwal?" she asked Bothrobim.

"No," he said. "Our journey lies to the southwest, around the main island. I must warn the friendly clans of what has happened to Belordoos."

73

WIDSEM

North of Gilgalem, Vaynland
Thawtide, 2269

Widsem preferred to travel alone or with the scouts whom he had personally trained. It was how he was trained in Donovan Colony, before there was a Frontier Corps. And before all the cooperative work with the barbarians.

Even so, Widsem did not mind riding with the Raffen to ensure delivery of Hilsingor's message to the Gallerlanders. Maybe it was because Walpert and his little troop could not speak Brintilian, so they could not pester him with questions. Or maybe it was because Walpert was focused on whatever Pendigied set him to do. Widsem respected that.

The wilderness path to Gilgalem was familiar to Widsem. He liked the roughness of the unsettled land, but knew it was only a matter of time before Gilgalem fell to the corps. Then the roads, settlements, and farms of Bram Province would swallow the area. Widsem hoped he would be able to work in the east afterward. He had grown bored with the Gallerlanders. They were all but defeated and the ranger craved the challenges of nearby wildlands.

Widsem knew his post as Hilsingor's top ranger was an honorable one, though he was not a knight and would never be. He was born to common folk, and, like his father, brothers, and eldest sister, the explorer spirit was in his blood. He loved the tracking, scouting, hunting, even the messengering. But it was taking those first steps in new lands that thrilled him.

When they were a half day's ride from the plain that led into the foothills of Gilgalem, Widsem parted ways from Walpert and his troops to seek out Ferndeath. He was confident Walpert would do as he had been instructed by the marshal. Walpert was to stab a spear into the ground within view of Gilgalem and fly the black flag of parley. To the spear they were to tie the parchments and Odon's ring, then leave so the Gallerlanders would retrieve it. Widsem doubted the message would make any difference.

74

RILDNING

Gilgalem, Vaynland
Thawtide, 2269

Rildning saw the confusion in Tirgranir's face as he sat upon his throne while the chieftains assembled. A Gallerlander scout stood by the throne holding a spear with a black flag tied to it. Tirgranir held a parchment and an electrum ring. The chiefs quieted down as the Vaynking spoke.

"We have received a message from the Raffen," he announced, then nodded to the scout to take over.

"We found this down on the plain." The scout held up the spear. "Left by Raffen riders in foreign armor. Our watchers in the fields saw a foreigner travel with them for a distance before disappearing in the woods. The writing on the letter isn't Raffen or Gali. But the ring found sewn inside is one of our own."

"It may be the foreigners' speech," Tirgranir said, looking hesitatingly at Rildning.

"Give it to him," the Sage said to the Vaynking, but he ignored the advice.

"We cannot read the letter," Tirgranir said, "but the message is clear enough with the black flag, which must mean death."

Rildning knew Tirgranir no longer trusted him after seeing the Frontier Corps banner fly from his tunic.

"Give it to him," urged the Sage again. Rildning had had enough and stepped up to the throne.

"This isn't a flag of death," Rildning said. "It is the black flag of parley, vice the white of surrender. It means the enemy wishes to speak to us as equals."

"And give us a gift of electrum?" Tirgranir mocked. "Perhaps they sent it to Rildning, since I and my chiefs already have one."

"The sky omens of this morning do not look well for those who play games," the Sage said. "Give him the message."

Reluctantly, Tirgranir returned the letter to the scout, then looked away, as if he had no part in the letter being handed to Rildning. Rildning patiently received it from the scout and scanned it.

"The ring belongs—belonged to Odon. The letter does not get any better."

"Odon?" Tirgranir asked.

"Read the letter, Rildning," the Sage said. And so Rildning translated it aloud to the assembly.

> Tirgranir, King of the Vayns,
> I am Hilsingor, marshal of the Frontier Corps. I write to inform you that Goynking Odon has surrendered and is now part of the Imperial Council of Pemonia in Eglamour. Attached as proof is his ring, which he hopes will convince you to lay down your weapons.
>
> In addition, Umbyrking Erambrin was killed in battle and his men scattered in the woods. We've executed one of your envoys, Yelgoram, and our allies captured another, Urgamdir. Your efforts to negotiate with the Rahlampians will come to nothing as well, while we have solid allies in the Raffen, Bronhildi, and others. You are surrounded and broken, and Gallerlandia is no more.
>
> I offer you the following terms of surrender, and I pray you accept them. You will remain Vaynking and your sacred mountain will be spared, if you join the imperial council and become a vassal of the Brintilian Empire. Join us, and save your people and your lands.

> I will await your answer on behalf of the exarch, who extends his peace to you, in the name of the emperor.
>
> Hilsingor of Ned Gollen
> Marshal, Frontier Corps

"Gallerlandia is no more!" a chieftain cried.

The assembly erupted into debate that Tirgranir could not control.

"It's a ruse!" shouted another chief. "Trickery to lure us away from our stronghold!"

"Perhaps we should consider surrender," said one of the Goyn chiefs.

"With Erambrin and Odon lost, there is no hope," agreed another.

"Vaynland is alone!"

"We cannot defeat the enemy that will soon encircle us!"

"This refuge has never fallen to an enemy. We won't be defeated!"

"If we do not accept the offer now, it will not be offered after our defeat!"

"There is no guarantee the foreigners will treat us as well as they say."

"The only certainty," Rildning yelled over the din, "is that the Frontier Corps will march upon Gilgalem when the snowmelt on the ground is dry. There is little time."

"You think we should surrender?" Tirgranir bellowed.

"No, but I think we can use this to our advantage. We could—"

"We should consider the terms," Rumban interrupted. "Consider the offer and what we face if we do not take it. All of the tribes have fought the foreigners and were either destroyed or came to terms. We shouldn't make the decision lightly in either case, but it seems certain we will share Odon's path or Erambrin's."

"The blood of the Vayns flows in me," a husky chieftain said. "I'll not submit, and I won't die easy either!"

"What about our families?" asked a chief who took a stand beside Rumban. "Are they all to be destroyed?"

"Gilgalem has never been destroyed or surrendered," Tirgranir repeated.

"The water of the wells is deep," Rumban said, "but the forest berries will only last so long after the landship food is gone. Gilgalem has never faced a famine like this."

The debate continued into the night without resolution. When Rildning had heard enough, he approached the Sage.

"I'll go north to get Urgamdir. And try one more time to make an ally of the Bronhildi."

"You will fail in both endeavors," the Sage said.

"Tirgranir is no longer a king. I can no longer help him," Rildning said.

"You are wrong in both statements," the Sage countered.

"Please, look after Enildir until Eniri returns."

75

PENDIGIED

Near Rachard, Bram Province
Thawtide, 2269

Pendigied looked out across the cold soggy plains of Bram. He was glad the heaviness of winter had finally faded as the new season would bring his next great victory. The sun-warmed ground was bare and saturated with snowmelt. Only the hollows of the valleys and other low places still sheltered significant snow.

The rivers were muddied and swelled, reaching beyond their banks for rocky cliffsides that were like tumbled tables, some flat and standing resolute against the rush, others half-submerged like neglected tombstones. Tiny yellow flowers dotted the new green and sprouted from the smallest cracks in the rocky banks.

Pendigied insisted on riding at the front of the half legion as they approached Rachard. Genthus was on his left, and one of his senior chiefs, Ligwared, was on his right. Alda rode behind him, and riding in his personal rearguard was his supposed ally, the Hral chieftain Shimga and a few of his men. Pendigied had yet to think of a role for them, but he had agreed to accept Shimga as a retainer as the exarch wished.

As the sun notched its midday height, the bustling stoneworks of Rachard came into view. Hilsingor's wooden castle was already dwarfed by the rising towers and walls of new-cut stone. In that moment Pendigied had a sudden understanding of the power and genius of his new allies.

He had seen the new capital of Eglamour, with its grand columned palaces. But seeing a rising fortified town on the frontier made him realize the empire would be a permanent part of the continent. No tribe had ever built such constructions on the frontiers of their enemies. Most tribes, including the Raffen, were skilled in stone-cutting and building, but not on this scale.

"A foreboding sight, my king," Alda said. "How long will it be before they build such fortresses in Raffen lands?"

"Quiet, you old goat," Pendigied said. "You've ruined the whole view that—"

"At least I'm not ruining your father's empire," Alda said.

The king turned to look at him. The wiseman had strongly opposed going to Rachard to deliver the cavalry. Pendigied was sick of the old man's stream of cautions and rebukes, so he had him shut into the great bed carriage during much of the journey. Only now did he order him released to witness their entry into the city.

"Take him down," the king ordered. Several Raffen warriors moved to pull the old man from his mount. "If you detest the empire so much, then don't taint yourself with a horse. And if you detest Rachard so much, then you shall pitch your tent outside it," Pendigied said with eerie calmness.

"May my words ring in your ears thereafter, as your father had wished," Alda said.

"My father is dead," the king said as he rode away from him. "Perhaps you should have died with him."

He sent his horse into a gallop, with his retinue coming close behind. The thudding roar of the hooves of his five thousand cavalry gave him great pleasure. He soon forgot about Alda as he neared the partial walls of Rachard.

76

HARSEN

Rachard, Bram Province
Thawtide, 2269

Behind King Pendigied's cavalry came the camp followers. From atop his wagon seat Harsen could see that the Raffen king and his retinue were met by a group of mounted knights who rode out from Rachard. They carried the banner of the Frontier Corps and a herald among them also held the emperor's flag, the golden-crowned white lion on a purple field, which Harsen took as a sure sign that Marshal Hilsingor himself had ridden out to meet Pendigied.

Harsen was stunned when he saw the construction of the place. When he entered the gates, he thought the city might rival Eglamour one day, given the broad foundations that had been laid. He had spent most of his life in the countryside, but even he could see that the pattern of the foundations was unusual for a city.

"You there, master merchant," hailed the quartermaster when Harsen stepped down from his wagon in the area allotted for the camp followers. "You'll make good coin if you help me move cargo between here and Eglamour. I can see from your load that you do a fine business, but I just don't have enough cart men, what with all the building going on here. The pay is good."

"No, sir," Harsen said, shaking his head. "I've come with the Raffen and I intend to follow them and the corps into the wilds. But I'll remember your offer when the barbarians are beaten."

"The campaign has yet to start," the quartermaster countered. "If not the road to Eglamour, perhaps you can lend your cart to the building of the roads. There is much stone to quarry and transport from the hills and much lumber to be cut from the forests. The marshal demands every wagon be put to work in some fashion. Pay is good."

"Then come find me as you will, but after my horses have rested from the journey," Harsen said.

"What is your name, merchant?"

Harsen hesitated, considering whether to provide a false name. But the quartermaster's piercing eyes seemed to discern lie from truth. Then he thought of Garonig, the camp follower who had spent a few years in Durgensdil Colony. He had also been a merchant.

"Harsen," he uttered. "From the Durgens."

77

WIDSEM

North of Gilgalem, Vaynland
Thawtide, 2269

Widsem frowned as he looked in his food satchel. He would wait one more day for Ferndeath. He mounted his horse and rode out into the cool morning to circle the route again.

It was only Thawtide but the signs of an early spring were easily seen in the forest. He wondered for how much longer Hilsingor would need Ferndeath. Once Gilgalem fell to the corps, Widsem might even be allowed to detain the little man for desertion. The ranger grinned to himself at the thought. He hated spending so many cold nights waiting for Ferndeath just to carry a tiny scrap of information to the marshal.

Widsem felt he was not alone. He slowed his horse and listened. No birds sang in this wood. He peered up into the black-boned trees, their swaying branches grasping at the wind. Here and there the melting snow on the ground was pocked with drips of water and slush, more than normal even for an early spring. He looked up again.

He kicked his horse forward and fitted an arrow to his bowstring. It would not be the first time the Gallerlanders had tried to ambush a lone rider. His horse grew anxious now, too, and sped up on her own. She whinnied and snorted, but Widsem would not let her go a different route.

As he set his eyes upon a path a ragged fur-cloaked man with a green-painted face jumped down from the branch of a leaning tree onto the path. Widsem cursed and steadied his mount.

"Man of the beasts!" the ranger shouted. "Why can't you signal or walk out like anyone else?" Widsem did not lower his bow.

"I'm not like anyone else, am I?" Ferndeath said. His matted hair and beard were stained with green paint and there was a wildness in his eyes. His Brintilian speech was coarse and unpracticed, and his stench of soggy earth and rotting fur carried on the wind.

"Do you have a message for the marshal?" Widsem asked.

"Yes, but I have no letter. I must tell you quickly, so listen. First, Rildning will soon leave Gilgalem to seek Harkarom of the Bronhildi, likely using the north road. Second, I think I've found a way to destroy the electrum forge of the mountain, but it could create an all-consuming fire. The marshal should tell me if he wants that."

Widsem eyed Ferndeath suspiciously. Ferndeath had always written something out on a scrap of parchment. But part of Widsem wanted to believe him.

"Is there anything else?" Widsem asked.

"What more could you want? The heretic will be on the road north and vulnerable. And I can melt all of Gilgalem if he wishes it. Tell the marshal I expect my reward to be great."

Ferndeath darted into the snow-slushy bushes and Widsem spurred his horse into a full gallop. He considered whether he should take up a position on the north road to bag Rildning himself. But there was a chance of trickery on Ferndeath's part. He would let Hilsingor decide what to do.

78

OWERDIR

Sipadshur, Naren-Dra Mountains
Thawtide, 2269

After the seneschals concluded their Council of Snowshelling and departed from Sarbondibum, Owerdir's training under Ankarmesh and others proceeded in earnest.

"Your first task shall be to learn medicinal alchemy," Ankarmesh said.

"I'm familiar with the healing herbs of my home forests."

"The methods of the Naren-Dra are different. You will practice on your own body, focusing first on your finger stubs so you can learn the effects directly."

Owerdir learned about the ingredients used to make the salve that the old woman had first applied to his wounds, including gourd warts, mud stalk, and clover gem powder. He learned where they could be found, not only in the high mountains but other common places of the Low Earth. Next, Ankarmesh and the others taught him how to communicate as they did outdoors.

"As you have seen, speech is difficult or dangerous when the cold winds blow," Ankarmesh said. "Our hand gestures and head jerking may not come easy for you at first, but you will need it."

"I'm used to making the calls of the birds and animals of the forest," Owerdir answered, "but I've come to enjoy the little bit I've learned from Urikimesh."

"Good, then your neck muscles have already begun to adapt. Regardless, the silent communication will be easier than learning to speak Nari."

Owerdir spent whole afternoons working on these "wind calls," as the Naren-Dra called them. As with the medical training, Owerdir worked hard and learned as much as he could, gaining confidence as he went. He only became uneasy when Ankarmesh took him to the smiths.

"I know your god prevents you from handling the metal," the seneschal said. "But you must see how all of this is made. Then we will modify it for your use."

Owerdir saw how they made tiny iron knives and darts, then he was shown how to do the same with stone and even wood weighted with lead. Fighting with stone knives was not new to him, but the Naren-Dra showed him how to perfect his technique with these smallest of blades.

When he had gained proficiency with these hidden weapons, Ankarmesh took him to the shroud alchemists.

"This is the school of alchemy that is the opposite of the school of medicine," he explained. "The techniques are offensive and illusory."

"I am ready."

"Good. First, you will learn the details of the red coughing cloud that afflicted you when you met the seneschals." Ankarmesh pointed to one of the alchemists preparing the mixture. "Observe: chalk rust, henbane oil, and the crushed shells of barb snails must be carefully mixed and slowly fed into the pinhole of a drained mountain bluebird egg. When properly thrown, the small egg will burst upon its target, sending the powdery cloud aloft."

"Why is the egg blackened?" Owerdir asked, fingering one from a specially built tray that stood the eggshells on end.

"Shroud alchemy eggs are usually coated black with kowl dust so they are more difficult to see when thrown. The sudden confusion makes the attack more effective, as you have experienced. The kowl dust also adds an extra layer of strength to the shell."

"Fascinating." Owerdir's eyes scanned the shelves of bottles, flasks, vials, and ingredient sacks. Everything was labeled with glyphs. "What else will I learn?"

"There isn't time to teach you everything, but you'll learn about powders that can temporarily or permanently blind a victim. Ones that cause a stupor, dizziness, or vomiting. Here, this you must learn . . ." Ankarmesh reached for a stack of bound reeds and a small, flexible vessel.

"This is a goat bladder that holds liquid poisons and straps to your side under your elbow, beneath your snow robe," the seneschal continued. "It connects to these jointed reeds that extend down your arm under your robe. When swiftly pressed against your body by hand or elbow, the poison will surge out through the reeds to the wrist, spraying the victim. Reeds can also be fitted to the chest, so that sprays can emerge from under the chin as a defensive technique."

Owerdir stared at the goat bladder, awed by the ingenuity of the Naren-Dra and thankful that his experience had been limited to the coughing cloud.

"And this shelf here holds the gifts of illusion," Ankarmesh said. "These are equally important for you to learn. Remember when I disappeared in a cloud earlier? It was this mixture." He picked up a clay jar and opened the lid. "Powdered snake molt, kowl soot, mica flakes, and powdered cave frog gastroliths. We call it a cloak, which can be used to hide yourself, others, or any object. Other powders and mists suspended in the air can dazzle, distract, or even take the form of a man. Still others muffle sound and some create or mask smells."

"How are they suspended in the air?" Owerdir asked.

"Hollow eggs are most often used, but also tiny trays of wood or bone that can be hidden in the palm of the hand, slid open with a finger, and then flicked or blown toward the target." Ankarmesh paused and held up a finger. "As a final lesson before you practice these things, you must always take note of the weather or any movement of airs inside a room. Weather and airs are fickle and thus the primary weakness of all shroud alchemy techniques, but especially those of illusion."

Owerdir was finally given the opportunity to test his crafting and execution, including against the other shroud alchemists. More than once he was choked by clouds, disoriented, and briefly blinded. But he learned quickly from his mistakes. He also impressed Ankarmesh and the others by mixing in his own Gallerlandia fighting techniques, such as running up walls as if they were trees and bounding off walls when trapped, all while throwing well-aimed alchemical eggs. Even with his handicapped hands, he was as nimble as any of the Naren-Dra.

During these trials, Owerdir noticed there was one among Ankarmesh's trainers who seemed to dislike him.

"His name is Hadanish," Ankarmesh said after an evening training session. "He was, until recently, a Hidden Eye."

"He is among those you chose to travel back with me?" Owerdir asked.

"Yes."

"I suspect he means me harm."

"He will not harm you. Stay focused on your training. Your time in the sacred mountains will soon end."

79

HILSINGOR

Near Rachard, Bram Province
Day of Wrethe Hunt, 2269

Hilsingor held the spear forward, its blade a dull gray in the dusk of the forest. Pendigied mimicked the marshal's movements with his own spear. All was quiet around them, then a horn called out through the brush. Hilsingor motioned for the Raffen king to ready himself.

They heard crashing in bushes nearby and the thud of small hooves. The wild boar burst out on Pendigied's right with high-pitched squeals. Pendigied jabbed at the animal but merely sliced its haunch.

The maddened animal charged the king with its menacing tusks wet with foam. Hilsingor quickly impaled it in the ribs. It screamed and wrenched the spear from the marshal's grasp, and still it charged. A last stab from Pendigied's blade finished it.

"An excellent kill," Arnolf said. He appeared with the hunters who had driven the animal to them.

"Hearty congratulations," Firkas said.

"Very well done." Hilsingor nodded to Pendigied.

"How refreshing," the king said. "A holiday for killing wild pigs! What was the name again?"

"Today is the Day of Wrethe Hunt," Hilsingor replied. "This mid-Thawtide festival celebrates two things. Firstly, the martyrdom of Prophet Hinund, who foretold the coming of God's messengers. And the second is the end of winter.

It's tradition that the boar is roasted with frozen wild blueberries, which these forests still offer in great supply."

"I look forward to the fine dish," Pendigied said as they walked back to the horses. "What does *Wrethe* mean?"

Hilsingor was pleased with Pendigied's interest in the history, customs, and religion of the empire—just as the exarch had said in his letters. Hilsingor was also pleased to educate the king, though he wondered if Ralmo had not given Pendigied an adequate education while in Eglamour. And Pendigied's legion of ten thousand cavalry and warriors appeared to be well trained by Firkas's provincials, even in a short time. Certainly well enough to run down Gallerlanders.

"Hinund was wrapped in a rope of sticks and straw and set alight by the pagans who ruled part of early Almeria, perhaps a thousand years before Lord Wilhargant defeated them and reunited the early Almerics," Hilsingor said. "We call this the Wreathing, or wrethe in the Arch Almeric tongue. Wreath-making symbolizes his martyrdom, which occurred as winter faded to spring. So by tradition we hunt to celebrate both."

"Fascinating," Pendigied said as he mounted his steed. "I believe I was born to be a Messengian."

"You clearly were," Hilsingor said. "May I say, your Brintilian speech has developed well since Genthus was first sent to you by the exarch."

"It is the language of a new era for our continent," the king said as he turned his horse.

Pendigied's wiseman, Alda, approached Hilsingor as he mounted his steed.

"It is *our* continent, master marshal," Alda said in a low tone. "Your folk are merely visiting for a time, but it won't last forever."

"If history is any guide, we'll outlast fossils like you," Hilsingor said. "I suggest you serve your king with an eye toward building the New World alongside us, else you become buried like the other fossils."

Hilsingor brought his horse close to Alda and stared long at him. The old man scurried aside, then Hilsingor turned to catch up to Pendigied.

80

MRIGAMAD

Bay of Pemonia
Thawtide, 2269

Mrigamad stood at the prow of the imperial ship as he did every morning. He made note of the features of the nearby coast and the heading of the ship in relation to the sun, as he had daily since the journey began. He had drawn a map in his mind to make sure the imperials took the correct way back when the time came for them to return home.

This morning was different.

"Today we will arrive at Port Rilhammor," Drigoman Trelnaf had told him and Anfinnan. "It was one of the first ports established in Pemonia by the Brintilian Empire, and the largest in Donovan Province. From Rilhammor we'll journey by horse to Eglamour."

"Thrilling!" Anfinnan said. "To see the exarch and his capital has been my great wish."

Mrigamad kept quiet. When they reached Rilhammor, they found it to be a bustling place not unlike the ports of Rahlampia, except the Brintilian ships were massive and the quays were full of them. There was also a sprawling shipyard where new vessels were being built.

"The finest sea-crossing ships hands can make," Trelnaf said with pride as they sailed by. "For a time, Rilhammor was the capital of the former Donovan Colony. This land is named after Helcirk Donovan, the founder of the colony, and Rilhammor, the name of his sword."

When Trelnaf had sauntered off to speak with the captain, Mrigamad spoke under his breath to the domnitar.

"They should have named this place First Theft of the Empire."

Anfinnan was not amused. "You gave me your word that you would support my efforts. That sort of talk is not supportive."

"My apologies, domnitar." But Mrigamad continued to think about how to frustrate Anfinnan's efforts.

When the captain found their berth, Anfinnan and his retinue were greeted by the governor of Donovan Province, whose knights escorted them to a large covered wagon pulled by a team of eight horses.

"A gift from the exarch," the governor said.

"Very kind," Anfinnan said, slipping his hand along the ornately carved rails and trim. He poked the goose-feather cushions and tried his smile in the polished electrum ornaments. "What do you call this?"

"A sleeping carriage," Trelnaf said. "You can sit on top for a view or go down below. There are a few beds, a wine cabinet, and washbasin. Every comfort for a king on the road. The exarch and the vassal-kings travel in nothing less, and neither shall you," the governor said with a reassuring smile.

Trelnaf pointed to mounted soldiers nearby. "We shall also have an escort of a half legion of knights, spearmen, and archers. No harm will befall you, as promised. We will arrive in Eglamour safe and well rested."

Anfinnan smiled broadly as he climbed into the carriage. Before the convoy set off for the road, flagons of Old World wine, bread, dried meats, and baskets of extra fur blankets were brought up to them. Domnitar Anfinnan, his son Morlbeag, Mrigamad, and drigoman Trelnaf climbed the ladder to view the city from the top. They all sipped the wine, which Mrigamad had to admit to himself was quite good. He watched the city and countryside pass by.

The farm fields, vineyards, orchards, and ranches of Donovan Province were vast, with cottages, barns, and villages dotting the land. Ominous castles perched on the high ground in the distance. The province as the foreigners had built it had a striking look of permanence very different from the marshland huts and salt-plant farms of his home or the forest dwellings of the Gallerlanders.

Mrigamad remembered Rildning and hoped the *Earthark* had arrived at Gilgalem safely. He wished he was with him, fighting alongside him against the invaders, rather than sitting here amid their luxuries and purchasing of kings. He hoped Rildning and the envoys found help more reliable than his own Rahlampians.

The convoy snaked through the elegant stone-paved streets of Eglamour, passing white stone palaces and spacious squares with fountains. When they arrived at the exarch's palace, Trelnaf prevented Mrigamad from following Anfinnan out of the bed carriage. Mrigamad moved to shove him out of the way, but Anfinnan intervened.

"I must speak of high matters with the exarch," the domnitar said to Mrigamad. "I don't require your counsel during this first meeting, so it's best if you go directly to our quarters and make sure everything is satisfactory."

"Yes," Trelnaf added, "the exarch is busy. And, as he said, you should have a look at the domnitar's villa to make sure everything is ready."

Mrigamad wanted to protest, particularly at the sudden role of being the domnitar's house warden, but he held his tongue. He decided to remain in Anfinnan's good graces if he wanted to have a chance to learn what the empire was planning. He also considered following them to the exarch, but a few palace guards closed him and Anfinnan's son back up into the carriage. The horses pulled away and they were taken to the domnitar's quarters.

It was a lavish villa that looked out onto a garden courtyard and similar villas for the other vassal-kings. Woven rugs of exotic patterns and tapestries showing grand scenes of hunts and battles adorned the domnitar's chambers. It made Mrigamad uneasy.

Alone with Anfinnan's infirm and unruly son, Mrigamad grew anxious. So he explored, leaving Morlbeag with the servants. He walked the halls and stairwells, making his way up into a tower where he found a room stacked with old books and parchment scrolls.

From a window he looked out onto Eglamour. He could see half the city, and the edge of it that was still being built out in all directions. He could see lines of oxcarts along the roads, laden with newly cut stone blocks and timber and slate roofing tiles. A pale blue river slithered through the middle of the capital, speckled with all manner of boats. The purple flag of the empire fluttered from every spire of the city's heights.

Beyond the city walls, which were still incomplete in some sections, there were vast stretches of farmland as he had seen outside Rilhammor. So different from the weathered coastal marshes of his people. He wondered how long it would be before the imperials outnumbered even the Gallerlanders.

Mrigamad was startled by the sound of shuffling feet behind him. An old scribe hissed at him and reached for a knife in his belt. Mrigamad escaped the room as quick as he could, with the old man's voice ringing down the twisting stairwell.

After exiting the tower he walked a hall and came to a great door with imperial insignia painted across it in purple and white. The soldiers guarding it attempted to speak to him in Brintilian. Mrigamad passed them by, trying to appear as if he belonged there and was too important to care.

As he walked toward the next hall, one of the soldiers followed him at a distance. When he turned a corner, he entered the first unlocked room. It was narrow and dark, with light beaming in around a door at the far end. As he approached, he could hear voices. He cracked the door open enough to see an immense, domed room. A wide ring of columns separated the outer wall from the inner area, where many cushioned seats were arranged in a half circle around the exarch's throne.

A cluster of men stood in the middle of the otherwise empty chamber. Mrigamad thought he could hear Anfinnan's voice, but he couldn't be sure. He slipped into the chamber and crept from one column to another to get closer. As he neared them, he could hear portions of what was clearly

Rahlampian and Brintilian speech flowing back and forth. Then he could see the domnitar, Trelnaf, and others.

". . . and the chiefs have agreed . . ." Anfinnan was saying. ". . . rivers, and the other territories . . ."

Mrigamad pushed farther to hear better, careful to stay in the shadows of the columns. As he stepped he felt cold metal press into his back ribs. He jerked away but found himself tumbling, with hard blows landing on him from every direction.

He sat up and found himself amid a jumble of long brass trumpets festooned with imperial banners and the insignia of many tribes. He had crashed into an iron stand of the trumpets near the column. The iron-shod boots of soldiers soon appeared around him. As he was lifted to his feet, he caught the venomous eyes of Anfinnan, along with Trelnaf and several other richly robed men.

Mrigamad was subjected to a vicious harangue from the domnitar that evening. His trespassing in the scribe's tower had also been reported.

"I'll send you back to Rahlampia early," Anfinnan said when his rage had subsided. "Not as punishment, but because the initial talks have gone well and already bear us fruit. You will sail back with Trelnaf. The two of you will inform the chiefs of my success in arranging peace with the empire. You will convince them to turn their weapons against the Gallerlanders to show our dedication to the arrangement."

"Our warriors are to be integrated into the Frontier Corps?" Mrigamad asked. "I can't tell the chiefs to—"

"You will. This is how the Rahlampians rise over our enemies. We will be unstoppable. Imagine fleets of landships with legions of cavalry among them."

"And you, domnitar? What will the foreigners give you for selling our people?"

"I will be crowned with the electrum, not as a true king for myself, of course, but as a representative of the chiefs. And I'll convert to Messengianism, as will you and the other chiefs. Lastly, we will provide hostages for a term of three years to guarantee our alliance, so you will provide summons to Denildon and a few others for them to come here."

"Hostages? I won't do this."

"It's what the other tribes have done. You and the others will serve me here, especially when I must travel back to Rahlampia."

"I won't do this, Anfinnan."

Anfinnan stepped close to Mrigamad.

"I'll ruin you if you don't. You think your clan would follow you if they knew the truth about Castracane?"

"What truth? The foreigners destroyed my cities . . . my family . . . We did what we could to—"

"Don't lie to me. You were settling scores with that Welkar chieftain, Chirog."

"He was killed by the foreigners," Mrigamad insisted. "We were trying to help them defend the coast."

"Except that you took the opportunity to hunt down Chirog when he hid in the woods. I don't blame you, I would have killed him too. But it cost you time, didn't it. Days that could have been spent defending your own coast. Your own family."

Mrigamad stared at Anfinnan. A grin crept across the domnitar's smug face.

"I said I don't blame you," Anfinnan continued. "But others might. If they knew that your personal score settling took priority . . . That you were romping in the woods while your towns burned, that might change things."

Mrigamad remained silent. He looked down, away from the truth in Anfinnan's ugly eyes.

"Now, you will carry my messages to our chiefs at once. They will respect your endorsement of my plans. Do not fail me in this task."

81

ENIRI

Western Coast of Nydenland
Thawtide, 2269

"I won't allow it," Bothrobim said, shaking his head. "I fear for the life of your companion, too, but . . ."

"What if we traded something for Tegmad?" Eniri asked.

"Even if we had something they wanted, I don't trust the Raffen enough to let them get that close."

Eniri looked toward the Raffen ship, merely a speck on the blue-gray horizon behind them. They had escaped Chadwoid and outrun the Raffen ship that followed them out. But the journey around the Nyden islands had been a sullen one for Eniri and Bothrobim.

"I'm not sure what we can do," Bothrobim muttered. "If we risk letting them catch up for a trade, then I risk the lives of my crewmen for one man."

"But our numbers are greater," Eniri said, gesturing to the six other ships that flanked them. "And you said more of your clansmen will join us as we sail around."

"Yes, we outnumber them by far. But what good is our speed if we must fight them anyway. If they don't agree to barter—and we have nothing to trade with—and we fight, they will certainly kill Tegmad before we can save him."

Eniri knew he was right, but she hated it. Tegmad had done what Rumban and Eniri asked of him. He had not agreed to escort her to Amlon and end up a Raffen prisoner or worse. She kept looking to the gray sky but the heavens offered no signs. She hoped time would provide some opportunity to save him.

"The war has begun anew." Bothrobim pointed to distant columns of black smoke rising here and there on the main island. "Toredwoak has no more brothers to restrain him now. Those who don't unite under him will fight, and most will perish, since he has the Raffen to help him. The Raffen fleets will sail over from their homelands and swamp our islands, as they have before. That is why we must warn the clans. Some will come with us; some will stubbornly stay and fight and die."

"What will you do, then?" Eniri asked.

"I would like to help your people, but it will be difficult to persuade my people to save yours from a far enemy while their homes are burned by a near enemy. However, the Nyden will never defeat the Raffen while they are divided against themselves."

"How long have the Raffen attacked your realm like this?" Eniri asked.

"For many generations. But only in the past few years has their conquest been helped so much by Toredwoak's men. All of the outlying islands were taken by the Raffen easily enough. It was the destruction of nearly every Nyden warship that ended the resistance.

"The Raffen brought a new weapon to the sea battles, which I saw myself. It was a fire that burned hotter than even the sea could quench. A hellfire that, once flung upon our ships with catapults, would chew our hulls even after the ships had sunk under the waves.

"One of these ships went down beside me. Stinking flames lit the depths even when the hulls were deep enough to be unseen. And the fires burned the wet debris that floated. After the burning of the fleets, Toredwoak wanted to make a deal to keep himself, and Belordoos, in power. So resisting the Raffen has been impossible, though many in the south still hold out in some places."

"I'm sorry for your people," she said. "Especially that, even in the face of such an enemy, they won't unite. It is the same for the Gallerlanders. Perhaps I'm wrong in asking for your help." She looked down at the water in shame.

"The Gallerlanders still have a chance," Bothrobim said. "Your kings don't welcome the enemy. And you have great lands. Surely the empire cannot infect all of Gallerlandia."

"The ivy-crowned underkings are scattered," Eniri said. "That is why I came. Our hope lies in whatever help we can find, and for Rildning to lead us."

"I'm sorry I cannot be of much help. Perhaps as we visit the harbors of the clans we will find more help," Bothrobim said.

"I would be grateful."

"Who is this Rildning you have spoken of? Is Tirgranir no longer the Vaynking?"

"He is still," Eniri said. "Rildning is . . . different." She explained how Rildning came to the Gallerlanders and became a leader among them. How he had been transformed "by the will of Wurumnak," but could not wholly accept his destiny. She told Bothrobim that the Sage believed him to be the next high king of the Gallerlanders and perhaps unifier all of the tribes. And she believed this also.

"You talk tenderly of this Rildning," Bothrobim said with a smile.

"He is my husband, and the father of my son," Eniri said. "I love him whether he is the next high king or not. My greatest hope is to see him again."

Bothrobim looked quietly out into the sea.

"I'm sorry if I've misled you," she said. "You resemble my Rildning and have saved my life more than once during my reckless quest to come here. I'll always be grateful."

"You did not mislead, nor are you reckless. Keep your hope alive, for his sake and yours. Your story has inspired me, and perhaps it will inspire others. Convincing my clansmen who already hate the Raffen and their puppet Toredwoak may not be so difficult. We must tell them that if we pressure the empire and the Raffen in Gallerlandia, that the empire will demand more warriors from the Raffen and thus reduce the Raffen in the Nyden islands.

"Since we can't properly fight the Raffen in Nydenland, we can fight them in Gallerlandia. Given that Toredwoak is the last legitimate king without an heir, perhaps the destiny of the southern Nydenland lies with the Gallerlanders, if they will open their eyes to it."

They continued their journey, stopping at harbors believed to still be friendly. More than once they encountered Raffen ships, but they were often burdened with too many men, horses, and loot to catch Bothrobim's small fleet. The few quicker scouting ships that persisted were defeated without much loss to Bothrobim's men.

Eniri finally felt free of her fear of the sea. After the dark cell under Toredwoak's castle, the clean openness of the sea, the daily view of the sky omens, and the relative plenty of the food was refreshing. Still, she remained worried for Tegmad, saw the faces of Rildning and Enildir in every sunset, and prayed for them all with every sunrise.

82

HARSEN

Rachard, Bram Province
Thawtide, 2269

"No one has seen that heretic in these parts for a while," said Henneth. "Not since the battles on the plains near Rachard six months or so ago. Ran with the other whipped heathens south to some damn refuge. An evil mountain built by Memelos, they say. Story is that the mountain was pushed up from the earth when Memelos down in his Depths sneezed on the sulfur and made a cavern swell."

Harsen nodded, searching for the useful information in this and every other tale he had heard in the tavern. He knew he had to be careful not to ask too many questions focused on his friend.

"And this mountain, why is it more a refuge than the others?" Harsen asked.

"They say it's some sacred place for 'em," Henneth answered. "No one has ever been there, except the Raffen folk, and I wouldn't trust them for all the electrum in this damn country."

"Where is it?" Harsen asked, a bit too quickly.

"Well heck, you want to pay 'em a visit?" Henneth chuckled.

"I reckon it must be stocked with their gold," Harsen said. He rubbed his hands together like the other greedy merchants did.

"May be truth in that," Henneth said. "But this town is flooded with the electrum as it is. Lowered its value a bit. The Frontier Corps is good at looting the villages and cemeteries before torching them. Otherwise the soft stuff would melt back into the Depths."

Harsen put a Brintilian gold coin on the table and slid it over, clinking it on Henneth's mug of spiced beer. "If you hear of any route, or any way to get there before the corps does, you let me know. There is much more where that came from."

Henneth pocketed the coin discreetly. "Fair enough, Harsen. But be warned, the corps plans to take the mountain and everything in it, soon as the buds open. Following a camp is dangerous enough. Wheeling ahead of the legions is worse still."

Harsen looked across the table at Garonig and Seef, who had accompanied him to the tavern. Garonig eyed Harsen suspiciously while the dim-witted Seef called for another flagon.

"Why risk your neck with the mountain alone, when you'll be able to buy the loot at an easy price from the soldiers?" Garonig asked. "And what's the heretic got to do with it?"

"Simple," Harsen said. He had prepared. "I think he's a heretic, but I've always wondered if he did it for the electrum. I bet he has a hoard stashed away, maybe at that refuge."

"But how would you get at it?" Garonig asked. "The heathens will be all over it."

"I hadn't figured that part yet," Harsen conceded. He hadn't thought out his lie that far either, but ideas were starting to roll in.

Garonig was unsatisfied. "Odd thing, if you ask me. Camp followers follow, not lead the legions, see? You'd get yourself killed," Garonig said.

"He is right," Henneth agreed. "I'll take your coins, but it sorta feels like stealing from a doomed man."

"All right, gather in close," Harsen said, getting ready to spill his conspiracy. They all leaned in to listen, even Seef, who drooled his drink a bit. "I want *him*, and the prize he'll fetch."

"The heretic?" Henneth grimaced. "You some kind of ranger?"

"Something similar, back in . . . I know the woods . . ."

Garonig shook his head. "Being a woodsman is not going to get you into that mountain, see? And you think that heretic is just going to walk down with you?"

Harsen knew Garonig wasn't buying it but the woodsman became agitated. "I gave the coin to Henneth, not you. Unless you know a route, I want to hear from him."

"If I hear of a route, I'll take your offer," Henneth said. "But your friend is right."

Harsen got up without emptying his mug and bade them all a curt farewell. Before he got a few steps toward the door, he heard Garonig come out behind him.

"Harsen! I ain't as stupid as Seef, nor as cold as that coin pincher back there. What are you trying to do?"

"I'm a merchant, same as you, but with an eye on a prize and the tracking skills to grab it," Harsen replied. "Just want to be the first to have a shot at catching him."

"That's not how this is done," Garonig said. "I've been a trader on frontiers for twenty-odd years, same as you claim to have been. But going where the legions haven't gone yet is foolery. And you don't look like the bounty hunter sort. We've become friends enough, and I'll help you get this Rildning if I can, especially if you will lend me your wagon. But—"

"I'm after the prize," Harsen said. "Nothing else."

"All right, then." Garonig shook his head and Harsen knew he still didn't believe him. Harsen turned to walk away and bumped into a man with the Frontier Corps starcross on his tunic. The soldier was interested in Harsen and Garonig.

"What—what name did you say?" the wide-eyed soldier asked.

"Rildning?" Garonig answered.

The soldier shook his head. "No, your name." He looked at Harsen.

"This is Harsen, an honest merchant," Garonig said.

"Come with me," the soldier said to Harsen.

"Why?"

"I'm Marshal Hilsingor's adjutant, Arnolf. Come with me."

Harsen looked at Garonig, who looked equally puzzled. Then he did as he was told. He walked to the wooden castle with Arnolf, who by then had summoned a few other soldiers with a snap of his fingers. Without a word they escorted him into the castle.

Harsen soon found himself waiting in a quiet anteroom. He could hear voices on the other side of the heavy oaken doors, but could not understand the words. He considered running, but he was gambling that he might learn something useful.

83

HILSINGOR

Rachard, Bram Province
Thawtide, 2269

"He's just outside, waiting in the hall," Arnolf said.

"What luck," Hilsingor said. "But curious that he is here in Rachard."

"Perhaps Harsen seeks vengeance on the Gallerlanders for having abducted him?"

"That's not it," the marshal said. "According to Rildning's journal, the woodsman wished to leave Gallerlandia and was not a vengeful man. No, something else is going on. There are many pieces moving on the board at the same time."

"Sir?"

"You said he claimed to be a merchant?" Hilsingor smiled. "Perhaps this is a lucky find, indeed. Arnolf, as my adjutant, you alone know Widsem meets with a special contact in Gilgalem. And as you know, Widsem returned yesterday with a letter from this person, Ferndeath is his name. If you ever repeat his name, by the way, I'll have your tongue out.

"Now, Widsem said Ferndeath claimed Rildning was going to leave Gilgalem—perhaps he already has—to take up Urgamdir's quest in Bronhildia. Stubborn man. Perhaps Harsen plans to help Rildning travel north."

"But how would the woodsman have known?" Arnolf asked. "He only just arrived, and Gilgalem is days away in the south."

"Whatever the case," Hilsingor continued, "we can help the pieces move where we want them. Ferndeath previously

371

assured us the Gallerlanders would sooner starve than surrender, and Gilgalem is a natural fortress never before taken in battle. We can certainly be the first to break their refuge, but what if we could draw out their warriors instead?"

"How is Harsen going to do that?"

"Given it's already spring, we can guess Rildning will take the shortest path to Bronhildia and back—the north road. That means he will come near Rachard. What if Rildning were to find his old friend Harsen on that road? He would probably be happy to see him, if what he wrote about their friendship in the journal still holds."

"I see." Arnolf nodded. "And Harsen probably does not know you have the journal."

"As you said, he only just arrived in Rachard," the marshal said. "Unless he is close friends with the pesky archbishop, Harsen won't know that we know his significance to Rildning. Therefore, we can send him on a special task up the north road, hoping the two will meet.

"Harsen's task will be to carry a sealed letter to Highchief Harkarom for me, ensuring that sooner or later the woodsman will encounter the heretic. The letter will, of course, instruct Harkarom to arrest both men and send them back to me.

"By holy Messenger Ibelan, such luck is rare! We'll finally have that heretic in our hands, and perhaps even draw out the Gallerlander when they realize we have him. And if not, the jailers—or Ravorglad—can make Rildning tell us the weaknesses of Gilgalem."

"Wouldn't it be easier to have Firkas's patrols simply pick up Rildning on the road?" Arnolf asked.

"Rildning will avoid the patrols, as Urgamdir did. If we try sending Firkas's men, we will lose him. Whereas he will be drawn to Harsen if he recognizes him. Besides, Highchief Harkarom won't miss the chance to prove his loyalty to the empire, if the letters from Eglamour about him are true. We can also promise a reward for the highchief's efforts, and this whole affair will strengthen the ties between the empire and the Bronhildi."

"My remaining concern," Arnolf said, "is that neither you nor I can write a message to Harkarom in his native tongue."

"Harkarom knows some Brintilian," Hilsingor said. "And he will have the imperial drigoman with him. Harsen is waiting and Rildning may be on the road, so fetch me the sealing wax and we'll do it now."

∞

"So, there it is," Hilsingor said to Harsen. "And your pay will be greater than what you'll make following the legions."

Hilsingor watched Harsen's face. Clearly he did not know what to say to the proposal. The marshal took it as a good sign Harsen was up to something by being in Rachard, and that perhaps his plan would work. The woodsman turned merchant was carefully considering what he had been told.

As the marshal waited for an answer, he noticed he had left Rildning's journal on the table. He motioned to Arnolf and the adjutant promptly shoved a pile of dispatches over the book.

"Well, perhaps your pay for delivering the letter will be higher still, since we have word that Gallerlanders are not using our newly built roads," the marshal said. "Please understand my proposal isn't a request, but an imperative, so I want to make sure you are properly compensated.

"And of course, I cannot guarantee the senior chieftains and the dangerous heretic himself won't try to use the roads to escape. They are like cornered animals. So you must use caution on the roads."

"Why me, my lord?" Harsen asked. "The scouts and couriers of the Frontier Corps are renowned for their bravery and swift riding."

Hilsingor smiled reassuringly. "I wish for this letter to draw less attention than usual. I want it to arrive by the hands of a merchant, not a soldier. This explanation should be sufficient for your purposes. Now, the new year comes soon and this business must be conducted in haste."

"Then I am honored to serve," Harsen said.

When Harsen had departed from the wooden castle with the letter, Hilsingor and Arnolf watched him from a window.

"What if he reads the letter?" Arnolf asked. "We may never find him again, or Rildning."

"That's what Widsem is for," the marshal said.

84

RILDNING

North of Gilgalem, Vaynland
Thawtide, 2269

Rildning hoped he would encounter a small Raffen patrol. He would pick them off with his bow, then steal a horse. Or perhaps he could sneak up on a camp and take one. Attempting to reach Bronhildia by foot and back would take months otherwise.

Before he had departed Gilgalem, the Sage insisted he take a Vayn or two to guide and help protect him. But Rildning knew the way himself, knew the risks, and did not want to wait for Tirgranir to agree to send his clansmen.

As he walked the woodland paths, he considered ways to speed his travel if he were unable to acquire a horse. He did not speak Raffen, so he could not pose as one. The green tattoos on his face and hands would be difficult to hide anyway. He could not pretend to be a Frontier Corpsman for the same reason. But he wondered how close to the frontier the settlers had come. The empire would grant the nobles new lands to farm and defend, as they had elsewhere. The settlers would have horses and carts aplenty.

For several days he trekked at a good pace, driven by thoughts of what would happen at Gilgalem if all the envoys failed, as he felt he had done. Did Eniri safely cross the sea? How had Owerdir fared in the Naren-Dra Mountains? He hoped Urgamdir would still be alive, and that Harkarom would be persuaded by the Gallerlanders' persistence, if nothing else. Perhaps he was naive, he thought, to go on this journey. But what else could he do at Gilgalem under Tirgranir?

As the days passed, Rildning saw more and more Frontier Corps scouts and Raffen patrols. They were always too many to ambush or too disciplined for him to sneak a horse, but he stayed close to the roads in case an opportunity presented itself.

One morning he was awakened by creaking wagon wheels and heavy hooves. It sounded like a single cart, so he arose and carefully followed the sound until he could see it clearly. A single covered wagon trundled north on the road with a Frontier Corps banner fluttering from a short pole. There were no mounted escorts, but Rildning knew soldiers could be inside. He followed the wagon all morning, trying to assess its cargo. Having only seen the one driver and worried about encountering soldiers on the road ahead, he took a chance.

He slung his bow over his back and broke into a jog toward the back of the wagon. The muddy slush was slick but he managed to catch up without spooking the horses. He grabbed the back of the wagon and hopped on as gingerly as he could without falling. He looked for a place to try and peek through the layers of canvas, but everything was tied up tightly. So he drew his stone blade knife and clenched it between his teeth.

He slowly picked his way around to the side of the wagon with his moccasin toe tips. The sway and jerk of the wagon threatened to buck him off his toeholds, but he finally managed to approach the heavy-hooded driver. Taking his blade in one hand, he sprang onto the driver's bench and put the knife to his throat.

When the driver yelled out, a sudden familiarity struck Rildning and froze his knife hand. Feeling the blade fall from his neck, the driver turned to look upon his attacker as he elbowed him in the face.

"Bandit!" shouted the man as his blow landed.

Rildning careened off the bench and into the icy mud. Holding his bleeding nose, he was stunned by what he had heard. It couldn't be, he thought. He sat unmoving in the mud as the driver lashed his horses onward.

After a moment, the driver slowed and then stopped them. When he jumped down from his bench, short sword in hand, Rildning pulled himself up. He looked around for his knife but not hard. He walked toward the wagoner.

The two men approached each other as if they had each seen a ghost. When they were close enough to hear the heaviness of the other's breath, they stopped. The wagoner did not lower his sword.

"Stop there," the man said in Gali.

Rildning couldn't bring himself to speak. The man looked him up and down, then swept back his own hood to reveal his thick brown hair and beard.

"Is it you, Rildning?" he asked, now in Brintilian.

"Harsen?"

Harsen lowered his sword and took a step closer. "You're no longer a wilderman. You are one of them. A true Gallerlander. Aren't you?"

"And you're no forester," Rildning said, glancing at the Frontier Corps banner. "Why are you out here?"

"I came to look for you," Harsen said. "I . . . I'm sorry, Rildning. For leaving after Nalembalen, especially the way I did. I'm sorry, my old friend."

"My friend . . . are you?"

"I saw what they did to the prisoners of the tree city," Harsen continued. "I saw what they did to Yelgoram, and the others. Then they forced Odon to join the empire."

"Yelgoram is dead? And Odon surrendered?"

Harsen nodded. "And every tavern from New Lorin to Eglamour to Rachard is posted with rewards for your death or capture. I'm wanted too, in New Lorin, so I left. But living under a hood is no life for me. I'm sorry I abandoned you, my friend."

Rildning shook his head. "You chose your own path. I never intended to drag you into a war between the empire and the natives. I never intended it for myself either, when we first set off with Varesig and Orren those four long years ago. But the forests of Gallerlandia changed me. The people changed me. I wed Eniri, in the fashion of her people. We have a son."

"A son . . . Must be quite a lad," Harsen said with a glowing smile.

"She is away, and I left him for the road," Rildning said. "The Gallerlanders and other tribes are on the cusp of defeat."

"How can I help?"

"No, my old friend. I was nearly responsible for your death in Nalembalen. You cannot—"

"I came to Rachard to look for you, whether you want me or not," Harsen said. "I won't be going back now. So here I am. Let me help your cause, or at least your family. I have no family left in New Lorin. There is no more trade with the Gallerlanders. Everything is war, the building of castles, the chopping down of the forests I once tended. There is no place for this forester but in the woods that still stand wild."

"These woods now have roads of stone," Rildning said, "for the marching of the boots of the Frontier Corps. They tame the wilderness as easily as they topple the tribes. I fear the struggle has already been lost, but I must continue trying to find help among the other tribes."

"Then let me help. Leave the mud and let my horses do the work. And I've got a wagonload of provisions. There is much for us to talk about."

"You shouldn't have come."

"You shouldn't have put a knife to my throat."

"I'll only endanger you."

"You can act as my slave if we are questioned. And you've got the nose to prove it. Sorry about that."

"I must go north, I don't have time to—"

"I'm going north as well, to Bronhildia," Harsen said. "Sent by the marshal himself."

"The marshal? Why . . . How . . . ?"

"Just climb aboard and we'll talk all about it."

⚘

It had been years since Rildning rode in a horse-drawn wagon. It felt good to rest and watch the horses carry them forward. He relished the fresh wheat roll slathered with onion butter and draped with cured beef. And the flagon of winter beer.

"So that's how it was," Harsen concluded. "I returned to New Lorin but after a while the old governor suspected me of having a hand in Varesig's death. I escaped to Eglamour before they came to arrest me."

"What is Eglamour like?" Rildning asked.

"The empire's new capital of all of Pemonia. The emperor's representative, the exarch, resides and holds his court there. It's called the Imperial Council, which Odon and the Raffen king just joined. The city is stunning. Grand palaces and such."

"I remember the title exarch," Rildning said. "The empire used them for far-flung imperial possessions, not colonies."

"Yes indeed," Harsen replied. "No more colonies, but provinces. Everything changed, as in old Almeria. The exarch's imperial council is made up of provincial governors and barbarian kings. It's a grand scheme."

"The building of the New World," Rildning mused. "And you mentioned Rachard."

"It's the marshal's new frontier city and the capital of a province they call Bram. I was just coming from there before you nearly knifed me. Aside from the town, Hilsingor is building something mighty big there. The foundations look like a castle, but much larger."

"You said the marshal himself sent you north?" Rildning asked.

Harsen nodded. "I signed up with the corps back in Eglamour, hoping I would find you out here. Not long after I arrived in Rachard, the marshal's men took me to him. He gave me a secret letter and told me to deliver it to the chief of the Bronhildi."

"You're going to Harkarom?" Rildning asked. It seemed too good to be true. Rildning looked up into the sky as the Gallerlanders did, trying to take note of everything he saw, to remember what a lucky sky looked like.

"Yes," Harsen said. "Hold up, what's this?" They looked up ahead. There was a cluster of horses and men walking about on the road.

"Raffen patrol," Rildning said.

"Remember, you're my slave."

Rildning noticed the Raffen did not appear alarmed, perhaps because of Harsen's Frontier Corps banner. But they grew suspicious when Rildning's green tattoos came into view. They stopped the wagon and tried to give Harsen orders in Raffen speech. Harsen simply shrugged. Finally, a Donovard soldier walked up to the road from a little encampment inside the woods.

"What is your business?" the Donovard asked.

"Messenger sent by the marshal, on the road to the Bronhildi," Harsen answered. He pulled the letter from his coat to show the soldier the purple seal. The Donovard was satisfied but Rildning saw the Raffen eyeing him warily. They spoke to the Donovard.

"Who's that savage with you?" the soldier asked.

"A slave I won from dice," Harsen replied. "He is my own business."

The Raffen were chatting now among themselves and to the soldier. Rildning didn't like the looks of it.

"Why is your slave armed?" the Donovard asked.

"Well . . ." Harsen hesitated. "Well, I want him to shoot if any more barbarians or wolves or outlaws jump out from the woods. As you can see from his face, if he gets unruly I handle him just fine."

"The only barbarian in these woods is the one sitting next to you," the soldier said. "You best not arm a slave you won from dice."

"You best leave me to my business of delivering the marshal's correspondence," Harsen said, "lest I report you to Rachard." The soldier backed down and waved the Raffen away from the wagon. The Raffen was still agitated but Harsen flicked the reins and sped away before they could protest further.

"Tell me about the letter," Rildning said when they were safely down the road. "Why did Hilsingor send you to Bronhildia?"

Harsen told him about the conversation he had had with the marshal. "I thought it odd," Harsen concluded, "that he wanted a wagoner newly arrived to the frontier for this task.

But he said he wanted the letter to be delivered without drawing attention."

"Strange," Rildning agreed.

"The thought crossed my mind that I had been discovered. But I had just arrived in Rachard and they didn't ask me about you. So I'm sure they didn't realize who I was. If they had, I'd have been arrested then and there. But the marshal did warn me about the dangers of this road and that Gallerlanders were using it. He even said chieftains and perhaps you might use it to escape Gilgalem."

"Why would they think we would leave our strongest refuge?" Rildning pondered. "If they thought we were about to escape they would more heavily guard the road."

"Perhaps they don't believe you will try to escape," Harsen said. "They simply wanted me to hurry on my way."

"Perhaps."

They continued up the north road, catching up on events and recalling many memories from days long passed. Rildning was glad to be in the company of his old friend. But his mind constantly wandered back to Hilsingor's task for Harsen, which seemed odd. But the good food, good banter, and improving weather easily distracted him back to the wagon ride.

85

ENIRI

Southeastern Coast of Nydenland
Thawtide, 2269

Eniri came up to the deck of the ship, as she always did, to watch the sunrise. The salty air was subtly warmer with the winds from the north. Perhaps it was also the view of the other ships plying the waves alongside Bothrobim's. The fleet now numbered more than thirty ships.

Bothrobim had done well recruiting from the various harbors as they circled under the southern part of the main island. Eniri didn't care if they were doing a favor for Bothrobim, wanted money, or simply wanted to flee the war, so long as she did not return to Gilgalem empty-handed.

The fleet was a wonderful sight, but its size must have finally scared off the persistent Raffen ship on which Tegmad was bound. After they visited the harbor of Ormy, the ship disappeared. Eniri had all but given up hope until she spotted a Raffen ship on the horizon. The crow's nest had seen it first. Bothrobim joined Eniri at the prow for a look.

"Tegmad's ship," he said. "They must have cut around while we were at Ormy."

"Why would they sail right into our fleet all alone?"

There was another call from the lookout above them. Bothrobim translated.

"They are not alone. A Raffen fleet is behind us."

382

Eniri became frustrated. She was satisfied with their numbers and was homesick. She wanted to return to Gallerlandia. "Can we outrun them?" she asked.

"We're going to try," Bothrobim said. Then he hurried off to give orders to his men. Eniri saw one of the crew raise a blue flag after Bothrobim shouted at him. The other ships responded by raising the same flag. Then all of the ships unfurled every sail to pick up speed.

As they neared the solitary Raffen ship, they saw a gangplank extend out the side of the ship. A man was shoved out onto it. When they got closer, they saw the man's feet were bound and attached to a rope held by several Raffen crewmen.

"It's Tegmad!" Eniri cried as Bothrobim returned to her. "Can we help him?"

Bothrobim shook his head as Eniri noticed something peculiar.

"Why is that Raffen crewman waving a yellow flag?" she asked.

"It's a request to stop, usually for deal making," he answered. "But they can't be trusted."

They watched as the Raffen ship veered out of the path of the fleet and let out its sails to keep up a bit. There was another furious waving of their yellow flags. A Raffen man prodded Tegmad off the gangplank with a spear. Eniri screamed when he crashed down into the water. They could see his arms flailing but his legs were still tethered to the ship with a long rope.

"I'm sorry, Eniri," Bothrobim said. "The Raffen do not want to deal. They're just . . . making a show of him. We've seen this before."

The Raffen gave a final wave of the yellow flags as their crew reeled Tegmad back in. But when they still saw no signal from the Nyden, they stopped reeling Tegmad in. After a few moments, they cut him loose. Eniri saw his body wash away lifelessly behind the Raffen ship. She buried her face in Bothrobim's shoulder. He shouted orders to the crew and a nearby ship.

Eniri clutched the side of the ship as she watched two Nyden ships swing over toward the slower Raffen ship.

When they came close enough, the Nyden archers filled the Raffen deck with volley after volley of arrows, then they sped away and rejoined the fleet. The dead of the Raffen ship littered the deck and hung from the rigging while the Nyden were untouched by the few Raffen archers who tried to respond.

"I'm sorry, Eniri," Bothrobim said. "I wish we could have done more."

"He is avenged," she said coldly.

"The Raffen fleet won't catch us, not until we reach Roydenwoap at least. We must stop there because I know many ships will join us before we sail to Aggarwal. If the Raffen are foolish enough to follow us to that harbor, then we will give them battle. But it will be worth the risk for us."

86

OWERDIR

Sipadshur, Naren-Dra Mountains
Thawtide, 2269

"Do you have everything?" Ankarmesh asked. Owerdir touched the gifts the seneschal had given him, hidden under his furs and snow robe. He could feel the belt of little bottles and powder eggs on his waist. There was the goat bladder and reed contraption on his handless arm. And layered inside his snow robe were small knives and darts of stone.

"I have everything," he said.

"And you won't forget what you have learned here?" Ankarmesh asked.

"I won't forget. And I have the *Book of Shroud Alchemy* as well."

Ankarmesh nodded his approval but was hesitant to bid farewell. Urikimesh stood nearest him, with four shell sleds and mountain goats ready. Six shroud alchemists were ready and waiting as well. Hadanish, whom Owerdir still suspected of being tasked by the other seneschals to spy on him, was among the six.

"I don't know how to thank you," Owerdir said.

Ankarmesh smiled. "I wish the council had done more. Best of luck to you and your people. The clouds are clearing and I'll be watching."

They bid each other goodbye and Owerdir stepped into Urikimesh's shell. Their descent through the ridges, snowfields, and rockfalls went much faster than when

Owerdir had come up the mountain. Although the giant tortoise shells protected them from the jagged rocks, Owerdir's head pained him until his ears finally popped.

Ankarmesh had been right about the weather. Every day was warmer and brighter than the last. Owerdir felt good about not returning to Gilgalem empty-handed as he had once feared he would. He would remember the two brothers who perished on the way up, for he never would have reached the Naren-Dra without them. His only regret was that the seneschals had not offered help. But he was grateful for Ankarmesh's hospitality and generosity.

Owerdir had learned enough of the Nari language to understand the outlines of the campfire banter. All of the shroud alchemists were honored to have been chosen by Ankarmesh for the dangerous task of helping the Gallerlanders. They did not appear to harbor any ill will against his people; in fact they were curious about going down into the forests of the Low Earth. But Hadanish, who rarely spoke to anyone, was not happy.

As Owerdir and the Naren-Dra reached the foothills, they came into view of a little cove fed by a long, narrow inlet that led out to the sea. The mountains guarded either side of the brackish inlet, which gradually necked down to this little cove. The cove was not empty. A dark blot interrupted the sunlight sheen. As they continued down, they could see it was a large ship anchored in the middle of the water.

"Not Rahlampian, nor Bronhildi," Urikimesh said. "My brother taught me the sails through the Window of the World."

"It must be the foreigners," Owerdir said. "A single ship could mean they are scouting this area. Perhaps not so far from the Naren-Dra as the council thought. Come, we must get a closer look."

"We may go, but it's time for the goats to return, if they are to find their way back," Urikimesh said.

"Then let us release them," Owerdir agreed.

The Naren-Dra emptied the shells and loaded the provisions and equipment onto their backs. They shed their snow robes and stuffed them into the shells. Without more than a swift hand signal from Urikimesh, the goats turned and dragged their empty shells back up into the mountains, one behind the other. Owerdir marveled at them, knowing he probably would never see such a sight again.

They continued on toward the cove, scrambling down slopes and rock ways wet with snowmelt. They saw a small boat depart from the big ship toward the steeply sloped shore. It was the only sandy beach within view. Owerdir and his men took care to keep out of sight, walking through ravines and gullies or behind bushes, coming out a few times to check the view. As they got closer the foothills became thick with hawthorns and rhododendron. The rocks became more rounded and less perilous.

An hour before sunset they reached a covered precipice from which they could observe the beach and the ship. They saw the little boat had landed there and the crew fanned out along the beach and into the reed-choked pools ringing the area. The gray shine of the crew's armor confirmed they were foreigners.

"Why are they here?" Urikimesh asked.

"As I told the council," Owerdir said, "the empire will come because they can."

"What should we do?" Urikimesh asked. Owerdir thought for a moment.

"We cannot let them gain a foothold here," he answered. "They could use this cove to bring the legions into Gallerlandia from a new direction, or into Naren-Dra or even Rahlampia."

"Then let us stop them," Urikimesh said.

"We will wait until nightfall."

❧

It was night when Urikimesh shook Owerdir awake. The shroud alchemists had also rested, but now it was time. They looked down into the cove and saw lamps aboard the distant ship. The beach was lit by campfire. Tents had been set up. There were barrels, crates, sacks, timber, and a Frontier Corps flag that was stabbed into the sand.

Owerdir and the Naren-Dra weaved down through the ravines to the beach. They could hear the foreigners drinking and singing merrily. The wind smelled of burning wood and wine. Owerdir gave the hand signal to split into two groups. There appeared to be less than a dozen foreigners in the camp.

Owerdir and a few others huddled behind the largest tent. One of the shroud alchemists took out a small blade and cut a neat slit into the side, then slipped inside. Owerdir could barely make out a muffled yelp. A moment later the alchemist reappeared and gave the signal that the tent was cleared. Owerdir looked across the fire to the other side of the camp, presuming the other Naren-Dra were clearing those tents as well.

He counted seven men around the campfire. Owerdir reached into his furs to his crafting belt. He counted the corked bottle tops with his fingertips. He pulled out the fifth, as agreed with Urikimesh, and aimed it carefully.

The half-drunken foreigners never saw the little clay bottle spin through the air, never heard it break upon the logs. Their song was broken by the flare-up of the fire and the sting that tore at their eyes and lungs. They never saw their masked attackers. The ambush was over as soon as it began. The fire died back down and the camp was quiet.

Urikimesh looked out toward the ship with Owerdir as the others rummaged through the tents for useful items. Hadanish sat alone by the fire, unconcerned with spoils or the ship.

"The ship is too distant to notice," Urikimesh said.

"We should go out to them," Owerdir said.

"But how?"

"Their little boat," Owerdir said.

Fear flashed across Urikimesh's firelit face. "We—we do not do floating," he said. "We ride the snows and the mountain winds, not the waves. The only Naren-Dra who swam were those who delved deep into the flooded caves of the mountains, where the giant crystals grew. But no longer. Not us."

"I'm from forest folk myself," Owerdir said. "But we must row out to them. When the sun rises, they will see what has happened here, and we will be outnumbered and forced to run, leaving them to their original task. Come, let us row out to them."

"What is rowing out?"

"Don't worry, the waters of a cove are calmer than the sea. Come with me."

After much delay and prodding, Owerdir succeeded in holding the hands of Urikimesh and one other man named Dimuzid as they stepped into the boat. They gripped the sides as if their lives depended on it, but breathed easier once Owerdir joined them. Hadanish came willingly, raising Owerdir's suspicions. The other shroud alchemists gave them some of the bottles from their crafting belts.

After brief instructions on the use of oars, the four rowed out into the dark waters. Fewer lamps were winking on the ship but they could see sentries walking up and down the deck. Owerdir gave a few head nods and hand signals. With strong hands and toes adapted to clutching the smallest of icy mountain ledges, Hadanish and Urikimesh crept up the stern of the ship while Owerdir tethered the little boat to the ship. Dimuzid stayed in the boat to ensure their escape route was protected. Owerdir leaped out of the boat and grabbed a rope Urikimesh lowered to him. His missing fingers hardly slowed him.

When all three were aboard and safely hidden in the shadows of the moon, they crept off one at a time to complete their tasks belowdecks. Urikimesh had to silence a sentry when he came too close.

Owerdir found a hatch and entered the ship. The snores of the crew and the creaking of the swaying ship was more than enough to hide his footfalls. With ease he made his way down to the bottom. He brought out seven clay bottles and emptied the green liquid contents onto the planks near the keel, where they puddled. The wood smoked as the mixture ate into the ship's belly.

He took out another bottle filled with a metallic powder. He dumped it into the smoking puddle, then retraced his steps to the door. He looked back, seeing the fog build and hearing the sizzle grow. He quickly returned to the deck without encountering a single foreigner.

All was still quiet and Owerdir could see no sentries. He crept back to the stern and looked down. Dimuzid was there, his masked face looking up at his. Owerdir slid down the rope.

"Where are they?" Owerdir asked. His voice was impatient. Before Dimuzid could answer, Urikimesh appeared stepping around the side of the hull like a furry masked barnacle.

"Did it work?" Owerdir asked when he had gotten into the boat.

"The fire should be starting now," Urikimesh said. "And the acid?"

"I think it worked," Owerdir said.

"Where is Hadanish?" Urikimesh asked. They were all growing anxious.

"I don't hear the sound of mass vomiting," Dimuzid said. "Maybe something happened to him?"

A few moments later they heard shouts from within the bowels of the ship, faint at first, then loud and panicked. The dark waters glimmered as more lamps appeared. Feet pounded inside the hull. Even from their little boat they could smell the burning and a strong sweet-salty scent.

"How long do we wait for Hadanish?" Dimuzid asked.

"We should wait no longer," Owerdir said after a few moments.

"He cannot swim," Urikimesh said.

"They may already have him," Owerdir said. But he did not think Hadanish was dead. He remained suspicious of Hadanish, who had disliked Owerdir from the start. He had been too silent during their journey and agreed too easily to come aboard the ship.

They heard more shouting and looked up. Sailors had spotted them. Urikimesh reached for the tether and cut it. They rowed away from the ship as Dimuzid broke a bottle of hiding smoke. The darkness enveloped them as an archer came to the side of the ship.

When they had gained some distance, they stopped rowing and watched as the ship teetered amid billowing smoke coming from belowdecks. The ship lurched and sat lower in the water as flames chewed through the far side. Men were throwing themselves overboard.

They rowed back to the beach and watched until the last flames dipped below the water. No crew made it to the shore. When the dawn appeared, only floating debris and bodies could be seen. None of them looked like Hadanish. The Naren-Dra were saddened by the loss. Even Owerdir lamented Hadanish's death and wished things had been different.

§

Their journey continued south and west until they reached trees and forests and paths Owerdir recognized. He felt more at ease without Hadanish's constant glare. And he was optimistic the shroud alchemists and his own new skills would benefit Gilgalem.

87

RILDNING

North of Rachard, Bram Province
Thawtide, 2269

Rildning and his friend made camp each night within the canvas of Harsen's wagon, using the cast-iron stove for light and heat. Slices of salted pork, leeks, and lentils stewed in the top while a small fire popped and sizzled in the bottom. Its four legs stood on a slate tile that protected the wooden planks of the wagon. For Rildning it was a luxurious setup.

They recalled more of their previous adventures, good times and bad, and their most fateful journey to explore Gallerlandia. That task seemed so naive to them now.

"I'm glad to have found you on the road," Rildning said.

"Me too," Harsen said. "We're quite lucky in this vast wilderness. It's like old times. Well, you're a greenskin now and I'm a false merchant for the . . ."

Rildning felt fear creep up on him.

"What is it?" Harsen asked.

"It is vast, isn't it?" Rildning muttered.

"Well, crisscrossed with roads now, but yes, still vast."

"Vast . . ."

"Of course. Say, you don't look well."

"It's too lucky . . . meeting each other on the road. Too lucky."

Harsen frowned. "Well, this is the only wagon road to the north. They couldn't have known you were—"

"One of my men went to Bronhildia before me. He was captured. They might have guessed I would try in his stead. Or somehow they knew I would go. That I have gone."

"If the marshal had a spy in Gilgalem, wouldn't the Gallerlanders have sniffed him out?" Harsen asked. "Maybe it's a coincidence."

"Where is the marshal's letter?"

"We cannot open it. The seal is our safe passage, as you have already seen. If we try to pass patrols without it sealed up, we won't make it."

"And what if we are riding into a trap? Safe passage into a trap. We must have a look at the letter."

Harsen reluctantly fished it from his coat and handed it to Rildning. He examined the outside of the parchment. On the front was written *Highchief Harkarom of the Bronhildi*, and the back folds were sealed with the purple wax of the high offices of the empire and stamped with the marshal's signet ring. Rildning tried to carefully lift the parchment with the wax but it was no use. The seal broke completely.

> Highchief Harkarom,
> Thank you for offering to ransom the barbarian Urgamdir. He is of little concern to me, except any information you may have extracted from him about Gilgalem, the refuge of his fellow Gallerlanders.
>
> However, the man who delivers this letter to you is of great concern. His name is Harsen and he is a wanted man. Most important, he may come to you with a companion who will appear to be a Gallerlander, but don't be fooled. He is Rildning, a high heretic and most wanted man.
>
> Should you have the fortune to detain them both, I would be grateful if you would send them back to Rachard under heavy guard and send word quickly. I would reward you with five thousand newly minted electrum emperor coins, which would be sent back with your tribesmen. If capture is not possible, I will gladly pay four thousand for their heads.

I will personally inform the exarch of your cooperation.

Hilsingor of Ned Gollen
Marshal, Frontier Corps

Rildning handed the letter to Harsen to read for himself. His reaction was the same as Rildning's: a clenched jaw and a new alertness to the sounds of the night outside the wagon tent. The wind whipped louder, the forest lions screamed more viciously, and the raking of branches sounded like someone walking.

"I'll burn it," Harsen said, opening the little door of the stove. Rildning plucked the letter from his hands.

"We cannot do that," he said.

Harsen became frustrated. "It is our death warrant. You were right, it's a trap. Let us destroy it and go to—"

"Go where?" Rildning interrupted. "If you go back to Rachard they'll know you read it and arrest you. If you go back to Eglamour, they will realize in time that you did not complete your task and they will find you. They may even have scouts following us. We must press on to Bronhildia, because I still need help from Harkarom. But this time we go a bit wiser and on our own terms."

"Can we write a new letter?" Harsen asked.

"We will gather up the fragments of wax and remelt it on the letter."

"It won't get past the patrols," Harsen said. "We lack the marshal's seal."

"Put your thumb on it and wave the parchment around. It's the best we can hope for."

"Risky." Harsen shook his head. "They will take a closer look than that, and Harkarom will know we've read it."

"We will already be in Harkarom's power by then," Rildning said. "We have to risk it."

"I'm not going to freely put my life in that vile heathen's hands!" Harsen cried.

"I didn't ask you to come with me," Rildning said.

Harsen put his hands in his face. "I'm sorry, Rildning. I let them use me as a hook; the carrier of a letter condemning us both. Such a fool!"

"My friend, how could you have known of their scheme?"

"I remember now." Harsen hung his head and shook it slowly. "I remember, back in his petty castle. Your book. The journal you kept . . ."

"My journal?" Rildning recalled all of the candlelit evenings, the bloodberry ink, the sanity those pages had provided him in dark times. He had lost the book when they fled Nalembalen and bitterly regretted the loss, as if part of him had died. But in time he was relieved, thinking of it as a break from his previous life. He now had Eniri and Enildir, and the freedom of the wilderness. Until the Frontier Corps came. He had given little thought to the journal until now.

"Then the marshal will know me well," Rildning said.

"I'm sorry, Rildning," Harsen continued. "I caught a glimpse of a singed, weathered book and didn't think twice, even when they hid it from me. Now I know it was yours. Somehow they found—"

"It means nothing to me," Rildning said. "But it means they certainly knew who you were. I'm sorry you are as wanted as I am."

"Let it be so!" Harsen now turned defiant. "If a man cannot stand beside his friend when most in need, then he is no friend and shall have none. Let us go to Bronhildia so you can make your requests to Harkarom. Come what may, this is a task I will complete."

"Come what may," Rildning echoed.

88

MRIGAMAD

Calbrian Sea
Thawtide, 2269

Mrigamad had been ashamed back in the domed council building of Eglamour, but not for the reasons Anfinnan might have thought. He felt ridiculous for falling into the trumpets, but he was ashamed to be there in that place at all, and to see the domnitar negotiating with the empire for a kingship. Mrigamad wanted no part of it. Most of all, he was ashamed that Anfinnan knew the truth about his delay in returning to Castracane when the foreigners attacked his home, and that the domnitar was using it against him.

Part of him was glad to be away from Anfinnan and the Brintilians. But when he arrived in Rilhammor and boarded the imperial ship, he lamented he had to share it with drigoman Trelnaf. He also regretted he had to carry the news of the domnitar's dealings and the summons for the hostages to guarantee the alliance with the empire. Even more, he hated the idea that the Rahlampian warriors would now be absorbed into the ranks of the Frontier Corps. This knowledge made him miserable throughout the voyage.

Standing at the prow, Mrigamad watched the chill waters of the dawn ripple as the ship pushed through the sea. Spring was coming, he could feel the change in the air. Now as they came within sight of the coastal marshlands of home, he was struck with a moment of clarity.

396

Mrigamad plucked the summons from his cloak. He crumpled it and ripped the neat row of colored wax seals from the parchment. Then he threw it all into the rippling water. He looked at the coastline. Not too far to swim, but the water would still be cold.

He rushed back belowdecks. The knights who had been sent to escort Trelnaf and protect Mrigamad were awake but concerned with breaking their fast. He hurried past their rooms and the crew quarters. He found the hatch down into the bowels of the ship. It was dark, with one oil lamp to see by. Once inside, he barred the hatch closed.

Mrigamad soon discovered where they had stowed his windrazor. But then he found something better: an ax. He shook his furs off and put on his reed armor. Unlike the heavy iron plates worn by the knights and Trelnaf's layers of embroidered robes, he knew the reeds would help him keep afloat, as proven in the estuaries of home.

He picked up the ax and hacked at the base of the mainmast where it was bound to the keel. The wood was exceptionally hard and it rang out an alarm along the bones of the ship. In his mind he could see the restless pushing of the cold water as it waited under the belly of the ship, waiting to flood in.

He knew it would fill every chamber and cavity, then pull the ship down into its deep beds. And with it the drigoman of the domnitar, he who would surrender his people to the wolves. Mrigamad had little concern for himself as he swung the ax. He would try to swim for the coast if he could, but he accepted with a grim smile that he might not have the chance.

By the time he had chewed halfway through the mast, there came shouting and beating on the hatch. He knew they had realized his disappearance and the chopping sounds meant sabotage. He happily continued his work.

Eventually they hacked through the hatch and Mrigamad was forced to answer them. He grabbed up his windrazor and, though difficult to handle inside the ship, he managed to aim its point up the ladder and through the breaks in the hatch. He repeatedly stabbed upward. Blood spattered down amid screams from above. He tossed his windrazor aside and returned to chopping the mast, but again they tried to force through the hatch.

As Mrigamad again left his ax to fight, there came a great groan from the ship. The wind blew and the ship rocked. Mrigamad threw himself down and covered his head as the mast tore, throwing long splinters and ripping the ribs of the ship.

He risked a look and saw the planks warp and burst. A white column gushed up into the ship. The smell of salt filled his nostrils as the cold water swirled around him. The decks above were torn open with the crush of the mast, sending down rays of morning light. He could hear men screaming and the banging on the hatch had ceased.

He sloshed over and took up the ax again from where the mast had thrown it. He hacked the ship's ribs to widen another wound in its belly. Before he could get far, the sea tore through and twisted the keel. A second smaller mast snapped like a broomstick. The death cries of the ship rattled up and down the keel.

Mrigamad's mind raced as he felt the cold creep up from his knees to his hips. He let go of the ax and took hold of two heavy earthen jars stoppered with lamp oil inside. When the water reached his neck he took one last breath and ducked under the foaming swirl. The seawater burned his eyes for a moment, but growing up in the coastal marshes and shrimp ponds allowed him to adjust quickly.

He looked above him and saw the air pocket vanish. He looked toward the ship's wound and saw it had widened. The weight of the earthen jugs was enough for him to push toward it and sink through. But then he struggled.

The ship was quickly being pulled down and started to roll over. He saw the morning sun flood into the darkness below him, then the ship's wound swallowed him in again. He kicked and closed his eyes to the stream of the water. He dropped a jug but grabbed the mouth of the wound and pushed himself against the stream.

His lungs heaved now as he swam for the darkness. The eerie groans and wrenching of the ship filled his ears. There was a great popping as the weight of the sea finally snapped the keel. The ship rolled over and the wound pushed him away.

Mrigamad let go of the second jar as he turned his eyes up to the light. He could see the debris clogging the surface. His body grew cold and his lungs begged for breath. At last he reached the surface, his reddened eyes full of sun and sky. He crawled onto a fragment of decking and collapsed.

When Mrigamad awoke, he was cocooned in raw wool blankets in a bed in front of a hearth fire where dry clothing and his reed armor hung. Without moving his body, he shifted his eyes to look about the room.

The crudely crafted rafters of the cabin were strung with smoked wild garlic, smoked salmon, and leafy herbs. A rusting longsword hung above the mantel. Then he saw a body, a man wrapped in wool on another bed, as he was. But Mrigamad could not see his face well.

Mrigamad listened for a while. Hearing nothing but the crackle of the fire, he sat upright slowly. The wicker door of the room was closed and he couldn't hear anything from the other side. He slid out from the blankets and with wobbly legs donned some clothing, a mix of foreign garb and Rahlampian woolens.

He crept toward the man who slept nearby. It was Trelnaf. His breathing was faint but he was quite alive. Mrigamad was disappointed to see him survive. He glanced at the rusting sword on the wall, then gazed at the fire. Returning to Trelnaf's helpless face, he prayed his breathing would stop. But he would not take his life in this way, despite the evils of this man.

There were no windows in the little room, only the wicker door. Mrigamad took the sword from the clay-brick mantel and crept to the door to listen. Just the sound of waves crashing on a nearby shore. Slowly he pushed open the door.

He was in a small, two-room cabin. Ahead of him was the outer door and windows on either side of it. A furry form was hunched beside a fire, silently stirring a clay bowl with a carved stick. Mrigamad froze, but heard the crackle of an old voice.

"Gali?"

"Rahlampian," Mrigamad said.

"Pity. You speak Gali?"

"Yes."

The hunched man, moving slowly, stood with the help of a walking staff and turned toward Mrigamad. His beard was long and matted, his hair unkempt. His eyes were dark and sunken, and his face was dirty and scarred. His hands were gnarled, and his fur tunic and cloak were a patchwork of rabbit and beaver.

Mrigamad's eyes quickly fell onto the clay bowl, wondering what was inside it. He did not know for how long he had been asleep.

"Who are you?" Mrigamad asked.

"A survivor, like you," creaked the man. He seemed somehow younger than the old husk of his body, then his gaze became distant. "Perhaps my solitude has been my salvation. But I was once called Ebeloft, before . . . before the storm."

"You are an imperial."

"I was."

"And you pulled me from the sea?" Mrigamad asked.

"The both of you. I buried the others, best I could. Made sure they were dead first. Did you meet . . . a storm?"

"You could say so."

"Why are you holding my sword?" Ebeloft asked.

Mrigamad lowered it and leaned it in the far corner of the cabin, making sure to keep himself between it and Ebeloft. "May I have a drink?"

The hermit pointed to a moldering bucket and gourd ladle. The water smelled fresh, so he drank deeply. Ebeloft used his little stick to flick roots roasting over the fire onto two small planks of wood. He handed one to Mrigamad. From the bowl he poured a brown dollop of thick meat-smelling sauce over the roots, and they ate the meager meal with their fingers. To Mrigamad the roots tasted raw and bitter, but he was glad to have something in his stomach.

"Thank you," Mrigamad said, "for all of this. Can you tell me where we are, and how you came to be here?"

Ebeloft pondered the questions before answering. "We are where the storms come from. The storms brought me here, and they keep me here. You know them, and have made them. Did you kill the others? Have you come to kill me?"

Mrigamad stared into Ebeloft's fear-filled eyes. He couldn't run or fight. His every movement was slow, his speech labored.

"I'm not here to harm you," Mrigamad said. "How long have you been here?"

"I cannot recall." Ebeloft rubbed his forehead as if trying to shake loose a memory.

Mrigamad glanced around the room. Handmade tools, old bits of ship rigging, sail cloth, and a broken windrazor. He stared at it for a while, noting it had been snapped close to the handle. It lay in a pile of wood shavings, as if used for carving. The whole cabin was undoubtedly built by this man by himself, log upon log with clay smeared in the gaps.

"Were you a soldier?" Mrigamad asked.

"Not I—no . . . I cured men's wounds. Used to."

"A healer, then. You've certainly nursed me back to health, and the man back in there."

"Doctor . . . before the storm."

"Tell me," Mrigamad said, "what happened in the storm?"

"Screaming," the hermit said, more timid than ever. "Much screaming . . ." He shook his head and clenched his eyes, as if wanting to be rid of the memory. "There was death on the wings of the air. Blades in the wind . . ."

"You were attacked." Mrigamad glanced at the broken windrazor.

"I went belowdecks, but it was no use," the hermit said.

Memories also flooded back to Mrigamad. The fire catapulted from the imperial ships. The burning of his home, Castracane, and the other villages of his land. The chasing of one of the imperial ships.

"What happened?" Mrigamad asked.

"A storm of cutting. Red rains . . . You killed them all . . ."

Mrigamad tossed aside the wooden plate and took hold of the hermit's tunic, jerking him to his feet and looking him in the face.

"You are not—we spared no one!" he cried. He shook Ebeloft, feeling the renewed strength in his own arms. The realization made him want to shake this man to pieces. His teeth gnashed until his mouth was numb. Ebeloft did not resist. The hermit's wide eyes gazed through the anger in Mrigamad's, resigned to fate but still fearing it.

"I survived . . ." breathed the hermit faintly.

Mrigamad let him drop to the floor as he retrieved the rusted sword. Ebeloft waited on his knees. He did not flinch when Mrigamad raised the sword, but fear laced his sunken eyes. He may have wished for death.

"You burned the cities . . . the people . . . my family!" Mrigamad shouted.

Ebeloft lowered his head. Mrigamad tightened his grip, but his arms would not swing the blade. His heart leaped from his chest, but he could not take a breath. Hot tears welled in his eyes. Mrigamad stumbled backward away from Ebeloft, who did not look up.

Everything about the massacre aboard the imperial ship came rushing back to him. The images of their dead mixed with those of the smoldering ruins of his home. The faces of his wife, his children. But his vengeance was spent. He looked with pity on the hermit, the healer who had been among the killers.

Mrigamad looked down at his hand and found it empty, the sword flung aside. Ebeloft finally looked up at him.

"You are in the land of storms . . . your land of storms," the hermit said. "Walk the path of the sun along the coast and you will see the ruins of our anguish." Ebeloft then buried his scarred face in his hands and slumped to the floor to weep.

Mrigamad stood and took a deep calming breath. He eyed the windrazor stub, the shipwreck, and the wicker door that hid Trelnaf. Then he turned toward the cabin door and walked out into the sunlight.

89

ENIRI

Northeastern Coast of Nydenland
Thawtide, 2269

Bothrobim promised Eniri that Roydenwoap would be their final stop to recruit Nyden warriors before sailing back to Aggarwal. But he warned her the Raffen fleet behind them would harass them, or worse.

When they arrived at the harbor, they found it still in friendly hands, but word of the war renewed in Chadwoid had already arrived. The taverns and quays where Bothrobim and Eniri recruited more ship captains quickly became rowdy.

"We're sick of fighting," said one Nyden captain. "My opinion is my own, but I favor submitting to Toredwoak rather than risk another generation of this war."

"The Raffen have us firmly by the neck, it's true," Bothrobim said. "We can regroup on the mainland, help the Gallerlanders and secure them as allies, then return to finish this."

"Go to Gallerlandia?" scoffed a Nyden chief. "Why risk the sea when I can fight the Raffen in the next town?"

"Will the tree dwellers send their warriors here to rid us of the Raffen after we help them? I think not," another said.

"None of this is easy," Bothrobim acknowledged. "But look out into the harbor there, and beyond. See how many others I've convinced of this. If you join us, our fleet will number over fifty ships, enough for this to work."

The men looked out to the harbor and saw the fleet taking on provisions for the crossing of the sea.

"Word is the Raffen are already on their way from Chadwoid," said a captain. "Maybe it's too late for us."

"We've been here in Roydenwoap for three days," Bothrobim continued. "We won't be staying a fourth. So if you want to join Toredwoak, then stay here and wait for the Raffen. But if you want a chance for freedom, come with us."

Most of the captains relented. When Bothrobim was satisfied, he hurried them from the town into the harbor to get under way. His watchmen saw them coming and unfurled the ship's great sails, displaying the sea-blue stripes of the Nyden. Like a wave, the other ships of the fleet did the same. Then two by two they sailed toward the open sea, with Bothrobim's ship near the front. As they neared the mouth of the outer harbor a ship ahead raised red signal flags.

"Look there," Bothrobim said to Eniri. "They have spotted the enemy."

As they rounded the last spit of land protecting the harbor, they could plainly see a Raffen fleet close, as if they had been waiting for Bothrobim's fleet.

"Looks like they want a battle," Bothrobim said. He stroked his blond tusks nervously.

"Surely we have more ships," Eniri said with hope.

"Number no longer matters, not since they brought their foul-burning weapon. And they do have fast ships; you've just yet to see them." He rushed off shouting orders to his crew and arranging signals to the fleet.

As she gazed at the billowing sails of the enemy, Eniri noticed a growing darkness beyond them on the horizon. She pointed as Bothrobim returned to her.

"An ill omen," she said.

"I see it," Bothrobim said. "We'll battle the storm or the Raffen, perhaps both." She looked at him worriedly. "The clouds don't appear to be blowing this way," he added. "We might steer round them yet."

Smaller Raffen boats were breaking away from their main fleet, coming close enough that Eniri could make out the brown wolf heads on their sails. Then she saw blue-striped sails among them.

"Nyden alongside the Raffen?" she puzzled.

"Toredwoak's Nyden," Bothrobim said.

Before long the little Raffen boats were close enough that their prows and sides, bristling with archers ready for battle, could be seen. Bothrobim yelled out the call to arms.

"Don't worry," he said. "We will defeat them. But you should go below."

"Nonsense. The women of my people are as brave and skilled with a blade and bow as any man."

"I have no stoneswords aboard," Bothrobim said. "But you are welcome to a bow. The quivers are—"

Before he could point them out, she moved to sling three quivers over her shoulder. He pointed up into the rigging.

"If your aim is good, take up a spot up there," he said. "The decks will be awash in blades if they board us, but you'll be shooting them well before we slash them down here. Watch their archers as well, as there is no room for fancy jumps to evade their shots up there."

Without a word she ran up the main mast and positioned herself on the platform below the crow's nest and alongside two other Nyden archers. The better view reminded her of being back in the trees. The storm was closer now.

Bothrobim's ship, the *Tasaloop*, turned along with others, forming a V for the approaching Raffen to sail into. Eniri saw they would hit them from both sides. Five of the Raffen fast boats were close now. Raffen battle cries rang up across the waters, and the Nyden responded in kind. Arrows shot up from a Raffen vessel and rained down on a Nyden ship named the *Woorasloop*, positioned next to the *Tasaloop*.

Six Raffen ships passed into the V and Eniri let loose her first volley, with every shot finding its mark. She was accustomed to shooting with the sway of a tree, and even while running. The challenge of aiming around the rigging and sails of her ship and theirs, with the lurch and roll of both ships and the gusting winds, was similar to shooting through branches waving in the high breezes of home.

She and the other archers shot fiercely. One of the Raffen ships grazed by the *Woorasloop* and the crew attempted to throw their grappling hooks over her side to board her. But the Nyden archers and spearmen responded swiftly, cutting their ropes. The Raffen passed by and engaged other ships. The other fast boats attacked elsewhere in Bothrobim's ten-ship V.

Next, from up ahead, came a formation of two Raffen quick boats and a larger ship with a catapult built on its deck. Eniri saw two clay barrels waiting in the catapult's bucket. Each was stoppered with a knot of rope set alight by the crew.

The captains of the Nyden ships closest to this formation frantically directed every archer to this catapult ship, taking down many crewmen. Eniri did so as well, until Bothrobim veered the *Tasaloop* away. Then she saw the catapult ship attack.

The arm of the machine tossed the two barrels with a single throw. One splashed into the water and disappeared in a sizzling spray of foam that shot up in a column. The other crashed into the hull of a Nyden ship at the waterline. Fluid spewed out and erupted in wicked flames. Eniri saw the part in the water ignite first, then spread up the hull and onto the deck.

Then came another volley from the catapult ship. Both barrels landed on the deck of the same ship. Nyden men who had been there were splattered with the fluid and set alight. They jumped into the water but Eniri saw the flames dance on their backs even as they tried to duck under the water. The water intensified the flames.

The fire chewed on the ship and leaped up into the sails. Eniri watched in horror as the remaining crew threw themselves overboard. There was no hope for a ship and her crew once stuck by the dangerous fire. One of the Nyden archers next to Eniri shook her to break her stare. He yelled something to her in the Nyden speech. She saw the formation had passed by and a second was headed toward the *Tasaloop*.

All the archers again concentrated on another catapult ship. Bothrobim expertly steered the *Tasaloop* out of the catapult's aim, but caused the V formation to split and give way to the sinister ship.

As the second Raffen formation cut by them, Eniri and the others unloaded on the catapult's crew, delaying their second volley after the first had hit the water. She aimed at one of the barrels but her arrow harmlessly punctured the clay. The archers beside her snickered.

"Shooting them won't do any good," said one.

"It's the water-fire they call quicklime," said the other. "You can't disable it. Shoot for the crew."

Bothrobim maneuvered the *Tasaloop* around behind the second Raffen formation. As they turned, Eniri could see another Nyden ship erupt in flames from the first catapult. Other Nyden were attempting to board the catapult ship, but its archer escorts made the task too costly.

As the *Tasaloop* gained on the second catapult ship, one of the fast boats darted in front. Another Nyden ship, the *Danusloop*, rammed the fast boat, causing it to take on water. As its archers struggled to shoot, spearmen on the *Danusloop* stabbed at the Raffen archers like fish in shallow water.

The catapult ship then flung a barrel at the stern of the *Danusloop*, and another barrel ripped through the main sail of the *Danusloop* and crashed into a Nyden ship beside it.

By now some Nyden warriors had boarded the other catapult ship and kept her crew too busy to lob more barrels. The fires of several burning ships released black streams of foul-smelling smoke that rolled along the water, obscuring everyone's view. But Eniri could see that Bothrobim kept up the *Tasaloop*'s speed and maneuvered around the stricken hulks to join another Nyden captain in boarding and destroying another fast boat.

Eniri glanced back at the catapult ship that had been boarded, seeing it was now on fire. Through the smoke she could see the Nyden who boarded were now scrambling off. She shot at the Raffen archers who tried to kill them as they fled.

The catapult ship lurched and a great column of water shot up from within it. The ship rolled violently and floundered, with foaming and hissing water tearing at its hull. The blaze was fueled by their store of quicklime, even as the broken ship sank below the waves. From her perch, Eniri could see it glowing down into the depths, leaving a trail of searing bubbles as it plummeted.

The Nyden gave a cheer but the tossing of the clay barrels from the other catapult ship soon ended the celebration. One barrel sailed over the deck of the *Tasaloop*. Eniri was close enough to catch its putrid smell.

She was down to her last quiver of arrows as she shot down on another Raffen fast boat. Then she heard a sickening tearing sound and the scream of one of the Nyden archers beside her. He fell off the platform onto the deck below. She and the remaining archer scrambled behind the mast as more arrows struck it.

Eniri grabbed for the spare quivers left by the killed archer. She popped up and shot at the catapult ship as it was lining up on the *Tasaloop*. She and the other archer were still under fire from a fast boat, so they took turns bobbing up and down.

This time the *Woorasloop* was able to maneuver behind the catapult ship. They got close enough to hook it and spearmen protected the Nyden as they jumped aboard. They ran to the catapult crew, whom Eniri could see were armored in metal. Unlike the first crew, they wore helmets. But it wasn't enough for the determined Nyden.

As they were winning control of the catapult, out of the smoke came a huge Raffen ship. Its prow was fitted with a ramming rod that had already speared and was dragging parts of a smaller Nyden ship. The greatship swept aside a Raffen quick boat, tossing several of its archers overboard. As it slipped out of the smoke, Eniri saw it had two large mast-like beams that were hinged on the sides of its top deck. They swept down like arms, and on the ends were long blades of hammered iron.

The greatship plowed forward, gathering the *Woorasloop* and the struggling catapult ship on one side and the *Danusloop* and the quick boat on the other. The greatship's arms struck all four ships, tearing their sails and rigging like paper and string. Their masts were cut in half. The greatship barely slowed as it ripped the broken masts from their decks.

The Raffen quick boat crumbled and was pulled under the greatship, while the *Danusloop* was dragged along by part of a mast. That arm of the greatship tore off and fell into the deck of the *Danusloop*, sinking it in a blink. The catapult ship went down in a flurry of flame and hissing foam, while the *Woorasloop* alone bobbed like a useless buoy in the wake of the greatship. A few of their warriors and crew jumped to other ships before it too disappeared under the swelling waves.

The greatship seemed to bring the storm with it. It took a while for it to turn for another pass, which gave Bothrobim time to decide what to do. He shouted orders and signal flags were raised. Eniri knew it was time to make an escape, and some captains had not waited for the signal to turn their ships toward the sea.

The rain became a torrent. It was with great difficulty and many arrows expended by Eniri and her companion that they hit their mark. She looked out through the holes in the sails of the *Tasaloop*. She could see the greatship coming for another plow with its one-bladed arm.

Lucky for her the greatship passed just out of reach of the *Tasaloop*, but it also had rows upon rows of archers. The greatship took down one other Nyden ship before turning back for the harbor. Eniri saw Bothrobim's fleet was probably too scattered and the storm too dangerous to make it worth the greatship's lumbering turns.

With the enemy gone, Eniri came down from the mast. She joined the others belowdecks as Bothrobim and a few others struggled to keep the *Tasaloop* afloat. She listened to the sounds of the sea as it pounded to enter the hull and the thunder and howl of the winds above.

The fleet would lose more ships to the storm that night than had been lost in the battle. When calmer winds greeted them with the dawn, many more had suffered broken rigging. A few were abandoned and two turned back to the harbor, willing to face the enemy again or surrender rather than sail further out to sea in an unworthy vessel.

The remaining fleet was scattered, so that even from the crow's nest Eniri could not see more than a dozen ships from horizon to horizon.

"Don't worry," Bothrobim said. "The captains know the way to Aggarwal."

"But will they be ready?" she asked.

"Don't worry."

90

RILDNING

Northern Frontier of Bram Province
Thawtide, 2269

The journey to Bronhildia continued without much problem for Rildning and Harsen. They passed several patrols much as they did the first, with none of the soldiers giving the blank seal a second look. Rildning and Harsen reasoned these patrols either didn't want to slow a messenger of the marshal or were lazy, since they knew patrols farther south had already inspected them. But one of the patrols was of interest.

"Broke in the cold," Harsen had told the soldier. "Dropped it in the wagon and cracked it underfoot. So I melted the seal to keep the parchment shut." The soldier rolled his eyes and waved them on.

"Wait," Rildning whispered to Harsen. He had to play the part of Gallerlander slave, but there was something about this soldier. There under his helmet Rildning noticed every lock of hair showed a knot of tight curls. "He's a Fernil," Rildning whispered. "Ask him."

Harsen squinted at the soldier. "You're a Fernil, of the Old World?"

"So I am." The soldier nodded.

"Beg your pardon," Harsen said, "but why are you this far south? I thought your folk were given Brewel Province."

"We're imperial subjects all the same," the soldier said. "Everyone knows most available troops are headed south. Even Arukans in the east have been called up. The last campaign to drive out the dirty Gallerlanders, like your slave there."

"Ah, well, we don't get all the news so quick down in Rachard, at least not men of the wilderness roads like me." The soldier gave Harsen an odd look as he flicked the reigns.

"Hilsingor is swelling his legions," Rildning said when they were out of earshot. "We have to hurry."

The following day they were surprised to find a small village built behind a road toll. From the looks of the horses and carriages stopped at the inn and tavern, Brintilian nobles from the Old World were traveling south. There were also Bronhildi tribesmen who wore imperial cloaks and armor.

They rode up to the toll and Harsen waved the letter and bellowed his orders, as he had grown accustomed to doing. This time the guards were cautious. They saw the blank seal and insisted on escorting Harsen and his slave to the newly appointed magistrate who was living at the inn.

"Why are you carrying a blank purple seal?" he asked suspiciously, turning the parchment in his hand and fingering one of the flaps. Rildning knew he was tempted to open it.

"As I told your men earlier," huffed Harsen, "my fool slave stepped on it. The many cold nights make these things brittle, so I remelted it shut."

"Careless for a trusted messenger to let this Gallerlander step on important correspondence. And why is a wagoner delivering the marshal's letters, anyhow?"

"I was given the letter by the marshal himself," Harsen answered. "He told me to make sure it arrived with as little attention as possible. Those were his exact orders, sir."

The magistrate was still not satisfied and continued to flick at the fold. He turned to Rildning.

"And what about this heathen? Why would the marshal permit you to carry important correspondence alongside this spawn of Memelos?"

"He's my slave."

"But I see no chains or sign of restraints of any kind." The magistrate frowned. "Most unusual." When he switched into Gali, it was clear this magistrate had served long in the region. "What do you have to say, Gallerlander? Tell me your name, clan, and village."

Rildning was caught off guard. He looked at Harsen as his mind raced for answers that would appease the magistrate. Harsen helped fill the void.

"Yes, you may answer this man," Harsen said slowly in Gali.

By then Rildning had it. He turned to the magistrate. "I am Bafimdir, of the Ulgol clan. I lived in Torfnar, before it was destroyed by the crusaders."

The magistrate pursed his lips and returned to Harsen. "How did you get him?"

"A game of dice, from some fool who captured him as he fled Umbyrland. Now, I must deliver the letter with haste, unless you prefer I take the long road back to Rachard with your name."

The magistrate stopped flicking the parchment. Without a word he reached for his wax and placed his own seal alongside the blank purple one.

"To ensure you have no further troubles," he said. "On your way then. I'll send two of my Bronhildi troops to escort you the rest of the way."

"Not necessary," Harsen said. "I'm to avoid attracting—"

"It is necessary," the magistrate interrupted. "I don't want the marshal's correspondence to be further delayed. It is my duty to see you safely arrive with that letter. They have their own horses and will not burden you. Be off."

❧

Rildning and Harsen felt uncomfortable being shadowed by the two Bronhildi. For the most part they kept to themselves, but Rildning and Harsen were wary that the magistrate had told these Bronhildi of his suspicions. On the first evening they made it impossible for Harsen not to offer to host them in the covered wagon. As the food cooked on the stove, the Bronhildi men watched them carefully, especially Rildning.

"He is a peculiar-looking Gallerlander," one of them said in rough Brintilian speech. "Is he Teshi?"

"No," Harsen said. "Umb-something-or-another. They're all the same to me."

"Not to me," the other Bronhildi said. "The Umbyrs are our neighbors." When Harsen moved about the wagon for his utensils, this Bronhildi chided him. "Careful not to break the second seal."

It was then clear to Rildning and Harsen that the magistrate had told them his concerns. The following day Rildning quietly urged Harsen to do all he could to avoid hosting them for meals, but it was no use. They were all companions on the road. Each evening was more tense, with more probing questions from them.

When at last they reached the first toll of the Province of Barres, which they were surprised to learn was part of the new Bronhildia, their escorts talked with the Bronhildi toll man. Five additional mounted tribesmen joined them. When Harsen asked why, he was told it was for his protection.

"What are we to do?" Harsen asked when they camped. For once, he and Rildning were left to themselves while all the Bronhildi dined together outside. "Should we try to sneak away?"

"We are already in the hands of Harkarom," Rildning said. "His tribesmen will make sure we go directly to him, which is what we wanted. He'll open the letter and we'll have our say. That's all we can do, but Gilgalem depends on it."

91

HILSINGOR

Rachard, Bram Province
Day of Farewell, 2269

Hilsingor raised a flagon of wine. They toasted to the new year that would dawn the next morning. Pendigied was intrigued.

"We do not count the seasons together as one as you do," the young king said. "Nor do we count the generations, as the Gallerlanders do. The Raffen count the seasons."

"We all mark time differently, yet it passes the same nonetheless," Hilsingor said with a smile.

"Wise counsel," Pendigied acquiesced.

The Raffen king's comment made Hilsingor think of his wiseman, Alda. Genthus had told the marshal that the old man was a constant irritant for Pendigied, and that Alda had been ordered to camp alone outside the city since their arrival. Genthus had urged the king to allow Alda to attend the Day of Farewell feast, insisting that it was proper. All of Hilsingor's commanders and councilors were present for the special wine and meat. But Pendigied forbade it, so Hilsingor wondered if the time for dealing with Alda's distractions had come.

The marshal looked out happily at the tables. There was moose steak rubbed with smoked salt, warty pig pie with butter bolete, twice-baked acorn squash with chervil cream, and candied plums—a sweet Brintilian tradition for the new year. The feasting was accompanied by music and dancing.

415

Long banners of the Raffen, the Bronhildi, and the Frontier Corps hung high in the rafters of the grand hall. The hearth fires glowed with every color of twisting flame, fed by pinecones rolled in orpiment, gley, and sand, as was the Brintilian custom to mark the passing of the year.

The talk at the marshal's table was of the victories of the past year and the brave souls that had been lost. This was also customary, and every commander vied for the highest honors among the living. Eventually they drifted into talk of the upcoming campaign.

Hilsingor thought now was as good a time as any to tell them about a change he had decided upon, while the wine slowed their wits and perhaps soothed those who would be quick to anger, namely Ravorglad. The marshal stood to address the hall.

"Honored knights and nobles and our brethren of the continent. I have news to relay to you for the new year that will be difficult for many of you who are so eager to serve. I've decided all the legions, veteran and newly formed, will fall upon Gilgalem together, rather than be split among other fronts. One legion will be left to garrison Rachard and the frontier forts. Everyone else will take part in tearing down their mountain fortress."

The commanders and councilors cheered at this, but the marshal raised his hand to stay their excitement.

"However," he continued, "I have also decided to delay the campaign." Shock and disappointment plastered each face at the tables. "I came to this decision because I have reason to believe the enemy may be lured out of their refuge, or even that their leaders will surrender."

"I oppose this plan," Pendigied said in rough Brintilian. "I did not march from Woudenhod to Eglamour to Rachard to allow them to surrender. We must make war on them!"

Some of the other knights and nobles joined his protest.

"The Raffen king is right," Ravorglad said. "We must crush them so they cannot rebel. We are ready!"

"Sir," Firkas said in a more respectable tone. "Perhaps the enemy will strengthen while we delay."

Hilsingor was prepared for those brave enough to grumble. He unfolded a parchment from his pocket and read it to them.

> Marshal Hilsingor,
> It is with great pleasure that I announce yet another barbarian chieftain has joined the empire, along with all of his people. Domnitar Anfinnan of the Rahlampians traveled to Eglamour and pledged his service to the emperor. He now sits beside Odon in the Imperial Council of Pemonia.
> Enclosed you will find a letter written by the domnitar himself, in Gali, for you to deliver to the Gallerlanders holding out at Gilgalem. The domnitar attempts to persuade the Vaynking Tirgranir to surrender to us. He repeats my generous terms that his people will avoid punishment for resisting us for so long, and that he would have an honored seat at the council, equal to Odon's status as a vassal-king, and remain ruler of the Vayns.
> Send them Anfinnan's letter at your earliest convenience. If at any time you determine it has not had the desired effect, then I urge you to spare no effort and no expense in besieging them. May God continue to grant you victory.
> Exarch Bredahade

The hall was silent as the commanders and the nobles considered the exarch's instruction.

"The domnitar's letter will be delivered," Hilsingor said. "Tirgranir will likely refuse, but we'll explore this possibility before we spend many months investing and besieging the mountain. If he does not surrender, I have an effort under way to lure some of their warriors from the refuge, which would make the siege that much easier. Don't worry yourselves over thoughts of lost glory and plunder. For you are likely to have your battles, maybe more than you realize.

"Let no one think Gilgalem will be like Nalembalen," he continued. "We walked into a forest, vice climbed up a mountain. And there are more Gallerlanders holed up in that mountain than we fought under Odon or Erambrin. The Frontier Corps has never besieged an enemy of this size in a natural fortress made by the hands of Memelos himself. The proper paths must be prepared.

"Now, enjoy the wine and meat! It will be another year before your bellies have it so good, and the savages of Gilgalem may stop you from seeing that day."

Hilsingor was pleased with himself as his men devolved to their own chats. He looked at each of his senior commanders and they nodded to affirm their loyalty to his plans. Then he left the table.

❧

As instructed, Widsem was waiting by the hearth fire of Hilsingor's chambers when the marshal returned from the feast.

"Have the arrangements been made?" the marshal asked.

"Yes, they're waiting for our signal," the ranger answered.

"Very well. While we wait for him, I have another issue for you. Read this." Hilsingor handed him the letters from the exarch and Anfinnan, then sat down at the fire. Arnolf prepared a plate of cheese and wine for Hilsingor.

"I did not expect this, sir," Widsem said.

"You don't think it will work?"

"I don't," the ranger answered. "Gilgalem is their last refuge. Most will choose death over the empire, as Erambrin did."

"Ah, but Odon surrendered, and we all said the same about him. Odon wanted to save his people. Erambrin did not have as many children and elderly as Odon did, and as Tirgranir has at Gilgalem. Perhaps the Vaynking will accept how well Odon and Anfinnan have been treated and will consider the exarch's offer."

"I tried to find Ferndeath again," Widsem said, "but he did not show. He could decide on his own to melt the mountain, whatever that means."

"It sounds like something that could disrupt our plans, which could deliver Gilgalem into our hands easily enough," Hilsingor said.

Widsem returned the exarch's letter to the marshal and put Anfinnan's in his pocket.

"Go ahead and deliver the letter, in the same fashion Walpert did," the marshal said. "Afterward, give Ferndeath a few days to come out."

"Shall I kill him?"

"Not yet. I want to know how the Gallerlanders react to all these messages. But if he insists on doing something that could disrupt our plans, well, we cannot allow that."

There was a knock on the door and Arnolf poked his head in. "Marshal, the Raffen king has arrived."

"Yes, we are done. Show him in."

"Thank you for the invitation," King Pendigied said as he walked in.

"Of course." Hilsingor smiled. "But before the tobacco and brandy, let me introduce to you my master ranger, Widsem. There is something we would like to show you. A gift, really. And it is up to you whether to accept it."

The marshal led Pendigied out to the balcony and pointed outside the walls.

"Over there . . . You see the torchlight on the edge of the wood, by the little tent? A few of Widsem's discreet scouts are waiting just there in the wood. I've heard from Genthus and others how much your wiseman Alda has pained you. How he has selfishly served the ghost of your father, rather than his flesh-and-blood king. And how he has tried to spoil our new partnership at every turn. Resisting the new era we will build together while casting shame on all of us.

"I want you to know those problems can end, right now, if you wish. The city guard will run out to his burning tent and report he died in his sleep after tipping a candle."

Hilsingor watched the king's eyes, fixed on the little tent.

"I have wished for his death many times," Pendigied said, "and have nearly taken his life myself. But I swore an oath to my father . . ."

"In the empire, oaths are very important," Hilsingor said. "You have sworn an oath to the emperor through the exarch.

And to God through the archbishop. I've sworn the same. And your men and mine are all sworn to duty in the legions. But we hold oaths to the living to be more sacred than those made to the dead, even upon their deathbeds. Our highest obligations are to the empire and to God. Any conflicting oath is made to be broken."

"My only regret will be not doing it myself," Pendigied said after a moment.

"This frees you from such a distraction," the marshal replied. "But only if you wish it."

"Light it then."

Widsem went back inside and returned with a lit three-pronged candelabra from the table, which he waved back and forth from the balcony. They saw three figures exit the wood. The one with the small torch waited behind the tent as the other two entered and then exited the tent as quickly as they had come. The fire was then touched to the base of the tent before they sprinted back in the moonlight.

"Great men often make hard choices for the good of their subjects," Hilsingor said as they watched. "And hard choices require sound advice from trusted councilors, which you unfortunately did not have in Alda. With this obstacle now removed, we will accomplish great things together."

92

TIRGRANIR

Gilgalem, Vaynland
Raingreening, 2270

The scout gave the message to Tirgranir, noting that it was found tied to a spear on the plains. Tirgranir ignored Rumban's expectant look and read to himself.

> King of the Vayns,
> Our peoples have warred for generations. But a new era has dawned, one the Gallerlanders have resisted as fiercely and courageously as any of the tribes. Despite our quarrels, I wish for peace. Do not wilt in the sun of a new day, but welcome it.
>
> I sit now at a council in Eglamour beside Goynking Odon and the other tribes. We talk of what this new era will hold for us. The kings of the council are brave and wise, having chosen life for their people, not death, and partnership with our new brothers from across the seas.
>
> I entreat you to descend from your mountain and accept the generous terms of the exarch, as we have. You can end this war with the steps of your feet. Your reward will be great, and your honor will remain intact. Come forth and join us in these better days. Landships of food will be only the beginning of new partnerships.
>
> Domnitar Anfinnan of Rahlampia

Tirgranir sighed as he dismissed the scout. Then he gave the letter to Rumban.

"Shall we summon the chiefs?" the steward asked after reading the message.

"No."

"They will want to—"

"It doesn't matter," Tirgranir said. "Half would probably support surrender, while the other half would put a stonesword in the hand of every old woman and child."

"Perhaps we can feign interest in the offer until more help arrives," Rumban said.

"Help from where? Sending envoys failed, demonstrating our desperation to the enemy. Crawling on our knees in winter to beg help from our enemies. Ha! No, we will answer this ourselves, one way or another."

"Perhaps the council will—"

"I am Vaynking!" Tirgranir shouted.

He despaired that it had come to this. The tiny unripened fruits of early spring were being rationed. Herb-sprinkled water and grass pastes served as nourishment for many. He could feel the strength and will of his people weakening.

93

RILDNING

Gradhild, Barres Province
Raingreening, 2270

Rildning and Harsen were not surprised when their Bronhildi escorts arranged for them to be detained upon arriving at the palisade gates of Gradhild. It no longer resembled the Umbyrland village it once had been. The Bronhildi had converted the place into earthen berm dwellings like what they used in the north. Harkarom's new capital was draped in a mossy bloom of tiny yellow flowers that opened with the first rains of spring.

They were finally ushered inside the main gates. Inside the berm wall were wooden buildings with sod roofs where new vegetables were sprouting in the sun. The paths were split logs and flagstone. Rildning could read the disgust in Urgamdir's face at the sight of the village's transformation.

They were brought to a central mound of earth, where an inner palisade protected the highest point in the expanding town. The mound, high enough to see the surrounding countryside from, was carefully terraced and crowned with a fortified house of rough stone and thick oaken beams. Its prominent supporting beams were fashioned like eagles' wings, and its roof curved steeply upward toward three central pinnacles, the middle having the highest spire. The roof was also sodded, and its walls were cloaked in yellow-bud moss.

The house's two-story windows were opaque and seamed, as if made with cloudy gems. Two great eagles of stone perched menacingly on either side of the threshold at the top of the ramp. One had the torn body of a fanged snake curled about its talons, while the other clutched a dying mountain lion.

Inside the grand house sat Highchief Harkarom. Rildning and Harsen were brought before the throne on a path of cloudy windows set into the floor, providing a view of the dimly lit tombs of dead highchiefs below. Rildning thought it was extraordinary that the empire had convinced Harkarom to move his capital further south to help lead the war, but Harkarom had gone further by moving even the bones of his forefathers. The cloudy window path led to the feet of the highchief himself. Several important-looking Bronhildi were clustered around him.

The tribesmen motioned to Harsen to provide his letter. The woodsman looked at Rildning. He nodded. Harkarom spoke at length with his tribesmen before reading the letter. Then, when he had finished reading it, Harkarom stared at the pair, pondering their fate.

"May I read the letter?" came a Brintilian voice creeping out from around the throne. A richly robed man with long silver hair came forward.

"Not at this time," Harkarom responded in heavily accented Brintilian. He was younger than Rildning had expected, a king with more stories of victory to his name than many kings twice his age. But it had not been enough to stave off the Frontier Corps.

"Highchief Harkarom," the Brintilian man continued, "I wish to remind you—"

"That the exarch sent you to be of service? Yes, I'm well aware," Harkarom said. The highchief continued to study Rildning and Harsen. "Leave us," he finally said.

"My lord?" The Brintilian was clearly surprised.

"All of you, except my brother Premarom," Harkarom said.

The tribesmen and the Brintilian filed out the doors. When the court had cleared, Harkarom gave the letter to Premarom. When he had read it Harkarom motioned to the fire pit.

"Burn it," he said.

Rildning and Harsen looked at each other. Without questioning his brother, Premarom tossed the parchment into the coals. It flared and turned to ash.

"My apologies for the rudeness of my drigoman," Harkarom said. "The exarch sent him as an envoy to broker peace and advise me. All of the tribes who have joined the empire have the misfortune of having them as minders. My people call them men of many tongues for their language abilities and also their tendency to speak truth one moment and lies the next."

"Perhaps the exarch has already sent a drigoman to Gallerlandia to prepare for your king's surrender," Premarom quipped.

"May I speak?" Rildning asked. Harkarom nodded. "There will be no surrender. The Gallerlanders will continue to resist the empire."

"Not much longer, I think," Harkarom said. "I'll be the first to lament the empire came to our realm at all. But my people are better off living as part of the empire than being destroyed by it. The Welkars tried to fight, and look what happened to them. Foolish.

"The wise recognize when they are defeated and look for the opportunity in surrender. You must convince the Gallerlanders to yield while the imperials are still offering good terms."

"Your sacred electrum should be an easy price," Premarom added. "If the imperials are so greedy for it, then give it to them. It will never be lost in the earth again, and your people will live."

"My people won't give up what is sacred to them," Rildning said. "They believe it ensures their safety in the next life."

"But you don't believe it," Harkarom said. "Tell me, how did they ever accept you?"

"There was a time when I was among the most dedicated knights of the colonies. But that was a long time ago. The beauty of this continent and its people changed me, and the Gallerlanders accepted me. I don't believe they should be imperial subjects. The empire will twist the New World like the Old World, and you will have helped them."

"I respect your courage, Rildning. And your candor and persistence. Your reputation as a heretic is well-known, but so are your admirable qualities. But you don't see the world for how it is. It is no easy choice, but if you love the Gallerlanders then you must change your path. Help them adapt to the modern times, as we have, not lead them into destruction."

"They will never surrender."

"King Odon surrendered," Harkarom continued. "He was wise to do so. I wanted to see his head on a pike above the walls of Eglamour, or at least killed in battle as Erambrin and Gratgofa. But he preserved his people. Let me tell you, there is nothing harder than what Odon did and what I have done. Leading your warriors into battle is glorious. Leading them into the hands of the enemy—well, I've made it palatable and found the opportunity in it.

"You are, of course, a most wanted man and have no hope of rejoining the world. But you can still persuade Tirgranir that a measure of freedom lies within surrender, even if not for yourself."

"I came here to persuade you to throw off those bonds," Rildning said, stepping toward the throne. "The Bronhildi, like others, have long been bitter rivals of the Gallerlanders. But think of what you are doing by joining the empire as one of many vassal-kings. They will make you like them, caught up in a whirlwind of conflict and coercion and conversion. This continent will soon mimic the repeating violence and grief of the Old World, an infection that will never be washed away."

"I have not been to their continent across the seas," Harkarom said, "but you are mistaken if you think this realm has not seen similar times. You see through the floor windows there. Most of the Bronhildi highchiefs in those stone coffins were killed battling the Gallerlanders or some other tribe. And when the empire came, there was the Frontier Corps to our south, crusading Fernils in our north, and innumerable ships on our eastern coasts. We were defeated and made peace where it could be found."

"You must submit," Premarom added. "Have you seen what the corps is building in Rachard? Unlike your clever victory in the Ardfalm Forest, Gilgalem will not be a victory for you. Stop this bloodshed, or we will stop you."

Harkarom glared at his brother before continuing. "There are no Bronhildi or Raffen slaves in the empire," he said. "I've been to Eglamour and seen for myself. They hold hostages to guarantee the peace, but only the Hrals and Welkars are slaves. Perhaps the winds of change will shift again with time, and the empire won't be dominant. But for my days, the winds blow against you and everyone sheltering in Gilgalem."

"Perhaps we will be the winds of change," Rildning said. "Why did you burn the marshal's letter? Are you not his ally and vassal?"

"The marshal never listens to me," complained the highchief. "He regularly demands my warriors for his provincial legions, but never seeks my advice or heeds my requests. So now I'll ignore his. You will be given safe passage back to the imperial lands, then you are on your own. And Urgamdir may go as well. I urge you to use this mercy to convince the Gallerlanders to surrender, before the legions march on the mountain."

"I'll take your mercy as a sign you can see the truth of my words. Perhaps with time you will abandon the empire. Surely there is opportunity in that. I hope not to see Bronhildi among the legions when the Frontier Corps comes to Gilgalem."

"It is a certainty that you will see us, and soon. Do not mistake me, I will not hesitate to kill any enemy, even those I respect. If you don't seek peace, then I wish for you a good death. Farewell."

Rildning and Harsen were led by a Bronhildi guard to the cell where Urgamdir was held. Premarom had wanted to escort them, but Harkarom kept him by his throne to talk. Rildning guessed the highchief did not want his younger, headstrong brother to cause problems.

The Bronhildi court customs were such that the guard took them to the prison area before returning to the throne hall. They were given to a warden who carelessly handed them off to a cell sentry.

"Thank the sky omens!" Urgamdir exclaimed when the heavy door was opened. He bear-hugged Rildning, lifting his feet from the straw-strewn floor. "I was sure they would sell me to the foreigners. How . . . what did . . . who is this?"

"All will be explained," Rildning said. "It is good to see you again, and to see you well. We must leave at once."

Urgamdir gave Rildning a solid look.

"We, as in, the two of us," Urgamdir said, gesturing to Kemet, who shared his cell. "Thank the signs, we'd have both been sold, or killed, if you didn't come for us." Rildning realized he was speaking so the guards could hear.

"Yes, of course. Both of you are released and will come with me," Rildning responded.

The sentry waited for Urgamdir and Kemet to exit before shutting the door. Rildning half expected the sentry or the warden to catch on, but they didn't. The message from Harkarom to the court guard to the warden to the sentry had become muddled, evidently.

They made their way back to Harsen's covered wagon without any delay and started down the road to the south, with their Bronhildi escort in the lead.

94

OWERDIR

Gilgalem, Vaynland
Raingreening, 2270

Tirgranir laughed bitterly. Owerdir had scarcely opened his mouth before the Vaynking shrieked with madness. The rest of his court was silent. When Tirgranir finally composed himself, he cast a dark look at Owerdir and his companions.

"You sacrificed the lives of two brave Gallerlanders in those mountains, and nearly your own, to bring back a mere half-dozen cloud-dwelling mud mixers? This is the army you brought us? I suppose you are not as much of a failure as Urgamdir and Arbardir. Well, what have you to say?"

Owerdir stared at the Vaynking with disgust. "No one wishes the two brothers were still here with us more than I. It wasn't easy to leave them buried in the vast and treacherous snow." Owerdir glanced around the court to address everyone, pointing the stump of his hand at all the staring faces.

"Who among you ventured out into the winter to foreign lands, to beg allies from our many enemies? Who among you?" he insisted, then returned his gaze to the king. "I'm troubled to hear the others have failed. I would have also, if it were not for the generosity of a single chief among the Naren-Dra. These men are not mud mixers. They are warriors the likes of which you have never seen. They are no army, but they are—"

"More mouths to feed," Tirgranir said in a low, disturbing voice.

Owerdir had learned about the sabotage of the food stores upon his arrival. Shamed by the Vaynking's reaction but glad the shroud alchemists could not understand Gali, Owerdir turned and left the hall with his companions. It was the Sage who caught up with him in the stone hallway first.

"You must understand that he is pained by the plight of our people. He expected an army, from somewhere, to help."

"Why do the Gallerlanders expect folk who were long our enemies to suddenly come to our aid? I've done what I could."

"Indeed you have, and returned to us alive and with wisdom. Tell me, what was the reaction of the seneschals to my letter?"

"They did not want to involve themselves in the affairs of the Low Earth, as they call our lands. All but one."

"Ankarmesh. Am I correct?" the Sage asked.

Owerdir's eyes widened. "How could you . . . ?"

"The World Watcher thinks he spies down on the Low Earth without anyone noticing. But he has never been on the receiving end of his far-eye, to see the glint of the sun or full moon upon it. Most observers will presume it is the shine of ice atop the peaks. But trust me when I say you are not the first to meet him, even if you were the first to meet him up there. But that is a long story for another day.

"You should know Rildning has returned from Rahlampia with even less help than you did," the Sage continued. "They sent food but ultimately joined with the foreigners. Because he is persistent, Rildning departed again for Bronhildia. That tribe took Urgamdir, despite our good-faith effort to talk with them. Rildning was determined to free Urgamdir and try once more to persuade Highchief Harkarom to turn away from the foreigners. I have no hope for that, and I save my remaining hope for their safe return. And the return of Eniri."

"She went with him?" Owerdir asked.

The Sage shook his head. "She took a ship to try and enlist the Nyden. She left soon after all of you did. We have not heard from her since."

"Poor Enildir. What can I do?"

The Sage let out a tired sigh. He looked more ancient than ever, weary with worry.

"Tirgranir is uncertain of what to do."

"What do you mean?" Owerdir asked.

"He has received letters from the enemy." The Sage told him about Odon, Erambrin, and Anfinnan, which left Owerdir speechless. "Your half brother Arbardir has also not returned. I'm sorry."

"Tell me what I can do," Owerdir said again.

"Unfortunately, Tirgranir's steward has counseled him to consider the foreigners' offer for us to surrender. I've known Rumban since he was a child. He means well but I believe it's a path of bad omens. We must wait for Rildning. He must return and lead, regardless of what Tirgranir does."

"Tirgranir has rarely listened to Rildning."

"It is worse now. Even after all this time, Tirgranir is contemplating whether Rildning is a spy. Even if he won't listen to Rildning, perhaps most of the Gallerlanders will. Until then, we must prepare. Gilgalem has survived on the Rahlampian food and foraging parties—some of whom have not returned. With the warmer days, the Raffen raiders now ride the foothills as they please and have even scouted alternate paths up Gilgalem. Perhaps while we wait for Rildning, your Naren-Dra will be of use helping to hide the foragers."

"Yes, we will."

"Owerdir, there is something else we learned from the letters of the enemy. If their words are to be believed—and we have little reason to doubt them—your father is dead. They say they executed him during the winter."

Owerdir turned away to hide his welling eyes. His chest heaved and he fell to his knees and grieved.

"Like many chiefs before him," the Sage continued with a hand on his shoulder, "he gave himself for his people. We will always remember him thus. When you rise and look to the sun, walk as he did. A chieftain who was protective of those under his care. Unblinking in the face of his enemies. And proud of the son he left behind."

95

RILDNING

Northern Frontier of Bram Province
Raingreening, 2270

Rildning, Harsen, Urgamdir, and Kemet were provided a few provisions from the Bronhildi warriors who escorted them to the border between Harkarom's Province of Barres and the marshal's Bram Province. From there they wasted no time in traveling back down south in Harsen's covered wagon. Rildning had let himself fall into a dark mood, despite accomplishing what he did in Gradhild.

"Defending Gilgalem will be much more difficult without breaking the Bronhildi from the Frontier Corps," he said.

"There is nothing more you could have told him that would have changed the highchief's mind," Harsen said. "We are lucky to be leaving with our lives."

"All this way . . . and spring has come. We have nothing to bring back to Gilgalem."

"Nothing?" Urgamdir chuckled. "I'm not the prettiest Gallerlander, but I did find this Bronhildi, Kemet."

Rildning wasn't amused. "Our hopes now lie with Owerdir and the cloud dwellers," he continued, "unless the Rahlampians also have a change of heart."

"The envoys have done their best. There are many fine Gallerlander warriors in Gilgalem," Urgamdir said. "And the refuge has never been taken."

"Gilgalem also shelters many of the very young and old," Rildning countered. "Our warriors will be outnumbered, underfed, encircled, and besieged by modern weaponry. Perhaps it has already started."

"Then let us bring our warriors out, if it's not too late," Urgamdir said. "The foreigners probably won't expect that. We could raid their camps before they have prepared themselves. Then we lie in wait for them in the forests that gird the foothills below Gilgalem, sabotaging their supply lines as we did in the Ardfalm Forest. We mustn't wait for them to climb up our mountain."

"Bringing the warriors out of Gilgalem wouldn't be wise," Harsen said. "The Frontier Corps and their allies know these lands well now. It's an old wisdom: keep a refuge while you have it."

"Gilgalem is a giant bramble thicket that we're trapped in," Urgamdir said. "It will be a tomb for all. Let us at least fight."

Rildning let them banter back and forth. The sun was warming, the flowers along the roadside were beginning to peek out, and the birds were melodious. But Rildning's head ached. Had he done everything he could to seek help from all quarters?

"I think we should abandon this cart and ride the horses as fast as we can," Urgamdir said. "When I came this way, I was hunted by a man of the shadows. The Bronhildi called him a ranger. Nearly killed me more than once. He is certain to be watching the road."

"Since when are you willing to ride a horse?" Rildning quipped.

"This cart, as you call it, cost me a great deal," Harsen said. "I'll not leave it on the roadside like a piece of junk. These draft horses can pull swift enough, just say the word."

"Your Gali needs more practice," Urgamdir muttered.

"Let us continue with the wagon for now," Rildning said. "If we encounter the ranger or patrols, we can all pretend to be Harsen's slaves."

"Easy enough," Harsen said. "Rildning, shall I join you to Gilgalem?"

"Tirgranir won't like it, especially unannounced like this," Urgamdir said. "Some think Rildning is a spy, but everyone will think you are one."

"He's right," Rildning said. "And I've been thinking about it. You cannot return to Rachard either, because the marshal will have expected you to have been detained or killed by Harkarom."

"He could tell Hilsingor that he delivered the letter to the brother of Harkarom, but that the highchief himself was away," Urgamdir said.

"The marshal could write to Harkarom's silver-haired drigoman, who would speak of Harkarom receiving the letter," Rildning said.

"Hilsingor might be too busy planning the attack on Gilgalem to bother," Urgamdir said.

"Still, it's a risk," Rildning said.

"I have no good choices," Harsen said. "So I'll take the risk of using Urgamdir's story and go back to Rachard where I can perhaps learn something of their campaign, if we're not too late." Rildning and the others nodded solemnly.

The trio continued on the road, driving the horses hard. They encountered several Raffen patrols led by knights but were not harassed. A speeding wagon with a Frontier Corps banner appeared important, so they cleared the road. When the time came to part ways, Rildning and the others said their farewells to Harsen, then they continued on foot.

PART III

ORIGINS

96

MRIGAMAD

Bodamweym, Rahlampia
Raingreening, 2270

All of the clan chiefs were there. Denildon of Swaleshil. Harnachar of Peridod. Largharra of Harmengaud. Balbeg of the Usodimare. Carn of Shadfoyle, who was the Keeper of the Rock. And many others.

The countless anxious eyes of the crowd spoke of too many rumors—or perhaps too much of the truth. They watched as the leaders congregated around Domnitar Rock, now splotched with drizzle under the overcast sky. Mrigamad looked around at the crowd circling the rock. Behind them were the stilted roundhouses of Shadfoyle and landships large and small that had brought the chiefs, heads of family, and other important Rahlampians to this convening.

When Mrigamad departed the shipwrecked doctor's cabin, he had gone straight to the wiseman of his clan, Loyth, and told him everything that had happened with Anfinnan. Loyth knew nothing of the domnitar's plan to join the empire. Neither did the neighboring clan chiefs. And so Loyth organized a clan summons at the rock.

The chiefs talked while they waited for everyone to arrive. Balbeg and Denildon were the only chiefs who had an inkling of Anfinnan's intentions, it turned out.

"Said he was going to talk," Balbeg told a cluster of the chiefs as they waited. "I said, 'Talk about what, the bounty of the shrimp ponds?' Anfinnan said that was just it, that there was bounty in the empire. And that's when he went down to Swaleshil to meet that Brintilian, Trelnaf. That was the last I saw of him."

"Same," Denildon said. "Troubles."

"I'm glad you did what you did," Loyth said to Mrigamad. "Otherwise we wouldn't know Anfinnan was planning to sell off his own people."

"Well, he's sold nothing," piped up Harnachar. "He lost his people by his own hand. When everyone has heard what Mrigamad has to say, we must vote Anfinnan out as domnitar. If he were here, I would decloak him myself. He's not fit to wear the clan symbols and certainly doesn't represent us, as did those that wore the symbols before him. Decloak him, I say!"

Garedrem of Crail, the last chief to get close enough to hear Mrigamad speak from the rock, swaggered up. His black beard was already drenched with brine rum, a distilled pickleweed mash. Were it not for his younger brothers, Garedrem wouldn't know which way to walk.

"I knew," he said with a belch. "But I didn't believe Anfinnan would actually do it." Garedrem teetered before one of his brothers righted him with an elbow. The surrounding chiefs shook their heads.

"If you had known what the domnitar was doing, you likely would have spoken or vomited your dissatisfaction," Largharra said. "It has become hard to tell the difference with you."

Garedrem's mind was too foggy for him to notice the insult. But his brothers were clearheaded.

"We support a vote for a new domnitar," one of them said.

"Before any decisions are made," another added.

"The tide is not on our heels just yet," Loyth said. "Let Mrigamad speak. There will be time for that talk after."

"So he'll stand on the rock, then?" one of Garedrem's brothers asked.

"As the Keeper of the Rock, I'll remind you that the rock has always been open to any chief or anyone sent on their behalf," Carn answered.

Then Mrigamad ascended Domnitar Rock, a giant boulder believed to have broken off the Anchiclade Mountains and rolled to this spot in the marshy plain. As he stepped higher he thought about the old tales. The Agnesci forefathers of the Rahlampians, banished from early Gallerlandia, first came to these soggy lands after seeing lightning strike the mountain. They heard the roar of the boulders and found their paths, wide ruts through the swamp and sward.

This boulder was the largest, and nearby Shadfoyle was built for the first Rahlampian kings who dwelled in great stilt castles long ago torn down. When the line of kings fell and the clan confederacy was born, the boulder remained the place where all important gatherings were held, and where the domnitars mediated disputes among the clans.

Although he had been chief of his clan since his father's death, Mrigamad had never stood in that honored place. He held out his hands to quiet the crowd. Then he told them everything. The secret visit of Trelnaf to see the domnitar near the ruins of Cadentod. The journey by ship to Eglamour. The white palaces of the empire. The treachery of Anfinnan. Mrigamad's destruction of the letter and his sinking of the imperial ship. All of it. And everyone listened to every word.

Then he reminded them of the attacks by the empire. The foul-fire catapults along his coastal villages. The inland incursion. The destruction of the Welkars. The Raffen raiders. And the slow crumble of Gallerlandia. He could speak as one who had witnessed it all.

"If the clans decide to join the empire on their own, I will consider it a mistake," he concluded. "But if you decide to keep your own lands and not become beholden to distant crowns, then I'll think it wise. But either way, that decision will be made here, at Domnitar Rock, not by a false domnitar sitting in luxury in a foreign capital."

The Rahlampians cheered Mrigamad as he descended the carven steps. He felt a great burden lift from his shoulders and his mind cleared. When he stepped down into the wet long grass, Loyth led him to the other chiefs. They presented him with a new windrazor and attendants clasped a new set of reed-plate armor onto his torso. The blade was of the finest craftsmanship, the pommel a great orb of heavy blue lead.

"For service very well rendered," said Strompeter of Anchiclade, known as the Keeper of the Mountain Paths.

Mrigamad bowed humbly. "Thank you for your trust."

The chieftains each took their turn upon the rock. All of them voiced their support for what Mrigamad had said and done. All of them rejected the notion of joining the empire. Even Garedrem was not too drunk to deliver a rousing speech. Harnachar of Peridod was the last to speak. He gave the final blow to Anfinnan's power by pretending to decloak Anfinnan, using one of his men as a prop. This won cheers from the crowd.

However, Mrigamad noticed Garedrem's brothers, especially the twins, were unhappy.

"We need a new domnitar, now," said one of the twins.

"Gives the empire a single man to lure, as they did Anfinnan," Strompeter countered, shaking his head.

"They whine because Garedrem's head is too sloshy to lead anyone," Largharra said.

"Too much brine rum, not enough votes," Harnachar added.

Garedrem didn't notice his lack of support among the other chiefs but his brothers reddened.

Mrigamad stepped in, realizing the twins' repeated efforts to elevate their brother would not cease, even now. "As long as we're united, the unpainted men cannot pick us apart," he said. "We can settle the matter of the next domnitar later. For now, let us think on the enemy."

"Right, the vote at the rock is to join the empire," Carn said. "All opposed?"

Everyone voiced their opposition, except Largharra.

"Any for?" Carn asked.

"I'm for offering each of the unpainted men exactly six feet of Rahlampian marshland," Largharra said. "Seven for Hilsingor, as they say he's taller than most!"

The chiefs laughed heartily.

"And a vote to send a landship fleet to aid Gilgalem," Mrigamad said.

"We'll need our ships to defend our own lands," Balbeg said. "Not those of our rivals."

"Gilgalem is the Gallerlanders' last refuge," Mrigamad said. "If it falls, the empire's legions will soon appear on the banks of the Pernadun River. And then you'll be sending your ships to Denildon instead. We must not wait."

"He's right," Harnachar said. "Better to fight over there than upset my shrimp ponds here."

"Right, the vote at the rock is to aid the Gallerlander sods," Carn said. "Any opposed?"

"Aye," Balbeg said.

"Any for?"

All but one chief supported Mrigamad's plan. Garedrem hiccupped in abstention.

"Who will lead the fleet?" Carn asked.

"I will," Mrigamad said.

97

HILSINGOR

Rachard, Bram Province
Midspring, 2270

Hilsingor rubbed his stubbled chin. "Harsen made quick time . . . very quick time."

"Apparently he returned several days ago, sir," Arnolf said.

"Before you summon him to me, tell me what he has been up to."

"Stealing swords, sir. Harsen has a wagon full of them along with other provisions. I wonder if he plans to supply the heathens."

"Odd. He must know they detest the metal. And no word on whether he met Rildning on the road?"

"The quartermaster has tried talking with him, as you instructed, but nothing about Rildning or what happened in Bronhildia. Perhaps we put our questions straight to him and threaten his life."

"My commanders and the Raffen king lobby me daily to commence the campaign to Gilgalem. I had hoped to remove Rildning or at least Tirgranir to soften the Gallerlanders before attempting to assault the mountain. Otherwise our losses will be heavy and our progress slow."

"Perhaps after you speak with Harsen you will know better how to proceed," Arnolf said.

"No, the time has come for action, regardless of what Harsen says. If the Vaynking has not responded to our offer of terms by now, then he is unlikely to. We are well into spring and the longer we wait the more time we lose for other tasks." Hilsingor paused as he considered options.

"Arnolf, summon Harsen. Perhaps he can still be of use as we start the campaign. We could let him carry away the stolen swords, presumably to the Gallerlanders, along with information we provide to him. Arnolf, what was the name of that little village sacked by the Raffen last autumn, not a day's ride northwest of Gilgalem?"

"Birom, sir," the adjunct answered. "But it's just a ruin of scorched huts now."

"Perfect," Hilsingor said with a smile. "That will do. Send for Harsen, then I want to see Widsem and the commanders afterward."

"Yes, sir."

Arnolf found Harsen at the tavern with the other camp followers. Harsen was not surprised to see the adjutant, who escorted him to the castle. The marshal greeted Harsen warmly and gave him a plate of good food and filled a silver goblet with wine. Harsen dined as he described his travel to Bronhildia.

"Lonely and uneventful ride," Harsen concluded.

"Excellent," the marshal said. "And Harkarom took the letter?"

"He wasn't there, my lord," Harsen lied. "But I gave it to his brother, Premarom, who seemed to be well trusted and in command during the highchief's absence."

"Very well," Hilsingor said. "I suppose you did as any imperial courier would have done. Well, now that you are safely back, I have another task for you. And I pledge that you will be granted the lucrative status of most favored merchant once we begin the campaign.

"We have begun preparations to assault the barbarians' mountain refuge," the marshal continued, "but I need to resupply a unit I secretly dispatched two weeks ago. They are hiding in Birom, a ruined village near Gilgalem. They will attempt to infiltrate the mountain to weaken the defenses of the enemy before the legions arrive. You will resupply them and provide a map of our marching plans so they know which defenses to weaken first. When can you go?"

Harsen hesitated. Hilsingor thought he saw a gladness of opportunity flicker in his eye.

"I'm ready," the woodsman said.

"Excellent. Arnolf will provide you the map before you leave in the morning. I don't have to reiterate the sensitivity of this document, and the importance of the new supplies for our men in Birom."

"I understand," Harsen said.

Arnolf assigned a soldier to accompany Harsen to the quartermaster with a list of supplies to obtain. When Harsen had departed, the adjutant summoned Widsem, Firkas, Ravorglad, King Pendigied, and Walpert to Hilsingor's feasting hall, where they dined late with the marshal.

"Why waste time playing games with these traitors and barbarians?" Ravorglad asked when Hilsingor told them of Harsen's trek to Bronhildia and Birom. "Are my crusaders not worthy enough to attack Gilgalem without so much trickery to precede them? It robs them of honor."

"And I for one did not bring myself and ten thousand of my finest warriors across the continent to sit idle while little birds flit back and forth with silly messages," Pendigied complained. "Let us end these games and strike the mountain. Spring greens around us with skies fair enough for the battle we have all been waiting for!"

"As I have said," Hilsingor began, "Gilgalem is no small task, though I don't doubt the abilities of the crusaders or the Raffen. It is a matter of proper preparation. The intent of sabotage is not to lessen the honor or sport of the battle, for which there will be plenty. It is to assure victory. It also preserves the lives of more soldiers, which will be needed for the campaign into Rahlampia and to finish the route to the Durgens.

"The battle for Gilgalem must be swift and decisive," he continued. "If we can tear them apart piece by piece before drawing swords, it is better. My previous efforts have deprived them of food and supplies. This new plan will try to isolate their best leaders. Do not think victory is assured at Gilgalem because of our victories over the Goynking and the Umbyrking. Preparation is the only assurance. This is how I defeated the Arukans in the Old World.

"Now, Widsem, when Harsen leaves with the false map, I want you to follow him. He will likely divert from the path to Birom and go south to Gilgalem instead. You and your archers will continue to Birom and be ready.

"Unless they suspect a trap, Rildning or Tirgranir may be unable to resist the temptation to attack Birom. You will ambush them. After they have taken casualties, they may retreat, in which case you will pursue and drive them onward. This is when the crusaders and Raffen will get their first blood, for we will have moved the legions into the field to cut off their return to the mountain."

"And if they don't take the bait in Birom?" Firkas asked.

"Then we march on Gilgalem anyway," Hilsingor answered, "having lost nothing at the chance of gaining much." The marshal turned to Pendigied and Ravorglad.

"This will mark the last of our preparations, then you will be immersed in the battle of your lives against a large, desperate enemy crouching on the ultimate high ground. Arnolf, you will ensure the Rachard garrison troops left behind know to arrest Harsen if he is foolish enough to return here seeking more secrets. Then send him to my field camp in chains."

"Yes, sir."

"How soon can we march?" Ravorglad asked.

"Speak nothing of this tonight," Hilsingor said. "When Harsen departs at dawn with Widsem's archers behind him, you may prepare your men. We will march out in two days."

98

RILDNING

Gilgalem, Vaynland
Midspring, 2270

"Thank the heavens, Gilgalem still stands untouched," Urgamdir said as he and Rildning came within view. The mountain was more beautiful than Rildning had yet seen it, having first arrived in the autumn. The tall spruce and firs displayed their brown and green cones, and their scents filled the air. It was refreshing after what had been a hard journey.

After Harsen took the road to Rachard, they left the road completely, keeping to the woods to avoid patrols and Urgamdir's hunter. They had been awoken only one night, unsure if they were being followed, and returned to the trail in the starry dark without further alarms. They were encouraged when they were first spotted by the Gallerlander scouts of the plains. They learned there had been no sign of a springtime attack as they had all feared.

Exhausted but grateful for having made it safely, Rildning and Urgamdir trekked up into the foothills and then up the switchbacks and cliff trails. The views of the green plains, empty of any enemy, lifted their hearts and gave them strength to climb onward.

Their confidence waned when they saw their people. Their bodies were thin and disheveled, their eyes dark from a long and weary winter of meager meals. There was no great feast to welcome their return, as there would have been in the days of plenty. Instead, Tirgranir granted them a full meal despite the rationing to recover themselves from the long journey. Although the Vaynking would not sit with them, Rildning took the food as a sign that perhaps his fury and distrust had subsided. Only the steward, Sage, and Owerdir talked with them at the table.

"I'm sorry to hear of everything that happened to you," Rildning said to Owerdir when the latter finished his tale about the Naren-Dra. "But I'm glad you survived. As you have now heard, our efforts with the Rahlampians and Bronhildi yielded even less than yours. It is difficult to see a way out of our situation."

"There is another way," Rumban offered. "The enemy has offered terms. Odon took that path, as many others have. Even the Rahlampians now."

"Anfinnan joined the empire?" Rildning was surprised. He had held out hope the domnitar and Mrigamad would have chosen to help the Gallerlanders.

"The domnitar wrote to Tirgranir saying so. He urged Tirgranir to accept the terms. Tirgranir would still be king of—"

"Of a land and people who are no longer his," Rildning interrupted.

His mood had grown gloomier since leaving Bronhildia empty-handed. He felt hopeless, too often reminded of the disunity of the Gallerlanders. More than ever Rildning longed for a normal life with his family amid undisturbed forests. But this was increasingly a flickering shadow of a dream.

"I did not expect the steward of Gilgalem, keeper of the refuge, to suggest surrender should even be considered," Urgamdir said.

"It shouldn't be considered," the Sage said. "We have faced hard times before, and these walls have always stood strong."

Rumban sighed. "These walls have never faced an enemy like the foreigners, and Gallerlandia isn't as it once was."

Rildning saw the steward did not like the notion of surrender but was resigned to it.

"Gallerlandia no longer exists," Rumban continued. "Only its soul remains in the hearts of we who have survived to witness its final collapse. Not even the electrum has been saved from the enemy's hands. We must reach an agreement with them, or else perish."

"That is not the way," the Sage said, turning to Rildning. "Did anyone ever explain to you why you survived the snake pit that Owerdir and his father threw you into when you first came to their village?"

Rildning and Owerdir looked at each other. The Sage continued before he could answer.

"Of course not, because they didn't know why themselves," he said. "But I do. You see, the venom of the black adder of Ondirhar and its blood—which you previously sipped—are two of the four ingredients used by the Hrals to concoct the drink that sends them into their dangerous, unstoppable frenzy we call *turserkgyn*.

"The secrets of these ingredients were known to the Gallerlander Council of Kings generations ago but kept hidden because we did not want our own warriors to turn themselves into animals or kill themselves, as the raging Hrals sometimes do. Have you continued to feel the effects, which can last years? Enhanced sight, smell, speed, and limberness?"

"Only now and again," Rildning replied.

"After being bitten by the adders, I'm certain you would have perished without drinking their blood. You didn't know it would heal you, yet you took a chance without knowing why." The Sage returned his gaze to Rumban. "Rildning ultimately survived because he did not surrender to death. He adapted to his surroundings and he sampled his enemy. The Gallerlanders must not give up. We must adapt and fight as Rildning has counseled, on the backs of horse beasts and with the enemy's metal if necessary."

"What?" the steward scoffed. "How can the Sage suggest such a thing?"

"I've read the sky omens, and they are dire, even as spring begins to bloom. We will not last the season unless Tirgranir pulls himself out of his doldrums, shakes off the enslaving terms of the enemy, and listens to one who knows the enemy best and yet remains loyal to his adopted people."

"Well, it's clear I'll have no consensus to bring to Tirgranir," Rumban said while rising from his chair. "The Vaynking and I are glad all three of you returned safely from your perilous travel. It wasn't as successful as we all wanted, but not for your lack of trying. Tirgranir is grateful for that. I bid you good night."

"Thank you, my friend," Rildning said to the Sage when the steward had gone. "All of us nearly sacrificed our lives. Owerdir lost his hand and companions, and Arbardir is lost for certain. If Tirgranir won't lead his own people to resist, then perhaps it's better we not drag other tribes into a battle we ourselves will not fight."

"Don't be so dour," the Sage said. "There is one who may yet succeed. Eniri has not yet returned, so there is still hope."

Rildning pressed his fingers to his eyelids and sighed.

"Stay strong," Owerdir said. "She is a warrior in her own right. She will return to us."

"Yes, she is an Umbyr," Urgamdir agreed.

"And whether she brings a fleet of Nyden warriors with her or not, we will prevail," the Sage said. "Wurumnak will guide us."

"It is good to be with you all again," Rildning said. "I must go see my son. And we must rest for the days ahead."

❧

The following day, the Sage again asked Rildning to join him for a walk down to the forges of the Maluram. Owerdir and Urgamdir accompanied them as well. When they all came to the great steam-fogged chamber, all of the Maluram were standing idle, watching. They seemed to be waiting for Rildning, their dirt-smeared faces lined up surrounding a pedestal. It was cloaked in one of the large burlap sacks used to cart stone out of the mines. The Sage led them to the pedestal and then turned to address everyone.

"Days darker than the mines lie ahead," he began. "Whatever path the Vaynking decides to lead us on, we will also have Rildning, the joiner of two worlds, with us. Rildning, you have proven your bravery and loyalty to your adopted people time and again, and we know you will stay strong in the final battle.

"Though you don't share our faith, I believe Wurumnak has a crown for you among the greatest of the high kings of old, the Thuraniparin. A crown that forever marks the greatest warriors for the final battle at the End Times. We may face that battle sooner than we realize.

"So, Rildning, come forth. You have been called Parinsogon for your struggle with the snakes of the blackest forest. But now, take up your new name, Aengturor, for you are recognized as the Small Sword of Wurumnak, the precursor to his great electrum blade."

The burlap was pulled off the pedestal to reveal a suit of gleaming scaled armor. Rildning was astonished.

"It's an alloy of electrum and cinder," Niberi said. "I call it elinderum. Each scale and plate is trimmed with the moonwood of the cave willows, to remind you of Gilgalem."

"Nothing like it has ever been crafted by the Maluram," the Sage said. "Gratgofa wore the electrum helmet of the high kings, and the Graparins once wore ornaments of the sacred metal. But nothing like this was ever sanctioned, until now.

"The Maluram believe in you," he continued, "and they are deeply proud to have crafted this for you, particularly Niberi. You saw her deft hands experimenting with the melding of the cinder and electrum. She also strengthened it with her alloys, and made you a suit of mail from cinder so you will resist fire. You are Aengturor, the Small Sword of God and the Joiner of Two Worlds. The high king of Gallerlandia!"

Rildning was nearly overcome with emotion. He was honored beyond words and grateful for the trust placed in him, but at the same time uncomfortable with being so exalted. Even after all the conversations he'd had with the Sage and Eniri, he did not consider himself the next high king. And with the loss of the Goynking and Umbyrking, he knew the post of high king could never be more than ceremonial. He looked at Owerdir and Urgamdir. They were proud and happy and seemingly without such doubts.

The Maluram helped Rildning don the cinder mail and armor, the gauntlets, and the greaves. He saw Niberi beaming at the sight of him in the armor, which was a perfect fit and not as heavy as it looked. He looked down at the breastplate on his chest. Every moonwood-laced electrum scale shone like a bright gem in dark waters. He flexed in the suit, thinking how its relative lightness was a fitting contrast to the burden he felt at the prospect of leading his people.

As he was about to speak his thanks, a commotion was heard toward the main forge. A Maluram smithy was clearly fighting with someone atop the furnace where the steam exited the rock and flowed up into the tunnels to vent atop the Pindoarig tower. Several of the miners rushed over to help. After a short tussle, the Maluram brought a scruffy-looking Gallerlander down for everyone to see.

"I caught him trying to bar all the steam hatches!" the smithy cried.

"He could have burst the furnace," one of the miners said.

"Or the mountain," another said.

"His Gali isn't so good," the smithy continued. "Smells odd, too."

The captured Gallerlander struggled and screamed, but the grasp of the Maluram miners was tight. Rildning soon recognized the glare of this Gallerlander. He had seen this tribesman watching him several times, but was never able to approach him.

"I know your face," Rildning said to the man. "Who are you?"

He glared in response. Rildning saw one of the Maluram inspecting the man's arm. Rildning could see it for himself. The man's tattoos were poorly done, as if he had painted himself.

"Who are you?" Rildning repeated.

The man spat at him. After one of the miners slugged him in the face, Rildning heard the man curse—in Brintilian. Rildning scowled with disbelief and disgust.

"Ah, Arvgred . . . It's been a long time."

99

WIDSEM

East of Birom, Vaynland
Midspring, 2270

Widsem was glad to return to the wilderwood without having to seek out Ferndeath and his little letters. As instructed by the marshal, Widsem had earlier tried to make contact with Ferndeath in the foothills of Gilgalem to draw out information on the Gallerlanders' reaction to his offering of terms. But Ferndeath never showed.

Widsem was glad Hilsingor was not surprised or irritated. The marshal had now focused on the campaign instead of dealing with the unreliable and foul-smelling Ferndeath. Among the little man's many fibs was his claim that he killed hundreds of Gallerlanders, stalking them from the giant ferns of their forests.

Widsem had on more than one occasion wanted to cut out his lying tongue. Now that the marshal had moved on to other things, Widsem half hoped he would encounter Ferndeath once more, just to put an end to that nuisance.

Following after Harsen was easy. The merchant's covered wagon could always be seen and heard. Widsem even hand selected several trainees among the few dozen rangers, scouts, and lightly armored soldiers he brought with him for the task.

As Hilsingor had predicted, Harsen took the path toward Gilgalem instead of continuing on to Birom. Widsem smiled to himself, thinking of all the traps he had plenty of time to set for the Gallerlanders. How glorious it would be to kill Tirgranir or Rildning at Birom. He imagined Ravorglad's face turning blister red until it burst. The highborn knight never appreciated the unsung qualities of rangers.

100

RILDNING

Gilgalem, Vaynland
Midspring, 2270

"It's another trap," Rildning said, trying to remain calm despite his irritation with Harsen for being duped twice. He was glad to see his old friend in one piece, and was glad the Gallerlanders watching the plains had allowed him to get close enough to offer what he had to bring. But it was the darkest of omens that Harsen had come to Gilgalem bearing a map allegedly revealing all of Hilsingor's plans.

"I know how these men think," Rildning continued. "They failed to kill me in Bronhildia with this trickery, and now they're trying to lure us out to some isolated place to try it again."

Tirgranir was unconvinced. It was the first of Tirgranir's councils that Rildning and his companions had been permitted to attend since returning from the north. Tirgranir claimed Harsen's Gali wasn't good enough, so he demanded Rildning's attendance.

"Do you know their minds so well because you are still one of them?" the Vaynking asked. For once his tone was flat and not accusatory, perhaps looking for a reason to trust Rildning again. "The foreigners' banner that Mrigamad pulled from your furs suggested you were with the enemy, as the filthy Rahlampians are now," Tirgranir said.

"As I've said before, it was a memento of my religion," Rildning said. "Nothing more." He kept calm, knowing Tirgranir's mood had become unpredictable.

Tirgranir looked at the parchment map again. Harsen had explained the notations, the path of the legions' planned march, and the location of the scouts in Birom that would weaken Gilgalem's defenses.

"This is an opportunity to crush the foreigners hiding at Birom," Tirgranir insisted. "If these men are hiding so close to Gilgalem, perhaps they are responsible for flooding our food stores. Not only can we punish them, but we can prevent more disruptions to our defenses."

"And if we inflict this rapid defeat on them at Birom," Rumban added, "perhaps the foreigners will think twice about coming up the mountain. Or it may place us in a better position to negotiate terms later."

"I know who destroyed the food stores," Rildning said. "His name is Arvgred. He is the one I asked Rumban to tell you about. He tried to bottle up the steam of the Maluram furnace, which they said would have ruptured the mountain. Perhaps Rumban forgot to tell you. I knew this Arvgred once. I don't know if the Frontier Corps sent him or if he is following his own lust for blood, but I'm sure he is the one who flooded the stores. I've tried to question him in his cell down below, but he will barely speak."

"How did you know this Arvgred?"

"It's complicated. Harsen and I used him as a guide for a short time. He was once a colonial soldier who lived as a hermit in the forest. He stalked Gallerlanders to kill them, not far from Owerdir's village."

"Why didn't you stop him?" Tirgranir asked. "You gave him the opportunity to come here and cause so much misery!"

"He abandoned us," Rildning said. The eyes of everyone demanded explanation. "It was before Harsen and I came to Owerdir's village. We thought he could help us, but he stole one of our horses and left. I never saw him again, and had no opportunity to—"

"I claim this murderer and my tribesmen will question him," Tirgranir said. "I'm willing to overlook your failure to kill him, and I'm willing to forget about the banner. But you must show support for killing these men hiding in Birom.

And you'll come with me to disrupt them before they come here."

"I'm telling you this is trickery!" Rildning cried. "A clever commander like Hilsingor would never give a map of his true intentions to Harsen."

"If you want to regain my trust, this is the way," Tirgranir said. "You will help me kill the enemy hiding at Birom, or you will not, for reasons that will be obvious to me."

Rildning was glad Tirgranir was finally acting like a decisive leader again, a burden Rildning hoped he would not have to carry for all of Gallerlandia. But now he considered how the Gallerlanders would view him if he refused to go with Tirgranir and the Vaynking was killed at Birom. He knew it was a trap, but he knew he had to go.

"I'll go with you, but we must not take an army," he said. "We will need to move quickly and return before the legions come."

"We leave tonight," Tirgranir declared.

န

Before Rildning departed with Tirgranir, he spoke with Harsen.

"My friend, the marshal knows who you are and what you are doing for us. I wish you had not risked your life so many times, especially to bring steel swords the Gallerlanders won't use. It was brave of you to play Hilsingor's games, but this time it is surely a trap we will not escape. And if you go back to Rachard once more, they will kill you too before this is over."

"I think the scouts in Birom could be real," Harsen replied. "It makes sense that the Frontier Corps would try to soften Gilgalem before they attack."

"Will you at least stay here, in Gilgalem?"

"This is an important time," Harsen replied. "I must return to Rachard to learn all I can. The Gallerlanders don't want a foreigner here anyway."

"I'm glad to have had you with me, old friend. But I fear for your life more than ever. I couldn't bear the guilt if—"

"Let go of your guilt, Rildning. You have carried so much for so long. Look what you have done for the Gallerlanders. You have given them more than hope, but leadership when they lacked it. I wish I had never abandoned you in the first place. Who knows what I might have done for them, for you. And perhaps I would have allowed myself some green paint and tattoos . . ."

"You have earned one or two tattoos." Rildning chuckled. "But they would be seen as brands of heresy back in the provinces."

"You think I intend to return to the old life? I'm with you and yours, Rildning, to the end. And now I go to the enemy's camp once again to learn what I can. Good luck with the Birom raid."

"The raid would go better if the Gallerlanders would use the steel blades you brought for them," Rildning said. "But we will do our best."

"Farewell then," Harsen said. "I'll see you after."

"And you as well."

⤫

Rildning's stomach ached as they neared Birom. It was the same feeling he had gotten when the Frontier Corps was bearing down on Nalembalen. But he didn't have much time to think about it. Rildning, Tirgranir, Urgamdir, and four dozen Gallerlander warriors handpicked for their quick feet rushed through the dark forests under a moon half-hidden with streaky clouds.

"Bad omens," Urgamdir whispered, looking at the sky when they stopped for a brief rest. "I believe you are right about a trap."

"We will find out soon, my friend," Rildning said.

Tirgranir gave them few breaks on their way down the mountain and toward Birom. As Rildning suggested, Tirgranir wanted to reach Birom before dawn. Rildning also urged the Vaynking to rush back to Gilgalem if the raid was successful, so the Gallerlanders were not without their best leaders for too long. Rildning could not imagine the raid going well, but he could imagine Tirgranir being captured and paraded in front of the mountain—thoughts he kept to himself.

When they neared the ruins of Birom most of the Gallerlanders went up into the trees. Rildning had long ago learned how to run up the trunks, trot among the branches, and leap between trees. It was an exhilarating dance, with the light and shade of the moon flickering across them as they sped through the trees.

When they finally reached Birom, all was still and quiet. They crept slow as snails now as they fanned out through the trees that ringed where the huts had once clustered. In the dim light they could see new weeds poking up from the ashes and in the breaks in the canopy where trees had been burned down. But there was no sign of anyone.

They waited, remaining still as if part of the trees. The rustle of leaves in the breeze, the scamper of mice, the flap of an owl, but nothing more. Crouched near Tirgranir on an oak branch, Rildning could sense the Vaynking's growing frustration. Tirgranir soon cast a dark glare at him, expecting answers. Rildning padded over to him.

"Where are they?" Tirgranir whispered. Rildning could hear the anxious grinding of his teeth.

"Bad sign," he replied. "Perhaps they will try to cut off our escape."

"My men are protecting the route back," the Vaynking said.

They sat for a while more in silence, listening to the night sounds of the woodland. Every eye in the trees scanned across the ruined village and trees beyond, but the enemy was not there.

"I've had enough of this," Tirgranir said. He motioned for the others to follow him in dismounting the trees. Rildning tried to dissuade him, but he wouldn't pay him any attention.

Rildning did not follow the Vaynking to the ground. Instead, he watched as Tirgranir and some of his tribesmen walked into the clearing and picked around the ruins, examining the tumbled logs and mounds of ash. No one saw from where the first arrow came, nor the second or third. Gallerlanders were falling dead by twos every moment. Then they realized they were surrounded. Shouts also came from those who had lagged behind to protect their escape route.

"To the trees!" a Gallerlander shouted in a nearby elm, his voice carrying across the ruins.

The thud of arrows biting into the trunks and branches was like a deadly rain all around them. Rildning saw Tirgranir and the others running, diving, rolling and running again as they tried to reach the trees. He saw the warriors form a protective ring around the Vaynking. They took arrows for him in time with Rildning's racing heartbeat. Rildning knew they wouldn't make it.

Urgamdir leaped from the branch near Rildning and raced to Tirgranir. Rildning readied himself to do the same, but felt a sudden pain shoot through his left arm. He instinctively jerked his hand but found it pinned to a tree trunk. An arrow had pierced clean through the middle of his shield hand. He saw a spurt of dark red that then trickled down the tree.

Rildning looked down below and saw Urgamdir and his Bronhildi friend Kemet had reached the Vaynking and were hustling him back into the brush toward the route from which they had come. There was still no sight of the enemy, but arrows continued to zip from every corner of the clearing.

Rildning took hold of the shaft of the arrow and bent it until the end snapped off. Gnashing his teeth to stay silent, he carefully pulled his palm away from the tree and slid his hand off the broken shaft. His brow dripped with sweat as his hand throbbed with pain. He felt the tender flesh and could see bone. He tucked his hand in his tunic and trotted through the trees toward where Tirgranir had gone, cursing himself for not having done more to persuade Tirgranir against coming to Birom.

When the survivors were far enough away and felt sure no one had pursued them, Tirgranir ordered a halt for rest. Sentries were posted in all directions. Dawn had broken and they were exhausted.

"What was that?" Tirgranir demanded. He was furious and confused.

"You could have listened to me," Rildning said, exasperated.

"To you?" His face was plum red, but he could not think of what to say.

Rildning saw Urgamdir had taken an arrow in the shoulder, the same one that had been wounded saving Tirgranir months ago at Fenthugren River. But the big Umbyr was unconcerned as two men tended to him and the other wounded Gallerlanders. Rildning began wrapping his own hand with bandages.

Tirgranir paced about, searching for answers inside his sweaty brow. Rildning let him stew. When he realized the Vaynking was incapable of deciding what to do, Rildning spoke up.

"We must make for Gilgalem, now," he said. "We are several hours away. This ambush was meant to lure us away from the mountain for a reason. We must hurry." Rildning's single comfort was knowing Owerdir remained at Gilgalem. He did not trust Rumban to lead a worthy defense, and the Sage was too feeble to do so.

Tirgranir was in a daze. Rildning knew he had realized his error, yet still Rildning felt terrible. He had known the enemy was waiting for them at Birom, but there was nothing that could have persuaded the Vaynking. Rildning wondered how he would lead Gilgalem. He could not wipe the vision of Tirgranir's defeated, dumbstruck face from his mind's eye as they ran back through the forest.

101

ARVGRED

Gilgalem, Vaynland
Midspring, 2270

Arvgred knew they had forgotten about him. When they pulled him from his cell, he heard them say Tirgranir wanted to question him. But Arvgred heard the others talking about the absence of the king. He soon learned that he and the heretic had left the mountain.

They had left Arvgred sitting in a side chamber adjacent to the throne room. He snickered to himself as he peered over his shoulder at his wrists, bound with flax rope. The Gallerlanders' lack of metal chains gave him great confidence he could escape. They had left him in there for hours, and he had been continually rubbing the rope against the rough-hewn stone walls.

It was still night when he felt the rope begin to fray. He tried to pull it apart, but it wasn't ready yet. Half an hour later he tried again and it relented with a pleasing snap. Then he smiled, having polished his plan while working the rope. He opened the door to the throne room, knowing after listening so long that no one was inside.

He went straight to the tables behind the throne where he had seen the guards loiter before he was jailed. As he expected, one obsidian spear lay on the table. He snatched it up and sprinted silently to the spiral stairwell. He went up and up until he came to the broad hallway with several doors. He had been here once before, some time ago, stalking and scouting and preparing.

The bed was empty, as he expected. While he hoped Eniri drowned in the sea, he wanted to kill Rildning himself. Later. For now, there was the little wicker cradle. He closed the door behind him and lurched toward the cradle, unable to contain himself when he saw the bundle wrapped inside. He raised the spear and hacked and stabbed, drooling and weeping tears of twisted joy.

When he came up for a closer look, there was no blood, no flesh. Torn wrappings and broken wicker, but no Enildir. Arvgred could not control his guttural scream at first, but then he muffled it and hopped about madly. Then there was the sound of a door opening in the next chamber.

He skipped to the door and into the hallway where a servant of the Vaynking's family was speaking. The hallway was darkened but Arvgred's aim was practiced. From a distance he deftly jabbed the obsidian spear into the servant's mouth and withdrew it just as quickly. He was bounding down the stairs before the body fell.

He sprinted out of Pindoarig tower as he heard the commotion build behind him. He was up in the higher terraces by the time anyone came out. Then he was gone, up over the rim of Gilgalem's bowl.

He snickered to himself as he skipped through the spruce. The baby had escaped him this time, but he would be back. First, he wanted to meet that damn ranger and tell him Rildning and the Vaynking had left the mountain. It would be the right time to attack, if the marshal would just listen.

Arvgred imagined building himself a castle made with the electrum bricks Hilsingor would surely give him as payment. His dungeon would be filled with Gallerlander slaves, and he would water the roots of the castle with their blood. The castle would grow, and the electrum towers would reach up to the moon. He could hardly wait to live on the white orb where he could watch the earth die. All he had to do was find Widsem and he'd see payment.

Several Gallerlander scouts down on the mountain side and in the foothills would never see death coming for them from the ferns. They would not see the flash of obsidian or the wild eyes that watched their last gasp with fevered delight.

102

HILSINGOR

North of Gilgalem, Vaynland
Midspring, 2270

Widsem's messenger from Birom reached Hilsingor sooner than the marshal had anticipated. Hilsingor had pushed the legions into a swift march once they left Rachard. And the eagerness of the troops and their commanders, along with the newly built road that stretched about halfway to the mountains, made the march that much easier and got them that much closer to Gilgalem.

"Sir, I have good news," the messenger said when he rode up beside Hilsingor's great charger. "The king of the Vayns and the heretic came to Birom during the night. We ambushed them, but some escaped through the trees. They are running toward the mountain, sir, with our rangers in pursuit."

"Very well. Widsem will drive them south and easterly, as planned?"

"Yes, sir."

Hilsingor nodded the messenger away and continued his ride. He turned to speak to King Pendigied, who rode nearby.

"You see, the sword is not always the best weapon for the moment. Some men call it trickery. I call it preparation."

"Impressive," Pendigied acknowledged. "However, trapping them in a ruin or trapping them on a mountain—I suppose it makes no difference—they still live."

"For a while longer," the marshal replied.

103

RILDNING

Northwest of Gilgalem, Vaynland
Midspring, 2270

Rildning could see the dread in the Gallerlanders' eyes. There were a few dozen of them left, including the shaken Tirgranir and the wounded Urgamdir. The others had been lost in the ambush or fell to the enemy that continued to pursue them.

And the Gallerlanders were exhausted. They had run through the night to Birom, suffered an ambush, and now fled back the way they had come. Their retreat was slower now with little rest. Dread of what they might find at Gilgalem weighed heavy on them.

Urgamdir trotted ahead with Kemet. They were the first to see the gray glint in the lowland meadows that swept up into Gilgalem's foothills. Like a silvery river bending around woods and hills, the army marched southward. Some places flowed faster than others, which they reasoned to be cavalry.

For a moment Rildning remembered Ankarmesh's far-seeing eye, as Owerdir had described, and he wished for it to better see this foe. But from this distance he guessed it was several legions, sent to destroy Gilgalem as Nalembalen had been destroyed.

The Gallerlanders tried to push ahead of the host in parallel, but it was clear they were behind, and that the legions might cut off their return to the mountain. Rildning saw Urgamdir, Kemet, and another scout run up to the ridge of the next hill. Upon reaching the crest, the scout was struck in the neck. Another arrow split Kemet's left ear. He and Urgamdir dove for cover.

Rildning and the rest surged up to him as the Frontier Corps soldiers raised their glistening swords. Rildning threw his stone knife, catching a lightly armored archer in the collarbone as Urgamdir struck down a soldier. Kemet, who had initially rolled away from them, sprang up and jabbed several soldiers.

Rildning picked up a steel sword and made quick use of it. The Gallerlanders had nearly defeated the small scouting unit, but Rildning saw more soldiers coming. They appeared to be the troops guarding the flank of the legions.

"Do not betray your own hands for their sake!" Tirgranir shouted. Rildning saw Urgamdir had picked up a fallen soldier's iron war hammer. Urgamdir ignored the Vaynking and continued crushing the enemy soldiers. The other Gallerlanders kept on with their stoneswords and arrows, but the soldiers kept coming. The fighting shifted against the Gallerlanders when the mounted knights arrived.

"Rildning!" a knight cried. He could not resist looking at the man who recognized him. In a flash he remembered Harsen's words that he was now a notorious heretic in the provinces, with a high bounty on his head.

"Come!" Rildning answered. He burned to meet the challenge of this man. "Here I am!"

The knight put his spurs to his mount. Rildning could feel the blood pulsing out of his wounded hand, and even the old Hral-inflicted wound in his shoulder tingled. But he waited, sword held high above his head. The knight approached and attempted to spear him with a lance. Rildning twisted, turning the lance aside, and fell to a knee to swipe at the horse.

The animal screamed and fell to the ground, casting the knight from the saddle. Rildning got to his feet and rushed to the knight. He hacked at his helmet, sending the knight back to the ground. By now foot soldiers had come to the knight's rescue and Gallerlanders to Rildning's. The knight did not succumb until he had taken two Gallerlanders' lives. The soldiers and knights kept trotting over and the remaining

Gallerlanders were tiring quickly. Rildning saw six or seven tribesmen lying dead among more than a dozen corpsmen.

"We must retreat!" Rildning cried. Tirgranir gnashed his teeth.

"We can't fight the whole enemy, not here," Urgamdir agreed.

Together they fought their way southward into a little wood, where the uncertain footing around a stream and the Gallerlanders' use of the trees to their advantage caused the soldiers to hesitate and fall back.

"We must follow this stream to its source in the foothills," Urgamdir said.

"It will be slower than the meadow paths," Tirgranir said. "But if we must . . ."

A half-dozen soldiers surprised them, leaping out of nearby bushes. Some of the Gallerlanders who had run up trees shot arrows down on them, but not before Rildning struggled hand to hand with one. When he stood, his tunic was hanging off him. Tirgranir saw the electrum armor the Maluram had made for him beneath the tattered tunic. Rildning tore off the rest of the tunic. Tirgranir's eyes were large and unblinking. He could not speak.

"Come, we must push on," Rildning said to the others.

They did not rest until the hoofbeats and clang of metal became faint behind them. They napped briefly in a dark glade until nightfall, posting watchers in shifts. Tirgranir kept as far away from Rildning as possible.

104

OWERDIR

Gilgalem, Vaynland
Midspring, 2270

"Who is with me?" Owerdir shouted. He looked at the faces packed into Tirgranir's throne room. They were the faces of uncertainty, frustration, and fear. Only one voice answered his call.

"You are not a king," Rumban said.

"No, he is not, and neither are you," the Sage answered. "There is only one Gallerlander king that remains alive in Gallerlandia. But as we just heard from the watchkeepers and scouts, Tirgranir is in grave danger, and so are we."

"I'm the Keeper of Pindoarig," Rumban said. "And as the Vaynking's steward, I will—"

"If we run out into the plains to try and save them," a Vayn chieftain interrupted, "we will be overrun and Gilgalem will be left unprotected."

"Keep quiet, I beg all of you," the Sage said. "Let Owerdir speak."

"Not everyone would go," Owerdir said. "The counterattack must be small enough to move quickly but large enough to defend ourselves if we cannot avoid the enemy. Perhaps three hundred men." He had stood atop the mountain with the Sage and had seen the host. He thought of Ankarmesh and knew he was watching from the Wheeled Window of the World.

"The enemy draws closer every moment," the Sage said.

"I'll go, and my warriors with me," a chieftain said. "We are Umbyrs from the north who fled to Nalembalen, then Gilgalem, and to places in between. I'm done fleeing."

"What is your name, brave chief?" Owerdir asked.

"Nodarim, and I bring one hundred stoneswords."

"We will go as well," another chief said. "I'm Oturbrin of the Tamturs." Owerdir remembered that was Eniri's clan. "If the princess were here, she would have us go."

"And I, Lemori," a Goyn chieftainess said. "In memory of the Goyns who fell, and to mark our sorrow for Odon. We will fight the fight he could not."

"We leave at once," Owerdir said.

He departed from Pindoarig tower with his shroud alchemists and climbed the terraces to the rim of the mountain where he waited for the rest. As he was thinking to himself that, once again, the difficult tasks fell to Umbyrs and Goyns, he was pleased to see a few others join him—including Vayns—who had not spoken up in the throne room. Owerdir got his three hundred and then some.

They camped in the wooded foothills that night. From there they could see the innumerable campfires of the Frontier Corps in the meadowlands down below. It looked like a second night sky of orange twinkling stars. On the horizon to the north, separated by a gap of darkness, was another vast cluster of lights.

"Another host comes to join the first," Nodarim said.

"There will be more still," Oturbrin said. "That is how they fight. Wave upon wave of sinister metal and horse beasts."

"We were all at Nalembalen," Nodarim said. "Do you remember so many?"

"We could not see them come as we do now," Oturbrin answered.

"I've seen something similar," Owerdir said. "After we brought Rildning to Nalembalen as our prisoner, we left to return to our village of Takumbyr. Not too far down the path we were forced into the trees. We watched them flow by, like shining packs of wolves, an unending sea of them. We eventually found an escape, creeping from bush to bush back to join the fight at Nalembalen. We knew Takumbyr had been destroyed. You all were fighting them in the tree city by the time we came."

"We shouldn't have been so divided among ourselves," Lemori said. "Had the clans come together early on, it would have been different."

"I remember Rildning tried," Nodarim said. "Many times, at Gratgofa's councils and Tirgranir's."

"I'll never ride on one of those four-legged beasts," Oturbrin said, "and I won't touch their cursed-earth metal. But I'll stand beside any clan to oppose these foreigners once and for all."

"What about those shady cloud dwellers?" Nodarim asked, jutting his chin at Owerdir's alchemists. All the chiefs stared at them.

"Can they be trusted?" Lemori asked.

"I lived among them, as Rildning has lived among us, and they taught me their craft," Owerdir said. "They may not have the stature or the strength of our people, but they are quick footed, silent, and deadly. You will see."

"I'll fight alongside any but a Hral," reaffirmed Oturbrin. All the chiefs and Owerdir nodded.

"Rildning fought the Hrals alone in the forest," Owerdir said.

"I knew I liked him." Lemori smiled.

"What will become of him," Nodarim asked, "when Tirgranir becomes high king?"

"Eniri will be high queen," Oturbrin said. "No mistake."

"Truly now," Nodarim continued. "The Sage says Rildning is a gift from Wurumnak. But where is our victory? We are trapped while our enemy burns our villages and takes our lands. Wurumnak did not save Nalembalen. How will Gilgalem be saved? By one man?"

"Perhaps, if this is the End Times, the moment has come for the Maluram to cast all the electrum in Wurumnak's sword," Lemori suggested.

"Don't be foolish," Nodarim said. "There's no time for that, even if we could get word to the forgers."

"None of us have the answers," Owerdir said. "We must remain steady and have faith. For me, Rildning has been brave and truehearted since I first met him as an enemy.

Since then, I've known his loyalty as a friend. Whether or not he is the next high king the Sage proclaims cannot be known to me. But he has always been beside us. He will help us defeat this enemy."

Satisfied, the chieftains broke their huddle. As they prepared to get some sleep, the occasional distant ting of metal and the echo of men shouting hinted at what awaited them with the dawn.

105

RILDNING

Northwest of Gilgalem, Vaynland
Midspring, 2270

Rildning and Tirgranir continued to lead their struggling men along the wooded creek toward the foothills. But they could scarcely go an hour without being harassed by archers at their rear or foot soldiers appearing from the legions' flank. What normally would have taken less than a day to reach Gilgalem was now going to cost them another night.

They found high sugar pines to rest in, but their sleep was fitful and interrupted. Every sound and the smell of campfires reminded them of their peril. Rildning believed they would be too late, and at best they would have to climb up Gilgalem by some other path.

They climbed down from the thinning trees before dawn broke to get a head start on the enemy. But soon after they found their pace along to the stream, they were again ambushed by a band of archers and a few knights who had taken up a position at their rear. Tirgranir was incapable of making a decision, so Rildning prepared to call for a retreat further into the woods.

Before he could, he saw a black-as-night smoke swirling about the archers' heads. They screamed as more puffs appeared, causing them to vomit and claw at their faces before falling over dead. Seeing this, some of the soldiers turned and fled back into the meadowlands, shrieking about

Memelos magic. But a few stouthearted knights and their squires were not so easily turned away.

Rildning saw a shimmer pass in front of him, like a shadowy reflection on water. Then he saw several of these blurs. The knights were torn from their mounts when black clouds burst around the heads of their horses. One sure-footed knight quickly regained his balance and ran as fast as he could back to the legions. The others were soon overwhelmed by a horde of Gallerlanders crashing out of the woods ahead. Rildning and the others cheered at the sight. Even Tirgranir became excited.

Owerdir and other men stepped out of a shimmering shadow near Rildning. Owerdir smelled of soot and rubbed metal, and he smiled when he saw Rildning's puzzled face.

"So this is your shroud alchemy?" Rildning asked.

"Only a taste of it," Owerdir said. "We saw the fighting from the mountain, and the word from the scouts was that you and the Vaynking wouldn't make it to Gilgalem without help. I've brought you three hundred volunteers."

"We are with you!" Nodarim said to Rildning and Tirgranir.

"What evil trickery have you taught my tribesmen?" Tirgranir demanded, glancing back and forth between the soldiers' corpses and Owerdir. There was a putrid, peppery stink on the breeze.

"I've taught them nothing," Owerdir said. "This is the work of the alchemists of Naren-Dra."

"I don't like it. Keep your cloud magic clear of me and my tribesmen."

"The alchemists screened us on our way," protested Lemori, "helping us to avoid the enemy." Tirgranir glared at her.

"You sent him," Rildning said to Tirgranir. "You sent Owerdir to those high mountains and he returned with those alchemists to help. Now you reject the help that saves you?"

"Their method is not an honorable way to fight," the Vaynking sneered. "The end has come! I'll not participate in evil methods when my time to join Wurumnak has come!"

"The end?" Rildning scoffed. "So many times it has seemingly come. And we have resisted it to live on."

"No longer . . ." Tirgranir said. Before Rildning could ask him what he meant, a trumpet sounded out in the meadowlands.

"The enemy approaches!" Nodarim shouted.

They hurried to the wood's edge for a view. The vanguard of the Frontier Corps was continuing its march south toward Gilgalem, which loomed close now. But another smaller group—Rildning reckoned perhaps five hundred—was forming ranks to charge them in the woods.

"Keep inside the woods, and keep your arrows on the mark," Rildning said. "Wait until they're within range before countering their charge."

The Gallerlanders readied themselves as more trumpets sounded. Urgamdir still had his iron hammer, but Rildning and Kemet remained the only other users of steel swords.

"I'll even ride a horse before it's over," Urgamdir said defiantly when he saw the newly arrived chiefs staring at him. "We have nowhere left to run, so Wurumnak forgive me for using their cursed earth against them!"

Remarkably, a few Gallerlanders followed his example and picked up steel spears and swords from dead soldiers. Tirgranir sulked about, pacing to and fro at the nearby creek. Rildning suspected he was going mad, but focused on the battle at hand.

The knights in the meadow lowered their lances and spurred their mounts, then the footmen followed after them. The archers filled the Gallerlanders' woods with volley after volley until the cavalry neared the wood line. Rildning stood at the edge of the woods to lead a counter-charge. As the knights punctured the woods, the Gallerlanders seized upon them from ground and tree. Only a few knights fell quickly, including one hammed by Urgamdir, while the rest wheeled around until the foot soldiers caught up to support them. There was a great clash of steel and stone, screaming and shouting.

Rildning tried to make his way to the knight commander who led the initial charge, but he was too far away. Ultimately, most poorly armored soldiers were no match for the quick-footed tribesmen who used the trees. The Gallerlanders were equally hard-pressed when drawn out of the woods, but in the end the knight commander ordered a retreat when he realized he was grossly outnumbered by the Gallerlanders.

Many Gallerlanders, led by Nodarim, chased after the enemy despite Rildning's attempt to hold them in the woods. When Rildning relented and followed after them, he gained a broader view of the meadowlands. The size of the Frontier Corps was not as large as they had imagined, but they had already set up extensive siegeworks in front of the mountain.

Rildning could see the long train of carts and covered wagons snaking back toward the horizon in the direction of Rachard. For a moment he thought of Harsen and wondered if he was still alive, or even among the wagoners. Rildning noticed many of the vehicles were filled with wooden beams.

"Siegecraft," he said to the nearby chiefs.

"Machines?" Urgamdir asked.

"Or walls?" Nodarim asked.

"Undoubtedly both," Rildning said. "Machines to batter Gilgalem, inner walls to protect the soldiers from Gilgalem, and outer walls to protect their soldiers. This is their way of besieging cities, now applied to the face of the mountain."

"So the path to Gilgalem is closed," Owerdir said.

"Look, they come again!" Lemori shouted.

Nodarim and the Gallerlanders who pursued the soldiers had turned around to flee back to the woods. The trumpets sounded as the Frontier Corps charged again, with most of the Gallerlanders now in the open field.

The cavalry cut through with ease, but the acrobatics of the Gallerlanders surprised them when they timed their jumps to land on the rumps of the horses. Several knights were killed from behind in this way, but none of the Gallerlanders attempted to stay on the flailing beasts.

More soldiers from the vanguard were coming to join the cavalry. They were starting to flank the Gallerlanders and would soon cut off their escape back to the creek woods. Knowing it was hopeless to continue the attack, Rildning called a hasty retreat back to the woods before it was too late. Covered by their archers, most of the Gallerlanders returned to the woods while the corpsmen fell back to regroup.

106

HARSEN

Rachard, Bram Province
Midspring, 2270

Harsen approached the gates of Rachard warily. Nothing looked unusual as he passed through. Then he noticed the camp that had been in the square near the gate was empty of the merchants and other camp followers. He drove his wagon to the spot and was preparing to unhitch his horses when a stableboy came out to meet him.

"Hallow, sir merchant. Why've you not gone with the corps?" The boy looked puzzled.

"I took the western road," Harsen said. He could feel his brow wrinkle with worry.

"You a'right, sir?" the boy asked. "If you hurry down the south road, you might catch 'em."

The realization that he had been twice fooled struck Harsen like a hammer. For a moment he could not hear anything and his eyes blurred. The squawking of the stableboy snapped him out of it.

"Sir! Sir, you want oats for the horses or no?"

As Harsen tried to force his brain to do something, he spotted the soldiers walking in a column toward him. He saw the gate as it was being shut. A few guards from there were also walking toward him. Harsen chose not to run. He steeled himself and waited for them. The stableboy ran off, leaving him standing alone.

Harsen spent the rest of the day shackled in irons and locked away in the new stone-block prison tower, with the promise of being sent to Hilsingor the next morning. From the tower Harsen could see much progress had been made in building Rachard and the marshal's new monster of a castle. Hilsingor's original wooden fort, once a lone outpost of the frontier, now appeared to be reduced to a barracks for the legion of masons, carpenters, and other craftsmen.

Harsen could see a garrison force remained in Rachard, but most of the soldiers had left. His solace was that Rildning had known from the start that Birom was a trap. He hoped his old friend had persuaded the Gallerlanders to stay in Gilgalem or otherwise survived whatever he himself had unwittingly made possible.

He hoped Rildning would forgive him, if he still lived. He vowed, should he ever again be free from the Frontier Corps, that he would never leave Rildning's side again.

107

RILDNING

Near Gilgalem, Vaynland
Midspring, 2270

The Gallerlanders crouched for a meager fast-breaking by the wooded creek. The enemy had not approached the woods since the previous day.

"What are they waiting for?" Urgamdir asked.

"My guess is they are focused on investing Gilgalem with their siegeworks," Rildning said. "They'll force the mountain to surrender, no matter how long it takes."

"All of Gilgalem?" Urgamdir shook his head. "It cannot be done."

"It can, my friend. The corps will build their giant catapults and far-reaching trebuchets on the crests of the highest foothills within range of the bowl of Gilgalem, or at least the paths leading into and out of the refuge. They'll build a palisade to protect these siege machines from a Gallerlander attack, and to prevent the inhabitants from escaping.

"Then a second palisade will protect the machines and legions from outside attackers like us who may try to relieve Gilgalem, meaning our approach will be blocked by two sets of walls and ditches. The palisades are prefabricated, their tree trunks and binding bars carted to Gilgalem by the legions for swift construction."

"I know you were a knight once, but how can you know this with—?"

"Such precision? The Brintilian Empire had used this model to destroy cities for centuries. I heard tales about Hilsingor when I was living in New Lorin Colony. He used this strategy to dislodge Arukan rebels from their fortresses in the Old World. The marshal is likely here to oversee this siege, as he was at Nalembalen, so this is certainly what he will do."

"What can we do?" Urgamdir asked. His face was sullen.

"I stayed up half the night pondering what to do. But Tirgranir is . . ."

"He's useless. He's in a daze, lagging behind even when fighting breaks out. Don't we have at least enough men to harass Hilsingor's flank?"

"Yes, but to what end? If the marshal decides to attack the woods, our small band will be overrun by his legions. It would not help Gilgalem."

"Then why hasn't Hilsingor made such a move?"

"I don't know. If the marshal's intention in using Harsen to lure the Vaynking out of Gilgalem was to kill Tirgranir, then this is the time to do it. Perhaps Hilsingor wants Tirgranir alive so he can be installed on the imperial council with the others."

"He didn't give Erambrin the chance," Urgamdir said.

They were interrupted by a rising clamor down in the Frontier Corps encampments in the meadowlands. Rildning and the others rose from breaking their fast and rushed to the wood's edge for a view. Rildning and Urgamdir joined the Gallerlander scouts posted in the trees.

It was an astonishing and most unexpected sight. The Frontier Corps was busy with building their siegeworks and much of the army was still camped on the plain below the foothills. But that broad swath of meadow littered with tents, horses, campfires, and wagons was being divided by what seemed like enormous plows.

"Landships!" Rildning cried. He nearly fell out of the tree as he trembled with excitement.

"The Rahlampians have come?" Urgamdir asked. His eyes grew wide at the sight.

"They have come!"

The Gallerlanders watched in wonder as the landships sailed across the plain, arranged in a wing formation. Their sails were full and nothing could stop the crush of their giant wheels. Men perished by the dozens every moment. What was not destroyed in their parallel paths was thrown into disarray as soldiers and horses struggled to move out of the way.

When the landships neared the edge of the sprawling encampment, they turned to make a second pass. By this time, commanders had organized rows of archers. The Gallerlanders watched as thick clouds of arrows rained down onto the ships. Volley after volley cleared their decks of Rahlampian archers and tore into their sails, eventually robbing a few landships of their speed. But, as Rildning had experienced aboard the *Earthark*, even the slower-moving landships were too high off the ground for even swift cavalry to attempt to board.

The body of the Frontier Crops was soon split in half by the Rahlampians' surprise attack. Some soldiers sought refuge behind the incomplete palisades and ditches of the siegeworks. Most of the others huddled in a bristling mass of spears and lines of archers who were now shooting flaming arrows at one of the landships. Soon its sails were full of burning holes that widened with every moment.

Lacking the equivalent of oars that would continue to propel a ship upon the sea, the landship creaked to a halt. The Rahlampians aboard it held out for a while, especially when other landships attempted to sail a protective circle around it. But when the arrows of the Rahlampian archers were exhausted, the corpsmen climbed up the wheels and seized the landship, which they torched.

Rildning could see the landships, twenty or so, patrolling up and down the gap they had cleared. The Frontier Corps had backed away but had archers with flaming arrows ready when a landship strayed too close. When it was clear Hilsingor's men were not going to attempt to retake the gap anytime soon, one of the landships approached the woods where the Gallerlanders crouched. Rildning saw Mrigamad climbing down ahead of his men, and he made sure he was the first to meet the Rahlampian.

"My friend!" Rildning shouted, hugging Mrigamad jubilantly. "The most perfect timing. How did you know we needed your aid in this moment?"

Mrigamad patted his shoulder and smiled. "We could hear the trembling knees of the Gallerlanders from across the meadowlands." The Gallerlanders within earshot of his jest were too elated to think ill of it. "We sent scouts here before the Frontier Corps arrived, even before you left the mountain. But I'm sorry the landships could not sail faster. The foothills of the east slowed us."

"I've heard tales of these landships," Nodarim said. "I swore as a young man never to let them said on Gallerlandia while I lived. I cannot keep that oath if we are to keep Gilgalem, and Gallerlandia. Welcome, friend!"

Mrigamad nodded uneasily before speaking. Rildning knew such cooperation was still so unnatural between both tribes. "Today, we are enemies no more," Mrigamad said. "Only one Rahlampian needs to perish under our blades, either stonesword or windrazor. Unfortunately Anfinnan is far away, enjoying the pampered life of an imperial puppet in Eglamour."

"He is a leader without a people," Rildning said.

"And you are a leader with many peoples," Mrigamad answered with a smile. "Most of our fleets are preparing to defend Rahlampia, but these are the ones we could spare. The chiefs I brought with me are here not only to defend Gilgalem, but to destroy this host. Will the Gallerlanders march out to follow their electrum-armored leader?"

"The men you see here are our best," Rildning said. "Gilgalem is full of the weakened, half-starved, and fearful. I think we should withdraw from the field and fight where we must inside the cover of the forest. Sabotage their supply lines and steal their horses. But some Gallerlanders will not agree to this. We must decide, and soon."

Mrigamad nodded in agreement. "We own the gap now, but by tomorrow the unpainted men will have turned their catapults away from the mountain and toward us. They have learned that fire can stop a landship."

"They may attack even sooner," Rildning said. "Marshal Hilsingor knows patience, but he does not wait unnecessarily."

"I'm glad you know the enemy so well. Too well," Mrigamad jested.

"I know them, but I'm no longer pampered as Anfinnan."

Mrigamad climbed back up the landship ladder. "I will return to hear the Gallerlanders' plan."

Rildning looked around for Tirgranir. He finally found him, sitting on a stone that jutted out into the stream, staring down into the water.

108

ARVGRED

Near Gilgalem, Vaynland
Midspring, 2270

Arvgred decided to take a chance. He had gotten close to the Frontier Corps encampment, crawling in ditches and from one grassy tuft to another. The wheeled ships had ruined everything. But it was too late to turn back and wait for nightfall. He had to get his information to Hilsingor quickly, but without the soldiers mistaking him for a heathen.

He had tried to rub the staining paint from his face and arms, but the green would not come off easily. Now he simply looked like a muddy heathen, but he comforted himself in knowing the soldiers would prize his information. And that damn ranger would vouch for him.

The wheeled ship that stopped at the woods was on his left. He could see the barbarians getting back into it. They had nearly run him over when they passed by, and he guessed they would come back. The edge of the encampment he had planned to approach was now a bloody heap of bodies, twisted wagons, and rutted earth. He would have to go farther. He looked at his bloody elbows. It was no use.

The wheeled ship near the woods was coming now. It knew where he was, perhaps smelling the information in his head. He brought his legs up, trying to decide whether to stay or run. He could hear the call of the giant wheels. They spoke to him, told him to run. The grass waving under his chin whispered for him to stay. It was coming closer now.

Arvgred bolted up and ran across the meadow. He kept his eyes on the destruction ahead of him. He could smell the death of it, and the freshly torn earth. It looked good to him, free of barbarians and their filth. A grin crept into the corners of his mouth. He never felt the spiked wheels catch into his back and crush him down into the earth.

109

HILSINGOR

Frontier Corps Encampment near Gilgalem
Midspring, 2270

"He played his part wonderfully well," Hilsingor said with satisfaction.

"The guards in Rachard rushed him here," Arnolf said. "Do you want him executed?"

"Not yet. Keep him in chains."

"May I have the honor when the time comes?" Ravorglad asked. "That barbarian-loving wagoner's schemes would have led to the deaths of my own men, had he peddled true information to the Gallerlanders. He should die for his treachery."

"He will," Hilsingor said. "But the headsman will see to it. It is beneath my most senior crusader to dirty his hands with such low filth. Now, we have more important matters to discuss. What do we know of these Rahlampians and their land-rolling ships?"

"They are one of the tribes Admiral Arnasbirg's fleet encountered in the east," Firkas said.

"And unlike the Gallerlanders, they make proper use of iron for weapons and, obviously, special machines," Arnolf added.

"Quite remarkable," Hilsingor said. "I've never seen nor heard of land-sailing ships."

"And deadly," Firkas said. "More than eight hundred provincials were killed by them or the archers on their decks. Tomorrow we should march into the gap with every archer of the legions and send them a wall of pricking flame."

"We will do better than that," Hilsingor said. "Chief engineer Bronderod has been preparing something special at my request, but Arnolf has confirmed with him that every catapult should be turned toward the gap during the night, while the larger trebuchets remain focused on the mountain."

"And I want the stone urns of Raffen quicklime to be brought to the catapults. The Raffen assure us their foul-smelling concoction can burn any ship."

"I thought the leader of the Rahlampians had traveled to Eglamour and joined the empire?" Ravorglad asked. "And yet here are his black-faced warriors, sailing through our encampment."

"Evidently the word has not reached his own chiefs," Firkas said.

"It's more than that," Hilsingor said. "All of the admiral's dispatches indicate the Rahlampians are longtime enemies of the Gallerlanders. For them to suddenly ally themselves with Gallerlanders against us while their leader is away in our capital suggests something is afoot."

"Can't they be bought?" Firkas asked.

"They don't use money of any sort," Arnolf said. "Everything is communal for them, from the domnitar as titular head down to the artisans and shrimp pond fishers, if the admiral's surveyors are to be believed."

"Arnolf, do you remember that lengthy dispatch from his surveyors? Over there in that stack, I believe. Tell us more about them."

"Here, yes," Arnolf began. "Their black body paints are unique among the heathens, supposedly made from the aged blood of crows. All of their folk have black hair and dark eyes. They are builders of ships, mills, foundries, and catapults—"

"They've used catapult ships to good affect against my provincials," Firkas added.

"They call their wheeled vessels landships," Arnolf continued. "But they are used upon lakes, rivers, and marshes as well. Like the Welkars, the Rahlampians build their houses upon those same types of waters, usually on stilts or mounds of earth and gravel.

"The Rahlampian chiefs often have higher-rising and stronger fort houses built on palisades filled with earth and complex bridge networks for defense. The Welkars, of course, had hillier terrain with stagnant swamps, which permitted them to have lower, stilted hovels.

"Rahlampia is said to be mostly flat marshland with thick grasses, thorny brush, and straightwoods. These plains rise gently toward the south where high mountains form a wall beyond which lies the sea. In the mountains they mine special ores to make their long razor-thin swords."

"I can add to that," Firkas said. "My men found these swords aboard the landship that was burned. The warriors who wielded them were fierce indeed. At first the soldiers could not even see the blades, causing much fear and confusion. Swords made by some Memelos craft. When wielded, they could kill across a distance of seven paces or more. They said it was impossible to see where the blade was, so many men simply watched the fat-pommeled handles in their hands, often misjudging the distance.

"Even when these warriors were outnumbered and surrounded at the end, they spun like a whirlwind and cut down all the soldiers within reach. If it were not for the provincial archers, once again, it would have been near impossible to get close enough to kill them."

"The admiral wrote that he found a hoard of strange ore," Arnolf said, "alongside hunks of bog iron at a foundry when he sacked an inland stilt town. He sent the ores back to the smiths at Port Rilhammor, but we did not hear the results of their examination."

"Memelos magic all," Ravorglad said. "We should sack their whole confederation after ending the green-skins' tribe, whether or not their leader sits in a council chair in Eglamour."

"All in good time," Hilsingor said.

Engineer Bronderod walked into the hall.

"Please sit," Hilsingor said. "Bring him some wine. Tell me, how is the special project?"

"I have more special projects now than ever," complained the grumpy engineer. "Nothing is special if everything is special. Custom, prefabricated palisades for a double-ringed siegeworks around a mountain. Dangerous barbarian concoctions for the catapults. Not to mention the largest castle man has ever attempted. And now all the goldsmiths and some carpenters are—"

"Come now," Firkas said. "What has the marshal put on your plate now?"

Hilsingor answered for Bronderod as the engineer took a long draft from the wine cup. "A surprise," he said with a smile. "For the enemy, but also for us. Let's just say not all of our electrum will be minted into coins. And we can thank Rildning's journal for the inspiration."

110

RILDNING

Near Gilgalem, Vaynland
Midspring, 2270

Dawn was delayed on the battlefield as ominous clouds hung low over ground saturated with heavy rains during the night. Rildning was glad most of the Gallerlanders camped in the damp creek woods were in relatively good spirits, despite the poor sky omens.

The sight of the Rahlampian landships smashing through the enemy on the previous day had bolstered their confidence, as did Rildning's rallying speech. He knew sullen-faced Tirgranir would not speak to them, so he had stood on one of the stream stones to encourage them.

"As we have just seen, when the clans and tribes unite, the enemy cannot stand," he had told them. "Take heart, these are your lands. The enemy is far from his home. You know every mountain, hill, and rill. Every patch of earth and rocky cleft. Every sacred forest and tree hovel.

"They can steal and burn, but they cannot rob you of your spirit, your will to fight and live free in the forests once again. The Gallerlander, Rahlampian, and Naren-Dra have joined hands against this foreign foe. Show them, here at the feet of Gilgalem, where their road ends. Let those who do not perish under our stonesword, landship, and alchemy flee back to their own lands with tales of fear, never to return!"

The melancholy Vaynking did not rise to join Rildning or add his voice to the cheers of the others, but Tirgranir no longer distanced himself from Rildning either. He tended to stay close, as if hoping to absorb the aura of leadership he had lost since Birom.

They had held a council and made a decision. To Rildning's disappointment, most of the Gallerlanders wanted to charge the Frontier Corps. They were still loyal to Tirgranir, even if they respected Rildning. He relented and prepared to lead them in Tirgranir's stead.

Mrigamad had come across in the rain, the mud-sucked wheels slower and the sails not as full as before. He advised Rildning to delay the charge, and so they did. When the weather finally turned, they went forward.

The enemy's catapults began lobbing what seemed like barrels of fire at the landships patrolling the gap. Rildning had watched as every cavalry unit sent out to probe the gap was obliterated or turned back by the landships. It was time.

The Gallerlanders rushed out of the woods toward the siegeworks that barricaded Gilgalem's northern approach. As agreed upon with Mrigamad, half of his landships sped toward the siegeworks ahead of the Gallerlanders, while the other half patrolled the gap. In this way, Rildning hoped to keep the Frontier Corps divided.

As the Gallerlanders ran, Rildning could see the corpsmen manning the siegeworks readying themselves and quickening the pace of their catapults. Two landships were destroyed and a third disabled from the fire barrels, but they could not stop all of them. The clash was so fierce Rildning could hear the mountains ringing back echoes.

The first landship to sail into the siegeworks was captained by Denildon the Riverkeeper. It had an iron beak-like battering ram on its prow that punctured the palisade with ease. The hull crushed through, making a path for the giant wheels to scrape down the wall and every soldier that stood nearby. Those soldiers who were tossed aside and survived found arrows in their bellies before they could stand.

Rildning saw Denildon turn his ship down into the narrow space between the inner and outer palisades, tearing through the soldiers and their catapults. When larger fortifications threatened to stall his movement, he swerved the landship out into the field again, bursting another hole in the palisade. Rildning urged his men to run toward both holes, but they were still some distance away.

Two other landships soon followed Denildon's example. One became wedged on its way out of the siegeworks and the Frontier Crops wasted no time in swarming it. When the Rahlampian archers and windrazors would not let them aboard, the corpsmen simply set it on fire, consuming part of the palisade along with it.

By now the path up through the foothills into Gilgalem had come alive like a giant caterpillar. Thousands upon thousands of Gallerlanders were rushing down to join the fight. The tribesmen with Rildning greeted the sight with a great cheer, and it was answered from those in the foothills. Rildning saw panic among the corpsmen manning the palisade, which now formed a complete barrier in front of the mountain, and yet the main Frontier Corps body on the other side of the landship-patrolled gap remained unmoved.

Finally, Rildning and his men arrived at the breached palisades. He could hear the knights rallying the soldiers on the wall. Stone and steel clanged as the struggle began. Rildning and Urgamdir were among the first group to run into an opening and ascend the wall.

They chopped and shot their way down the palisade, fighting a mix of provincial soldiers and Raffen tribesmen. Enemy archers were crammed atop watchtowers. They fought their way to a command fort, one of a dozen or so positioned along the siegeworks at intervals. That was when the crusaders came out.

Rildning saw the gleam of the knights' armor and the glint of their steel longswords. The knights fought in pairs, back-to-back, as they were accustomed to when surrounded by the natives. For an instant his mind recalled the arrival of the first crusaders from the Old World, back when he had just come down from Mount Tremvig. And the training of other knights to fight with them. They were Old World nobles, seeking glory, wealth, or service to God. All were committed to the quest of purging the New World of its original peoples.

Rildning blocked a swipe from a tall fully armored crusader. He felt his shoulder burn, remembering the Hral poison-tipped barb that long ago bit into him. He felt his age as this strong young man hacked ruthlessly at him, one blow after another. Rildning lost his balance and the next glancing blow sent him teetering off the wall, his sword flying from his hands.

He landed on a wood pile, one side of his face lacerated by rough-cut bark edges. He could hear the knight laugh above him, then he heard the din of the fight around him vanish with an earsplitting roar. Splinters shot through the air like knives. The iron beak of Denildon's landship had ruptured the command fortress, making it a tomb for the crusaders still inside.

With his landship hopelessly wedged and his masts torn down, the Riverkeeper and his crew leaped onto the wall and joined the Gallerlanders. Their long windrazors passed effortlessly through the palisade planks and steel armor. The Rahlampians fanned out to fight alone, clearing a circular path all around them. Only the archers in the watchtowers above could strike them easily, but they were forced to aim at the Gallerlanders assailing their towers.

By now, the Gallerlanders who had raced down from Gilgalem arrived at the inner palisade walls. Rildning regained his feet and picked up a dead soldier's sword and shield. It was the first time he had held a real shield in years. He led the charge toward a small gate where they overwhelmed the soldiers and allowed the newly arrived Gallerlanders into the siegeworks. Soon that area was flooded with Gallerlanders and their allies, and they pushed down the siegeworks in both directions.

Rildning rejoined Urgamdir and Kemet. They dispatched a soldier guarding one of the high watchtowers. The stout door was locked, so Urgamdir moved to run up the tower as if it were a tree. His wounded shoulder caused him to move slower than he wished, and he cried out in pain.

Rildning would have followed if not for a spearman who came around the corner, determined to fight them both. When Rildning evaded his initial stab, the spearman attempted to skewer Urgamdir as he climbed. Rildning quickly closed the distance and ran his sword through him as Kemet killed two other soldiers coming toward them.

Rildning looked up to see Urgamdir with his ax within reach of the archers, who did not see him. One perished before the other archers in the next tower spotted him. Time slowed as Rildning saw them hit Urgamdir. His great form plunged to the earth. His eyes were open skyward, unmoving, when Rildning came to him. Rildning could see Urgamdir's barrel chest fall as his last breath escaped him.

While Rildning and Kemet were crouched over Urgamdir, the door of the watchtower burst open and a soldier with a spiked mace lashed out at them. Rildning turned and rolled, then sprang upon the soldier with a crushing blow that caved in his mail coif with a sickening crack. Rildning bounded over his body and flew up the stairs where he silenced the bows of every archer, then picked up a bow and shot at the neighboring tower, forcing them to take cover.

Through the wooden crenel barriers of his tower Rildning saw Denildon down on the ground attracting the attention of crusaders who insisted the archers keep out of their fight. The Riverkeeper now had a windrazor in each hand. Rildning recalled Mrigamad's talk of him being one of a few who had the strength and skill for this technique. Even these crusaders were in awe of him and desired the glory of killing him, yet none could approach his whirling form.

Denildon soon tired of the game and sliced toward their faces with the invisible blades. It was the first time Rildning had ever seen the well-disciplined crusaders run from an opponent whom they had already engaged.

The battle ebbed as the Frontier Corps retreated behind the walls built between sections of the palisades. Rildning knew this was by design, in case one section fell. He helped reconsolidate the Gallerlanders and Rahlampians as one of the landships crashed into the next section of palisade. It caused enough distraction among the Frontier Corps ranks that the Gallerlanders were able to break through the section wall.

The enemy was ready for them. Rildning saw a well-armored troop of provincials and Raffen, led by a mounted knight. They charged at each other. Rildning fought through the ensuing melee, trying to reach the commanding knight. Then he saw Owerdir and his shroud alchemists throw a dark cloud at the knight. The knight leaped off his horse before the cloud could smother him, ripping off his helmet to vomit.

"You!" the knight shouted between coughs as Rildning approached him. He resembled someone Rildning knew from long ago. "You!" the knight repeated as he came to his feet, his nose broken and bloodied, his eyes filled with rage. "You killed my brothers!"

The knight drew his sword and came at Rildning. As he parried, Rildning realized who this man was.

"Yield, Firkas! I did not kill them!"

"For Onas!" Firkas shouted as he swiped at Rildning's head. "For Rekef!"

"No!" Rildning cried. He tried to get a word in while blocking and evading Firkas's slashing. But he could not bring himself to fight, which only fanned the knight's fury.

"Fight me! I will avenge my brothers!"

"Yield! I will not fight you!"

"Fight me, damn you!"

But Rildning would not. Firkas's fury blinded him and he tripped and fell headlong into the soggy turf. Rildning turned to run but the knight sprang to his feet and swiped again.

"Onas was killed by the Ollohd, and Rekef by the Hrals," Rildning panted. "I swear it. I was saddened by their—"

"Lying heretic!" Firkas charged him. By now another soldier had stumbled toward them and Rildning was forced to defend himself. He killed the soldier and narrowly missed being hacked by Firkas. He turned and swiped defensively as Firkas recklessly leaned in for another jab. Firkas's throat opened and blood spewed onto Rildning.

Shaken by the deaths of Urgamdir and Firkas, Rildning ran for a corner hidden by a wagon to take a breath. Owerdir and Kemet followed him.

"We have to press on," Owerdir insisted.

"Something has changed across the gap," Kemet said. "The main body of the enemy may be moving, and the Frontier Corps are rallying on the other side of the palisades. Golenrad, vassal-king of the Ollohd, is leading them."

"We must focus on breaking the siege and leave the main corps to Mrigamad's landships," Rildning said. "Only then can we face the legions on the field with hope of drawing them into the woods."

As they moved to rejoin the fight they heard Nodarim shout out to the Gallerlanders. He was standing atop the outer wall where the most recent landship had crashed, pointing out toward the meadowlands. Then other Gallerlanders on the wall saw what he had and froze, uncaring of the soldiers that came at them. Only the Rahlampians resisted distraction.

Rildning, Owerdir, and Kemet rushed up to the wall for a look. A tall, gleaming structure was being raised in the distance, just beyond a small woods on the far flank of the Frontier Corps's main body. The narrow end of the structure pointed toward the sky. It was green-golden, like electrum. The sun burst from the clouds as its massive form rose higher and higher.

"A giant sword," Rildning whispered to himself.

"The sword of Wurumnak!" Nodarim cried.

"A miracle?" Owerdir asked.

The other Gallerlanders shouted excitedly. Rildning was confused and feared for them. From his vantage point on the wall, he could not see how the great sword had risen up from the earth, but he did not believe it was a miracle. He was confident the Sage would have told him about the forging of the sword, which the stories said the Gallerlanders would do for the End Times. Yet there it stood on the crest of a hill, alone and glistening.

"Stand your ground!" he called out to the Gallerlanders when some climbed down from the wall and walked back out into the plain. But in no time at all they were trotting out toward the sword. Nodarim eyed Rildning.

"If you are truly one of us, you must let them rally to our god. The End Times are upon us!"

"Have you not learned this enemy will use any trick to assure their victory?" Rildning asked.

Nodarim ran off with the others. Rildning looked out and saw that the Rahlampians and Gallerlanders who remained were struggling. Rildning took hold of Owerdir's shoulder.

"You must stop them," Rildning said. "Convince them this is not right." But even Owerdir was torn. Rildning saw his friend look up into the sky. The sun shone brightly on his face. Rildning could see the words forming on his lips.

"This sky will deceive you!" Rildning shouted. He shook Owerdir to get his attention. "You must tell them!"

Owerdir did his best, but those who had seen the giant sword would not listen. The Rahlampians chided and condemned the Gallerlanders who left their side in the midst of the battle. Rildning could see the panic spread. The remaining men of both tribes who were too hard-pressed to notice the giant sword now struggled to keep the breaches open, much less push farther into the siegeworks. Rildning rushed back up into the watchtower, with Kemet close behind him.

They saw the Gallerlanders fan out into the meadowlands toward the risen sword. Their scattered numbers forced a few of the landships still patrolling the gap to veer away to avoid crushing them. And yet, even now, the main body of Hilsingor's army remained in place, not taking advantage of the distracted and scattered natives.

Perhaps it was the snap of a rope or the glint of a chain that Rildning saw just before the great sword wobbled. When he saw this, there was no doubt in his mind it was a ruse. Some Gallerlanders had now reached the towering electrum and stood in awe.

They next saw the movement in Hilsingor's lines. Several signal flags waved up and down the ranks. A massive force of cavalry flowed out toward the giant sword, while another group charged the landships' gap.

The first group ran down the scattered Gallerlanders like a wind in leaves. They headed toward those clustering around the giant sword and were joined by infantry hidden in the nearby woods. The second cavalry group rushed past the landships toward the siegeworks, with all of the legions following behind them. Rildning could see a purple-bannered retinue front and center. He knew it was Hilsingor leading the charge.

A great cry of panic rose up from among his warriors. They abandoned the breaches as the thunder of the cavalry grew louder. A group of Gallerlander archers and scouts tried to concentrate their arrows at Hilsingor's retinue, but their resolve broke as the ground quaked and they were overwhelmed. Those who tried to flee were pinned between the cavalry and the siegeworks, where they were promptly slaughtered.

111

MRIGAMAD

Near Gilgalem, Vaynland
Midspring, 2270

Mrigamad had seen the giant sword and knew it was a ruse. He signaled the landships to follow him toward it, abandoning the gap that was already overrun by the legions. There they crushed through the Frontier Corps's lines.

Mrigamad spotted the Raffen cavalry and King Pendigied leading the charge toward the Gallerlanders gathered near the sword. He gave the signal to veer over and cut off the charge, breaking the riders and their horses like twigs. When his and the other landships sailed through, he looked back to see that Pendigied and his retinue had narrowly survived.

The landships pivoted their sails to come around again. Mrigamad directed his archers to one side to better shoot at Pendigied. He saw the Raffen king jump down from his horse as his commanders fell around him. His horse took the arrows and fell. Before Mrigamad sailed out of view of the king, he saw that Pendigied still stood, clutching an arrow that had bitten into his shoulder.

Mrigamad looked toward the electrum sword. He could see the soldiers propping up the sword with poles and chains from behind the hill on which it stood. He steered the landship toward it even as the Gallerlanders were drawing nearer to it, with looks of awe still on their faces. But they heard the rumble of his landship and leaped out of the way. So too did the soldiers holding up the sword.

Mrigamad's landship crested the hill as the sword tilted backward. The hull crashed into it, splintering the sword's log backings and shaking the electrum plates off like leaves. The landship's front half became airborne as it jumped the hill, crushing many of the soldiers upon landing.

The Gallerlanders rushed to the sword. Their grief changed to anger when they saw what the corpsmen had done. The soldiers who survived the landship were brutally killed.

Mrigamad was glad the Gallerlanders had awoken from their daze, but when he turned his ship he saw the legions swarming over them. They were scattered and well outnumbered, and one of his landships was on fire.

His and the other landships made several passes through the Frontier Corps, but when it was clear the Gallerlanders would be annihilated and the archers focused on the landships with flaming arrows, Mrigamad gave the signal to return to the siegeworks.

112

RILDNING

Near Gilgalem, Vaynland
Midspring, 2270

Rildning and Kemet came down from the disheartening view in the watchtower and gathered everyone around Tirgranir. A core group of about eight thousand Gallerlanders were still in or near the siegeworks. Others were picking off soldiers with arrows shot from the forest edge, and more Gallerlanders were still coming down from the foothills.

The Rahlampians were many fewer in number, but their landships continued to plow through the Frontier Corps while Denildon and others fought on foot with their windrazors.

Owerdir and his alchemists found ways to pinpoint their debilitating attacks on knight commanders and key choke-points. But for Rildning a direct fight was not the way to defeat the Frontier Corps.

"All is lost," Tirgranir said when he came near.

"We could punch back through the breach toward Gilgalem and take refuge," Owerdir suggested.

"Too late," Kemet said. "The legions are here."

Before Rildning could answer, the purple-bannered knights crashed into the breach nearest them. He heard the shout of a Brintilian.

"Prince of heathens and heretics, face me now!" the man cried as they entered the courtyard between the siegeworks. Rildning saw the banners and knew it was Hilsingor.

"Take the Vaynking," Rildning ordered Owerdir. "Use your shroud alchemy and mask the path behind you. Take him to Gilgalem, or wherever you can find refuge." Tirgranir did not resist as Owerdir steered him away.

Rildning looked around him at the chaos in the bright sun, the cries of defeat jammed into his ears. He and others descended the stairs as Hilsingor removed his gilded helmet and tossed it with a grim smile.

They looked upon each other, one standing in the bloodied mud, his shoulders slumped with fatigue and pain, and the other comfortably mounted on his fully armored warhorse. The fighting around them blurred as Rildning stared at Hilsingor. Kemet stepped toward the marshal, sword drawn.

"This is my fight," Rildning said, waving him off.

The marshal threw down his lance and unsheathed his sword. The steel rang with a cold eagerness, calling for blood. Rildning raised his blade as Hilsingor charged. A moment later the marshal slammed his sword down on Rildning's shield. He felt the pain in his Hral-bitten shoulder again. The strength of the aging marshal surprised Rildning, but he moved to ready himself for the next charge.

When Hilsingor came at him again, Rildning took another strike with his shield but still could not get positioned to slash the marshal or his steed. Hilsingor's third charge was cut short when the hind legs of his horse parted from its body. Rildning saw Denildon's dual windrazors had swept near them by pure fortune. All of the tribesmen were either drawing away with Tirgranir or being pushed closer by the corpsmen.

Rildning wasted no time in rushing upon the marshal as he struggled to roll away from the crushing body of the flailing animal. Rildning tried for Hilsingor's unprotected head, but one of his mounted knights came to his rescue and deflected the blow. This knight jabbed at Rildning with his lance while screaming profanities through his visor. A second knight ran up and put the horse out of its misery before helping the marshal to his feet.

"No, Ravorglad!" the marshal shouted at the first knight. "He's mine! Wilsig, stop him!"

Kemet landed a blow to Ravorglad's armored leg and he cried out as Wilsig stepped toward them. Before Wilsig could break them away, the front half of Ravorglad's horse fell away from his saddle and he collapsed into the animal's gushing corpse. Rildning caught a glimpse of Denildon whirling his windrazors around for another swipe, which narrowly missed Ravorglad but took off Wilsig's leg and sent him screaming down into the mud.

As Rildning turned to find Hilsingor again he felt a glancing but sharp pain in his back and found himself facedown in the mud. He tried to roll but the muck pulled at his electrum armor. He heard the single-word shouting of Denildon and the shrill tings of steel all around.

Rildning managed to push up with his hands and knees and grasped for a broken lance that lay nearby. He saw blood drip from his mouth as he felt the throb of the new wound in his back. In the corner of his eye he saw Denildon and Kemet distracted elsewhere.

"Come now, you've muddied your sacred heathen armor!" Hilsingor said. "You'll still make a fine corpse."

Rildning threw the lance at him to buy time for a sword. He took up Ravorglad's as that knight still found himself entangled in the muck and the remains of his horse. Rildning raised the sword in time to deflect the marshal's patient fury, his dark eyes aflame and fixed upon him.

The strokes between them were swift and determined, but each was skillfully parried by the other. Both were without shields now, and the mud that pulled at their feet promised to tire them quickly. They breathed the breath of the other, felt their strength sap with every moment of the struggle.

Rildning's mind fluttered with the sharp pain in his back and shoulder. He blinked and Hilsingor landed a crushing blow from above, shattering Rildning's sword hand. He cried out, dodged another strike, and lunged for his dropped sword with his shield hand. He yanked on it but it wouldn't lift. It wasn't his sword but a heavy windrazor. He jerked the heavy pommel into Hilsingor's face.

As the marshal recoiled Rildning noticed purple-bannered knights ringed around them to watch. He did not see Kemet, nor any Gallerlanders or Rahlampians nearby, though he could still hear fierce fighting all around. Rildning struggled to master the mud-caked windrazor with his tired shield arm, knowing it was meant for two strong arms. He mustered all his strength and whirled it overhead.

Hilsingor rushed toward him again, deflecting Rildning's heavy downward strike, which cleaved the marshal's sword in half. Hilsingor held fast to the fragment and stabbed into the electrum scales of his armor.

Rildning cried out and brought up the heavy pommel again but missed the marshal's face. Hilsingor landed his own gauntleted fist into Rildning's jaw. Then Rildning felt pain in his ribs and a blow to the back of his head. He felt himself falling, hearing Hilsingor speak before he blacked out.

"Take him back to . . ."

113

ENIRI

Gilgalem, Vaynland
Midspring, 2270

"Tell me everything," Eniri said. Her face was flush and her eyes glared dangerously. Behind her stood Bothrobim and several Nyden captains who had come with her from the coast. Owerdir, Mrigamad, and their followers were also with her. Every chieftain who had survived the battle crowded into the throne room.

"You've no right to make demands," snapped Rumban. "You were not here."

Tirgranir slowly climbed onto his throne. He sat sullenly, noticing nothing. Eniri had waited until they were safely in Pindoarig before asking what had happened, but she was done waiting.

"I have every right," she said. "I'm effectively queen of the Umbyrs now, and I'm his wife. What happened?"

Owerdir stepped in. "Just before you arrived near the foothills, we were doing well getting Tirgranir out of the siegeworks, while Rildning and others had stayed behind. But then the enemy charged us. My alchemists did not have enough smoke to cover our path, and too many tribesmen had followed us anyway. The foreigners rode into us. That was when you and your Nyden friends arrived."

"Why were the Gallerlanders outside Gilgalem at all?" she asked. "That is our stronghold."

"We thought he had an opportunity to surprise the enemy in the woods," Rumban said. "But one of Rildning's men, a foreigner, deceived us!"

"Harsen did not deceive," Owerdir said. "He had been tricked by the enemy, as Rildning said, but Tirgranir believed the trickery anyway. When Tirgranir and the others were attacked in the woods, I took three hundred warriors down from the mountain to help. Then the enemy attacked in full force."

"And Rildning?" Eniri asked.

"He fought the marshal," Kemet said, whose eyes were hidden behind a bloody wrap. "That was the last I saw of him. The last I saw of anything."

"Who are these strangers?" Rumban asked.

"I'm Bothrobim, and these are my clansmen. We have brought a fleet, anchored on the western coast. My warriors wait there. We have come to fight our common enemy alongside you."

"A fleet," Tirgranir chuckled. He did not speak further.

"Unless they are Rahlampian landships, your sails are useless here," Rumban said. "How many men?"

"Seven hundred warriors and crew," Bothrobim said.

Tirgranir chuckled at his pride.

"A paltry sum," Rumban said. "Each of the foreigners' legions has ten thousand and we don't know how many are upon us."

"I would wager any of my sailors against any three of their foot soldiers," Bothrobim said.

"And how do we know your men are not Raffen spies?" prodded Rumban.

"Given that the imperial army surrounds you here and are rebuilding their siegeworks, I think spies are the least of your concerns," Bothrobim said.

"These men are the enemy of the Raffen," Eniri insisted. "Even now, war has resumed on their island against the Raffen and those whom they control. Yet they braved the seas to offer help to you. And you insult them?"

"I speak for the Vaynking!" Rumban shouted.

"You cower behind a throne that has not had a worthy leader sitting in it for years," Eniri said.

"Enough," came Tirgranir's weak voice. "If the omens are favorable with the dawn, I'll walk down the mountain and surrender." A hush came over the stone-hewn court. Many faces were blank with shock. "It's what Odon did," Tirgranir continued. "It's what Erambrin should have done. It's what the Bronhildi and the Raffen and the Rahlampians did."

"Gratgofa would have never . . ." Eniri's voice wavered.

"All of this started with his failure!" Tirgranir shouted. "The failure of the Gallerlanders of the north."

"You betray the memory of those who died," Owerdir said. "We may have failed to stop the flow of a great river, but you will set fire to your own house."

"When I have taken my place at the imperial council, you will be nothing," Tirgranir said.

"So you join Anfinnan," Mrigamad said. "A vassal-king without a people to follow you."

"Those who don't follow the path of peace will surely die," Rumban said.

"What will happen to Gallerlandia?" Eniri asked. She could not believe her ears. She looked toward the Sage. He was holding his brow, tired and frail.

"There will be no Gallerlandia without the empire," Tirgranir said. "Nothing is left, except this tired mountain."

"So, this is how you will make yourself high king then? Crowned by the enemy who destroyed our people. A slave of the enemy."

"Enough, woman! I will have you—"

"Enough, coward!" she cried. "Whether the dawn brings sky omens that are good or ill, I'll go down into the meadowlands. We will find Rildning and the others, and find a way to defeat them!" She turned her back on him and started toward the door.

"And I'll go with her," Owerdir said, signaling his shroud alchemists to follow him.

"And me," said the blind Kemet.

"Our clansmen will go also," said the chieftains Oturbrin and Lemori.

"The Rahlampians won't surrender," Mrigamad said. "We will go."

Later the Sage caught up to her. She saw grief in his eyes.

"My child, all share the hurt you feel," he said. "I disagree with Tirgranir as much as you, but your anger won't prevent him from relinquishing his ivy crown. He has abandoned himself, and us."

"I will no longer try to change his mind," Eniri replied. "The Gallerlanders will remain divided, as they always were. Even Rildning could not mend us."

"Perhaps he may yet," the Sage said. "He may yet . . ."

"Do you think he lives still?"

"Let me tell you, child, the view from Gilgalem was, and still is, frightful. The spring meadows are muddied, bloody, and gray with the cursed-earth metals of the foreigners. No one can free us from this host, even if Tirgranir had remained a true king. I struggle to see any omens that suggest we could prevail."

"You said you once had a vision," Eniri said. "You said you saw the first Agnesci man and woman at peace then troubled and then finding peace again. And that my joining with Rildning mixed the ancient bloodlines, a change that would bring the prophesied peace between Almeric and Agnesci. You said Rildning would be our high king, and that our son, Enildir, would be a unifier of many peoples."

"I still believe," the Sage said, shaking his head. "But perhaps the prophecy won't manifest itself in the way I once thought."

"I will find him," she said.

"You must hurry. The foreigners have made repairs on their walls and positioned their troops and catapults. They will surely attack soon, perhaps before Tirgranir has had a chance to surrender," the Sage said.

"If Rildning is our high king, as we have believed," she said, "then I must save him first."

"May Wurumnak guide you."

114

HILSINGOR

Frontier Corps Encampment near Gilgalem
Midspring, 2270

Hilsingor looked about his tent, spacious and richly decorated. Ceremonial herbs smoldered on two braziers, the smell of recent victories. Food was piled high on his table. But he wasn't hungry.

He studied the myriad trophies scattered around his tent. The drying ivy crown of Erambrin hung like a wreath from a cross beam, but his favorite had always been the antlered electrum helm of Gratgofa. His ivy crown had long since crumbled into dust. But his new favorite was Rildning's armor. A servant had cleaned the blood and muck from the scales and plate, making it shine again. Hilsingor could not help but smile.

Then there was his journal, weathered and worn, sitting on a table beside the marshal's chair. Hilsingor had read it many times and felt he intimately knew the adversary he had beaten. Hilsingor knew the Gallerlanders' defeat was assured, and Gilgalem would be an imperial possession.

And yet, his victory would still be incomplete. His carefully laid plans had done everything he needed except unearth the one mystery in Rildning's journal that eluded him. The next few moments would probably be his last chance to find the answers he was seeking.

Finally Arnolf reentered his tent. Behind him soldiers carried a limp, dirty bundle of a man. They shuffled in and sat him upright in the empty chair opposite Hilsingor. The

507

marshal waved the soldiers away and Arnolf found a chair near the door so he could watch in silence.

Hilsingor stared at the man. His bandages were blood-soaked and falling apart. The man was hunched uncomfortably, holding himself together with one bandaged hand held close to his chest and the other propping his body on the chair. His breathing was labored and he smelled of mud and infection. Yet his eyes glared with a cold sharpness. Hilsingor stood and poured two goblets of wine from the table.

"For your pain, Rildning." He offered the cup to the man. "The finest vintage of my home in Ned Gollen. I have one precious case left, so I share it with those whom I respect the most."

Rildning grasped the cup with his good hand and held it aloft for a moment. Hilsingor sipped quietly, watching. Rildning tipped the cup, pouring it out onto the marshal's fine Eadish rugs, then he let the cup fall. Hilsingor forced a smile.

"You could have chosen not to take the cup," he said.

"Do I have a choice to sit with you?" Rildning asked.

"No, you cannot stand, so you must sit. And talk with me."

"If I could stand, talking is not what I would choose to do," Rildning said.

Hilsingor pursed his lips. "Do not be so ungrateful for having been spared."

"Have I been spared?"

"You will have the opportunity to spare yourself," Hilsingor said. "We could have cut you down like the other savages. But I respect your persistence and courage. Your determination. You could have made a fine general of a legion, had you not been so naive." Hilsingor picked up Rildning's journal from the table. "I know you well, you see? Better than any except probably your heathen woman. I know your past, have walked with you in your troubles, watched as you deceived the barbarians into thinking you could save them, and—"

"I deceived no one," Rildning said.

"Come now," Hilsingor scoffed. "You've no secrets. You have long doubted both your role in the forests and the Gallerlanders' own ability to properly defend themselves. Always sparring among their clans and sub-clans and families and all their many divisions. If the Gallerlanders had been half as unified as the Arukans back home, they might have stood a chance against the legions. You knew this, yet you encouraged them for so long, even after the legions girded the foothills of Gilgalem."

"I believe in them," Rildning answered. "They deserve the peace they enjoyed before my forefathers came to the New World."

"Listen to yourself," Hilsingor said, "still naive. Despite what others think, I know you share few of their savage beliefs. And what peace have they had? You know as well as any that the tribes and clans of Pemonia have fought each other continuously, otherwise they would have colonized us first. War is their nature, and only the strong hand of the Brintilian Empire can break them from it. We will provide peace for them."

"A tribe of this continent is no different from the noble houses of Almeria," Rildning countered. "The empire will not solve petty conflicts between tribes and clans any more than it has feuds and wars between Old World rulers."

"There is truth in that," Hilsingor conceded. "But when we make war, it is civilized. Man to man. None of this running in the trees or sneaking around in the bushes like green weasels. Can you really think the barbarians are the Agnesci from the ancient days?"

"You have my journal," Rildning said. "You have the stories about the Cataclysm. Perhaps we would know more if you had not torched Nalembalen."

"It was necessary to destroy that city," Hilsingor said. "In hindsight, I would have liked to have captured the Graparins' archive, if only to give the Church the proper tools to fully expunge the influences of Memelos on this wild continent."

"If you have seen the truth in that book," Rildning said, "and you still believe the natives are Memelos spawn, then you are more ignorant than those who have not seen the truth at all."

It was difficult for Hilsingor to avoid a grin. Truth was exactly what he was seeking. The key to the mystery plaguing his mind since first reading about the Gallerlanders' secret histories.

"Truth?" Hilsingor said. "Then what about the ships of the air, mentioned in your book?"

"What?"

Hilsingor opened the journal and found the page easily. "Allow me to paraphrase: Eniri said the Agnesci Seafathers who had discovered Cedelaebos, that is, the Old World of Almeria, found it after many long journeys sailing through, and I quote, 'sea *and clouds*.'"

"And there is another part," Hilsingor continued, "back in your translation of the Cataclysm scroll. Here it says, 'But waves of sea *and wind* no longer to divide the brothers.' Now, what is a wave of the wind? How does one sail through clouds? This sounds like the ancient Agnesci learned how to build ships that sailed in the air."

Rildning looked at him strangely.

"Well?" the marshal said. "Did they build such machines? Surely they did not banish their shipbuilders after the Cataclysm just to avoid normal seafaring thereafter."

"There is no such thing as an airship," Rildning said. "Those banished shipbuilders became the Rahlampians. You see the ships they have; they sail upon the land."

"Yes, but at some point did they teach their wheeled ships to fly?"

"Those words, *and clouds . . . and wind*, are nothing more than descriptive language," Rildning answered. "Or perhaps my own poor translation."

"Don't be coy. Tell me how they made them or where I can find one. Is it the magic of Memelos or some mechanism hidden in the belly of Gilgalem? Perhaps you have seen a peculiar hull in—"

"There is no such thing."

"Rildning, if you tell me about this ancient secret, then I'll spare your life. I'll tell Archbishop Ralmo that the most vile heretic of Pemonia was killed in battle here. He will be disappointed you could not be flayed and burned at the stake. Then I would secure a secret pardon from the emperor and ensure you lived out the rest of your miserable life in peace in some wilderness cottage. But only if you share your knowledge of the ancient flying machines of the Agnesci."

Hilsingor could read confusion and distaste in Rildning's eyes.

"I have no emperor," Rildning answered. "And I have no need of your mercy."

"Not even for your woman? Your son?"

Rildning remained silent.

"Then you will be executed. And I'll enslave every Gallerlander that survives our march into Gilgalem. You will so stubbornly allow this, when simply speaking the truth alone could free them, and you?"

"Even if such an impossible thing as an airship existed," Rildning said, "I wouldn't give it to you. As for the Gallerlanders, they will fight your every step into the mountain. Your legions will disappear there, as they did in the Ardfalm Forest. The Gallerlanders will not so easily fall as the Bronhildi or the Raffen."

"You are wrong," Hilsingor said. He pulled a small parchment from the table and handed it to Rildning. "This was delivered by my chief ranger during the night."

> Honorable Marshal of the Empire,
> We accept your terms. I will surrender at dawn.
> Vaynking Tirgranir

Rildning looked up from the note with glassy eyes, but his face was hard.

"So you see," Hilsingor said, smiling, "the Gallerlanders fall like the rest. But make no mistake, I can still enslave them if you won't cooperate on the airships. The choice is yours. Needlessly forfeit your life for a people who have already abandoned you, or save your life with a pardon and rejoin your family by helping me find the greatest mechanical mystery in history."

"I expected this from Tirgranir eventually," Rildning said. "But like Anfinnan he is a leader without people. Even if you take the mountain, you will never conquer the depths of every great forest of Gallerlandia. Some may submit for a time. But your life, and those of men like you, will be shortened in the end."

"Not as short as yours," Hilsingor quipped. "My only regret in having you burned after accepting Tirgranir's surrender in the morning is you will perish before seeing the same thing happen to Eniri and every other savage you have ever called friend."

115

ENIRI

Gilgalem, Vaynland
Midspring, 2270

Eniri looked down into Enildir's moonlit face. The sleeping child had the look of his father. She did not like putting the drops of spruce beer and honey in his cup, but he needed to sleep quietly in this dangerous time. She also did not want to give him up. He was wrapped in fox fur and rested easily in the sling about her body. She carefully removed the sling and hesitated. Then she handed Enildir over to chieftainess Lemori. She felt her eyes well.

"Don't worry," Mrigamad said. "We will protect him with our lives. Lemori will wait with the others in the woods. When your task is done, I'll come with the landship and recover you, then we will pick all of them up from the woods. Then we will sail to your Nyden friends on the coast."

"It's a good plan," Owerdir said. Blind Kemet nodded as well.

"If we fail," Eniri said, "please take Enildir far from here. No matter what happens." Mrigamad and Lemori nodded.

"Queen Eniri?" They turned to see a woman standing behind Eniri. It was Niberi, the Maluram smith who had made Rildning's electrum armor.

"I'm no queen," Eniri answered. She was flattered but knew it was a hollow title.

513

"You are the rightful queen of Umbyrland," Niberi insisted. "And all Gallerlandia, as far as most of us Maluram are concerned. I have something for you, from all of us."

Niberi handed her a long roll of woven willow cloth. Eniri unfurled it and found a sword of black and green-golden glimmer. The blade was smooth in places and rough cinder in others, with edges shaped like waves.

The hilt and handguard were electrum chased with moonwood. The pommel was capped with a polished jewel that shifted from gold to purple in the light. It was much lighter than Eniri had imagined.

"It is elinderum, like Rildning's armor," Niberi said. "It was made to pair with the armor, but I was not finished in time."

"The use of electrum for weaponry is forbidden," Eniri said. "Only the Graparins can wield shards of Wurumnak's sword."

"This was sanctioned by the Sage because pure electrum does not form a naked blade," Niberi answered. "And it was fashioned with no other metal, only cinder. The jewel symbolizes the heart of the Maluram, tough and true. Too many of our stoneswords are too weak against the foreigners' metal, but this one has a sacred strength."

"Thank you, Niberi," Eniri said. She clasped the new sword across her back where Enildir's sling had hung. "Will you stay with the Vaynking?"

"Most of the Maluram wish to escape with you," Niberi said.

"Then go with Mrigamad," Eniri said. "We are happy to have you."

"Our hammers and picks will always be yours," Niberi said.

Eniri looked about her. Owerdir and his shroud alchemists would be important for this raid. Bothrobim and his Nyden would be fierce fighters, and she was grateful for the ones waiting on the coast. Kemet was eager for vengeance for Urgamdir, as Rildning undoubtedly was, but the blinded Bronhildi would stay with Mrigamad. A few of the Rahlampians also agreed to come with her.

She glanced back up the mountain behind them. Gilgalem was quiet and still, its people resigned to the fate Tirgranir had chosen for them. She wished she could take more Gallerlanders with her, but the ships would already be overflowing. And many wanted to stay and follow Tirgranir, the last king.

She wondered whether the foreigners would make him a vassal-king or if they would secretly kill him to keep the Gallerlanders divided. She thought of the Sage as she turned from the mountain. Frail in his old age, he refused to escape or surrender.

"Do not fear for me, child," he had told her. "My tomb in the heart of the mountain already waits for me, under the branches of the cave willow of Ubromynir, where those who came before me rest. I'll lock the doors tight, and the tunnels will be barricaded and hidden to the enemy. The foreigners will not find the sacred places."

"And what about the electrum and the mines?" she had asked.

"The Maluram will seal them as well. Forever."

"Will the Maluram no longer hunt for the shards of Wurumnak's sword?"

"They will probably leave, child, and may Wurumnak guide them. Tirgranir has never treated them as well as he should."

"Am I doing the right thing?" she asked.

"I foresee Rildning's survival, but his liberation of the Gallerlanders is clouded to even my eyes. I still believe in him, but the light of that knowledge is passing from me to another. Wurumnak keep you safe and grant long life to Enildir. Gallerlandia will live on in your hearts."

Eniri had wept when the old man descended into the mountain for the last time. But the sky omens of the night sky were favorable and remained so as her group left Gilgalem toward the meadowlands where the encampment of the enemy lay sprawling and asleep.

Eniri, Owerdir, and their warriors darted from one wooded foothill to another. Passing through the siegeworks would be much easier with the help of the mists from Owerdir's alchemists. They could see from the moonlight glint of the soldiers' armor that the palisades were well-guarded at the breaches that were not yet fully repaired. But the stretch closest to the woods was less guarded and its construction incomplete.

It was through this series of narrow runs that they passed. One guard came close to stumbling into them, but he never had the chance to see them. A puff of glittering blue powder swirled about his head, and the attacking alchemist caught his body before it hit the ground, which he then hid in a ditch.

Once they reached the outer palisade, they could see that the bulk of the soldiers was still camped in their original places beyond the gap once patrolled by the landships. Several landships were still there, blackened hulks with charred bodies strewn about. A few still smoldered.

It would be dawn soon so they wasted no time in picking their way through the ditches and long grass toward the camp. They trotted between tents and used the alchemists' mist when needed, being careful to avoid the field stables and campfires. Few soldiers were awake and none had to be silenced.

Finding the tent of the marshal was easy enough. It was in the largest cluster and bedecked with purple pennants fluttering in the predawn breeze. Nearby were a few smaller, heavily guarded tents. Eniri gave the signal for the raiding party to split into their groups, then they all hurried off.

116

HILSINGOR

Frontier Corps Encampment near Gilgalem
Midspring, 2270

Hilsingor awoke to a loud commotion. He sat up as Arnolf dashed into his tent.

"Something has happened in the camp," the adjutant said. "Seems it's near Pendigied's tent. There is fighting."

"Perhaps with Firkas dead and Ravorglad bleeding in a bed, the crusaders have finally seized the opportunity to stoke the Raffen to great anger," the marshal said grouchily as he swung his tired legs out of bed. "Tell the guards to put an end to it."

"Yes, sir!"

"Never mind, get my sword! I'll tend to this myself. I'll not have anything disturb Tirgranir's intent to surrender."

117

ENIRI

Frontier Corps Encampment near Gilgalem
Midspring, 2270

The Nyden warriors burst into the prisoners' tent with Eniri and Owerdir close behind. Gray sooty clouds broke around them and blood dripped from their short ship blades. They found Rildning unconscious, sweat-soaked, and shivering. Bothrobim scooped him up and they all exited. Eniri and Owerdir were the last out, but just before they left they heard a weak sound. Then a voice broke from the gloom at the back of the tent.

"It is I . . . his friend," the voice said amid the clink of chains.

"Who?" Eniri asked.

"It sounds like Harsen," Owerdir said. The two hurried to him. He lay with his feet chained to stakes driven deep in the turf.

"I'm sorry . . . so sorry," Harsen muttered. "He is nearly gone, isn't he? I knew when they didn't bother to chain him that it was bad. And his breathing . . . Rildning has not been able to speak with me since the evening. I'm so sorry."

"Can the Maluram sword break his bonds?" Eniri asked. Owerdir shook his head.

"An elinderum sword is not a windrazor," he said. Owerdir flittered his fingers around the bottles in his belt. He found a small jar and poured the sulfur-smelling contents into the lock at Harsen's feet. The fluid sizzled and smoked, stinking bitterly. After a few moments they were able to jerk the lock open and rip the chains away. Meanwhile, the shouting outside had begun.

"Can you walk?" Eniri asked, lifting Harsen to his feet. "The Rahlampians' diversion won't last."

"There is one more thing," Harsen said as they stepped out into the break of dawn. He led them toward Hilsingor's tent.

"We have no time," Eniri said. Harsen broke away from her and pushed into the tent, so she followed. She sighed with relief when they found it empty. "What are you doing?" she demanded. Harsen rummaged around the tables, tossing parchments and wax about and flinging the marshal's cheese platters onto his carpets. Then he found what he was looking for and held it up for her to see.

"Rildning's journal," she gasped. "They had it all this time?"

"Not anymore." Harsen grinned.

Eniri knew leaving the camp would not be as easy as entering it. The diversion of sending the Rahlampians and two shroud alchemists to stir trouble among the Raffen had clearly worked, but Eniri knew the agitators were in trouble because the Rahlampians had not come to the back of the marshal's camp, as they had all agreed.

"Owerdir, the sun has risen. Take the remainder of the Naren-Dra to the Raffen camp and return our friends to us. We will meet you in the gap at the last burnt hulk."

Owerdir and the alchemists ran off and disappeared, while Eniri, Bothrobim, and the others rushed for the gap. They fought with waking soldiers as they emerged from their tents and bedrolls.

❧

The light of a beautiful morning shone through the broken ribs of the landship where Eniri and the others had taken refuge. Eniri cradled Rildning's head as he lay lucid.

"Wh . . . Where?" he croaked.

"Hush now," she whispered to him. "You are with me, and your wounds are cleaned and bound. But you must rest."

He smiled faintly as he relaxed. "My love . . . I . . ." His face tensed again. "Harsen?"

"I am here, my friend."

"We are hiding," Eniri said. "But not for much longer. Rest now." But she could see Rildning was still fevered. His wounds were deep and his skin was pale. But now that she finally held him, she would not let go of hope.

"Enildir?" Rildning whispered.

"He is safe," she answered. "With Mrigamad. We will meet them in the woods. I've brought you a Nyden fleet."

It was not much longer before they could see Owerdir and the others running across the gap. The clamor of the enemy could be heard behind them, but the gray alchemy smoke trailed and obscured them. Bothrobim again scooped up Rildning and they prepared to exit the hull to race toward the siegeworks. As Owerdir approached, Eniri shouted for them to keep running.

She was relieved to see Mrigamad's landship cruising on the other side. His archers were preparing the way by firing on the soldiers perched on the palisade. Two quick-footed Rahlampians even appeared on the wall, cutting down two or three soldiers with every windrazor sweep. Owerdir and the alchemists tossed a variety of bottles to clear the rest of the soldiers. Once inside the siegeworks, they found a troop of crusaders waiting for them.

"You have stolen your way through for the last time," the commanding knight said. "You've no army, no landships. And your king descends from the mountain even now. Surrender or perish!"

Owerdir pointed his finger stubs at the knight and then pulled his elbow in toward his body to mash the goat bladder hidden under his tunic. He felt the warm liquid surge through the reeds along his arm. A brown stream shot out from his wrist, well-aimed at the knight and the crusader beside him. They screamed and threw down their swords, and the knight frantically clawed to lift his visor. They could hear him vomiting inside his helmet. The other crusaders did not wait for further orders.

The Gallerlanders and corpsmen charged into each another. Eniri was pleased with her new sword, which shred most armor lacking the steel plate of the wealthier crusaders. Only the windrazors of the Rahlampians were effective against their armor.

Eniri ordered Bothrobim and a Rahlampian to the walls to clear the archers who had appeared. Then she saw the charge of a mounted knight out of the corner of her eye. The crusader was nearly upon her when one of the shroud alchemists showered his horse's face with a bundle of small throwing darts.

A second mounted crusader surprised her a moment later. She could hear the hoofbeats as she rolled forward, ducking under a crusader's sword swipe. At the end of her roll, she bounded up toward the rear of the horse. She grasped the tail of the animal, found a flash foothold on its kick, and then grasped for the leather straps trailing the knight's saddle. It felt like running up into a tree. When she landed behind the knight, she jerked him off to the side. To her surprise and brief horror, she found herself riding for a moment before being thrown off into the mud.

As the crusaders thinned, Eniri directed the Nyden who were carrying Rildning to run toward the inner palisade. When they had pushed through safely, she yelled for the others to follow. Eniri was among the last to head for the breach, glancing back at the bodies of one Nyden and one Rahlampian left behind. She finally felt Rildning was going to be safe, but it was a joy laced with the pain of what his rescue had cost.

She turned from the carnage and ducked into the breach. She felt her leg surge and kick out from under her and then she fell to the ground. She glanced down and saw a wet, red arrow head protruding from her thigh, cruelly pointing in the direction of where the others had escaped. She cried out and tried to stand with her elinderum sword.

Smoke swirled all about her when she opened her eyes. She tasted metallic soot and heard the voices of Owerdir and Bothrobim. Pain bolted through her body as she felt strong arms lift her. She heard more shouting and the clash of swords, but soon they faded behind. She squinted through her pain and smoke, seeing green hills ahead. And then Mrigamad's landship rolled into view.

118

ANKARMESH

Sipadshur, Naren-Dra Mountains
Midspring, 2270

Ankarmesh lifted his wooden mask for the best look. He had watched the glittering gray snake up the mountainside before cresting the rim of Gilgalem. He saw it enter and spread within the bowl. He stepped back from the eyepiece of the Wheeled Window of the World and let out a long sigh.

He told himself he should not be surprised. He had long known this would be the result. But Owerdir's arrival had been unexpected. It had given Ankarmesh a small bit of hope, maybe more than he realized since he had been willing to send Urikimesh and the others with the Gallerlander.

He took one last look through the lens. Gilgalem was awash with the glittering gray, but there was no sign of smoke or large fire. At least it was not Nalembalen, he told himself. As he walked away from the lens and down the spiral stairs, he thought of the lone landship he had seen depart toward the west. Could it be survivors? His view of their route was obscured by clouds, but he presumed they would make for the coast.

Ankarmesh considered what more could be done. The whole of Gallerlandia would now belong to the empire. The Rahlampians would surely be the next target. He thought it unlikely the empire would attempt to climb the mountains of his people. On this he agreed with the other seneschals.

But now he would tell them of the fall of Gallerlandia when the Council of Sunstepping convened in a few months. By then he would know what to say. He would try to convince the seneschals to act, even if it was only to direct the Clan of the Hidden Eyes against this new enemy.

119

BREDAHADE

Eglamour, Donovan Province
Midspring, 2270

"So I insisted that he cease such ungodly behavior," Ralmo said, "which was certain to—"

"Please, archbishop," Bredahade said as he reached for the messenger's letter, "let us continue this discussion another time." The exarch stifled a yawn as he opened the letter.

> Your Eminence,
> I'm pleased to report the Frontier Corps have captured the last capital of the Gallerlanders after a short siege. Gilgalem Mountain, which had served as a refuge for the Vaynking Tirgranir, his people, and the refugees from the north, fell easily into our hands once Tirgranir surrendered. He will accompany me to Eglamour as soon as possible and is eager to join the imperial council.
>
> Despite his surrender, we suffered several notable losses. Please relay my condolences to Chancellor Sarnaker for the death of his son Sir Wilsig, who died after he lost a leg to the barbarians. Sir Firkas, general of the provincial legions, was also killed, and Sir Ravorglad of the crusader legions was grievously wounded, though he will survive.

All of them fought admirably, as did King Pendigied. He was wounded and lost most of his top commanders, including the high Hral chieftain Shimga, but Pendigied will survive. King Golenrad of the Ollohd was killed in the siegeworks. Hunedorat of the Teshi unfortunately defected along with his closest commanders. We are culling his remaining tribesmen and attempting to find him.

I do not expect to campaign further this year, though I will think on how best to conquer the Rahlampians next, as we have discussed. I've already dispatched my chief ranger to the east to scout future routes for the legions. After I visit you in Eglamour, I'll return to Rachard to carve Gallerlandia into provinces as we have agreed. I'll also make sure the building of the warcastle is on schedule, and I will discuss with you my ideas to build more of them.

Finally, I'm proud to report the high heretic Rildning is no more. He was found dead on the field, along with his commanders, apparently killed by crusaders who sacrificed themselves for the honor. I ordered his body to be burned and his ashes cast into a stream, so he will be forgotten forever.

As for the journal that Ralmo had requested for Rildning's trial, I presume it was on Rildning's body when he was burned. Suffice it to say, the only trial Rildning will have at this point is before God, after which his place in the Depths of Memelos is assured for eternity.

Marshal Hilsingor

Bredahade put down the letter and described the contents to Ralmo.

"Vile heretic!" Ralmo sneered. "To perish on a crusader's sword is too honorable for Rildning."

"Even so, Rildning and the Gallerlanders are no longer a problem," Bredahade said. "We have more important things to attend to. The provinces have multiplied, their wealth is inexhaustible, and more nobles from the Old World arrive weekly to join the crusade and stake their claims to land. And the imperial council heaves with vassal-kings and princes now loyal to the empire. It feels like a new golden age, perhaps brighter than even Lord Wilhargant's ancient times."

"And God's church on earth is strong." Ralmo nodded. "No savage kingdom can stand against the holy Brintilian Empire."

"Quite right," the exarch said. "Now, let us begin the twelve days of feasting and celebrate the Gallerlanders' defeat. Eglamour is already blooming with merriment."

120

ENIRI

Aggarwal Sea
Midspring, 2270

"His fever has not subsided," Owerdir said. "And his wounds are slow to heal."

"Do you have anything for him?" Eniri asked. Enildir slept peacefully in her arms. Owerdir tapped the bottles on his belt and gestured to the other shroud alchemists.

"We gave him a syrup of balm garlic and poppy to ease his pain. His wounds are bound with willow leaves, solin, and honey. There is not much else . . ."

They looked down at him, wrapped in wool and shivering in his sleep as Bothrobim's ship rocked to and fro. Bothrobim had told Eniri he was confident he could reach a safe place in Aggarwal.

"How much longer?" she asked him now.

"The river is behind us," he said. "Just a few more days on the Aggarwal Sea following the coast. That's if the winds are good and if we don't encounter an enemy fleet. The Raffen should stay near Amlon and shouldn't follow us too far east anyway. We're going to dunelands where the Raffen will not go. They believe that particular coastal land is haunted. The Gallerlanders who still dwell there are untouched by the empire for now."

"Surely the foreigners will go there, even if the Raffen will not," Owerdir said.

"It's the closest, safest place that we could think of," Bothrobim said.

"Can we trust them?" Owerdir asked.

"The Gallerlanders of Aggarwal were originally Vayns," Eniri said, "but their lands at the southern edge of Gallerlandia are isolated by the mountains. Tegmad, who was from the Aggarwal clan, told me his family was from the valleys of Emeagwal beyond the coastal dunelands. They will surely give us shelter, for a time at least."

"I've been there once," Bothrobim said. "There is a natural harbor where a river empties into the sea. There we will sail upriver until it becomes white with rapids. Then we will anchor at the broad sandbanks near the village of Emeagwal, which is said to be there. Should be safe."

"Gilgalem was not safe," Owerdir said. Eniri looked out across the waters.

"Where will the Nyden fleet go?" she asked. "And can Mrigamad's landship go up to the river?"

"His landship can go many places mine cannot," Bothrobim said. "As for my fleet, I'll order them to patrol the coast. They will raid any Raffen ship that comes this way, until you decide on our next refuge."

Eniri nodded her agreement.

It was two long days before Bothrobim found the mouth of the dune river. Rildning was kept asleep by the alchemists' syrup, but when they reached the village she told them to give him less, hoping he would wake and see her.

୨୦

Eniri stood at the landship's bow with Owerdir as Rildning slept. They watched as Mrigamad steered into the mouth of a river that parted the coastal dunes. They were like mountains of white sand, studded with tufts of long grass waving in the wind.

"I'm worried about taking Rildning to Emeagwal," Owerdir said.

"I've not been there before either," she said, "but I trusted Tegmad and I trust Bothrobim. And we need a place to settle for a while."

"I suppose it is better than being trapped in Gilgalem."

"I wish there was more we could have done," she said.

"There was nothing we could have done. Tirgranir failed the Vayns."

"And all of Gallerlandia . . ."

"What will become of our home?" Owerdir asked.

"We no longer have a home."

They silently watched the water glide by and listened to the Rahlampian crew working behind them. The dunes finally gave way to gentle hills. The Emeagwal Valley was beautiful, with pink and white trees flowering under a bright sun. Soon the ship began to toss and jerk.

"Hold fast! Watch the rocks!" Mrigamad shouted from the stern. Bothrobim appeared beside him, pointing him where to go.

Eniri and Owerdir looked ahead. River-lashed boulders jutted up from the water, some large enough to host a single scraggly tree. They gripped the railing as the ship lurched left, then right. The river raged over the side, clawing at the planks of the landship's underbelly.

"Why doesn't he just drop anchor!" Owerdir shouted above the rush.

Eniri glanced toward the steep riverbanks on either side. "He knows what he's doing."

The Rahlampian sailor up in the crow's nest began shouting. Everyone looked ahead. A giant boulder loomed, with a large chunk split off but still supporting a half-submerged tree. A recent collapse, Eniri guessed.

"Hard to starboard! Hold fast!" Mrigamad howled.

Eniri nearly lost her footing as the ship wrenched to the right. She and Owerdir crouched low when the crash came.

"Port front wheel!" cried the sailor in the crow's nest a moment later. "Port mid wheel!"

Eniri jumped to her feet and looked overboard. Pieces of the shorn-off wheels tossed away.

"Come around!" Mrigamad shouted. "Portside inlet— Watch the shoals!"

Eniri looked ahead again, seeing only white water and rock. But to the left was a calm stretch sheltered by broad sandbars and fed by a small tributary.

"Come around . . . Gently, gently . . ."

Eniri felt they were moving too fast. The still water was not a long haven. Soon they heard the scrape of sand along the length of the hull. The ship slowed only a bit. Eniri's eyes widened as the end approached.

"Gently, gently . . . Hold fast!"

They threw themselves to the deck. An earthquake seemed to rattle every plank and nail as the bow of the ship turned upward with a brief scrape. Then they could hear the stubborn creak of the wheels coming out of the water. The bow dropped again when the front starboard wheel shattered without its partner on the port side. They heard the middle starboard splinter but it held. There was a collective sigh of relief when at last the ship stopped.

"This landship has never failed me!" Mrigamad laughed heartily. Not all the Rahlampians were so gleeful, particularly the sailors who climbed down from the mast.

"You consider this a success?" Owerdir asked. "How will we ever get out of this place?"

"It will be some time before my men can repair the wheels," Mrigamad acknowledged, "but she is still seaworthy."

"Expertly done," Bothrobim said, though he was clearly shaken. "We have to walk through the woods to the village of Emeagwal anyway. A short walk made shorter by the fact that we're actually on the beach."

Bothrobim, Owerdir, and his shroud alchemists descended first. Eniri, with Enildir wrapped in a sling around her, helped Kemet find the ladder. Harsen and Niberi followed after. Rildning, still asleep, was lowered down by a crank wheel. Mrigamad personally oversaw the task but Eniri held her breath until he was safely down and placed on a sled.

"How long will this take to repair?" Harsen asked.

As they all looked back at the landship, the starboard middle wheel splintered again and collapsed, dropping the hull down into the sand. The two remaining back wheels slowly rolled back into the water. A Rahlampian on deck released the anchor. It thudded onto the sand and the ship stopped. He shrugged and got back to work.

"The hull seems to be intact, so we could sail tomorrow if we chop the back wheels," Mrigamad said. "But to sail the land again, about three months, give or take. The Emeagwal folk will have to supply good lumber."

"Don't worry," Bothrobim said. "My Nyden fleet is not far. We can leave anytime we need to on proper sea vessels."

"Proper?" Mrigamad said.

Bothrobim turned toward the woods. "There's a path just up here."

The group followed after as the Rahlampians tended to the ship.

❧

"That's no mere village," Owerdir said as they came within view.

"Seems they've expanded since I was here," Bothrobim said.

"Refugees," Eniri said. "We're not the only ones to have fled here."

"Can you describe it for me?" Kemet asked.

"Well," Eniri began, "I see a small river snaking through the middle of a white sandy plain, bordered on all sides by the forest. The huts are stick and sand brick, and log canoes are as plentiful as our sandy-footed brethren. Salt is in the air. Very different from the forests and rocky plains of your Bronhildia."

"Look." Harsen pointed as a group of villagers walked toward them.

"An electrum circlet," Eniri said. "It's Serusi, the chieftainess of Emeagwal."

"Welcome," Serusi said as they approached. She clasped Eniri's hands in a warm greeting, then laid a gentle hand on Enildir's brow. "We had heard the princess of the Umbyrs was at Gilgalem. And this must be your son, born from the foreigner. But seeing you here, and without the Vaynking, tells me the worst has happened."

"Gilgalem has fallen. Tirgranir surrendered the mountain. We bring wounded." She gestured to Rildning, Kemet's bloodstained eye scarf, and the others with minor wounds. Serusi pointed to Eniri's leg.

"You need rest and healing, too. Consider yourselves at home and—" Serusi stopped and cocked her head, staring at the unconscious man on the sled. "You brought the Joiner of Two Worlds?"

"Rildning is in great need of care," Eniri said. "If you can spare the room."

"It is my great honor," Serusi said. "Our hands are many, the wood is strong, and the sand brick is quick to set. We have huts for you now, and many more will be built as others arrive. Come."

121

RILDNING

Emeagwal, Aggarwal
Midspring, 2270

When Rildning awoke and the blurriness faded, he found himself in a hut. The woven wood reminded him of the reeds of Rahlampia and for a moment he was brought back to that place, feeling the pressure to persuade that tribe to help the Gallerlanders.

He closed his eyes again and remembered the feeling of excitement when he first found the Gallerlanders long ago, and the anxiety of not knowing what Yelgoram and Owerdir would do with him as their prisoner. Pain shot through his back and snapped his eyes open again, returning him to the present.

"I'm sorry, my friend," a voice said. He turned his head slowly to see Owerdir seated beside him. "Your wife asked me to give you no more syrup for sleeping the pain away, so you would wake with a clear mind."

"Where are we?" Rildning asked.

"Drink this."

Rildning turned to see Eniri nearby. She came over and gently lifted his head and he sipped from the cup, salty water laced with the smell of roses. "We are gone from Gilgalem," she said, "thanks to Mrigamad and the Nyden, and the courage of our many friends."

Rildning noticed her limp. "You are wounded."

"I will heal," she said.

"What has become of Gilgalem?" Rildning asked.

"The Vaynking surrendered," Owerdir said. "Despite all we did . . ."

"Enildir?" Rildning asked.

"Our son is safe, here with us," Eniri said.

"And you had mentioned the Nyden?"

"A whole fleet has come," she said with a proud smile. "War has unfortunately returned to their islands. War among themselves. I found a brave warrior who recognized their fate was intertwined with the Gallerlanders. Unfortunately, it's too late for all of us."

"We are now in Emeagwal in southern Vaynland," Owerdir said. "The enemy has not reached this place. Not yet."

Rildning lay in silence. He looked up at the stick-woven roof of the hut and shivered. He could feel his body growing cold and he felt so tired. After a few moments Eniri spoke again, and he could feel her hand squeeze his.

"The herbs are working to cool your fever. How is your pain?"

Rildning took a deep breath, wincing as his back and ribs pinched. He wiggled his fingers but was startled when his toes did not move. He tried to sit up but Owerdir moved to restrain him.

"What's wrong?" Eniri demanded.

Owerdir glanced at her as he settled Rildning back down. Rildning looked back and forth at their faces, blinking away his welling eyes. He saw a realization in her eyes as he, too, understood. He held up a hand to stroke her face.

"My legs sleep, my love," Rildning said as she began to weep.

"I'm sorry, my friend," Owerdir said. "I tried to . . ."

"They served me well and long," Rildning said.

Owerdir squeezed his hand too, then left him with Eniri.

They talked about everything that had happened since they left Gilgalem as envoys for the Gallerlanders, and their longing for one another and for Enildir. They held each other and Eniri tended to his bandages. Then he fell asleep again, knowing she would stay by him.

When he awoke again, he found Enildir waiting in Eniri's arms. Rildning could not help but weep for joy at holding his son's hand. The innocence of his little face, his happy smile, his little fingers. Owerdir soon appeared with food and a message from the others.

"They wish to see you."

"And I wish to see them," Rildning said. He kissed Enildir's hand as Eniri brushed away a tear.

Harsen and Mrigamad were the first to enter the hut. His old friend greeted him warmly.

"You didn't lie around this much when the Hrals' poison arrow got you," Harsen jested. "Seems you've gotten soft with a lovely wife to care for you."

"And you didn't look this ragged when we were lost in the wilderness," Rildning countered. "How are you, Harsen?"

"Well enough, though I'd sooner spend a day in Hilsingor's jails than continue crashing in landships."

"You imperials aren't tough enough," Mrigamad said. "There's no better craft for land and sea."

Bothrobim came in behind them. "Yes, but better crafts for the sea, I assure you. As for his wife, Eniri has not made Rildning soft. Her bravery in these lands and in my home proves she is no mere princess of the treetop courts."

"You have my thanks," Rildning said, "for helping Eniri and bringing the Nydens."

"Wish more of my countrymen could have come," Bothrobim said. "But more may come yet."

Kemet entered next, guided by Niberi. "It is I who regrets the choices of his countrymen," said the blind warrior. "I'm ashamed to be the only Bronhildi here, and of little use now."

"Urgamdir told me of your bravery," Rildning said. "He was proud to have fought alongside you, and so am I. You may have lost your sight, but your heart remains strong. As for Highchief Harkarom, in time he may come to see the empire for what it is."

"I hope to live to see that day." Kemet smiled.

"Niberi, I must confess to losing the elinderum armor to Hilsingor. I deeply regret it."

"One of many thefts from our realm, but I can build another suit for you," she said. "And swords, as Eniri has proven the worth of an elinderum blade."

"What will become of the Maluram?" Rildning asked.

"They have scattered and will do what they do best: hide and work underground," Niberi answered. "We Maluram will continue the search for electrum, wherever it can be found.

"Just as we will continue the fight," Owerdir said.

They all looked to Rildning. He could feel the sweat of his fever burn again on his brow. A peculiar hot numbness crept into his wounds. He felt the urge to speak quickly.

"I know you wish to hear me say I will rally your hearts to defend Gallerlandia and your other native lands, but I have no more to give. If Tirgranir's surrender is true, then there are no kings of Gallerlandia. Or queens." He squeezed Eniri's hand and looked into her eyes. "But we have not shed blood for naught, and the dead have not died in vain.

"There is another path, not merely to survive, but to thrive," he continued. "While remembering the many sacrifices, we could accept the yoke of the empire that has been forced upon us, and in doing so shape the future. From within the empire you can subvert it. It can only collapse from within, perhaps many years from now."

"You would have us surrender?" Owerdir asked.

"Sabotage from within," Rildning said. "Remember what we did in the Ardfalm Forest? We posed as wagoners, destroyed their supply lines, confused their night watches, and cut down that legion bit by bit. You must use the same tactics. I see no other way, given the scale of the empire's victories and the wedges they have driven between the original peoples of Pemonia. Target their imperial governors and vassal-kings. Find them in their comfortable courts. Then rebuild the tribes of elected kings on their ashes."

"Will you not lead us in this endeavor?" Mrigamad asked.

"Death lurks near me," Rildning answered, struggling not to wince. "But you will know what is best, should you choose the path of submission with subversion, as I would."

"Will you name this people from many tribes who will walk this path?" Owerdir asked.

Rildning looked up into the woven ceiling, recalling the Cataclysm scroll, the old Graparin's tales, and High King Gratgofa's words.

"Gratgofa once told me he dreamed of white flames atop stones before I came to Nalembalen. Later I learned about the Agnesci's disastrous voyage to Cedelaebos in search of prophetic fulfillment. Similar to Gratgofa's vision, the Agnesci compared their journey to bringing candles of ancient truths to a cold, stony shore. Let your symbol be the candle flame flickering atop the stone. The flame shall symbolize our undying hope, while the stone will represent our unending resolve. Let the name be the Order of the Candlestone.

"Do not look so sullen, my friends," he continued. "I cannot be the high king some had hoped, but you are men and women of great courage, skill, and quick wits. I'll not be the last to unite the defenders of the original lands, and many will rise even when you are gone."

"You cannot leave us, my love," Eniri said. "It is too soon for your people. And too soon for us."

"You have faced down death before," Harsen added. "This cannot be your end."

"We all ponder life's end: when it will be, what form it will take, and the nature of the afterlife. For myself, I have not dwelled on these timeless questions or their elusive answers, but rather attempted to make the most of life's fleeting winds . . ." He winced and squeezed Eniri's hand.

"All good orders have oaths," Harsen said. "We should have one for our task and to each other." The companions nodded in agreement.

Owerdir spoke instinctively, and they repeated: "Like the long memories of the trees, we will never forget the prophecy and sacrifice. Like the electrum of the earth, we will be unseen until our time has come. Like the flame, we will keep the ancient truths alive. And like the stone, we will find strength in ourselves and each other. We will carry the truths and defend the original lands . . . Until the End of Days."

Rildning listened silently as everyone repeated Owerdir's words. He focused on Eniri's voice. He saw the dark creep over his eyes and looked to hers until the last moment. He closed his eyes and felt the grasp of Eniri's hand. Then he let his last breath pass from him.

EPILOGUE

Thorendor Castle, Wallevet Ministry
Midautumn, 3032

"So the old tales about how he died were lies," Marlan said.

"Correct," Arasemis said. "Begun by Hilsingor himself, as proved by the marshal's own dispatches, and then perpetuated by kings who preferred to snuff out Rildning's light."

"I see now why the rise of Candlestone was such a surprise to the imperials back then. The Brintilians thought the Gallerlanders' resistance died with Rildning and the surrender of Tirgranir."

Arasemis nodded. "Candlestone was feared for many centuries before gradually unraveling and fading into history. Although the Order became concealed, it did not go extinct. You're no doubt familiar with their later achievements, such as the assassination of Emperor Vikenbirg, the burning of the Temple Curia's hall, and the sinking of King Athelreew's ship in calm waters off the Austveede coast. But now you know that, despite the ups and downs, the Order has survived and accomplished great things since the very beginning."

"I look forward to learning more," Marlan said, looking around Thorendor's vast library. "I wish to open each dust-clad binding, study every cracked vellum page, and decipher every archaic language that you can teach me."

Arasemis smiled. "You shall, in time. As one of my first apprentices, you already know so much. But if we are to act upon our knowledge and properly revive Candlestone, we need to carefully recruit more pupils for the task. Only men and women truly worthy of Rildning's legacy should be chosen. Recruits who do not fear the dark paths toward what lies hidden from the world, and which must come to light once again."

APPENDIX

BRINTILIAN EMPIRE

OLSKEROTH: Emperor of the Brintilian Empire. Resided in
   Almeria.
BREDAHADE: First exarch of Pemonia. Resided at Eglamour
   in Donovan Province.

   His Court
      SARNAKER: Chancellor of the Imperial Council of
         Pemonia.
      RALMO: Archbishop of Pemonia.

   His Imperial Drigomen
      GENTHUS: Envoy to the Raffen Tribe.
      TRELNAF: Envoy to the Rahlampian Tribe.

   His Tribal Vassal-Kings
      GOLENRAD: Half-Brintilian king of the Ollohds.
      HUNEDORAT: King of the Teshi Gallerlanders.
      SHIMGA: False king of the Hrals.

HILSINGOR OF NED GOLLEN: Marshal of the Frontier
   Corps of Pemonia and former marshal of the Rivercross
   Corps of Arukia. Resided at Rachard in Bram Province.

   His Lieutenants
      FIRKAS: General of the Provincial Legions of the
         Frontier Corps.
      RAVORGLAD: General of the Crusader Legions of
         the Frontier Corps and grandmaster of the
         Order of the Red Garland.
      ARNASBIRG: Admiral of the Imperial Naval Fleet of
         Pemonia.
      ALPENING: Frontier Corps general, protector of
         Durgensdil Colony.

WILSIG: Frontier Corps knight-treasurer, son of Sarnaker, and member of the Order of the Harbor Thorns.

His Support Staff
ARNOLF: Adjutant.
WIDSEM: Master ranger.
BRONDEROD: Chief engineer of the Frontier Corps.

Colonists
HARSEN: Woodsman, merchant, and camp follower of the Frontier Corps.
GARONIG: Merchant and camp follower.
SEEF: Merchant and camp follower.
HENNETH: Commoner in Rachard.
EBELOFT: Shipwrecked doctor.

BRONHILDI

HARKAROM: Highchief of the Bronhildi Tribe. Resided in Gradhild.

His Brothers
PREMAROM: Chieftain of the Emodony Forest.
NATHOM: Envoy to the Imperial Council of Pemonia.

His Subjects
ISBEREN: Chieftain.
KEMET: Warrior, brother of Dombrad and Danyhad.
DOMBRAD: Warrior.
DANYHAD: Warrior.
YORIKSA: Warrior.

GALLERLANDERS

GRATGOFA: Deceased high king of the Gallerlander Tribe.
   Resided in Nalembalen.
RILDNING: Gallerlander warrior and former colonial knight.
ENIRI: Umbyr princess and warrior of the Tamtur clan.
ENILDIR: Son of Rildning and Eniri.

Umbyr Subtribe
   ERAMBRIN: King of Umbyrland.
   URGAMDIR: Chieftain.
   BIDAGDIR: Chieftain near the Nake lands.
   GOMBIR: Rhymer.
   NODARIM; Chieftain.
   OTURBRIN: Warrior of the Tamtur clan.
   HEGDIR: Deceased Graparin and former keeper of
      the Cataclysm scroll.
   GOFALNIG: Deceased son of Gratgofa.

Goyn Subtribe
   ODON: King of Goynland.
   YELGORAM: Chieftain of Takumbyr.
   OWERDIR: Warrior, son of Yelgoram.
   ARBARDIR: Warrior, son of Yelgoram.
   LEMORI: Chieftainess.
   BRUGMIR: Chieftain who accompanied Urgamdir.
   GIRTIMIR: Tribesman.

Vayn Subtribe
   TIRGRANIR: King of Vaynland.
   SABANI: Queen of Vaynland.
   TIRANI: Princess of Vaynland.
   RUMBAN: Steward of Gilgalem, keeper of Pindoarig.
   THE SAGE: Chief priest and diviner of sky omens.
   BIRNIM: Tribesman and mountain climber.
   FELBANIR: Tribesman and mountain climber.
   WENDON: Tribesman.

Maluram Branch of the Vayns
    NIBERI: Goldsmith.

Aggarwal Branch of the Vayns
    TEGMAD: Tribesman and guide to Eniri.
    SERUSI: Chieftainess of Emeagwal.

NAREN-DRA

ANKARMESH: Seneschal of Sarbondibum, shroud alchemist, and former member of the Hidden Eyes.

His Relatives
    TIZKARMESH: Grandfather of Ankarmesh and inventor of the telescope.
    URIKIMESH: Brother of Ankarmesh and a shroud alchemist.

His Subjects
    RIMUSHIRA THE GATHERER: Master alchemist, healer, and crystal farmer.
    DIMUZID: Shroud alchemist.
    HADANISH: Shroud alchemist.

NYDEN

BELORDOOS: Twin king of the Nyden Tribe and brother of Toredwoak. Resided in Chadwoid.
TOREDWOAK: Twin king of the Nyden Tribe and brother of Belordoos. Resided in Chadwoid.

BOTHROBIM: Chieftain, merchant captain, and nephew of the twin kings.

RAFFEN

PENDIGIED: King of the Raffen Tribe. Resided in Woudenhod.

His Relatives
HRUSTHIED: Deceased father of Pendigied and former king of the Raffen.
WALPERT: Warrior and cousin of Pendigied.

His Subjects
ALDA: Wiseman and political counselor.
WOLLEM: Courtier.
BROEN: Chieftain.
LIGWARED: Chieftain.
NORBAER: Chieftain.

RAHLAMPIANS

ANFINNAN OF BODAMWEYM: Domnitar of the Rahlampian Tribe. Resided in Bodamweym.

His Son
MORLBEAG THE INFIRM

His Chieftains
MRIGAMAD OF CASTRACANE: Chieftain.
-- MEARNSOD THE FLOODBRINGER: Deceased father of Mrigamad.
-- LOYTH OF CASTRACANE: Wiseman of Mrigamad's clan.
BALBEG OF THE USODIMARE: Chieftain and keeper of the Lowlands.
DENILDON OF SWALESHIL: Chieftain, keeper of the Lowlands, and Blade of the River.
CARN OF SHADFOYLE: Chieftain and keeper of Domnitar Rock.
GAREDREM OF CRAIL: Chieftain.
HARNACHAR OF PERIDOD: Chieftain.
LARGHARRA OF HARMENGAUD: Chieftain.

GLOSSARY

Aengturor: A name given to Rildning by the Sage of Gilgalem meaning Small Sword of God in the Gali language.

afban: A Gallerlander flatbread often eaten with herbs or berry spread.

Age of Calming Winds: The intermediate period between the chaotic Dark Age that followed the collapse of the Almeric Empire and the rise of the Brintilian Empire during the Silvern Age.

Age of Earthmaking: The period in the Old World at the beginning of the First Era, after God made the Almerics and the Agnesci. Few records exist in modern times of the mythical Age of Earthmaking, but the original peoples were given the power to multiply and form the land. This period was followed by the Lost Age because many Almerics had fallen into paganism by worshiping their own created works.

Age of Exploration: The period of the Brintilian Empire's expansion across the seas into the equatorial islands and eventually Pemonia.

Aggarwal: A minor subtribe of Gallerlanders who lived in the coastal wooded dunelands south of the mountain range that included Gilgalem.

Agimdir: The Agnesci Seafather who voyaged to Cedelaebos and was among the few to survive the Cataclysm and return to Aprelaebos. He wrote the Cataclysm scroll and became the first Graparin.

Agnesci: In Messengian religious tradition, the Agnesci were one of the two original peoples created by God. They originally inhabited the southern continent. See also *Almerics*.

airship: The Brintilian Empire believed the ancient Agnesci built airships and that the Gallerlanders hid them from the colonists. The rumors were based on two passages from Rildning's journal, including a possible reference to airships from the Cataclysm scroll.

Alemacingem: An alternative name for the Brintilian Empire's use of "Almeria" to refer to the whole of the northern continent. Used by some peoples of the Old World who resented Brintilian dominance.

Alemben: A failed Brintilian colony in Pemonia.

Almeria: The continent to the north of Pemonia. Also known as the Old World. The collective inhabitants of Almeria are known as Almerians. See also *Brintil* and *Alemacingem*.

Almeric Empire: The first unification of the Almeric peoples. Founded by Lord Wilhargant in the year 1, marking the beginning of the Second Era.

Almerics: In Messengian religious tradition, the Almerics were one of the two original peoples created by God. They originally inhabited the northern continent of Almeria and later founded the Almeric Empire. See also *Agnesci*.

amber resin: A soft, flammable stone that is fossilized spruce sap. It was used by Gallerlanders as incense and as a fuel to illuminate caverns.

Amlon: A port city in Aggarwal.

anchiclade: A metal ore named after the western mountains of Rahlampia from which it was mined. The Rahlampians alloyed the ore with bog iron to forge windrazor swords, which were exceptionally thin, light, strong, and resistant to rust.

Anchiclade Mountains: A mountain range in western Rahlampia.

Aprelaebos: The Almeric name for the continent inhabited by the Agnesci peoples. See also *Pemonia*.

Arasemis: A Donovard warrior-scholar who was involved with the Order of the Candlestone nearly eight hundred years after Rildning's time. He was the keeper of Rildning's journal and Enildir's books. Arasemis was the youngest brother of the House of Reimvick who resided at Thorendor Castle in Wallevet.

Arch Almeric: An Ancient language descended from the original Almeric of creation.

Arcodum: An Etekus shrine island in the Old World that was converted into a prison by the Brintilian Empire following the defeat of the Arukan Rebellion. One-tenth of the survivors of the Arukan capital were imprisoned here as punishment for the revolt.

Ardfalm Forest: A forest straddling Wallevet and Barres Provinces where Rildning and his companions destroyed an entire legion after the burning of Nalembalen.

Arembenel: A failed Brintilian colony on the mainland east of Leauvenna.

Arukan Rebellion: A revolt against the Brintilian Empire by Arukan peoples that began in the Ned Frosel region of Almeria and eventually ignited all of Arukia. The rebellion was defeated by Hilsingor and the Rivercross Corps.

Arukia: A region of Almeria that was home to the Arukan peoples and kingdoms.

Arvgred of Durnam: A Brintilian general and first governor of Donovan Colony following the death of Helcirk Donovan.

Asgemdirhar: An ancient giant tree forest in modern Donovan that was harvested by the Agnesci to build the ships used to voyage to Cedelaebos.

Ashlands: The name used by the Brintilians to refer to the extensive burned forests of Nalembalen.

Athelreew: A king of Austveeden believed to have been killed by the Order of the Candlestone.

Austveeden: A small, modern kingdom wedged between Donovan and Calbria that was formerly part of Vaynland and includes the Gilgalem Mountains.

Balanland: The Gallerlander lands that comprised Nalembalen and its environs, including forests and numerous villages and towns. Eniri's Tamtur clan ruled Balanland during the reign of High King Gratgofa.

bane wolf: The tall brown wolves of western Gallerlandia known for roaming in large packs and their willingness to attack groups of travelers. Their saliva was known to cause wolf fever, which often killed those who were bitten.

Barres: An imperial province founded by Hilsingor in northern Gallerlandia and ruled by the Bronhildi.

Basket of Onitgora: The vast food stores under Gilgalem that was excavated and stocked by High King Onitgora's administration many generations prior to Gratgofa's reign.

Battle of Deadfoot: A decisive battle between New Lorin Colony and a Hral clan of the northern Bomlofoss Mountains. The battle resulted in the destruction of the clan, thereby ending Hral raids into the colony for several years.

Belordoos: A twin king with his brother Toredwoak of Nydenland.

Birom: A Gallerlander village northwest of Gilgalem.

black adder: The giant snakes of the Black Forest of Ondirhar in central Gallerlandia known for potent venom. The venom and its antivenom blood were two ingredients used by the Hrals to create a tonic to stimulate their turserkgyn fighting trance. Drinking the black adder blood also saved Rildning's life when he was bitten in Ondirhar and later prevented his death when he was bitten a second time in Yelgoram's snake pit.

Black Forest: See *Ondirhar*.

Bodamweym: A stilt-house city in central Rahlampia that served as the meeting place for the clans and a residence for domnitars. See also *Domnitar Rock*.

***Book of Shroud Alchemy*:** A book given to Owerdir by the Naren-Dra seneschal Ankarmesh. It was later used by the Candlestone warrior-scholar Arasemis to revive the ancient alchemical methods of the Naren-Dra.

Bram: An imperial province founded by Hilsingor in central Gallerlandia.

Brambruk Valley: A river valley in southern Umbyrland.

Branbyen: The disputed hinterlands near the original New Lorin and Donovan colonies, claimed by both colonial governors. The presence of Hrals also delayed settlement.

Brewel: An imperial province in northern Bronhildia.

Brintil: The ruling family of the Kingdom of Almeria that expanded its influence over Alemacingem and founded the Brintilian Empire.

Brintilian: The language of the majority of the Brintilian Empire and the primary linguistic descendent of the Almeric languages. The term was also used to refer to subjects of the Brintilian Empire originally from the Kingdom of Almeria.

Brintilian Empire: An Old World empire that began its rise to power around the year 2010. The Brintilians oversaw the restoration of civilization in Almeria after the tumultuous periods that followed the Almeric Empire's collapse. The Brintilians eventually reconsolidated the Old World kingdoms and led the Age of Exploration to the New World.

Bronhildia: A tribal realm in north-central Pemonia inhabited by the Bronhildi.

Cadentod: A Rahlampian city in Swaleshil destroyed by Raffen raiders.

Caribania: A tribal realm in southeastern Pemonia inhabited by the Caribani.

Castracane: A Rahlampian coastal city.

Cataclysm: The Gallerlander term for the Almeric massacre of the Agnesci after they crossed the seas to Cedelaebos. Only one Agnesci ship that arrived in Cedelaebos returned to Aprelaebos. Among the survivors was the Seafather Agimdir, who wrote the Cataclysm scroll and became the first Graparin.

Cataclysm scroll: The Gallerlander document written in secret by Agimdir to preserve the history of the Agnesci's travel from Aprelaebos to Cedelaebos. The scroll was believed to have been lost when Nalembalen was destroyed, but Rildning preserved a version of the scroll in his journal.

cave willow: The white trees with blue foliage that grew beneath the mountains of Gilgalem, sacred to the Gallerlanders. They believed the trees represented Nawurihar, the White Forest of Heaven. See also *moonwood*.

Cedelaebos: The Almeric name for the created continent of the Almerics. See also *Almeria*.

Chadwoid: A port city in northern Nydenland that served as the seat of the Nyden kings.

chaurik: A frothy beer-like drink cherished by Umbyr Gallerlanders. Made by fermenting the juice of chaurik root.

cinder: A rough, porous volcanic rock originally mined by the Maluram beneath the mountains of Gilgalem. Naturally heat-resistant, it was used by the Maluram smiths to make shoes, gauntlets, greaves, and mail. The Gallerlanders believed cinder received its many pits and cavities from the searing glow of electrum when locked away in the darkness of the rock.

Cloud Hollows: A foggy basin near the Hesid's Teeth area of the Naren-Dra Mountains.

Colbrint: A frontier town between Eglamour and Durgensdil used to stage the building of a road through the wilderness between the two settlements.

Council of Kings: The infrequent Gallerlander meetings that comprised the high king, the Sage, and the three kings of the Goyns, Umbyrs, and Vayns.

Council of Snowshelling: The wintertime gathering of the Naren-Dra seneschals to Sipadshur in Sarbondibum.

Council of Sunstepping: The summertime gathering of the Naren-Dra seneschals to Sipadshur in Sarbondibum.

Crail: A region of Rahlampia.

Crusade, First: The Martinus of the Messengian Church declared the First Crusade as a means to organize the Old World kingdoms against the conspiracy of the Kingdom of Arukia and its allies to overthrow the Brintilian Empire. In 2255, Marshal Hilsingor led the Rivercross Corps to put down the revolt prior to his sailing to Pemonia to join the Second Crusade.

Crusade, Second: The Martinus of the Messengian Church declared the Second Crusade to encourage Old World noble families and commoners to flock to the New World to establish colonies and subdue the natives. Although the crusade began before his arrival, Marshal Hilsingor's sailing to Pemonia to lead the Frontier Corps signaled the height of the Second Crusade.

crusader: An honorary title given to nobles and knights who joined a crusade as officially declared by the Martinus. Four crusader orders were among the founders of the Frontier Corps in Pemonia.

Cryphanic Temple of the Holy Messengers: The center of the Messengian Church, built on the hillside where it was said that Martinus Arnabin, the first of God's Messengers, preached. The Third Messenger, Ibelin, was later buried within the temple.

cyser: A wine made with honey, apples, and spices.

Danusloop: A Nyden ship.

Dark Age: The period in the Old World following the collapse of the Almeric Empire. Followed by the Age of Calming Winds.

delver's eye: The Maluram used these small electrum spheres as a natural light source while mining in the caves beneath Gilgalem.

Demfrebra: Ominchar's future snake form at the last battle of the End Times.

Depths, the: A term similarly used by the peoples of the Old and New Worlds to refer to a hellish realm beneath the surface of the earth. Most of the Old World peoples referred to the ruler of this underworld as Memelos, while the Gallerlanders used the name Ominchar.

domnitar: After the downfall of the Rahlampian kings, the most respected elder elected by the Rahlampian confederation was given the title of domnitar. He was also given a black cloak with the insignia of the clans to symbolize the unity of the tribe and his role as impartial mediator between clans.

Domnitar Rock: A giant boulder in the marshlands of Bodamweym believed to have been struck off the Anchiclade Mountains by lightning. The boulder has served as a speaking platform for Rahlampian kings, domnitars, and chiefs since the Tarborchast.

Donovan: One of the first colonies of the Brintilian Empire in Pemonia, Donovan later became the largest province in Pemonia and hosted the imperial capital Eglamour.

drigoman: The noble warrior-scholars of the Brintilian Empire sent to tribal leaders in Pemonia as an emissary to facilitate communication, trade, and the absorption of tribes into the empire. Drigomen usually spoke the language of the tribe they were sent to, having learned from captured or friendly natives, and knew something of local customs. During the Age of Conquest, they were appointed by the exarch and were loyal to the empire, but they traveled with their assigned tribal leader as an official interpreter and adviser. The use of drigomen in Pemonia was modeled on their use in the Old World. The term was derived from the name of Drigom, who was an interpreter used by Lord Wilhargant of the Almeric Empire.

Durgens, the: A rocky cliffside realm overlooking the Sea of Nore between Hrallandia and Raffenia.

Durgensdil: An imperial colony and later province of the Brintilian Empire in the Durgens area of western Pemonia.

Dustbeard: A Kerchinfolk character in the Gallerlander fable "The Tale of Rustbeard and Dustbeard."

Earthark: A Rahlampian landship that was sent full of food to relieve starvation in Gilgalem.

Earthgate: The mountains in western Naren-Dra that mark the start of high peaks.

Edgewaters: The massive whirlpools in the seas between the Old and New World continents.

Eglamour: The imperial capital of Pemonia.

electrum: A natural alloy of gold and silver with traces of copper. It was believed by the Gallerlanders to be sacred shards of Wurumnak's sword that must be gathered and reforged for use against Demfrebra at the End Times. The Brintilians minted the electrum into coins, but the varied composition led them to fall out of favor among wary merchants unable to consistently determine their worth. In the mines of Gilgalem, electrum was often found alongside cinder and sometimes obsidian.

elinderum: An alloy of electrum and cinder developed by smithy Niberi of the Maluram to make a suit of armor for Rildning and a sword for Eniri.

Elmbrel: A mountain in northwestern Goynland considered by the colonists to be the western gateway into Gallerlandia.

Elrid: An eastern Vaynland village nearest Rahlampia.

Emeagwal: A Gallerlander village in coastal Aggarwal that sheltered many Gallerlander refugees from the north.

Emmedollen: A city in Almeria that hosted a military order that was one of many to contribute knights to the Crusade in Pemonia.

Emodony Forest: A region of Bronhildia ruled by Premarom.

End Times: According to Gallerlander religious traditions, Wurumnak will fight Ominchar at the end of time with an electrum sword, when the latter transforms into the snake Demfrebra.

exarch: The personal representative of the Brintilian emperor and highest-ranking ruler in realms often too distant for the emperor to rule through the traditional noble hierarchies.

Far East: A region of Pemonia that was largely untouched by the Age of Exploration, though Arukan explorers and missionaries did penetrate into a few tribal lands. The Far East and its native peoples were not well understood until the modern era.

faststicks: A traditional Gallerlander technique of fire starting. A straight, smooth stick was stood upright in a boat-shaped strip of wood with tinder. The stick was quickly rubbed back and forth in the palms to cause heat that would eventually ignite the tinder.

fathong: A unit for measuring distances. One fathong equates to twelve marqs.

Fenthugren River: A river valley in Umbyrland.

Fernil: A kingdom of the Old World and part of the Brintilian Empire.

firkerg: The Raffen term for quicklime. See also *quicklime*.

First Era: An Old World term for the period starting with the earth's creation up to the coronation of Lord Wilhargant and his establishment of the Almeric Empire.

Fort Arbuth: An imperial outpost on the eastern frontier of Bram Province.

Fort Rommested: The primary imperial fortress on the eastern frontier of Bram Province.

Frontier Corps: The first united army of Old World crusaders and provincial legions formed during the colonization of Pemonia to defeat the native tribes. Led by Marshal Hilsingor during the Second Crusade, the Frontier Corps later garrisoned castles across the frontier and were responsible for carving out many new imperial provinces from tribal lands.

Furnace of the Wild: The Brintilian name for the burning of Nalembalen. Soldiers who witnessed the aftermath noted molten pools of electrum and iron among the giant felled trees. The area later became known as the Ashlands.

Gali: The language of the Gallerlanders.

Gallerlandia: A tribal realm in western and central Pemonia inhabited by the Gallerlanders.

gastrolith: Small stones ingested by animals inadvertently while feeding or purposefully to aid food digestion. The Naren-Dra shroud alchemists powdered tiny cave frog gastroliths and other ingredients to make a cloaking cloud.

Gilgalem: The mountain refuge that served as the spiritual center of the world for the Gallerlanders in Vaynland. The throne of the Vaynking, the electrum mines and forge, and ancient burial caverns were also at Gilgalem. Gilgalem was a dormant volcano whose heat and steam powered the electrum forges of the Maluram and kept the inhabitants relatively warm during winter.

Gilgalem Mountains: A mountain range of southern Gallerlandia that separated Vaynland from Aggarwal.

Glom Stimril: A Wilhargantian knight of the Almeric Empire.

Glombruk River: A major river in northwestern Gallerlandia.

Golden Age: The period in the Old World that ended the Lost Age and began with the crowning of Lord Wilhargant and the establishment of the Almeric Empire. Followed by the Dark Age.

Goyn: A major subtribe of Gallerlanders who lived in Goynland in northwestern Gallerlandia. They were ruled by the Goynkings who resided in Yoredgoyn.

Gradhild: The capital of Barres Province and new seat of the vassal-king of Bronhildia. Formerly the Umbyrland capital Gradumbyr.

Gradumbyr: The capital of Umbyrland prior to becoming Gradhild, the capital of Barres Province.

Graparins: The Gallerlander warrior-priests who were responsible for religious teaching and safeguarding the secret histories of the Cataclysm and the related prophecy. The last Graparins were killed during the destruction of Nalembalen.

Gray Summers: The Naren-Dra name for two consecutive summers long ago that were remembered for their darker skies. Much later it was understood to be caused by ash clouds that drifted from the volcanoes in the Far East, but at the time the Naren-Dra interpreted the darkness as an ill omen against the overlords who ruled Naren-Dra. This caused conflict among tribal factions that pulled down the overlords and established the clan confederation that Owerdir witnessed.

greatship: A Nyden term for a large ship with mast-like bladed weapons that hinged on their hull sides to sweep across enemy ships.

Gustbeard: A Kerchinfolk character in the Gallerlander fable "The Tale of Rustbeard and Dustbeard."

Gwarun: The Gallerlander name for the first Agnesci woman created by Wurumnak.

Hangodir: A clan of the Umbyrs.

Haldembalir: The Gallerlander name for the world, literally meaning "the Tree of the World."

Harmengaud: A region of Rahlampia.

Harsen: A New Lorin woodsman, merchant, and close companion of Rildning.

Helcirk Donovan: A Brintilian general who founded the colony of Donovan.

Hesid's Teeth: The jagged western edge of the Naren-Dra Mountains.

Hidden Eyes: The Naren-Dra shroud alchemists sent to secretly watch and sometimes kill the leaders of tribal enemies. Also called Clan of the Hidden Eyes.

High Earth: The Naren-Dra term for their mountainous realm.

Hiltsfrad: A deceased Donovard crusader and member of the Order of the Knights of Hovedollen.

Hinund: The Messengian prophet and teacher of morals and ethics who lived during the Lost Age, when much of the Old World had fallen into paganism. Hinund foretold the coming of God's Messengers and the reuniting of the Almeric kingdoms, which peaked with the reign of Lord Wilhargant and the rise of the Almeric Empire during the Golden Age.

Holy Father: See *Martinus*.

horse beast: The Gallerlander name for Old World horses that were brought to Pemonia.

Hrallandia: The term used by the Brintilian Empire to refer to the tribal realm on the western coastlines of Pemonia inhabited by the Hrals.

Hrusthied: The father of Pendigied and a deceased former king of the Raffen who resided in Woudenhod.

Ibdahar Forest: A large forest that straddled Gallerlandia and Rahlampia.

Ibelan: In Messengian religious tradition, Ibelan was God's Third Messenger.

Imperial Council of Pemonia: The court and high council of the Exarch of Pemonia formed in 2269 to bring together provincial governors and allied tribal vassal-kings. It represented all of the possessions of the Brintilian Empire in Pemonia and served to advise, petition, and take direction from the exarchs.

Joiner of Two Worlds: A name given to Rildning by the Sage of Gilgalem.

Kalbum-Nuna: The Naren-Dra term for the Wheeled Window of the World telescope.

kerchinfolk: The short peoples featured in traditional Gallerlander fables such as "The Tale of Rustbeard and Dustbeard."

knight-treasurer: During the Brintilian colonial conquest of the New World, the Frontier Corps employed the sons of the high nobility to oversee the confiscation of precious metals from native tribes and the subsequent minting of imperial coins. In addition to serving as paymasters and fighting in battles, knights-treasurer were responsible for ensuring sufficient money was available to bribe native leaders to lay down their arms.

Knower of Change: One of the names of the Sage of the Gallerlanders, which referred to his role as the senior-most diviner of the sky omens.

kowl: Black, crumbly stones that were burned by the Naren-Dra instead of scarce wood to heat homes. The kowl smelled oily and gave off thick black smoke, and its dust was used to paint weapon eggs and as a face paint for shroud alchemists. The Brintilian term evolved as *coal.*

landship: The large six-wheeled ships built by the Rahlampians to sail across land, lakes, rivers, ditches, etc. Travel in a landship was noisier and more jarring than on a traditional seagoing vessel. Some were equipped with catapults but most had archers and ringstone throwers. See also *seaship* and *ringstone.*

Leauvenna: An imperial province comprising islands in the Bay of Pemonia that were previously inhabited by the Teshi Gallerlanders. See also *Teshdembal.*

Lost Age: The period in the Old World during the First Era that followed the mythical Age of Earthmaking and ended with the Golden Age of Lord Wilhargant. Many of the Almeric kingdoms fell into paganism during the Lost Age. Few records exist in modern times of the Lost Age.

Low Earth: The Naren-Dra term for any realms that existed outside their own mountain realm. See also *High Earth*.

Maluram: A minor subtribe of Vayn Gallerlanders who lived in the mountains of Gilgalem and a few other areas of Gallerlandia. They were responsible for mining and forging electrum and were seen as untouchables by other Gallerlanders because they used metal tools for mining and smithing.

Mandegar: The clan of Gallerlander High King Gratgofa and his son Gofalnig.

Marlan: A student of Arasemis and a member of the Order of the Candlestone.

marq: A unit for measuring distances. Twelve marqs equates to one fathong.

marshal: Within the Almeric and Brintilian Empires, a marshal was the highest military rank, answering exclusively to the emperor or his exarchs. Marshals commanded large groups of legions called corps, while the generals beneath them commanded legions of up to ten thousand soldiers each.

Martinus: The title used by the head of the Messengian Church. Named after God's first Messenger, Martinus Arnabin. The Martinus dwells in the Cryphanic Temple of the Holy Messengers in Almeria and is advised by the Temple Curia. The Martinus is also referred to as Temple Father or Holy Father.

Martinus Arnabin: In Messengian religious tradition, Martinus Arnabin was God's first Messenger who formally established the Messengian Church in Almeria during the Lost Age and was believed to have lived four to five hundred years before the reign of Lord Wilhargant. Martinus Arnabin was a great teacher of God's laws and prophesied the coming of the second Messenger, Rashelum. He was traditionally referred to by his given name followed by the town of his birth, Arnabin, to distinguish from those who served with the title Martinus to lead the church between the lives of each Messenger.

Messengers, the Three: In Messengian religious tradition, this phrase is a reference to the Messengers Martinus Arnabin, Rashelum, and Ibelin together.

Messengianism: The dominant religion of the Old World. Named after the Messengers, the great teachers believed to have been sent by God.

moonwood: A decorative, gleaming white wood harvested sparingly from cave willow trees in Gilgalem. The Gallerlanders used moonwood for decorative inlays in stone and electrum.

Mordheyri: An Old World pagan tribe allied with Arukia against the Brintilian Empire during the Arukan Rebellion. Defeated by Hilsingor.

Mount Tremvig: A mountain and colonial fortress in western New Lorin where Rildning fought the Hrals as a colonial knight.

Nakeland: The Brintilian name for the peninsula east of Umbyrland inhabited by the Nake peoples.

Nalembalen: An ancient giant tree forest and city in central Gallerlandia that served as the seat of high kings. The tree city and much of the forest was burned down by the Frontier Corps in 2267 and was later known as the Ashlands.

Napargaros: The Gallerlander name for an ancient Agnesci contraption used to light the burial caverns under Gilgalem, literally meaning "Big Light-bringer." The original designer of Napargaros was among those banished to what became Rahlampia after the Cataclysm.

Nari: The language of the Naren-Dra.

Naren-Dra Mountains: A tribal realm in the high mountains of central Pemonia inhabited by the Naren-Dra.

naval knights: The Brintilian knights specially trained for combat at sea and coastal raiding. Their numbers grew exponentially during the Age of Exploration and continued to be used into modern times.

Nawurihar: The Gallerlander name literally meaning "White Forest of Heaven."

Ned Frosel: A region of Almeria where the Arukan Rebellion began before spreading to Arukia.

Ned Gollen: A region of Almeria and birthplace of Hilsingor.

New Hovedollen: An imperial province east of Donovan.

New Lorin: The first Brintilian colony in Pemonia and Rildning's birthplace.

New World: See *Pemonia.*

Nore: A large island west of Hrallandia populated by the Noric tribe.

Nydenland: A tribal realm of the Nyden located on an island in southwestern Pemonia.

obsidian: A glassy volcanic rock mined by the Maluram beneath the mountains of Gilgalem. The Maluram smiths made sharp obsidian swords and spears for the guardians of Gilgalem.

Old World: See *Almeria.*

Ollohdia: A tribal realm of the Ollohds in northwestern Pemonia that was absorbed into Donovan Province.

Ominchar: The devil of Gallerlander religious tradition.

Onas: A knight of New Lorin and brother of Rekef and Firkas.

Onas Marshes: The marshlands south of Mount Tremvig and New Lorin.

Ondirhar: Gallerlander name for an ancient forest south of Goynland, literally meaning "Black Forest."

Onitgora: An ancient Gallerlander high king.

Order of the Candlestone: A secretive order founded in 2270 by a mix of Brintilians and natives from across western Pemonia. The Order's original goal was to undermine the Brintilian Empire's colonization of the New World.

Order of the Harbor Thorns: A Brintilian military order of naval knights founded by the explorer Rin, who discovered Pemonia. The oldest knightly order of the New World, the Harbor Thorns protected the first colonial settlements along the northern coastlines of Pemonia and served aboard trade ships that sailed between the colonies.

Order of the Knights of Hovedollen: One of the knightly orders that comprised the original crusaders of the Frontier Corps.

Order of the Red Garland: The largest and most powerful of the religious military orders that formed the Frontier Corps. Sir Ravorglad was the grandmaster of the Red Garland and later became the general over all crusaders of the Frontier Corps. The Frontier Corps crusaders adopted a red stripe on their shields thereafter, similar to Red Garland's own emblem.

Ormy: A port city in southern Nydenland.

Orren: A scribe and tribal expert of New Lorin who accompanied Rildning into Gallerlandia.

Pagdorat: A Teshi Gallerlander raised by a Donovard priest in Leauvenna. He helped teach Rildning to speak Gali but perished during the fall of Nalembalen.

Pemonia: The New World continent south of the equator that was discovered by the explorer Rin. Pemonia was named after Empress Pemony, who helped drive the Age of Exploration. Many tribes inhabited Pemonia prior to the arrival of the Brintilian Empire, including the Gallerlanders, Rahlampians, and Raffen.

Peridod: A region of Rahlampia.

Pernadun River: A river that separated Gallerlandia and Rahlampia.

Pindoarig: The Gallerlander name for the central tower of Gilgalem and literally means the "Tower of Steaming Stone," a reference to the volcanic steam furnaces of the Maluram.

Plains of Ambrist: A broad flat plain in eastern Bram Province.

provincials: The Brintilian legions assembled from provincial and colonial nobles, volunteers, and conscripts that were distinct from the crusader knightly orders. In Pemonia, provincial legions rotated between protecting their home provinces and serving in the Frontier Corps.

Questioner of New Graparins: One of the names of the Sage of the Gallerlanders that referred to his role in challenging the knowledge of new Graparins.

quicklime: A caustic mineral made from burning limestone that would ignite when coming into contact with water. It was discovered by the Raffen for use as a fertilizer and cement but was later used for naval warfare against the Nyden. It was adopted by the Brintilian Empire for use on land and sea after the Raffen joined the empire. The Raffen called it firkerg, Gallerlanders and others called it a foul-smelling fire, and later peoples also called it burned lime.

Rachard: The capital of Bram Province and headquarters of the Frontier Corps under Hilsingor.

Raffenia: A tribal realm in southwestern Pemonia inhabited by the Raffen.

Rahlampia: A tribal realm in central Pemonia inhabited by the Rahlampians.

Ramunhavin: The city in Almeria of which Sarnaker was once mayor.

Rashelum: In Messengian religious tradition, Rashelum was God's Second Messenger.

reed-plate: A Rahlampian armor made of thick bundles of dried marsh reeds and strengthened with hammered bog iron plates. It was light, flexible, and rust-resistant.

Regnarul the Bound: A notorious heretic during the Age of Calming Winds.

Rekef: A knight of New Lorin and brother to Onas and Firkas.

rhymer: Gallerlander minstrels known for their stories, kennings, and quick wits.

Rilhammor: A large port city in Donovan. One of the first major ports to be established in Pemonia by the Brintilian Empire. Also the name of Helcirk Donovan's sword.

Rin: The Brintilian adventurer who discovered the New World during the Age of Exploration.

ringstone: Rahlampian throwing stones specially carved with crisscrossing rings for gripping. Typically used to defend landships when archers were unavailable.

Rittonrewk: A Rahlampian city in Swaleshil destroyed by Raffen raiders.

Rivercross Corps: The eight imperial legions led by Marshal Hilsingor against the Arukan Rebellion in the Old World during the First Crusade.

Roydenwoap: A port city in northern Nydenland.

Rustbeard: A Kerchinfolk character in the Gallerlander fable "The Tale of Rustbeard and Dustbeard."

sand brick: A concrete of coastal sand and riverstones used by Gallerlander Vayns in Aggarwal.

Sarbondibum: A Naren-Dra region ruled by Seneschal Ankarmesh. See also *Sipadshur*.

Seafathers: The leaders of the Agnesci who voyaged across the seas from Aprelaebos to Cedelaebos.

Sea of Nore: The sea between the island of Nore and mainland Pemonia.

seaship: A Rahlampian term used to distinguish from landships.

Second Era: The Old World term for the period starting with the coronation of Lord Wilhargant and his establishment of the Almeric Empire and continuing without a clear transition. There was much debate among historians and politicians over whether a third era had begun earlier, such as with the discovery of the New World.

Shadfoyle: A region of Rahlampia noted for the stilt-house city of Bodamweym and the Domnitar Rock.

shroud alchemy: A Naren-Dra school of offensive and illusory alchemy that built on traditional medical teachings. Most shroud alchemists served as Hidden

Eyes, and their knowledge and techniques later heavily influenced the methods of the Order of the Candlestone.

shulmel crystal: Quartz-like crystals mined beneath the Naren-Dra Mountains. The Naren-Dra ground the crystals into a powder that was heated to purge it of impurities, then melted and cast into lenses for use in telescopes.

Silvern Age: The period in the Old World that saw the rise of the Brintilian Empire and restoration of civilization following periods of upheaval created by the collapse of Almeric Empire more than a thousand years earlier.

Sipadshur: The Naren-Dra name for the dwelling of Seneschal Ankarmesh, literally meaning "the Mountain Mast." Sipad is also a name for a long-stemmed cave flower native to the region. The settlement, located in the Sarbondibum region, was one of the highest in the Naren-Dra Mountains and since ancient times served as a meeting place for the Council of Snowshelling and the Council of Sunstepping. The ancient Naren-Dra overlords also dwelled at Sipadshur.

Sky King: See *Thuranmaret*.

skystones: The Raffen term for meteorites that were hard iron-nickel alloys and exceptionally difficult to work with. The most famous Raffen use of meteorites was the grotesquely fashioned crown of the Raffen kings. Also called sky-iron.

Slimethorn: A forest in the Gallerlander fable "The Tale of Rustbeard and Dustbeard."

Solemn Journey: See *Tarborchast*.

solin: A leafy medicinal herb used by the Gallerlanders to heal wounds.

spruce beer: A Vaynland beer made with spruce needles and having a floral, citrusy scent.

starcross: The primary Messengian religious symbol referencing the star that shone above the hillside where Martinus Arnabin preached into the night.

stonesword: A Gallerlander short sword fashioned from stone, typically gneiss, feldspar, or flint.

Swaleshil: The Rahlampian lands east of the Pernadun River.

tabakat: Dried tabakat leaves were smoked by Gallerlanders in thin, curly pipes similar to the tobacco smoked by peoples of the Old World. The smoke was described as intense, with flavors of pepper, crabapple, and licorice. It was later cultivated and exported to the Old World by the imperial colonies, fueling violence between rival merchants known as the Smoking War.

Takumbyr: An Umbyr village of which Yelgoram was chief.

Tamtur: The clan of the Umbyrs that Eniri belonged to.

Tarborchast: The Rahlampian term for the expulsion of the Agnesci shipbuilders and others into the hinterlands east of what became Gallerlandia following the Cataclysm. These banished people were the founders of the Rahlampian tribe.

Tasaloop: A Nyden ship captained by Bothrobim.

Temple Curia: The court of the Martinus that served as the highest religious and administrative council of the Messengian Church. Each Curian served as an adviser to the Martinus on a specific issue.

Temple Father: See *Martinus.*

Thorendor Castle: The residence of Arasemis, a Donovard warrior-scholar who was involved with the Order of the Candlestone. Located in northwestern Wallevet.

Teshdembal: The Gallerlander name for modern Leauvenna, literally meaning "Teshi Island."

Teshi: A branch of Goyn Gallerlanders who lived in modern Leauvenna.

Thigor: An ancient king of the Welkars.

Thuraniparin: The Gallerlander name for Wurumnak's warriors chosen from the most courageous high kings and other Gallerlanders to defend Haldembalir during the battle at the End Times. Literally meaning "Spirit Kings."

Thuranmaret: One of the names of the Sage of the Gallerlanders, literally meaning "Sky King," which referred to his role as the senior-most diviner of the sky omens.

Thurondsogon: The Gallerlander name for the final battle at the End Times, literally meaning "Day of the Black Snake."

Tolnarp: A village and farmland on the frontier of New Lorin Colony.

Toredwoak: A twin king with his brother Belordoos of Nydenland.

Torfnarbruk: A river near Donovan Colony.

turserkgyn: A Gallerlander term literally meaning "shrieking lion warriors," or simply "wild fighters." It was used to describe the Hral warriors who drank tonics of adder blood and other ingredients that pushed them into an unstoppable frenzy. They fought to the death or died from drinking the tonic. See also *black adder*.

Ubromynir: A cave willow in the burial cavern of Gilgalem that symbolized Nawurihar. Considered the sacred heart of Gallerlandia.

Ulgol: A Gallerlander clan in Goynland and Umbyrland. One of the first clans to be displaced by Donovan Colony and the Frontier Corps.

Umbyr: The largest subtribe of Gallerlanders who lived in Umbyrland of northern and central Gallerlandia. They were ruled by the Umbyrkings who resided in Gradumbyr.

underkings: A reference to the Goynking, Umbyrking, and Vaynking who served under the High King of Gallerlandia.

Urgamdir: An Umbyr chieftain and close companion of Rildning.

Usodimare: A region of Rahlampia noted for its extensive marshlands.

vassal-king: The title given to tribal kings who joined the Brintilian Empire as rulers of their own lands under the emperor. All of them were given seats on the Imperial Council of Pemonia in Eglamour.

Vayn: A major subtribe of Gallerlanders who lived in Vaynland of southern and eastern Gallerlandia. They were ruled by the Vaynkings who resided in Gilgalem.

Velpia: A tribal realm in north-central Pemonia inhabited by the Velps.

Vikenbirg: An emperor of the Brintilian Empire assassinated by the Order of the Candlestone.

Wadrulir Mountains: A mountain range in Umbyrland.

Wallevet: An imperial province established by Hilsingor in central Gallerlandia, including the ruins of Nalembalen.

Welkaria: A term used by the Brintilian Empire to refer to the realm of the Welkars in central Pemonia.

Wheeled Window of the World: A Naren-Dra telescope invented by Tizkarmesh and later refurbished and used by Ankarmesh. It was used to gaze down at other tribal realms around the Naren-Dra Mountains and beyond. See also *Kalbum-Nuna*.

wilderman: A Brintilian term for a woodland hermit or other reclusive person who was not of tribal heritage.

wilderwood: A Brintilian term for the unexplored forested interior of Pemonia.

Wilhargant, Lord: An ancient king who founded the Almeric Empire more than two thousand years before the rise of the Brintilian Empire. Wilhargant's reign was the first consolidation of the Old World kingdoms.

Wind Seer: One of the names of the Sage of the Gallerlanders that referred to his role as the senior-most diviner of the sky omens.

windrazor: A Rahlampian sword crafted from bog iron and anchiclade ores, which made the blade sharp, exceptionally thin, and difficult to see in battle. They were unusually long, often twice the height of the wielder, and rust-resistant. Their bulbous pommels were extra heavy to balance the long blades, often made of lead with ornate carvings and enamels. Rahlampian warriors used special sheaths at their waists that were open ended and unsnapped to allow the sword to be swept out away from the body, rather than upward. These swords could cut through most Brintilian steel except heavy-plate armor.

woodsprite: A mythical evil spirit of Slimethorn Forest in the Gallerlander fable "The Tale of Rustbeard and Dustbeard."

Woorasloop: A Nyden ship.

Woridam: The Gallerlander Umbyrking prior to Erambrin. Killed by Ravorglad after the fall of Nalembalen.

Wrethe Hunt, Day of: A Messengian religious festival in mid-Thawtide to mark the martyrdom of Prophet Hinund and the ending of the winter season. Wrethe was an Arch Almeric word meaning "wreath," which symbolized the burning of the prophet. The wreaths are orange, like the color of Messengianism, to signify the berries of the buckthorn branches that were used for Hinund's pyre.

Woudenhod: The capital city of the Raffen.

Wurumnak: The god of the Gallerlanders.

Yoredgoyn: The capital of Goynland.

Zebfargir: The Gallerlander name for the first Agnesci man created by Wurumnak.

Zimberdet: The overlord of Naren-Dra when the Welkars were at the height of their power and attacked the Naren-Dra. He was the father of Zimudar.

Zimudar: The overlord of Naren-Dra who created shroud alchemy. He was the son of Zimberdet.

ACKNOWLEDGMENTS

Thanks and appreciation to many for lending an ear, providing encouragement, and mending my scribbles. To my mother, who taught me to love books and to explore the art of writing. To my father, who taught me hard work and perseverance. And to my editors Anne McPeak and Tricia Callahan, for their talents and guidance.

ABOUT THE AUTHOR

Christopher C. Fuchs writes the Earthpillar novels and half-tales with flavors of fantasy, historical fiction, adventure, and steampunk. His debut novel, *Lords of Deception*, is the core of a nonlinear matrix of books that allow readers to wander and explore an epic alternative Earth that blends new continents and peoples, political intrigue, fictional materials, and customized medieval and early modern technologies.
He writes from Virginia.

To stay informed of upcoming books and receive discount codes, subscribe to the mailing list at
EarthpillarBooks.com.